GREG PAK • TAKESHI MIYAZAWA • TRIONA FARRELL

MECH CADET YU™

VOLUME TWO

BOOM! STUDIOS

Series Designer
MICHELLE ANKLEY

Collection Designer
JILLIAN CRAB

Editor
CAMERON CHITTOCK

Special Thanks
ERIC HARBURN

ROSS RICHIE CEO & Founder
MATT GAGNON Editor-in-Chief
FILIP SABLIK President of Publishing & Marketing
STEPHEN CHRISTY President of Development
LANCE KREITER VP of Licensing & Merchandising
PHIL BARBARO VP of Finance
ARUNE SINGH VP of Marketing
BRYCE CARLSON Managing Editor
SCOTT NEWMAN Production Design Manager
KATE HENNING Operations Manager
SPENCER SIMPSON Sales Manager
SIERRA HAHN Senior Editor
DAFNA PLEBAN Editor, Talent Development
SHANNON WATTERS Editor
ERIC HARBURN Editor
WHITNEY LEOPARD Editor
CAMERON CHITTOCK Editor
CHRIS ROSA Associate Editor
MATTHEW LEVINE Associate Editor
SOPHIE PHILIPS-ROBERTS Assistant Editor
GAVIN GRONENTHAL Assistant Editor
MICHAEL MOCCIO Assistant Editor
AMANDA LaFRANCO Executive Assistant
KATALINA HOLLAND Editorial Administrative Assistant
JILLIAN CRAB Design Coordinator
MICHELLE ANKLEY Design Coordinator
KARA LEOPARD Production Designer
MARIE KRUPINA Production Designer
GRACE PARK Production Design Assistant
CHELSEA ROBERTS Production Design Assistant
ELIZABETH LOUGHRIDGE Accounting Coordinator
STEPHANIE HOCUTT Social Media Coordinator
JOSÉ MEZA Event Coordinator
HOLLY AITCHISON Operations Coordinator
MEGAN CHRISTOPHER Operations Assistant
RODRIGO HERNANDEZ Mailroom Assistant
MORGAN PERRY Direct Market Representative
CAT O'GRADY Marketing Assistant
CORNELIA TZANA Publicity Assistant
LIZ ALMENDAREZ Accounting Administrative Assistant

MECH CADET YU Volume Two, October 2018.
Published by BOOM! Studios, a division of Boom
Entertainment, Inc. Mech Cadet Yu is ™ & © 2018 Pak
Man Productions, Ltd. & Takeshi Miyazawa. Originally
published in single magazine form as MECH CADET
YU No. 5-8. ™ & © 2018 Pak Man Productions,
Ltd. & Takeshi Miyazawa. All rights reserved.
BOOM! Studios™ and the BOOM! Studios logo are
trademarks of Boom Entertainment, Inc., registered
in various countries and categories. All characters,
events, and institutions depicted herein are
fictional. Any similarity between any of the names,
characters, persons, events, and/or institutions in
this publication to actual names, characters, and
persons, whether living or dead, events, and/or
institutions is unintended and purely coincidental.
BOOM! Studios does not read or accept unsolicited
submissions of ideas, stories, or artwork.

BOOM! Studios, 5670 Wilshire Boulevard, Suite 400,
Los Angeles, CA 90036-5679. Printed in China. First
Printing.

ISBN: 978-1-68415-253-7, eISBN: 978-1-64144-115-5

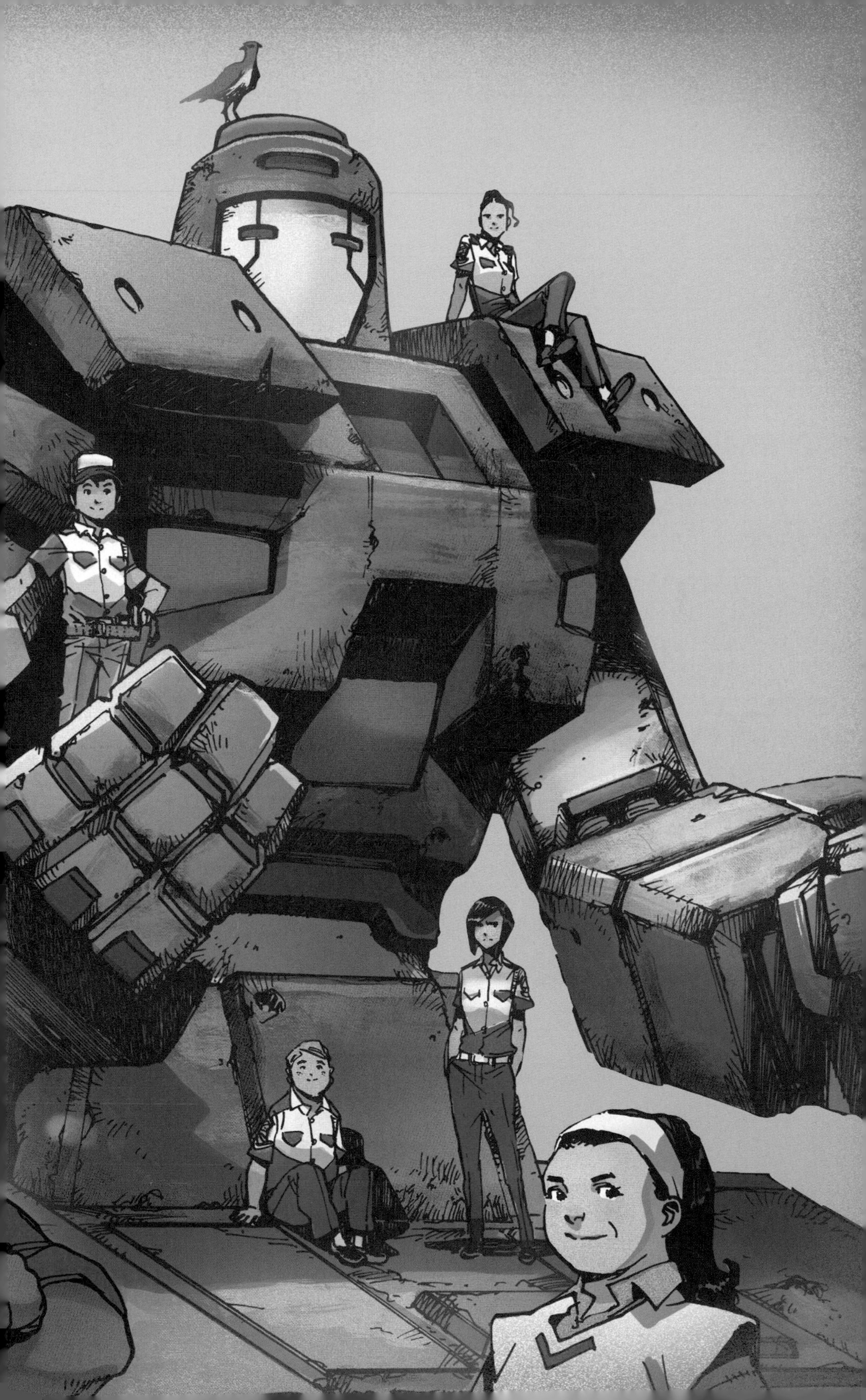

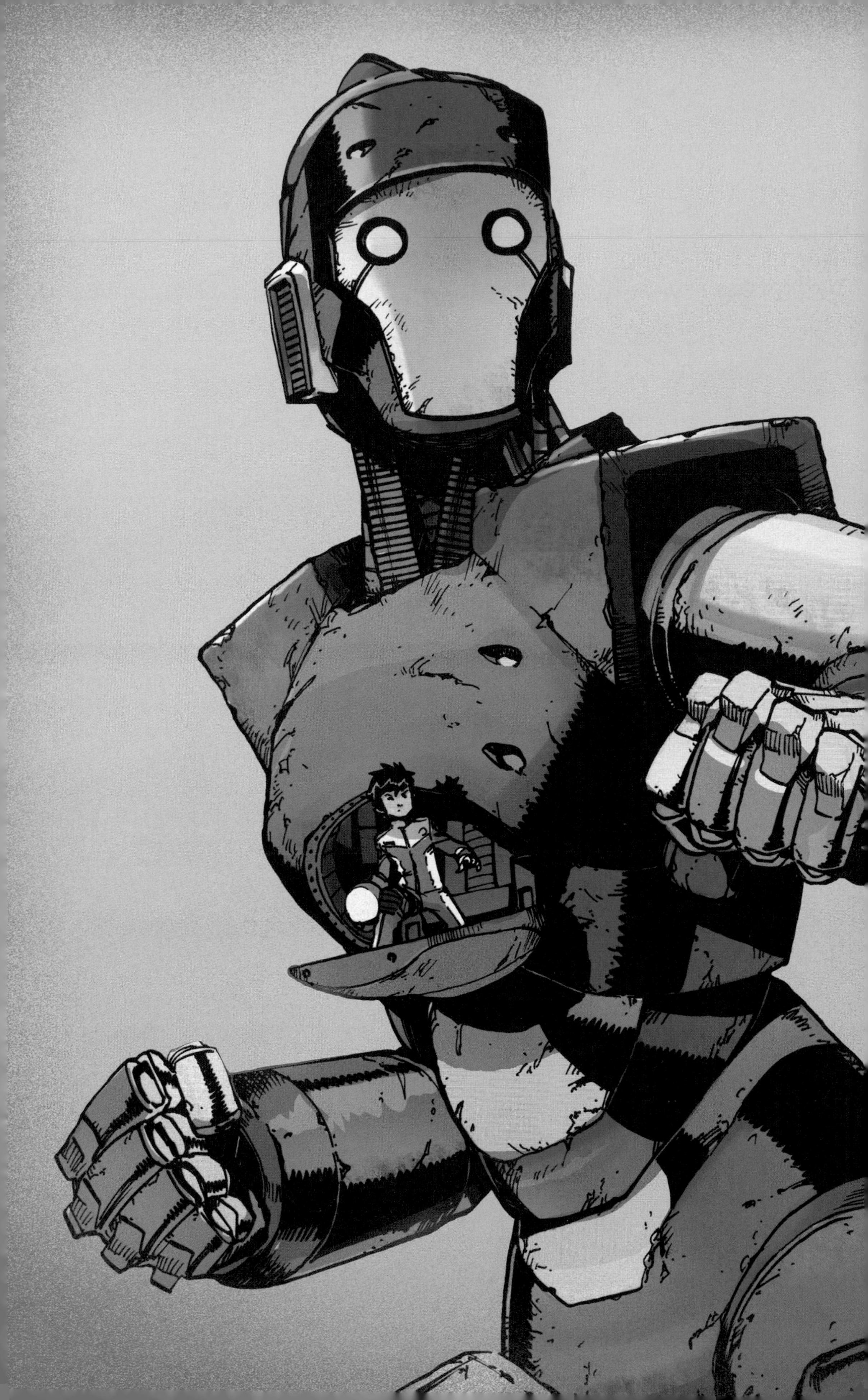

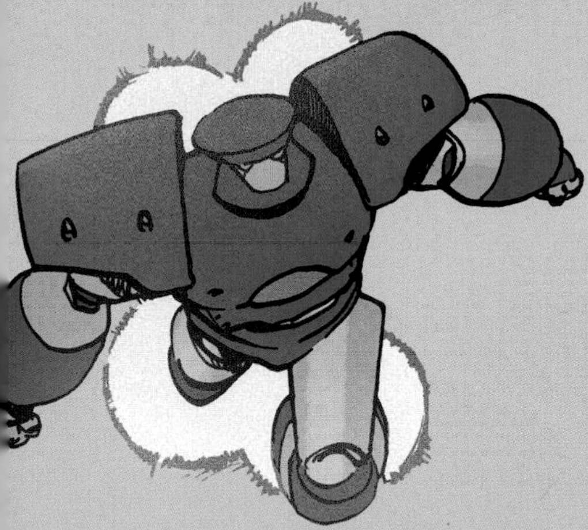

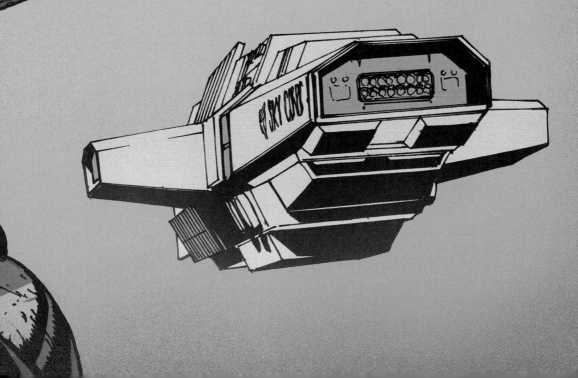

Written by
GREG PAK

Illustrated by
TAKESHI MIYAZAWA

Colored by
TRIONA FARRELL

Lettered by
SIMON BOWLAND

Cover by
TAKESHI MIYAZAWA
with colors by **RAÚL ANGULO**

Created by
GREG PAK & **TAKESHI MIYAZAWA**

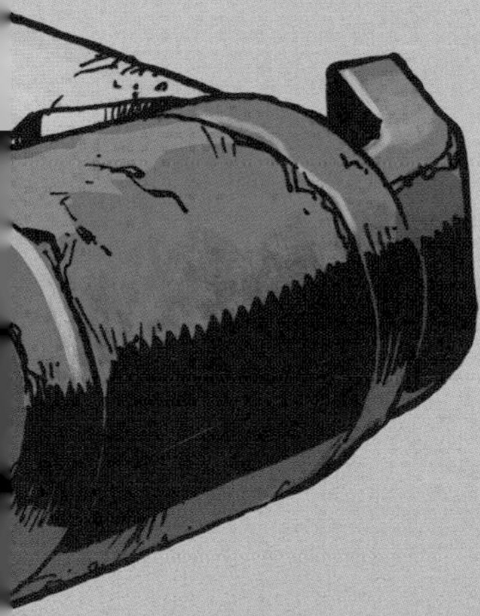

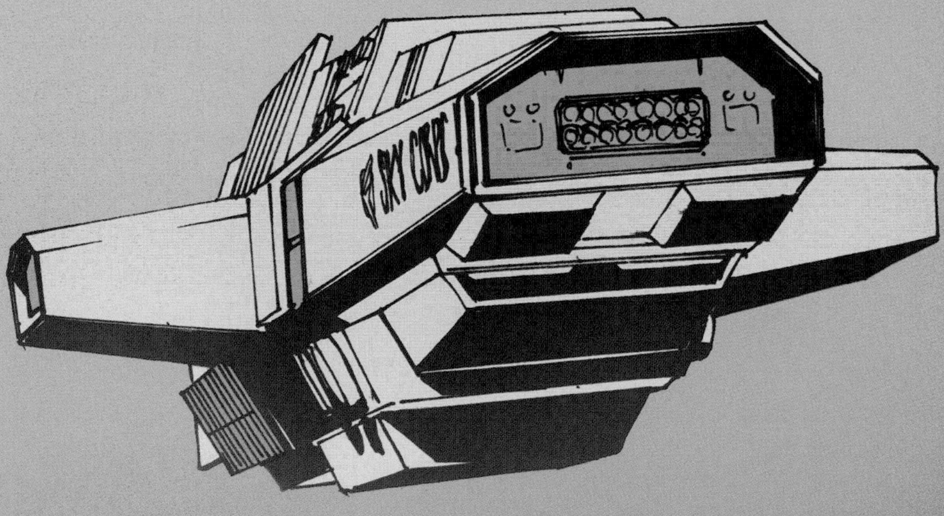

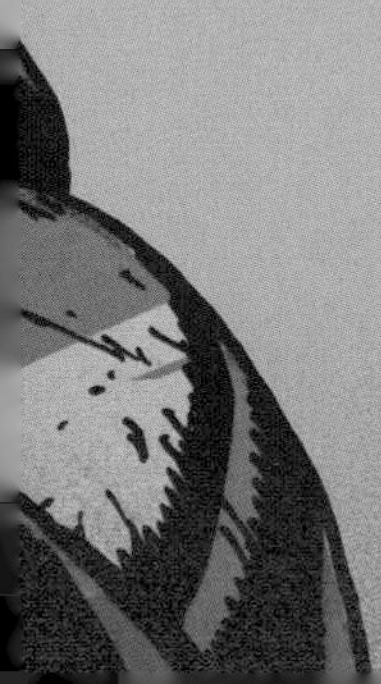

CHAPTER **FIVE**

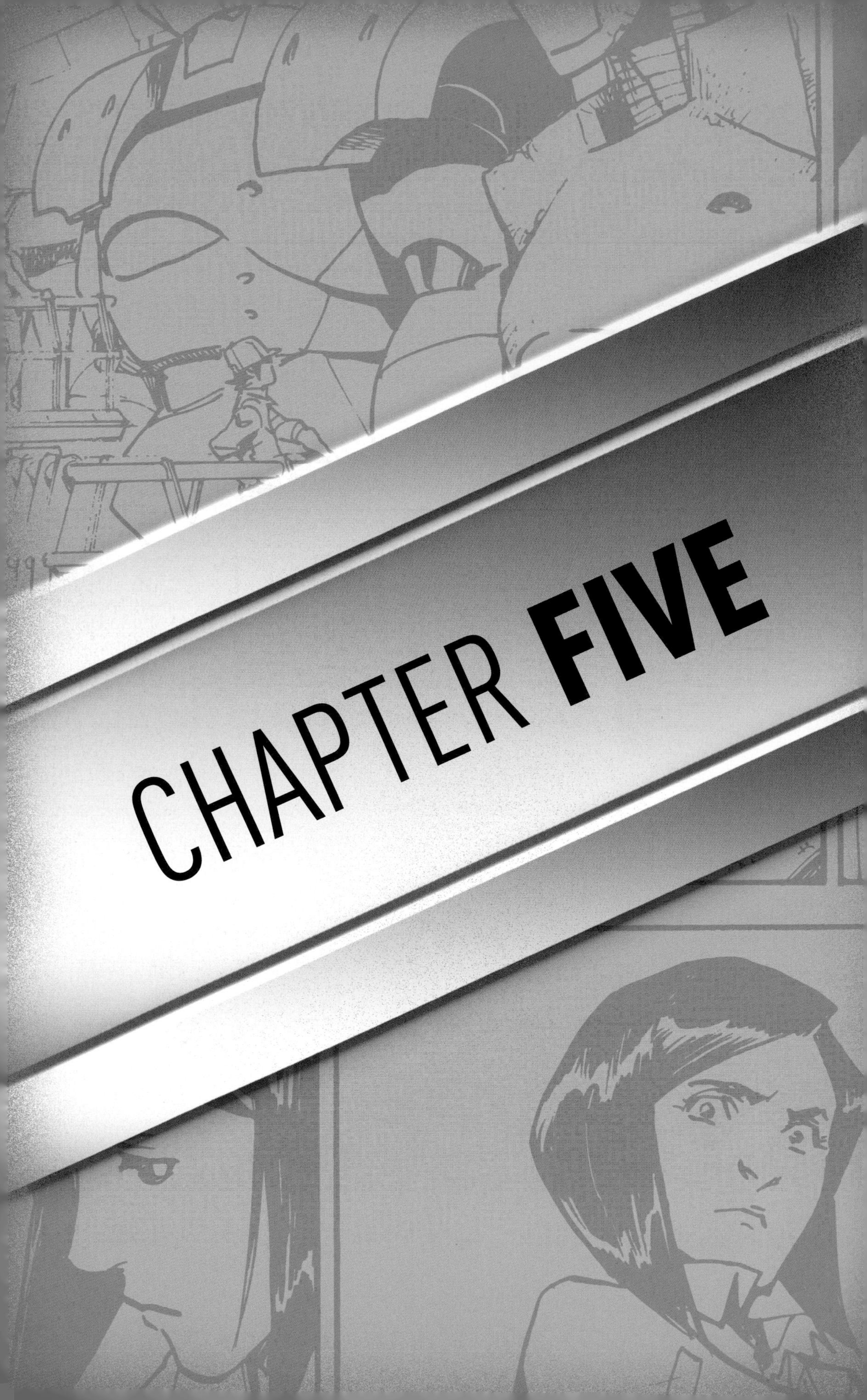

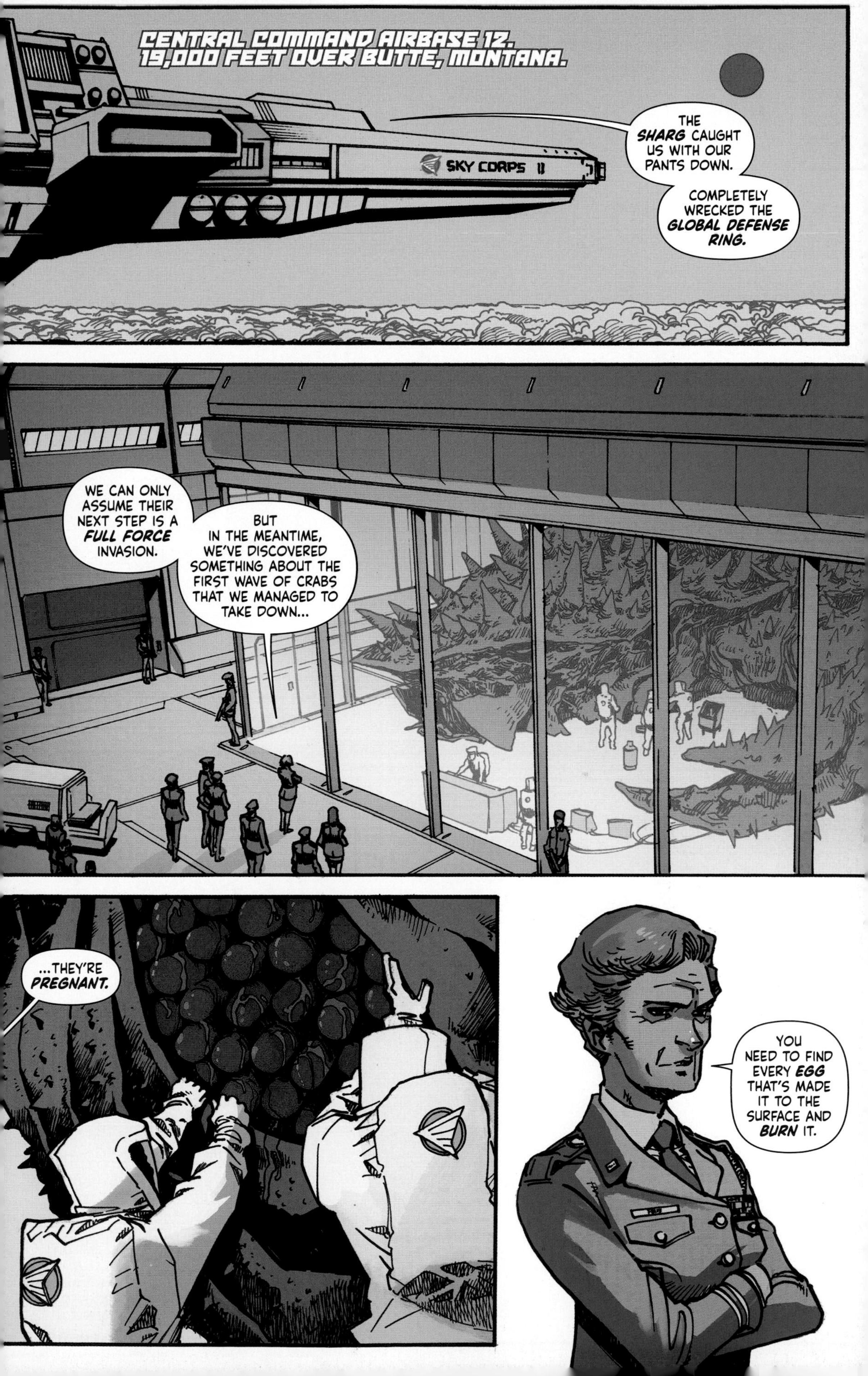
CENTRAL COMMAND AIRBASE 12.
19,000 FEET OVER BUTTE, MONTANA.
SKY CORPS II
THE SHARG CAUGHT US WITH OUR PANTS DOWN.
COMPLETELY WRECKED THE GLOBAL DEFENSE RING.
WE CAN ONLY ASSUME THEIR NEXT STEP IS A FULL FORCE INVASION.
BUT IN THE MEANTIME, WE'VE DISCOVERED SOMETHING ABOUT THE FIRST WAVE OF CRABS THAT WE MANAGED TO TAKE DOWN...
...THEY'RE PREGNANT.
YOU NEED TO FIND EVERY EGG THAT'S MADE IT TO THE SURFACE AND BURN IT.

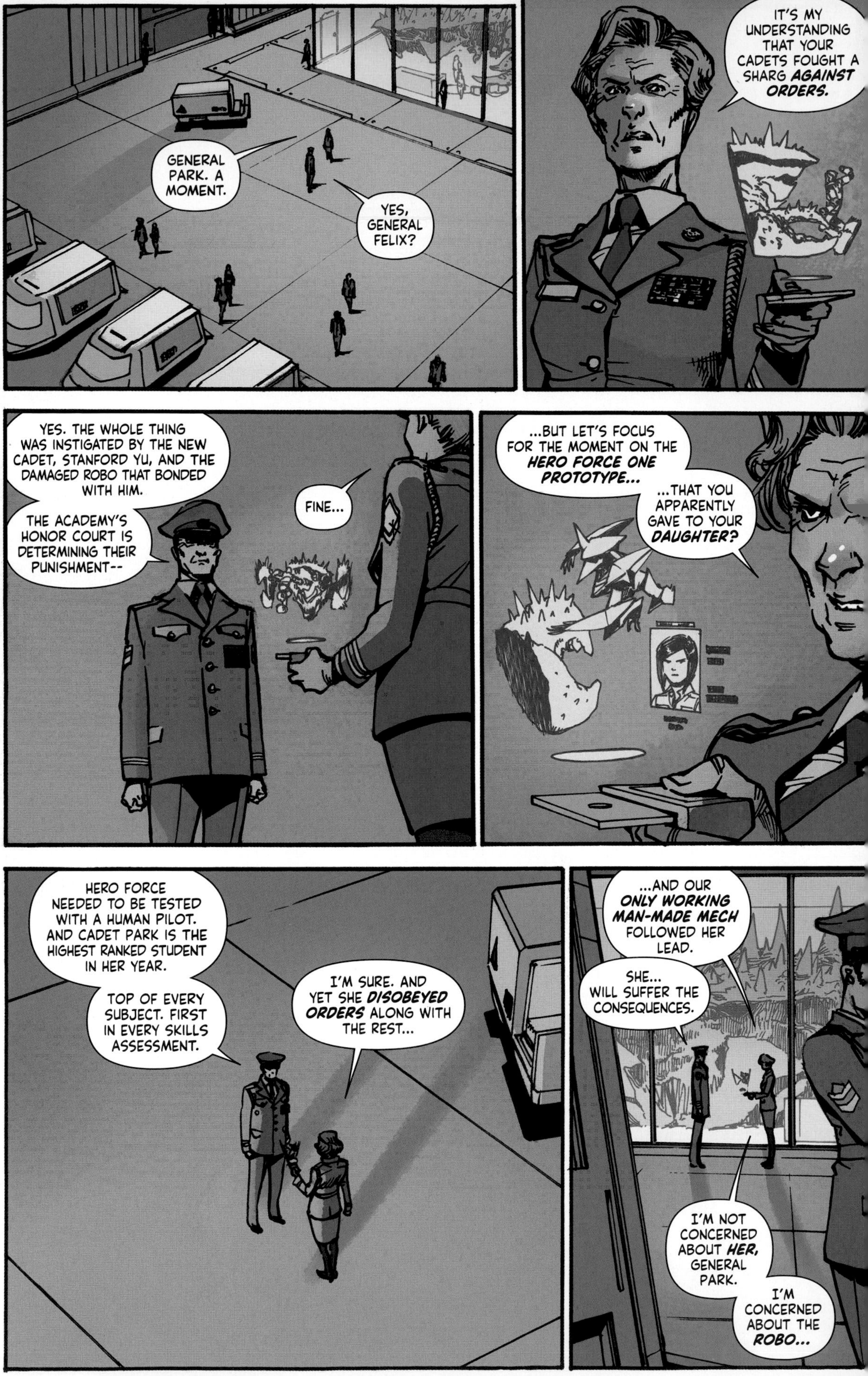
GENERAL PARK. A MOMENT.
YES, GENERAL FELIX?
IT'S MY UNDERSTANDING THAT YOUR CADETS FOUGHT A SHARG *AGAINST ORDERS.*
YES. THE WHOLE THING WAS INSTIGATED BY THE NEW CADET, STANFORD YU, AND THE DAMAGED ROBO THAT BONDED WITH HIM.
THE ACADEMY'S HONOR COURT IS DETERMINING THEIR PUNISHMENT--
FINE...
...BUT LET'S FOCUS FOR THE MOMENT ON THE *HERO FORCE ONE PROTOTYPE...*
...THAT YOU APPARENTLY GAVE TO YOUR *DAUGHTER?*
HERO FORCE NEEDED TO BE TESTED WITH A HUMAN PILOT. AND CADET PARK IS THE HIGHEST RANKED STUDENT IN HER YEAR.
TOP OF EVERY SUBJECT. FIRST IN EVERY SKILLS ASSESSMENT.
I'M SURE. AND YET SHE *DISOBEYED ORDERS* ALONG WITH THE REST...
...AND OUR *ONLY WORKING MAN-MADE MECH* FOLLOWED HER LEAD.
SHE... WILL SUFFER THE CONSEQUENCES.
I'M NOT CONCERNED ABOUT *HER,* GENERAL PARK.
I'M CONCERNED ABOUT THE *ROBO...*

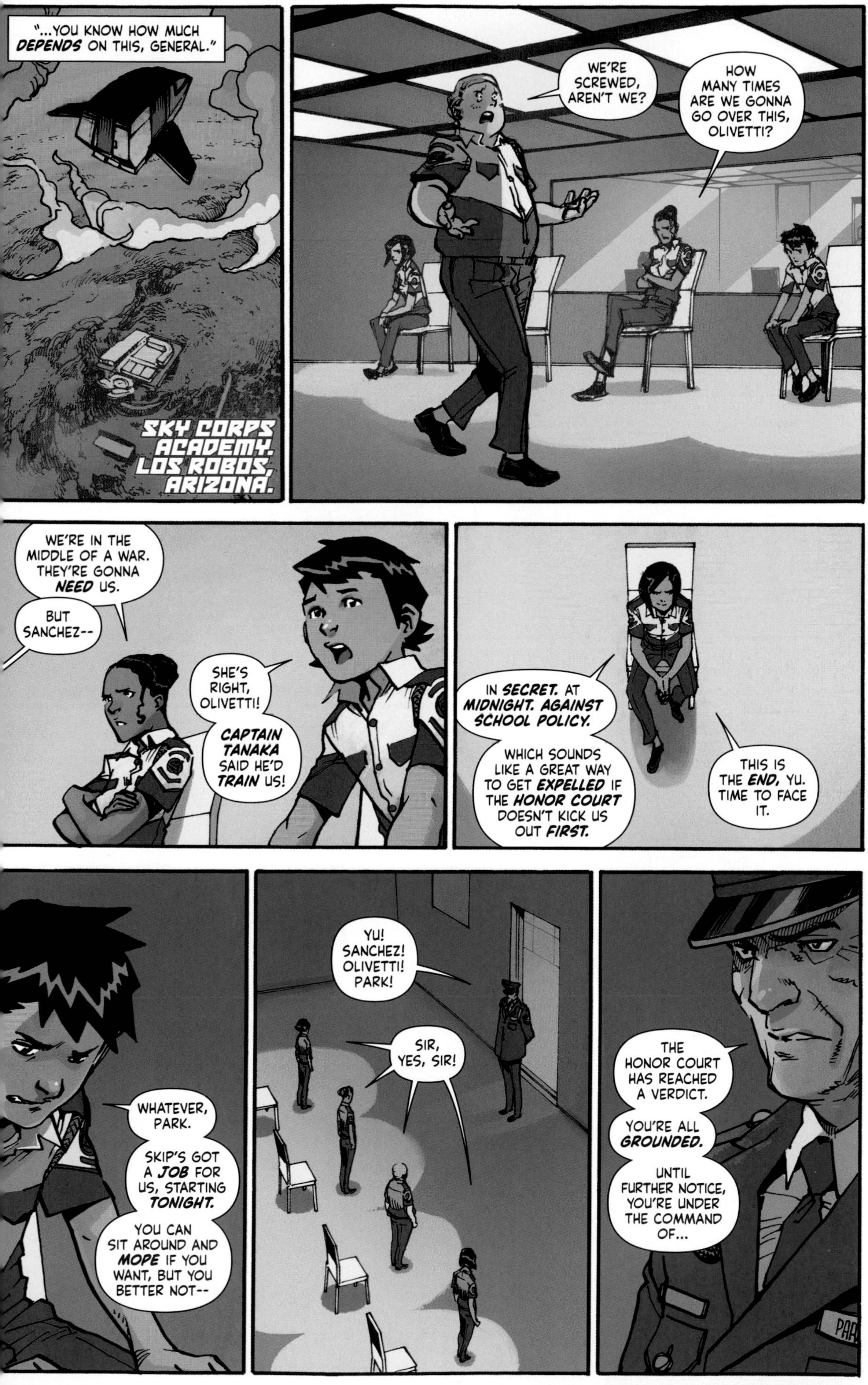
"...YOU KNOW HOW MUCH DEPENDS ON THIS, GENERAL."
SKY CORPS ACADEMY. LOS ROBOS, ARIZONA.
WE'RE SCREWED, AREN'T WE?
HOW MANY TIMES ARE WE GONNA GO OVER THIS, OLIVETTI?
WE'RE IN THE MIDDLE OF A WAR. THEY'RE GONNA NEED US.
BUT SANCHEZ--
SHE'S RIGHT, OLIVETTI!
CAPTAIN TANAKA SAID HE'D TRAIN US!
IN SECRET. AT MIDNIGHT. AGAINST SCHOOL POLICY.
WHICH SOUNDS LIKE A GREAT WAY TO GET EXPELLED IF THE HONOR COURT DOESN'T KICK US OUT FIRST.
THIS IS THE END, YU. TIME TO FACE IT.
WHATEVER, PARK.
SKIP'S GOT A JOB FOR US, STARTING TONIGHT.
YOU CAN SIT AROUND AND MOPE IF YOU WANT, BUT YOU BETTER NOT--
YU! SANCHEZ! OLIVETTI! PARK!
SIR, YES, SIR!
THE HONOR COURT HAS REACHED A VERDICT.
YOU'RE ALL GROUNDED.
UNTIL FURTHER NOTICE, YOU'RE UNDER THE COMMAND OF...

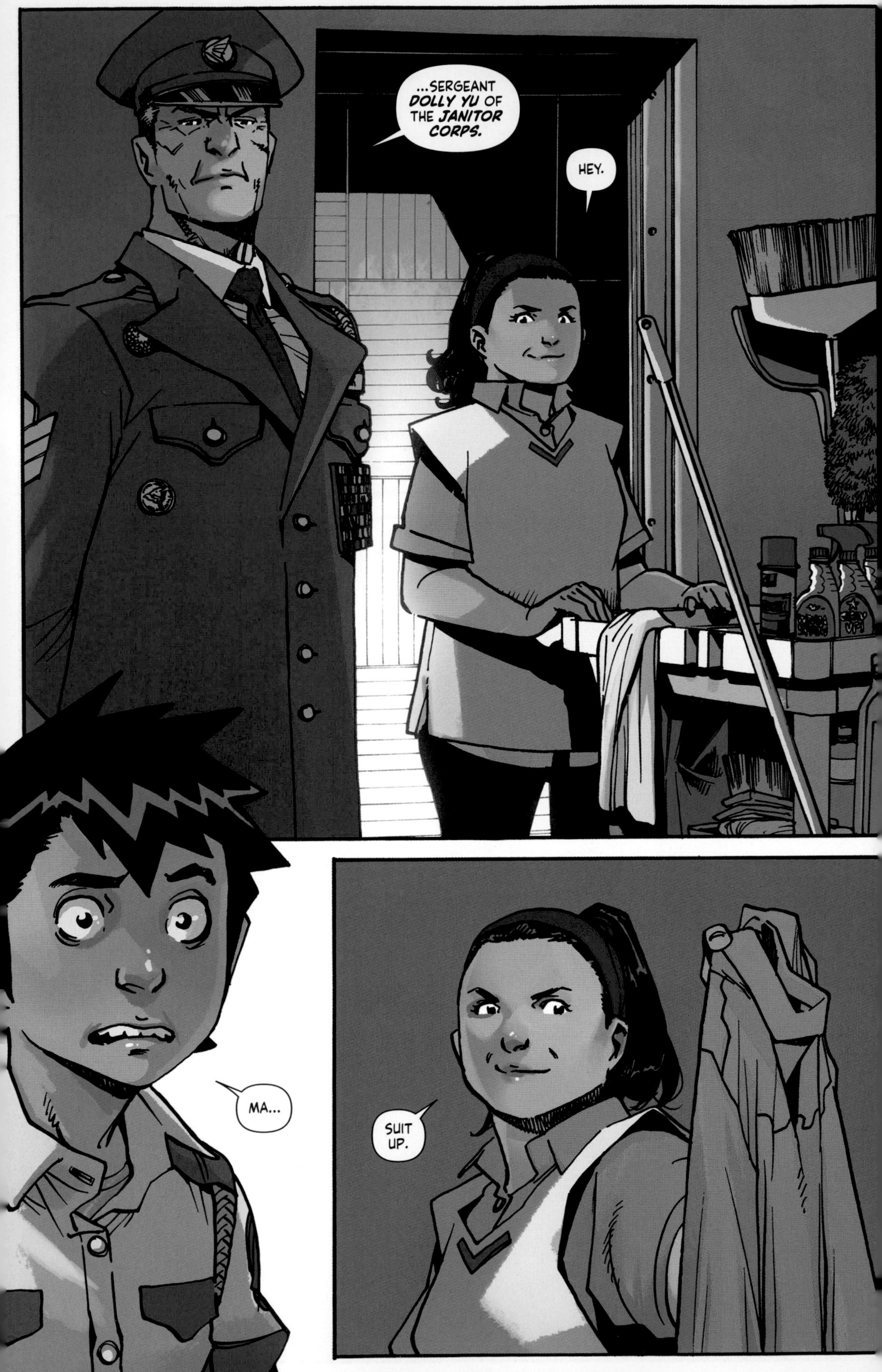
...SERGEANT DOLLY YU OF THE JANITOR CORPS.
HEY.
MA...
SUIT UP.

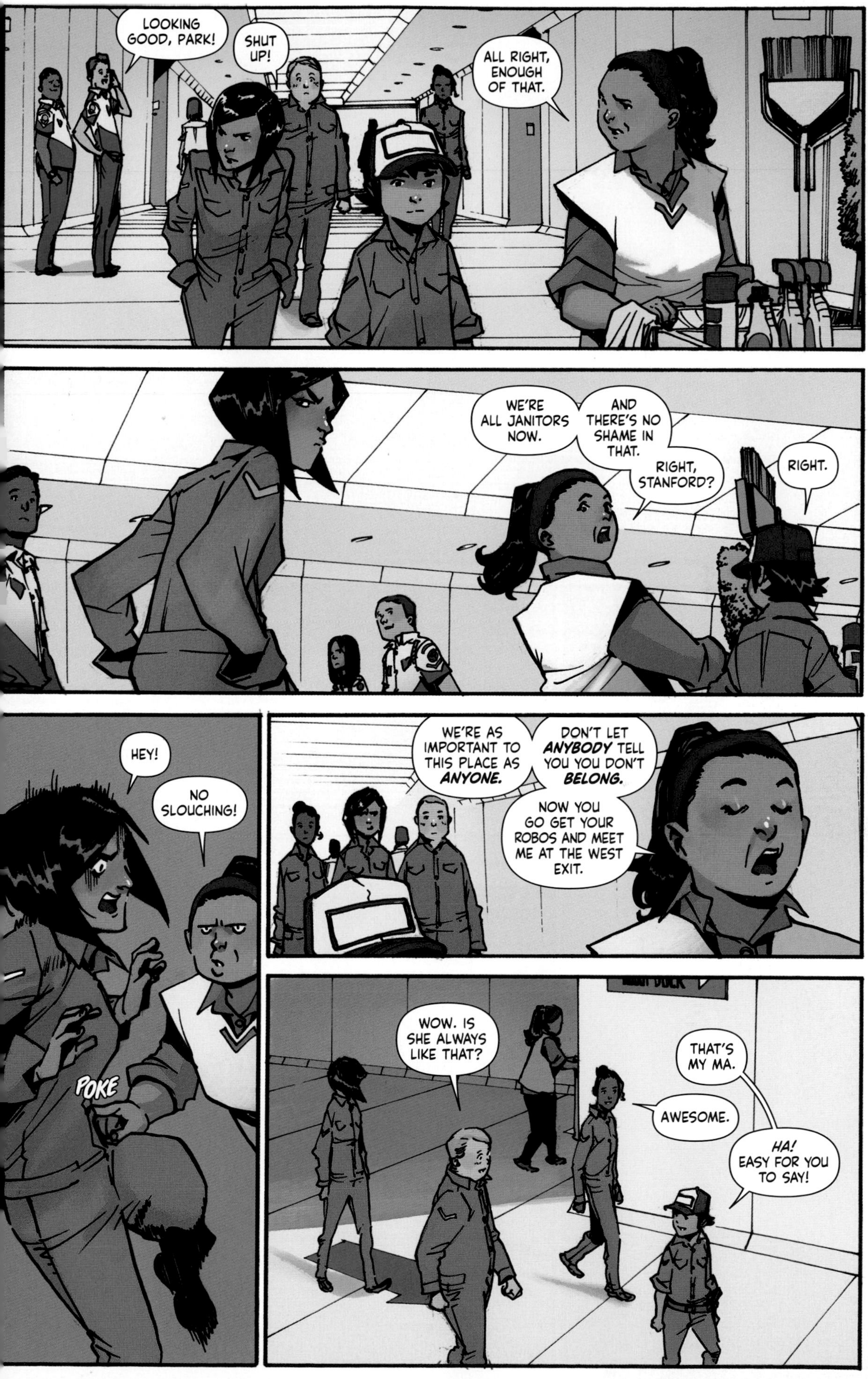
LOOKING GOOD, PARK!
SHUT UP!
ALL RIGHT, ENOUGH OF THAT.
WE'RE ALL JANITORS NOW.
AND THERE'S NO SHAME IN THAT.
RIGHT, STANFORD?
RIGHT.
HEY!
NO SLOUCHING!
POKE
WE'RE AS IMPORTANT TO THIS PLACE AS *ANYONE.*
DON'T LET *ANYBODY* TELL YOU YOU DON'T *BELONG.*
NOW YOU GO GET YOUR ROBOS AND MEET ME AT THE WEST EXIT.
WOW. IS SHE ALWAYS LIKE THAT?
THAT'S MY MA.
AWESOME.
HA! EASY FOR YOU TO SAY!

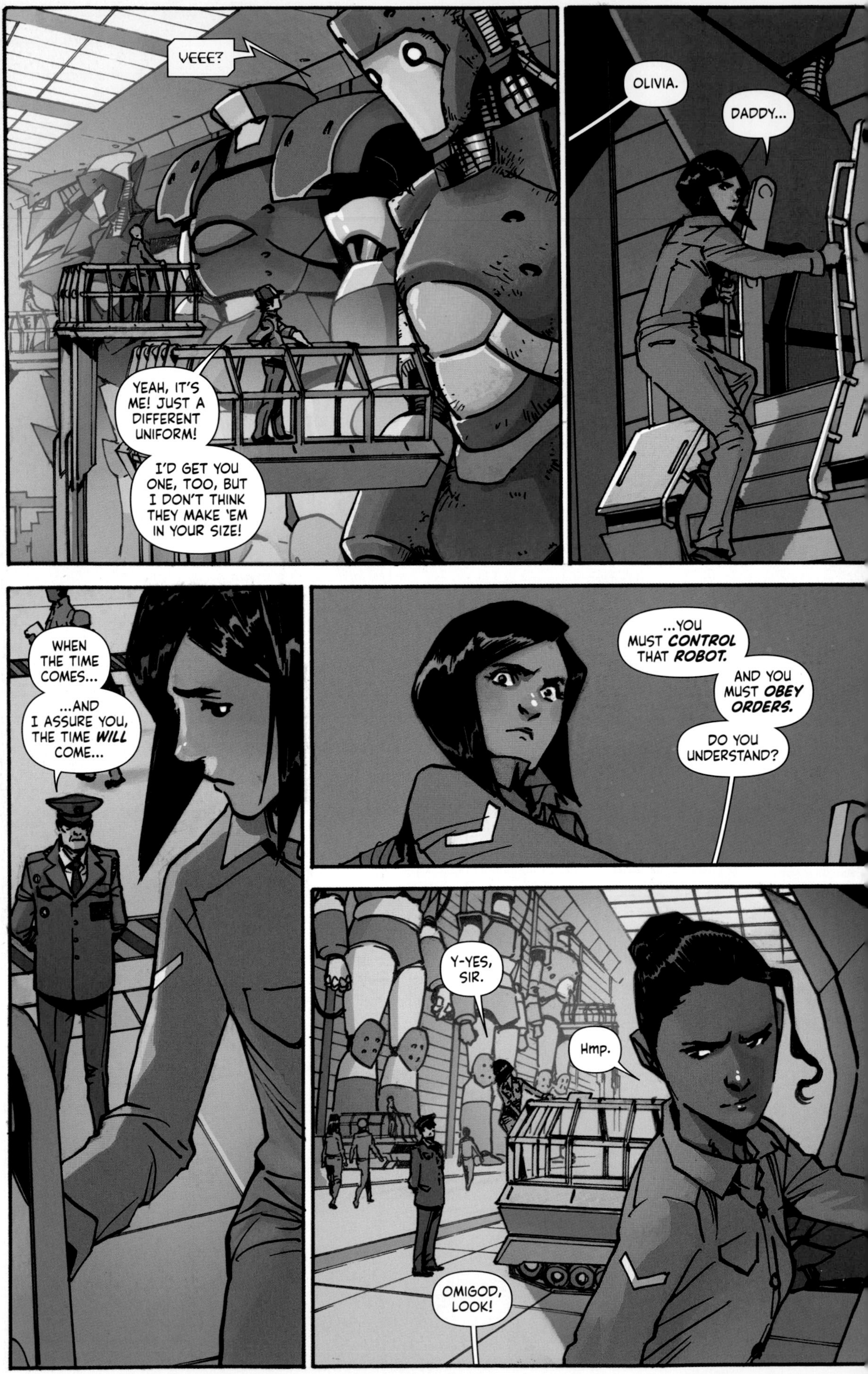
VEEE?
YEAH, IT'S ME! JUST A DIFFERENT UNIFORM!
I'D GET YOU ONE, TOO, BUT I DON'T THINK THEY MAKE 'EM IN YOUR SIZE!
OLIVIA.
DADDY...
WHEN THE TIME COMES...
...AND I ASSURE YOU, THE TIME WILL COME...
...YOU MUST CONTROL THAT ROBOT.
AND YOU MUST OBEY ORDERS.
DO YOU UNDERSTAND?
Y-YES, SIR.
Hmp.
OMIGOD, LOOK!

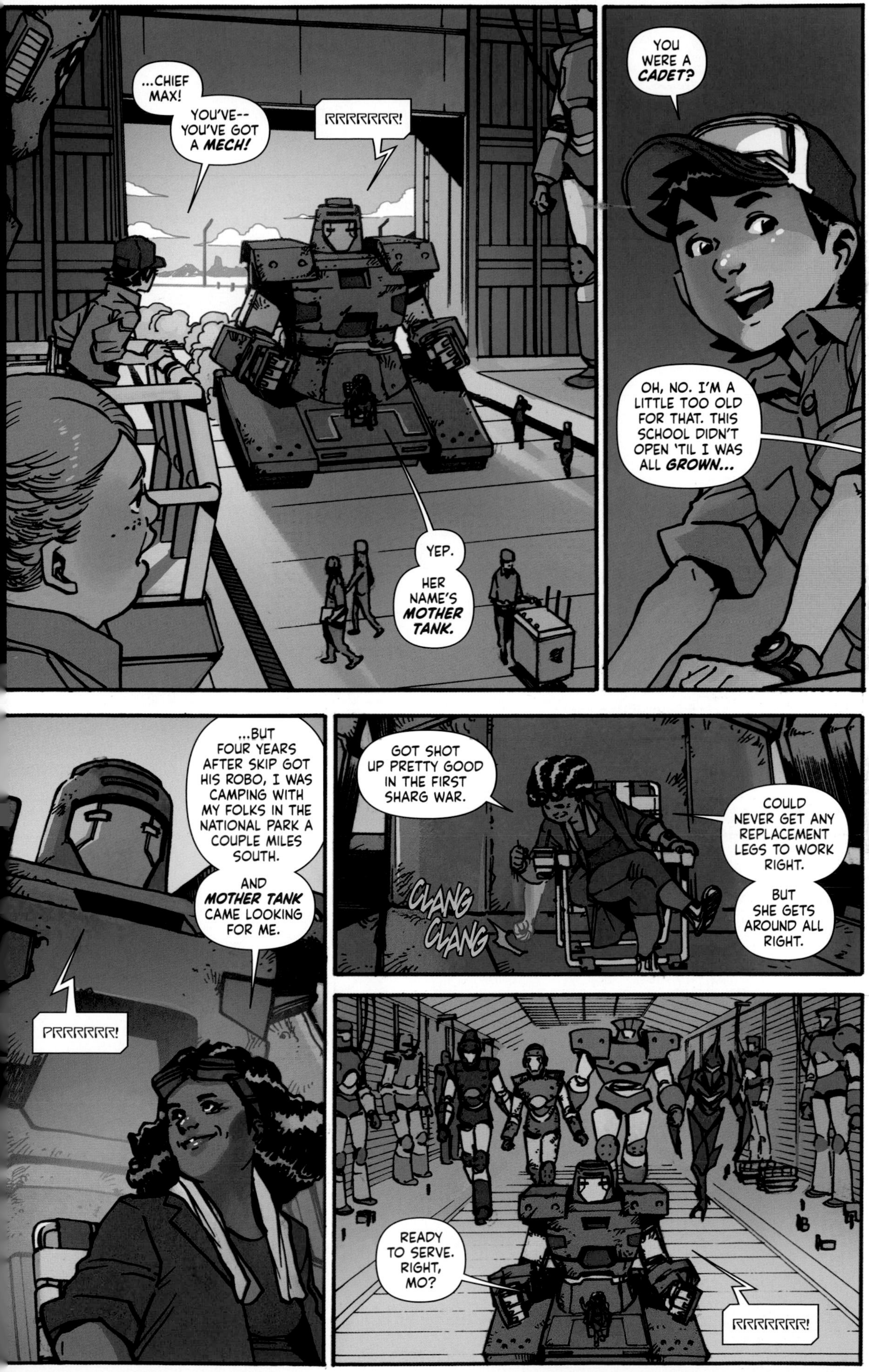

...CHIEF MAX!
YOU'VE-- YOU'VE GOT A MECH!
RRRRRRRR!
YEP.
HER NAME'S MOTHER TANK.
YOU WERE A CADET?
OH, NO. I'M A LITTLE TOO OLD FOR THAT. THIS SCHOOL DIDN'T OPEN 'TIL I WAS ALL GROWN...
...BUT FOUR YEARS AFTER SKIP GOT HIS ROBO, I WAS CAMPING WITH MY FOLKS IN THE NATIONAL PARK A COUPLE MILES SOUTH.
AND MOTHER TANK CAME LOOKING FOR ME.
PRRRRRRR!
GOT SHOT UP PRETTY GOOD IN THE FIRST SHARG WAR.
CLANG
CLANG
COULD NEVER GET ANY REPLACEMENT LEGS TO WORK RIGHT.
BUT SHE GETS AROUND ALL RIGHT.
READY TO SERVE. RIGHT, MO?
RRRRRRRR!

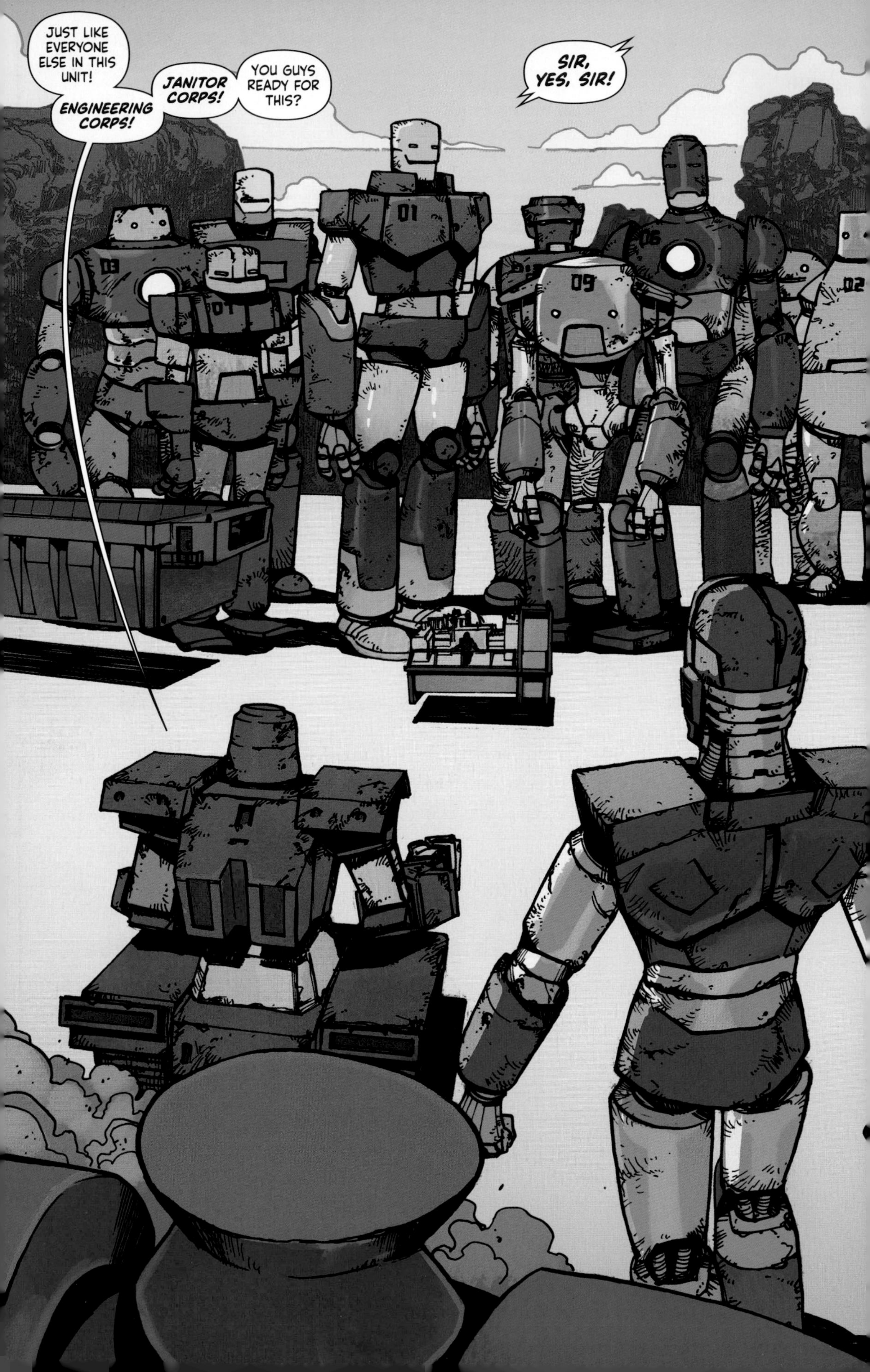
JUST LIKE EVERYONE ELSE IN THIS UNIT!
ENGINEERING CORPS!
JANITOR CORPS!
YOU GUYS READY FOR THIS?
SIR, YES, SIR!
01
03
01
09
06
02

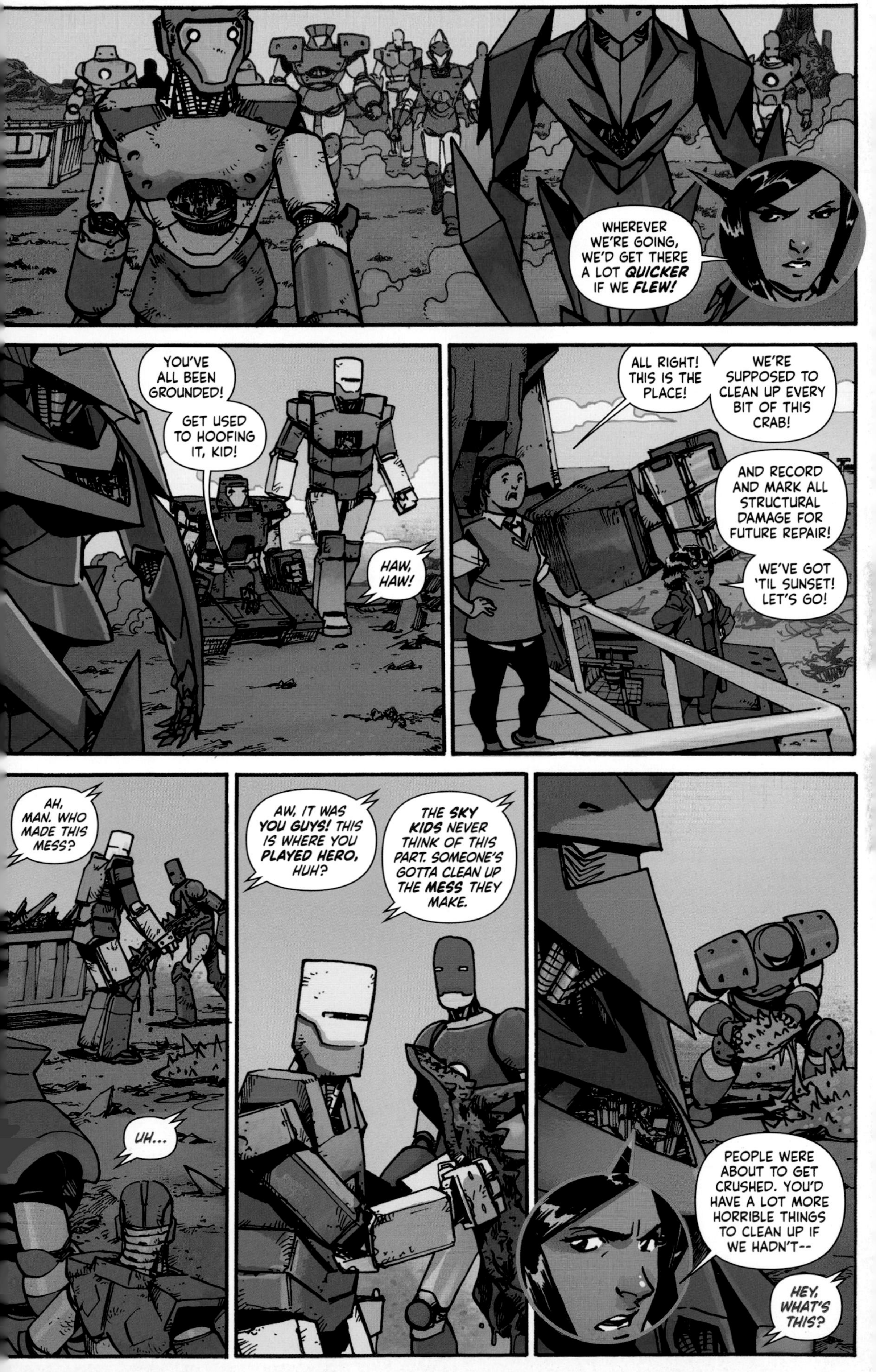
WHEREVER WE'RE GOING, WE'D GET THERE A LOT QUICKER IF WE FLEW!
YOU'VE ALL BEEN GROUNDED!
GET USED TO HOOFING IT, KID!
HAW, HAW!
ALL RIGHT! THIS IS THE PLACE!
WE'RE SUPPOSED TO CLEAN UP EVERY BIT OF THIS CRAB!
AND RECORD AND MARK ALL STRUCTURAL DAMAGE FOR FUTURE REPAIR!
WE'VE GOT 'TIL SUNSET! LET'S GO!
AH, MAN. WHO MADE THIS MESS?
UH...
AW, IT WAS YOU GUYS! THIS IS WHERE YOU PLAYED HERO, HUH?
THE SKY KIDS NEVER THINK OF THIS PART. SOMEONE'S GOTTA CLEAN UP THE MESS THEY MAKE.
PEOPLE WERE ABOUT TO GET CRUSHED. YOU'D HAVE A LOT MORE HORRIBLE THINGS TO CLEAN UP IF WE HADN'T--
HEY, WHAT'S THIS?

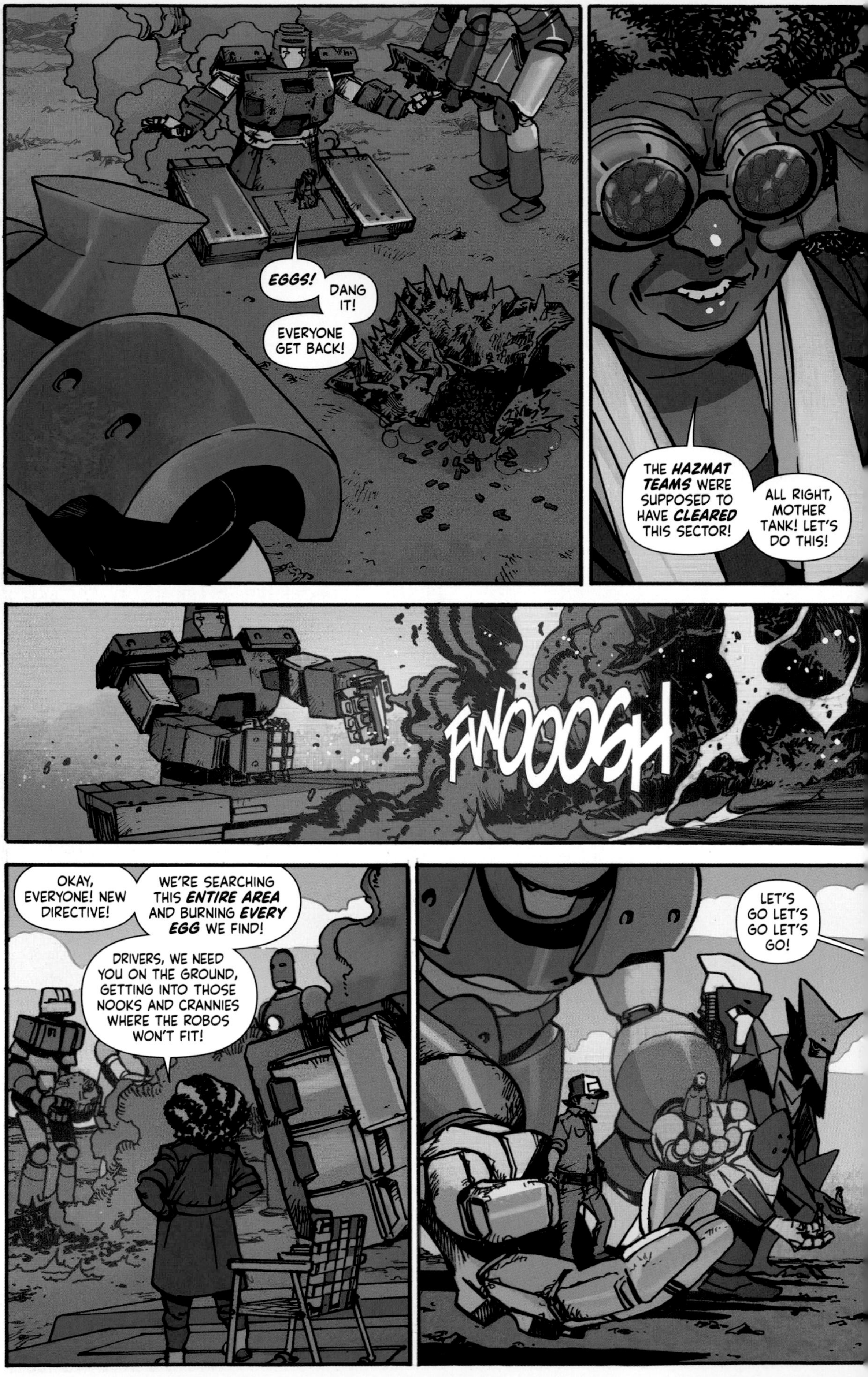
EGGS!
DANG IT!
EVERYONE GET BACK!
THE HAZMAT TEAMS WERE SUPPOSED TO HAVE CLEARED THIS SECTOR!
ALL RIGHT, MOTHER TANK! LET'S DO THIS!
FWOOOSH
OKAY, EVERYONE! NEW DIRECTIVE!
WE'RE SEARCHING THIS ENTIRE AREA AND BURNING EVERY EGG WE FIND!
DRIVERS, WE NEED YOU ON THE GROUND, GETTING INTO THOSE NOOKS AND CRANNIES WHERE THE ROBOS WON'T FIT!
LET'S GO LET'S GO LET'S GO!

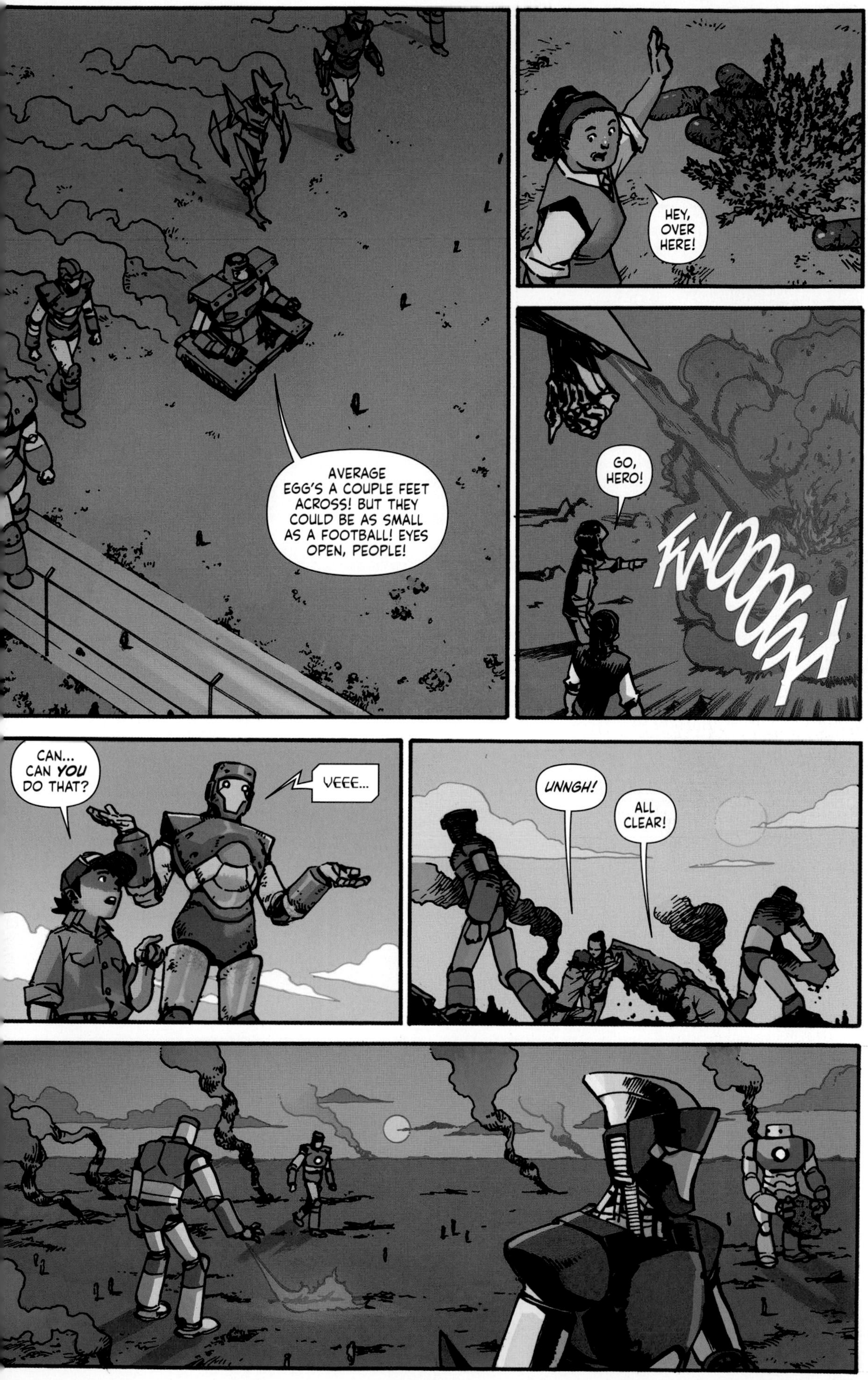
AVERAGE EGG'S A COUPLE FEET ACROSS! BUT THEY COULD BE AS SMALL AS A FOOTBALL! EYES OPEN, PEOPLE!
HEY, OVER HERE!
GO, HERO!
FWOOOOOSH
CAN... CAN *YOU* DO THAT?
VEEE...
UNNGH!
ALL CLEAR!

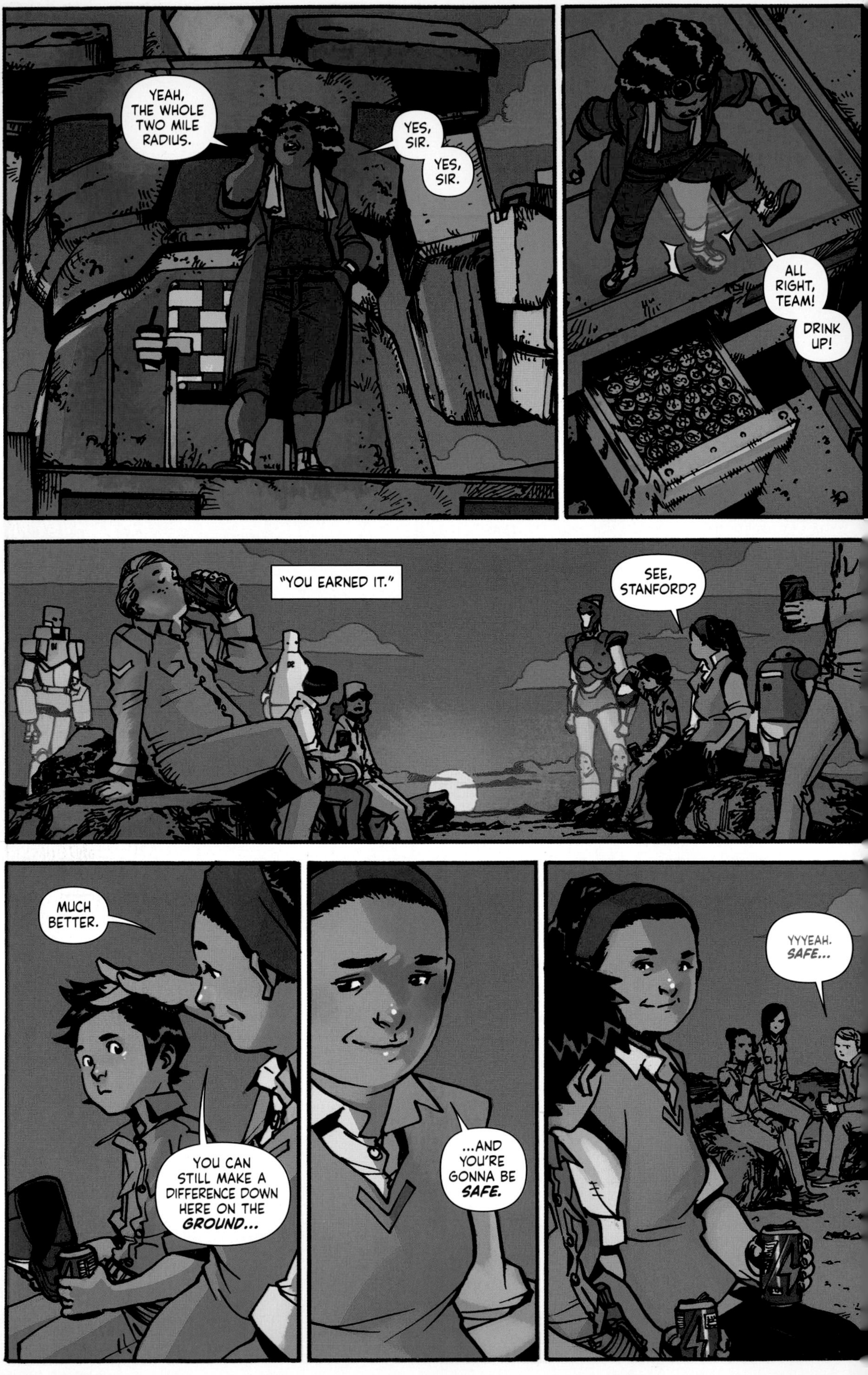
YEAH, THE WHOLE TWO MILE RADIUS.
YES, SIR.
YES, SIR.
ALL RIGHT, TEAM!
DRINK UP!
"YOU EARNED IT."
SEE, STANFORD?
MUCH BETTER.
YOU CAN STILL MAKE A DIFFERENCE DOWN HERE ON THE GROUND...
...AND YOU'RE GONNA BE SAFE.
YYYEAH. SAFE...

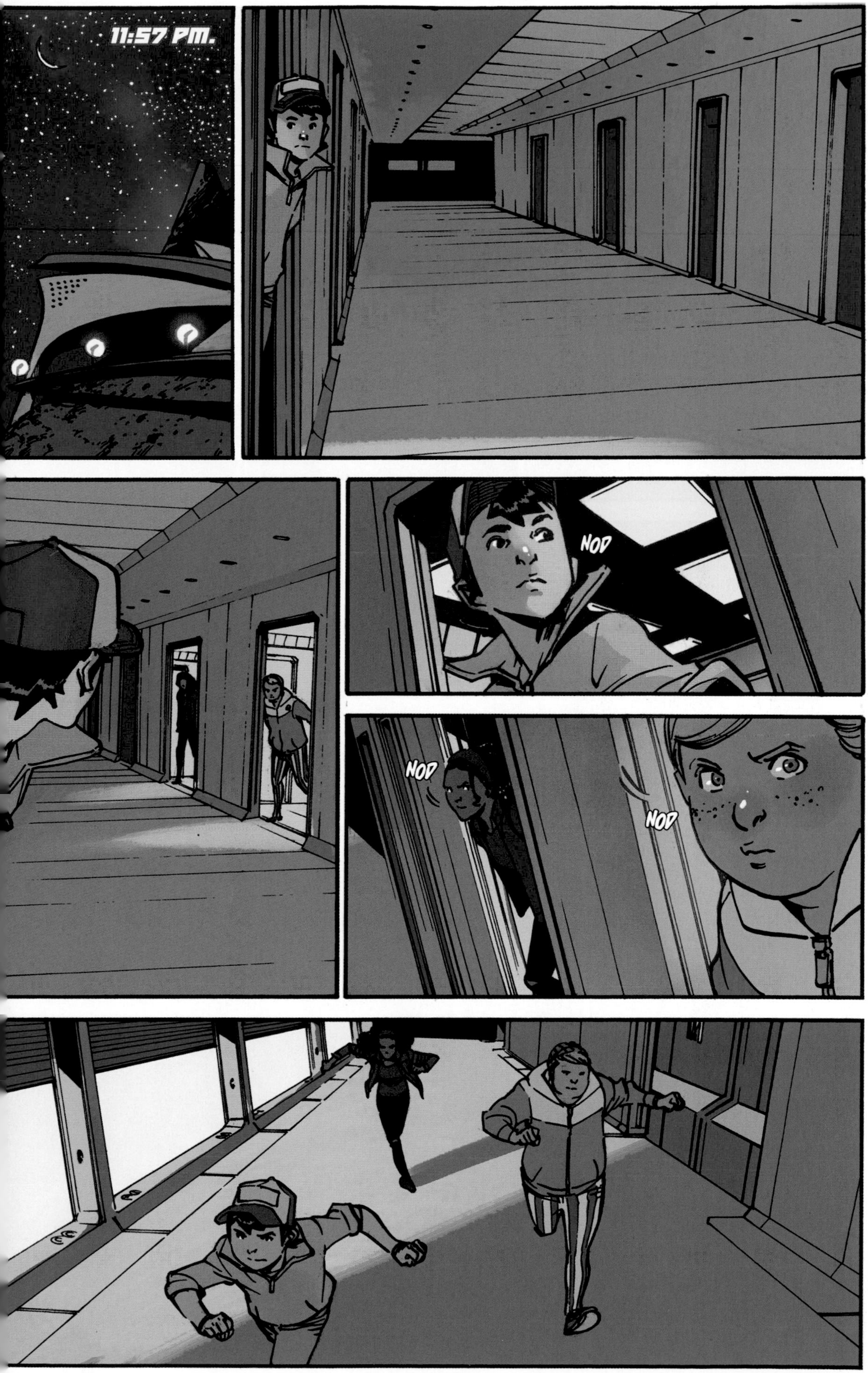
11:57 PM.
NOD
NOD
NOD

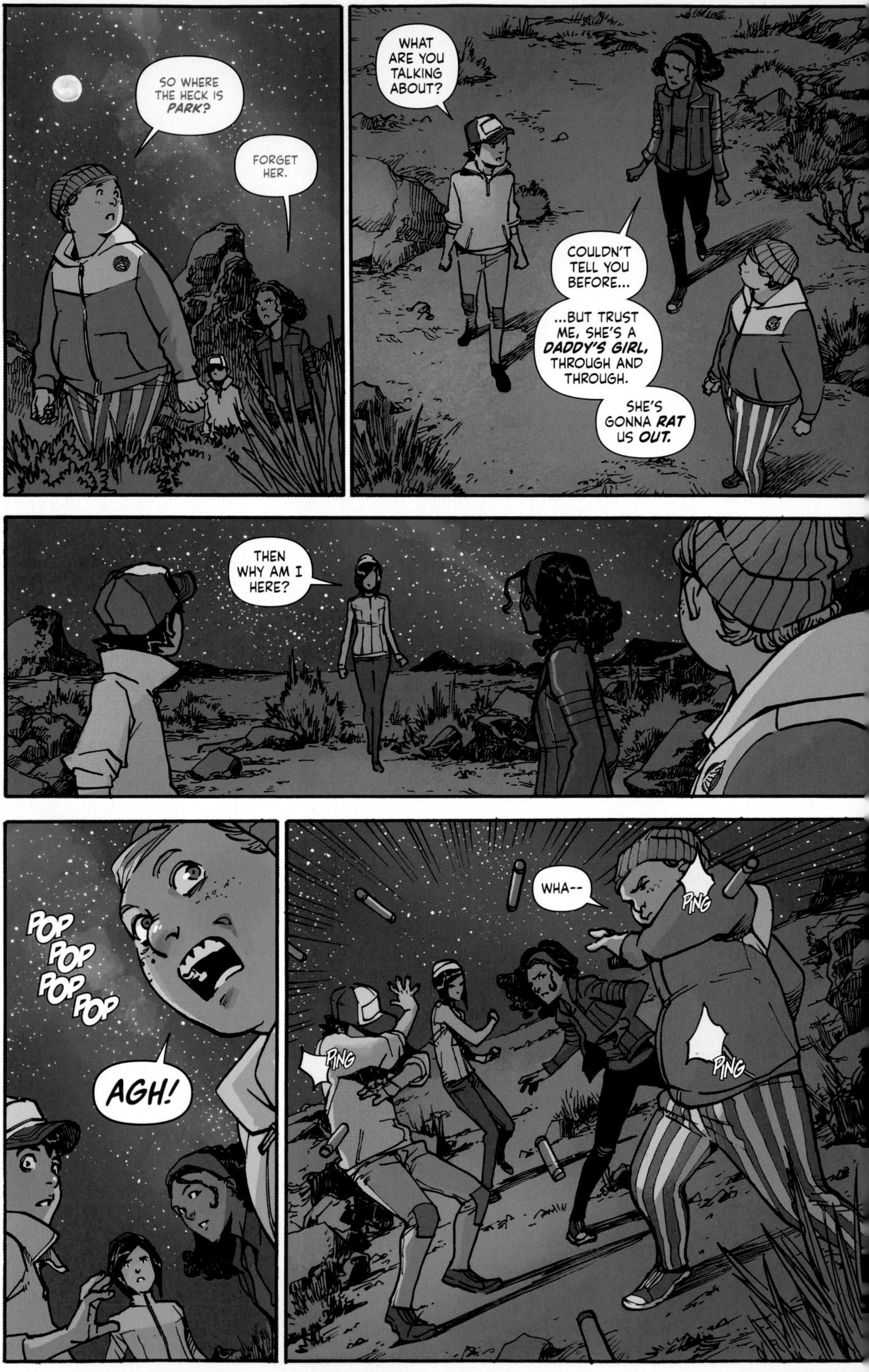
SO WHERE THE HECK IS PARK?
FORGET HER.
WHAT ARE YOU TALKING ABOUT?
COULDN'T TELL YOU BEFORE...
...BUT TRUST ME, SHE'S A DADDY'S GIRL, THROUGH AND THROUGH.
SHE'S GONNA RAT US OUT.
THEN WHY AM I HERE?
POP POP POP POP
AGH!
WHA--
PING
PING
PING

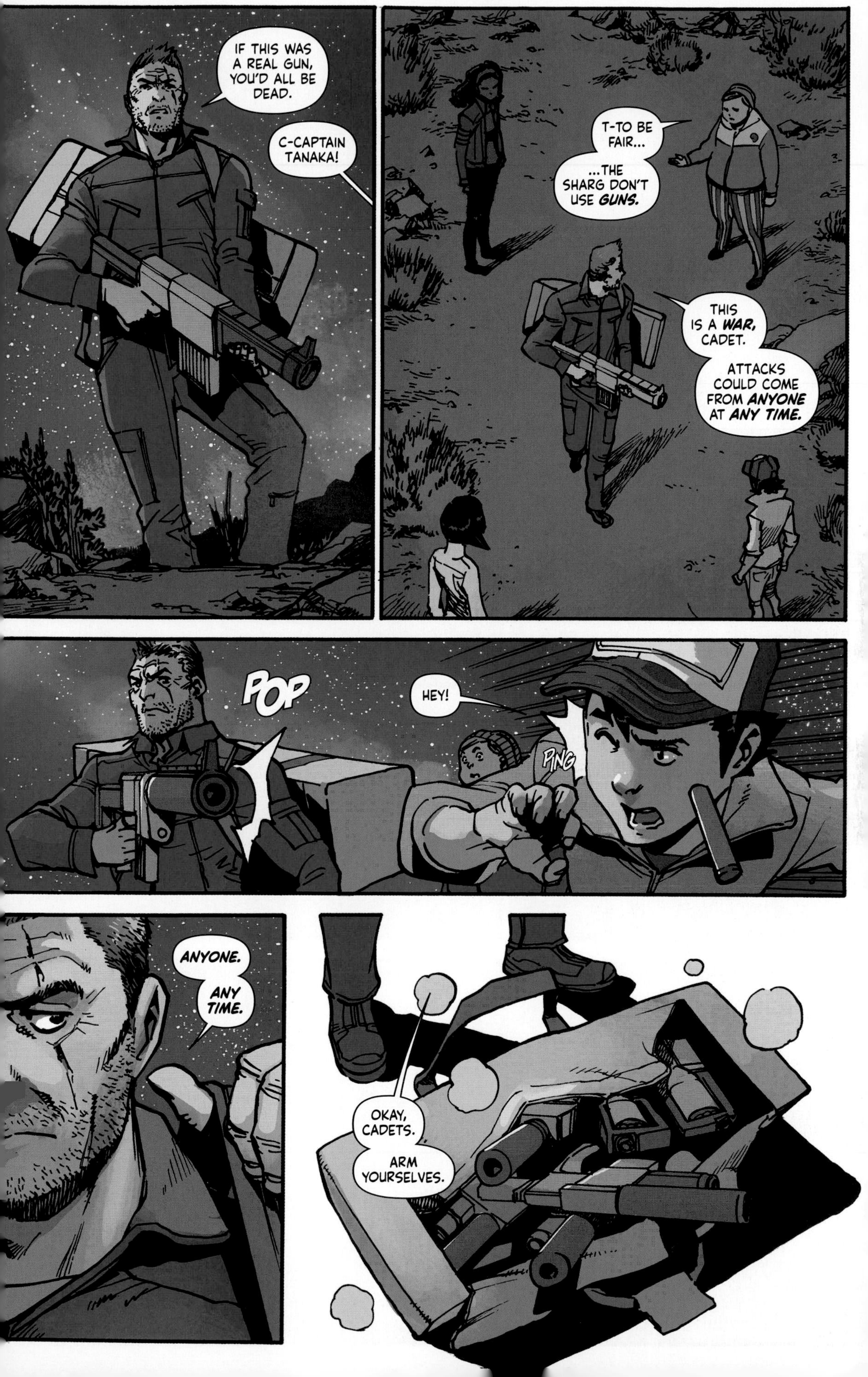
IF THIS WAS A REAL GUN, YOU'D ALL BE DEAD.
C-CAPTAIN TANAKA!
T-TO BE FAIR...
...THE SHARG DON'T USE GUNS.
THIS IS A WAR, CADET.
ATTACKS COULD COME FROM ANYONE AT ANY TIME.
POP
HEY!
PING
ANYONE.
ANY TIME.
OKAY, CADETS.
ARM YOURSELVES.

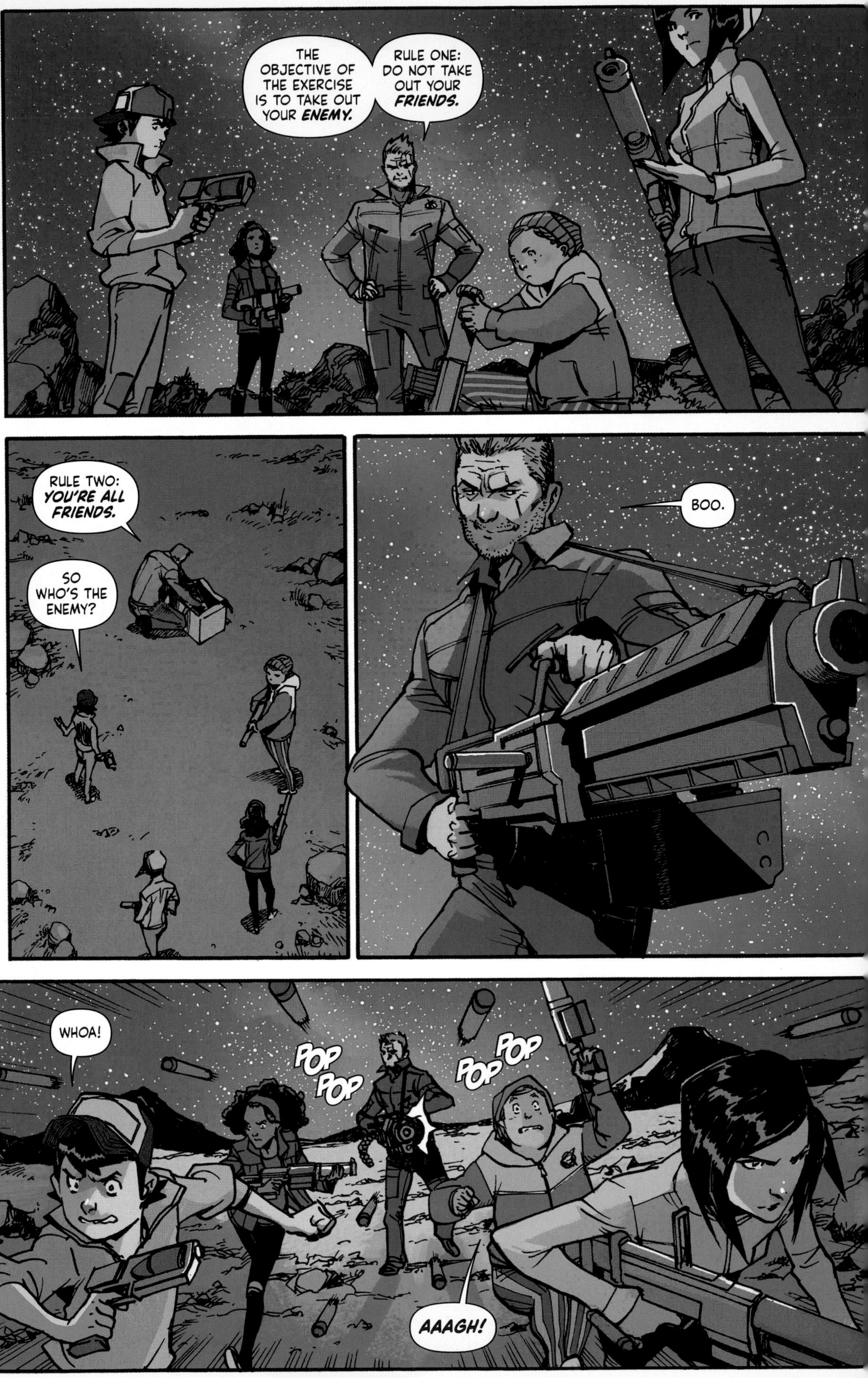
THE OBJECTIVE OF THE EXERCISE IS TO TAKE OUT YOUR ENEMY.
RULE ONE: DO NOT TAKE OUT YOUR FRIENDS.
RULE TWO: YOU'RE ALL FRIENDS.
SO WHO'S THE ENEMY?
BOO.
WHOA!
POP POP
POP POP POP
AAAGH!

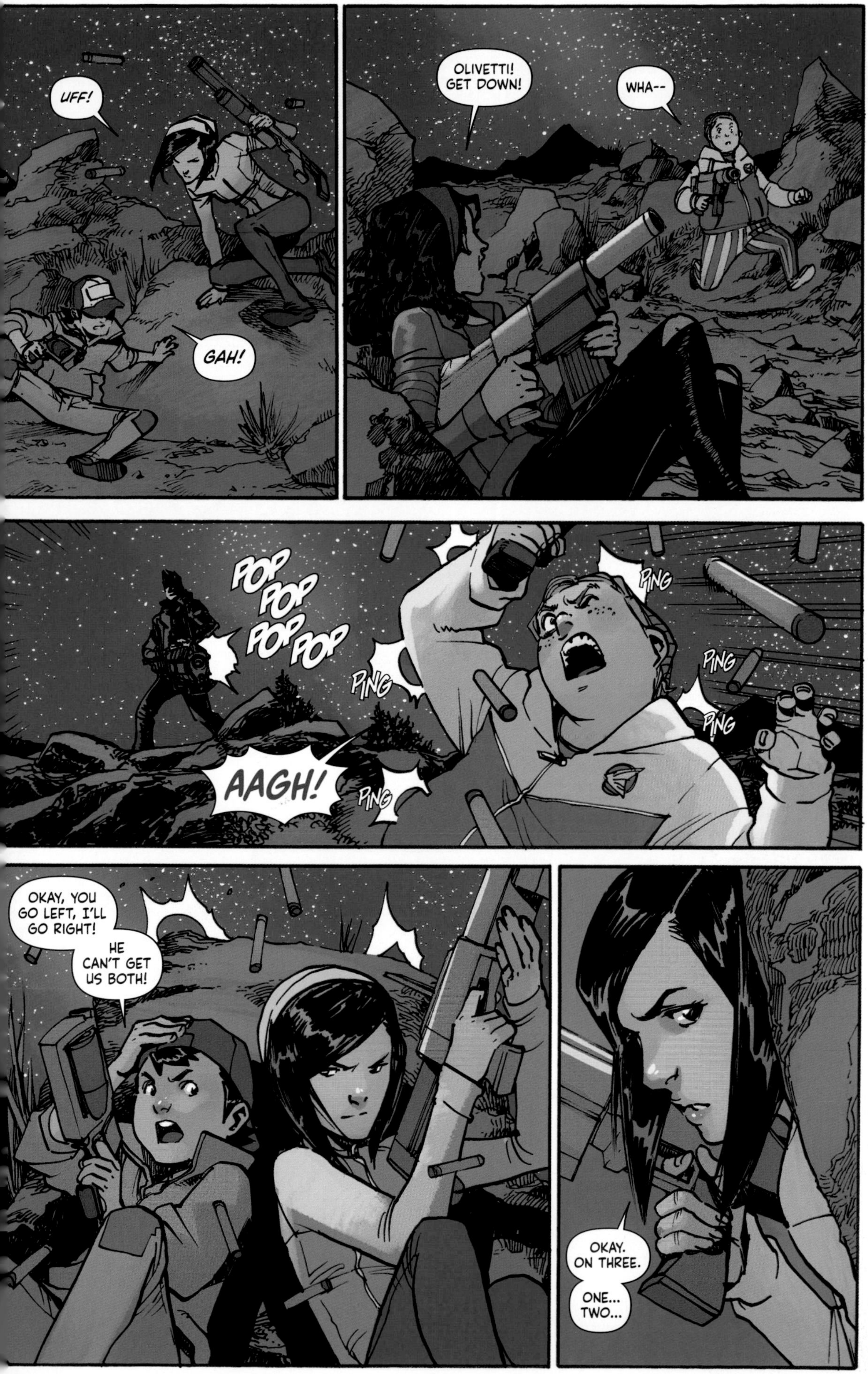
UFF!
GAH!
OLIVETTI! GET DOWN!
WHA--
POP POP POP POP
PING
PING
PING
PING
AAGH!
PING
OKAY, YOU GO LEFT, I'LL GO RIGHT!
HE CAN'T GET US BOTH!
OKAY. ON THREE.
ONE... TWO...

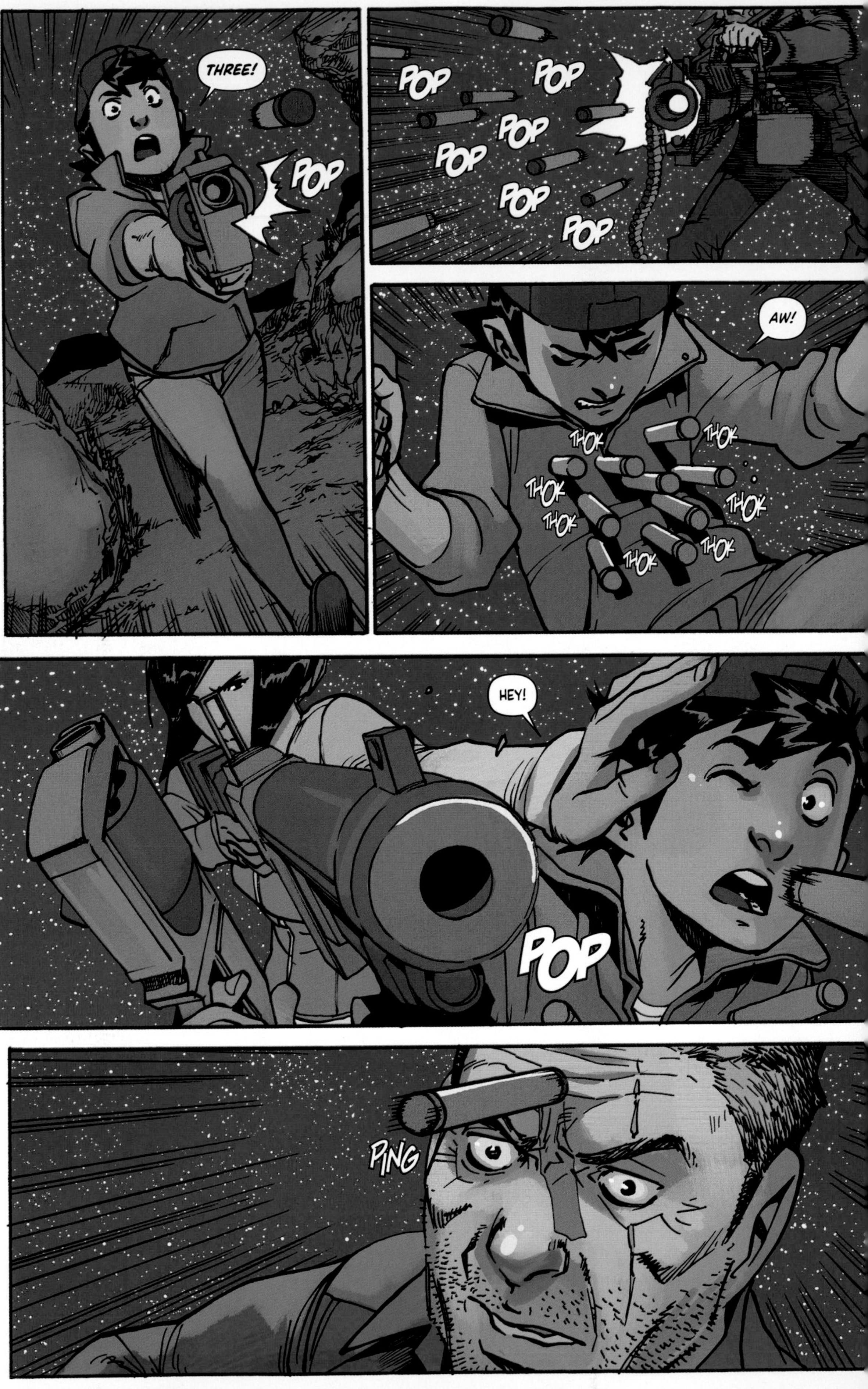
THREE!
POP
POP
POP
POP
POP
POP
POP
AW!
THOK
THOK
THOK
THOK
THOK
THOK
THOK
HEY!
POP
PING

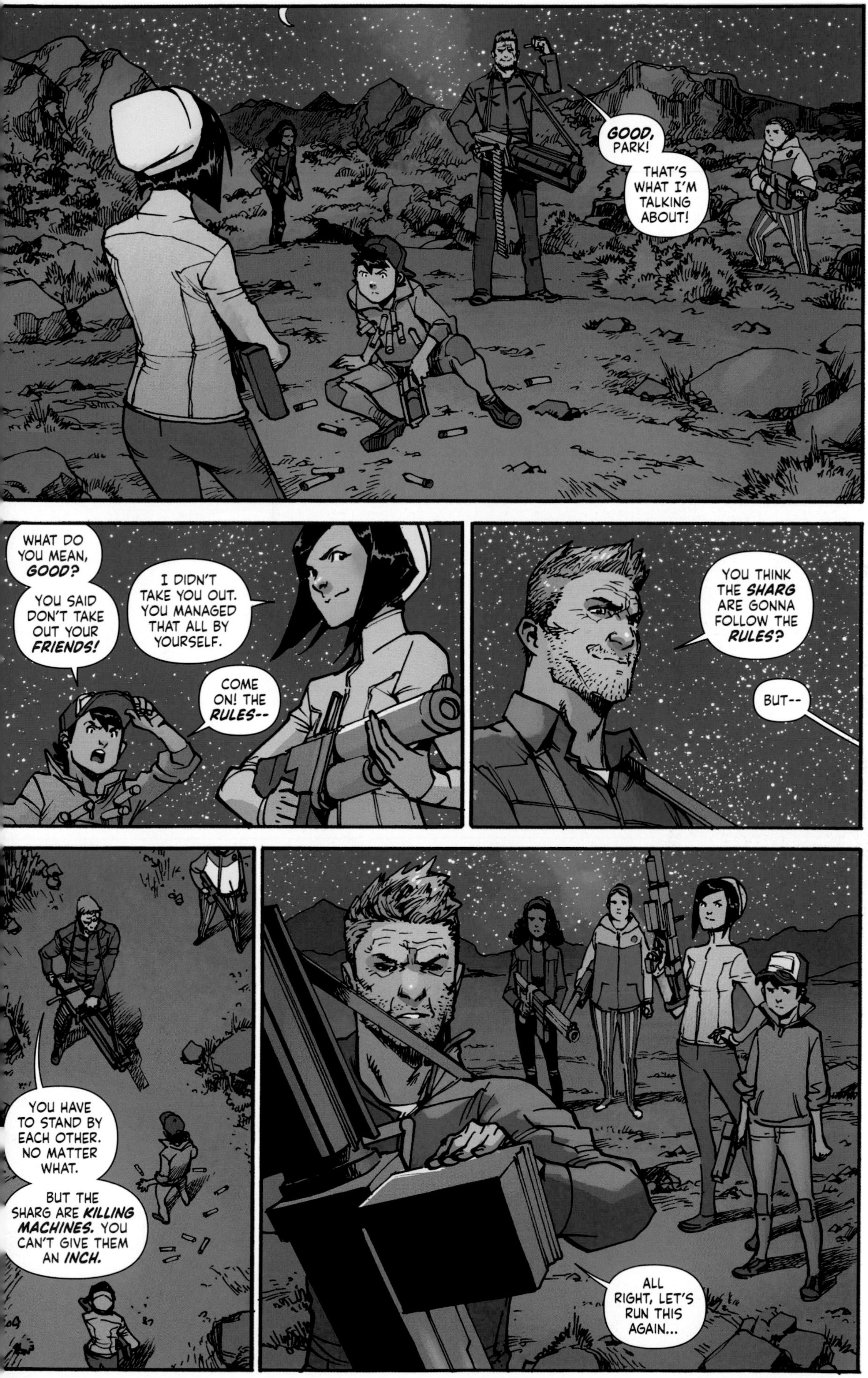
GOOD, PARK!
THAT'S WHAT I'M TALKING ABOUT!
WHAT DO YOU MEAN, GOOD?
YOU SAID DON'T TAKE OUT YOUR FRIENDS!
I DIDN'T TAKE YOU OUT. YOU MANAGED THAT ALL BY YOURSELF.
COME ON! THE RULES--
YOU THINK THE SHARG ARE GONNA FOLLOW THE RULES?
BUT--
YOU HAVE TO STAND BY EACH OTHER. NO MATTER WHAT.
BUT THE SHARG ARE KILLING MACHINES. YOU CAN'T GIVE THEM AN INCH.
ALL RIGHT, LET'S RUN THIS AGAIN...

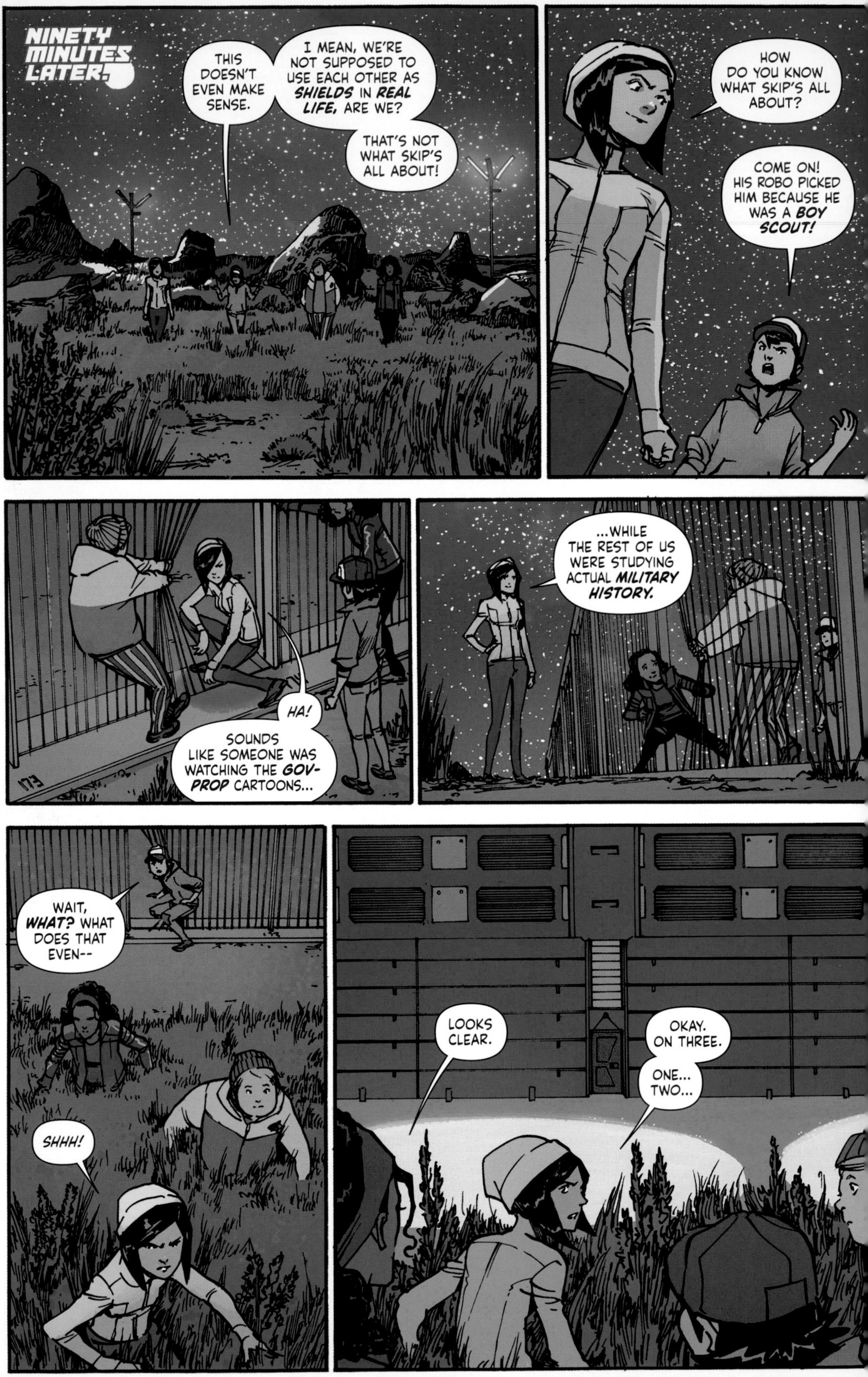
NINETY MINUTES LATER.
THIS DOESN'T EVEN MAKE SENSE.
I MEAN, WE'RE NOT SUPPOSED TO USE EACH OTHER AS SHIELDS IN REAL LIFE, ARE WE?
THAT'S NOT WHAT SKIP'S ALL ABOUT!
HOW DO YOU KNOW WHAT SKIP'S ALL ABOUT?
COME ON! HIS ROBO PICKED HIM BECAUSE HE WAS A BOY SCOUT!
HA!
SOUNDS LIKE SOMEONE WAS WATCHING THE GOV-PROP CARTOONS...
...WHILE THE REST OF US WERE STUDYING ACTUAL MILITARY HISTORY.
WAIT, WHAT? WHAT DOES THAT EVEN--
SHHH!
LOOKS CLEAR.
OKAY. ON THREE.
ONE... TWO...

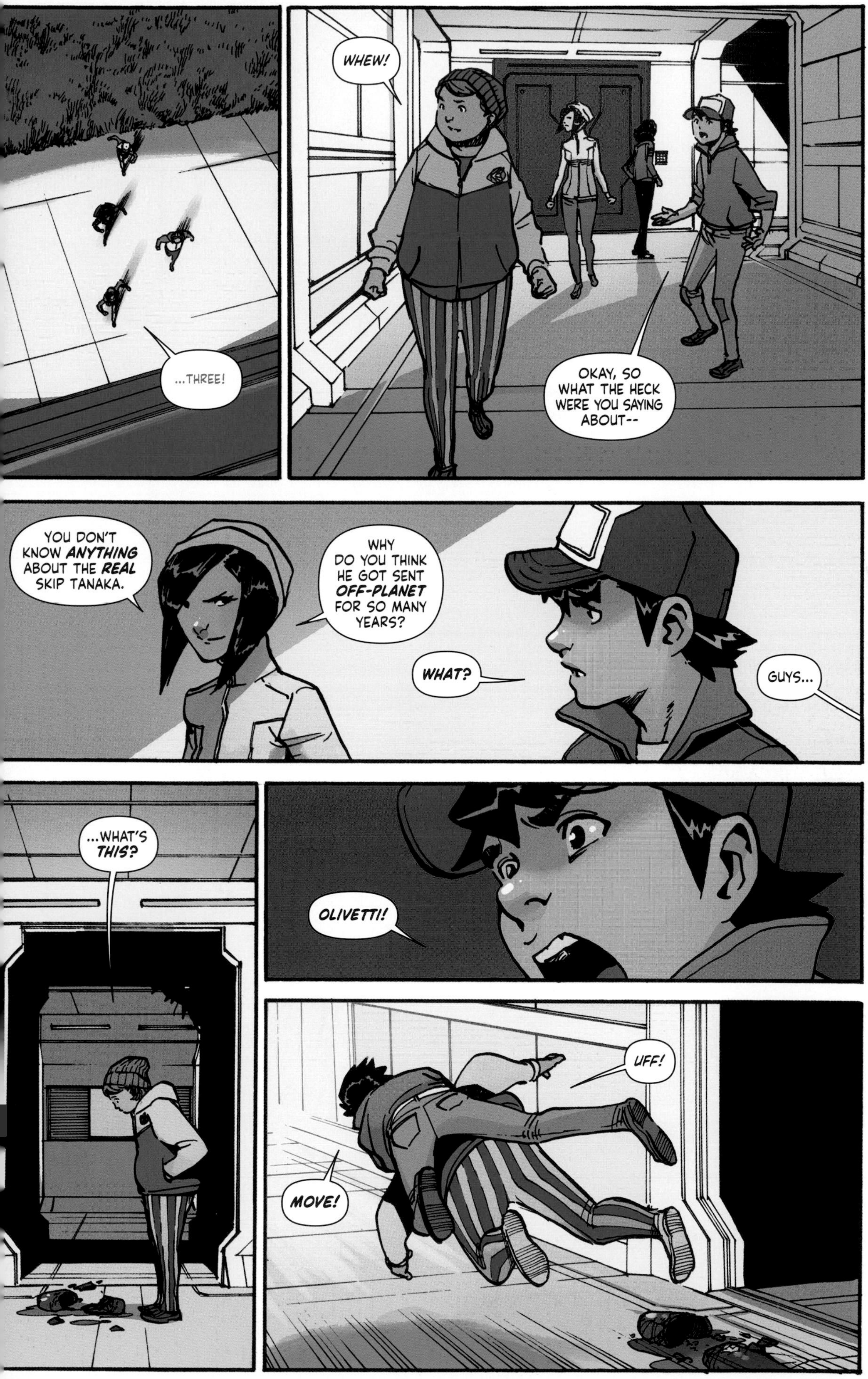

...THREE!
WHEW!
OKAY, SO WHAT THE HECK WERE YOU SAYING ABOUT--
YOU DON'T KNOW ANYTHING ABOUT THE REAL SKIP TANAKA.
WHY DO YOU THINK HE GOT SENT OFF-PLANET FOR SO MANY YEARS?
WHAT?
GUYS...
...WHAT'S THIS?
OLIVETTI!
UFF!
MOVE!

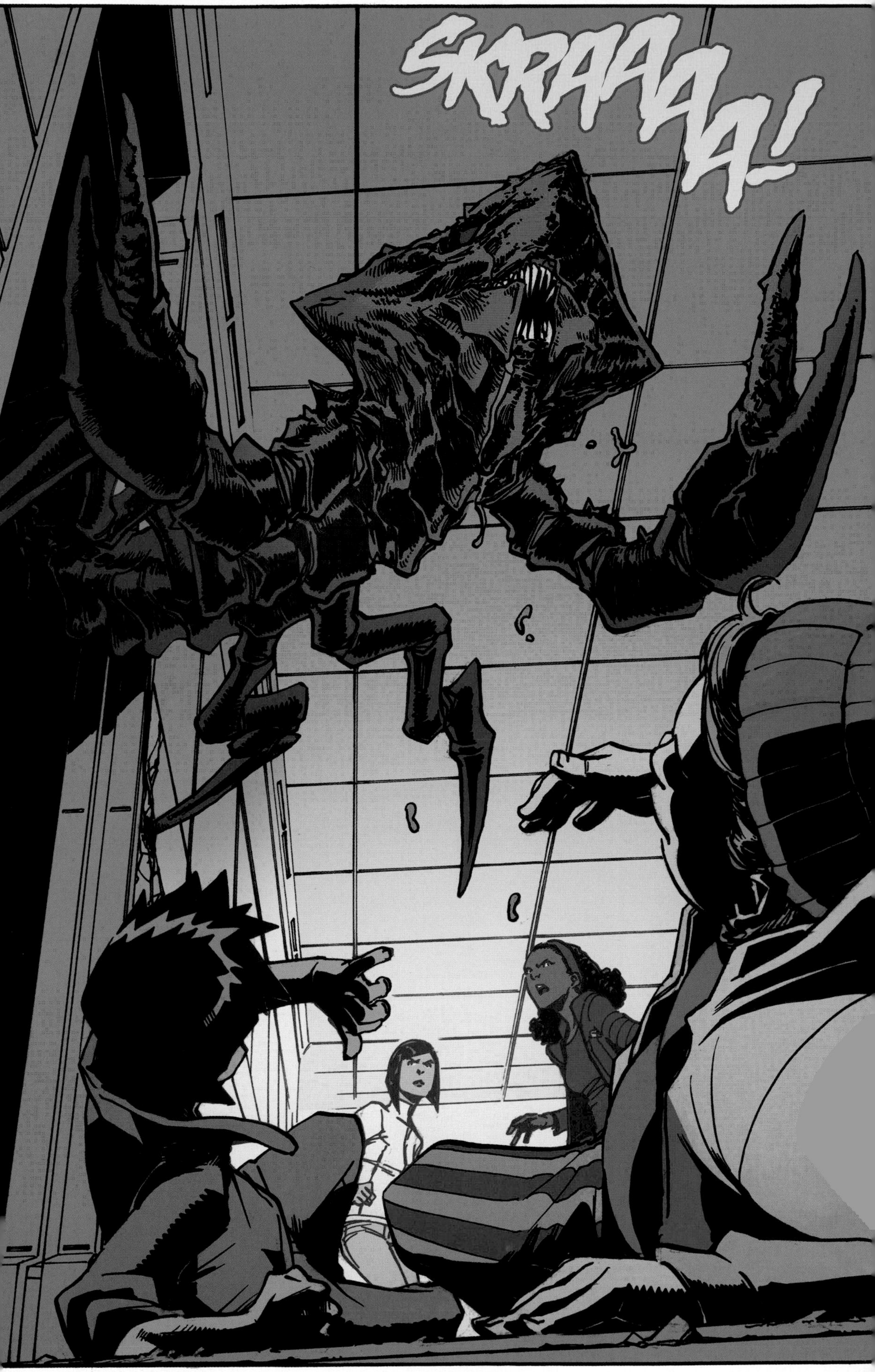
SKRAAAAA!

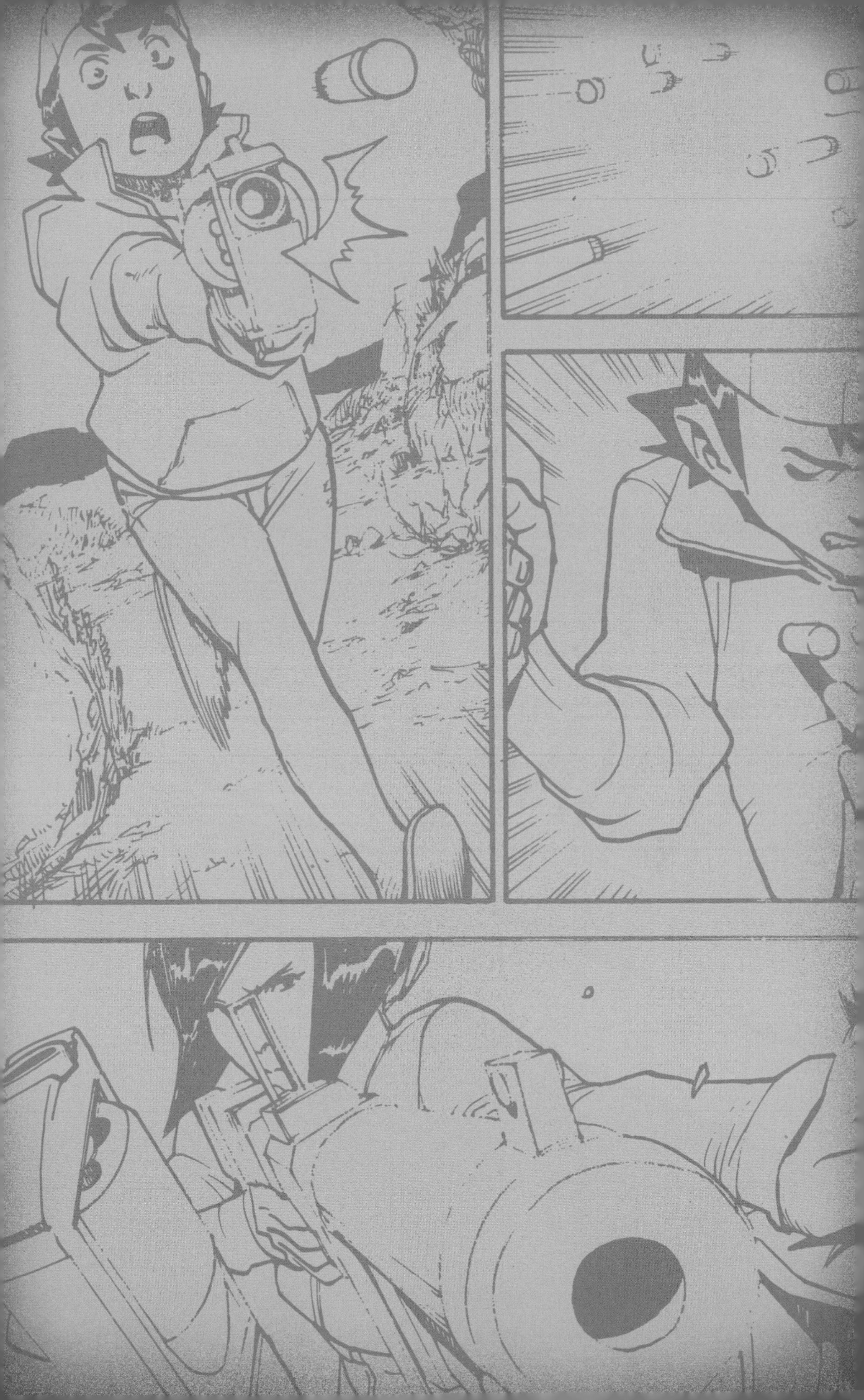

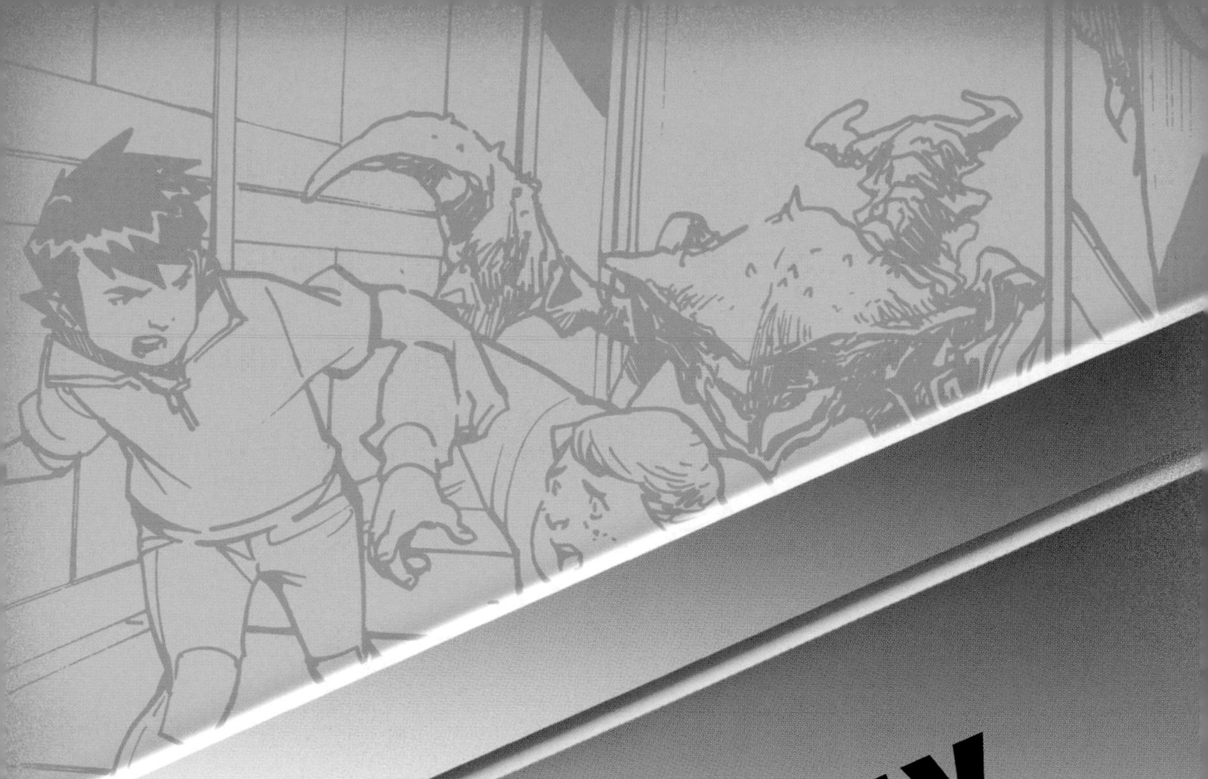

CHAPTER **SIX**

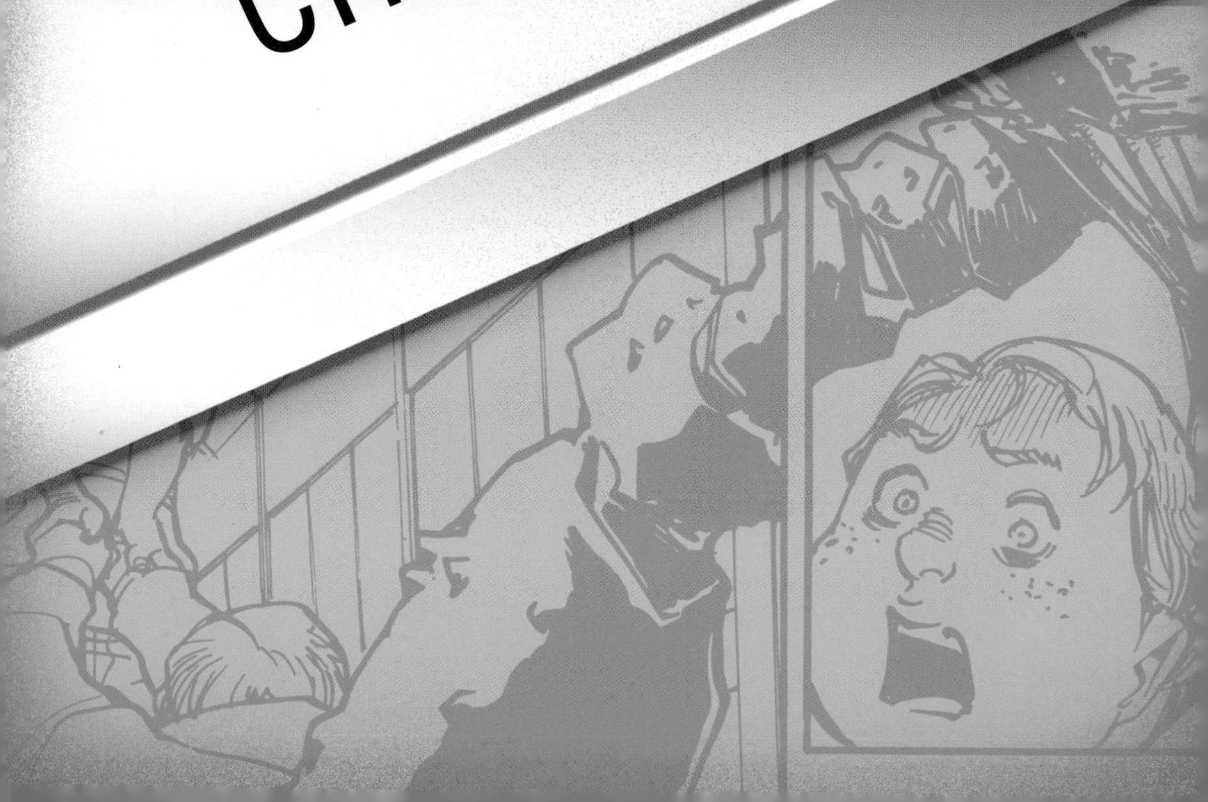

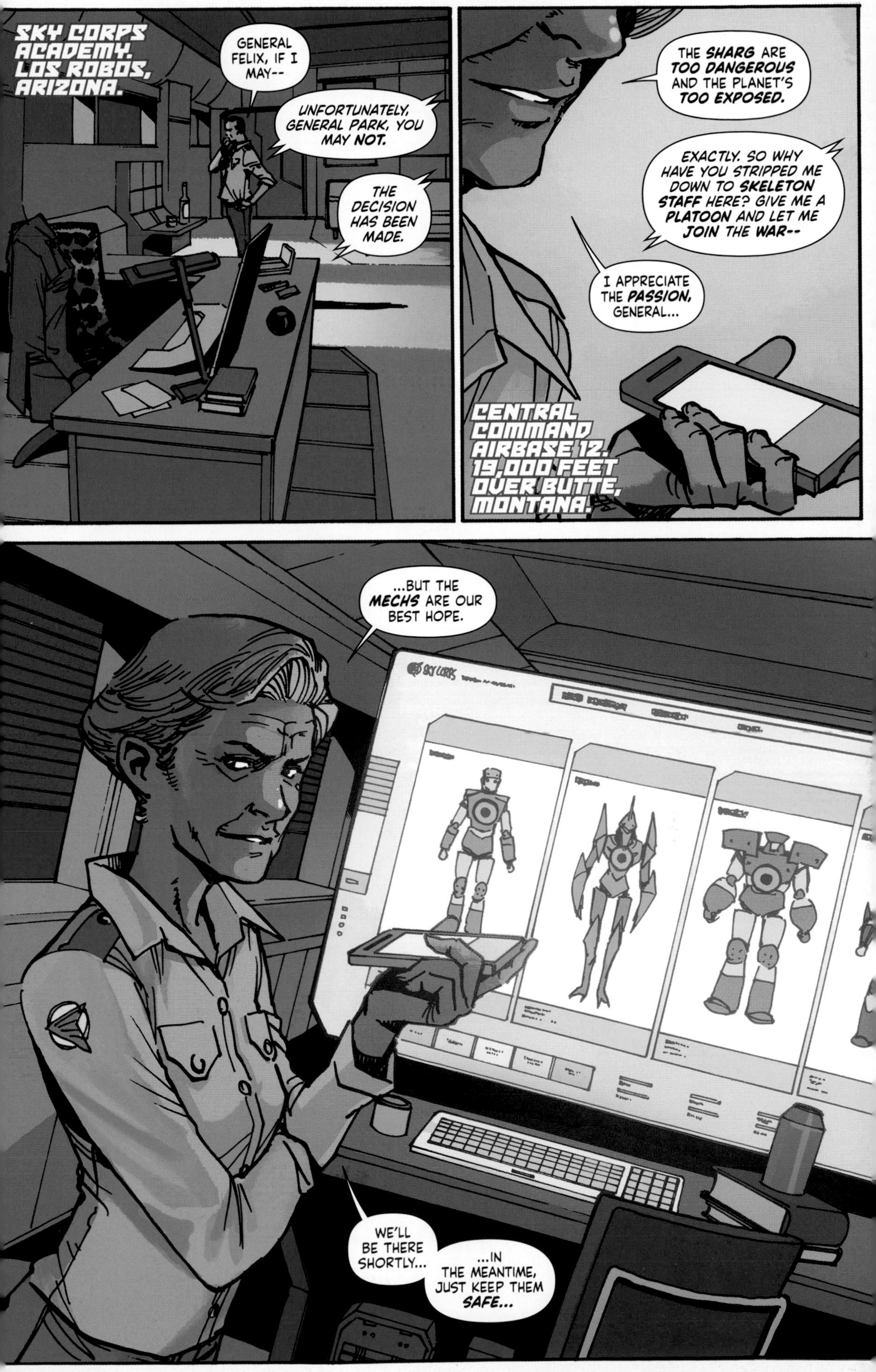

SKY CORPS ACADEMY. LOS ROBOS, ARIZONA.
GENERAL FELIX, IF I MAY--
UNFORTUNATELY, GENERAL PARK, YOU MAY NOT.
THE DECISION HAS BEEN MADE.
THE SHARG ARE TOO DANGEROUS AND THE PLANET'S TOO EXPOSED.
EXACTLY. SO WHY HAVE YOU STRIPPED ME DOWN TO SKELETON STAFF HERE? GIVE ME A PLATOON AND LET ME JOIN THE WAR--
I APPRECIATE THE PASSION, GENERAL...
CENTRAL COMMAND AIRBASE 12. 19,000 FEET OVER BUTTE, MONTANA.
...BUT THE MECHS ARE OUR BEST HOPE.
SKY CORPS
WE'LL BE THERE SHORTLY...
...IN THE MEANTIME, JUST KEEP THEM SAFE...

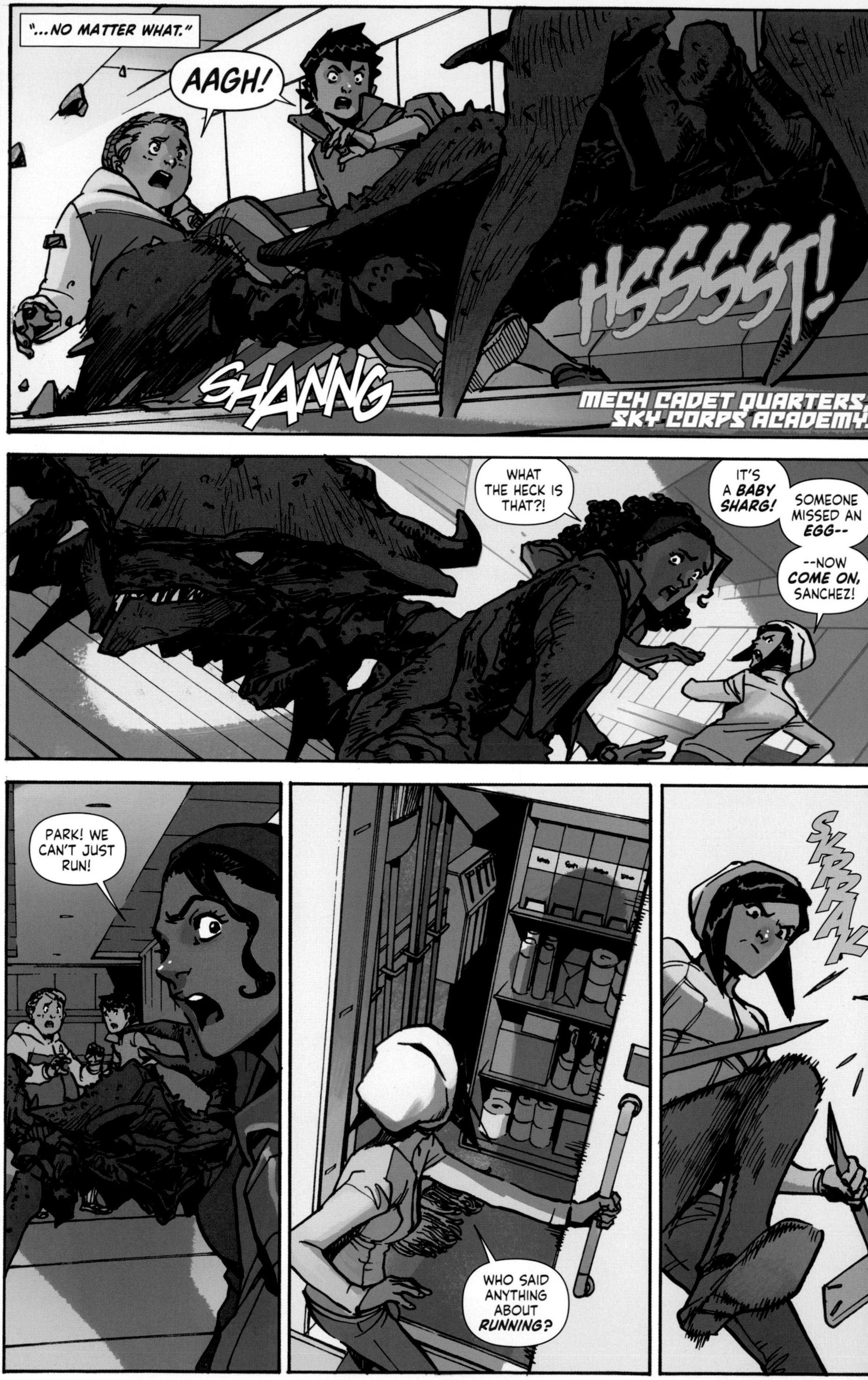
"...NO MATTER WHAT."
AAGH!
HSSSST!
SHANNG
MECH CADET QUARTERS, SKY CORPS ACADEMY.
WHAT THE HECK IS THAT?!
IT'S A BABY SHARG!
SOMEONE MISSED AN EGG--
--NOW COME ON, SANCHEZ!
PARK! WE CAN'T JUST RUN!
WHO SAID ANYTHING ABOUT RUNNING?
SKRRAK

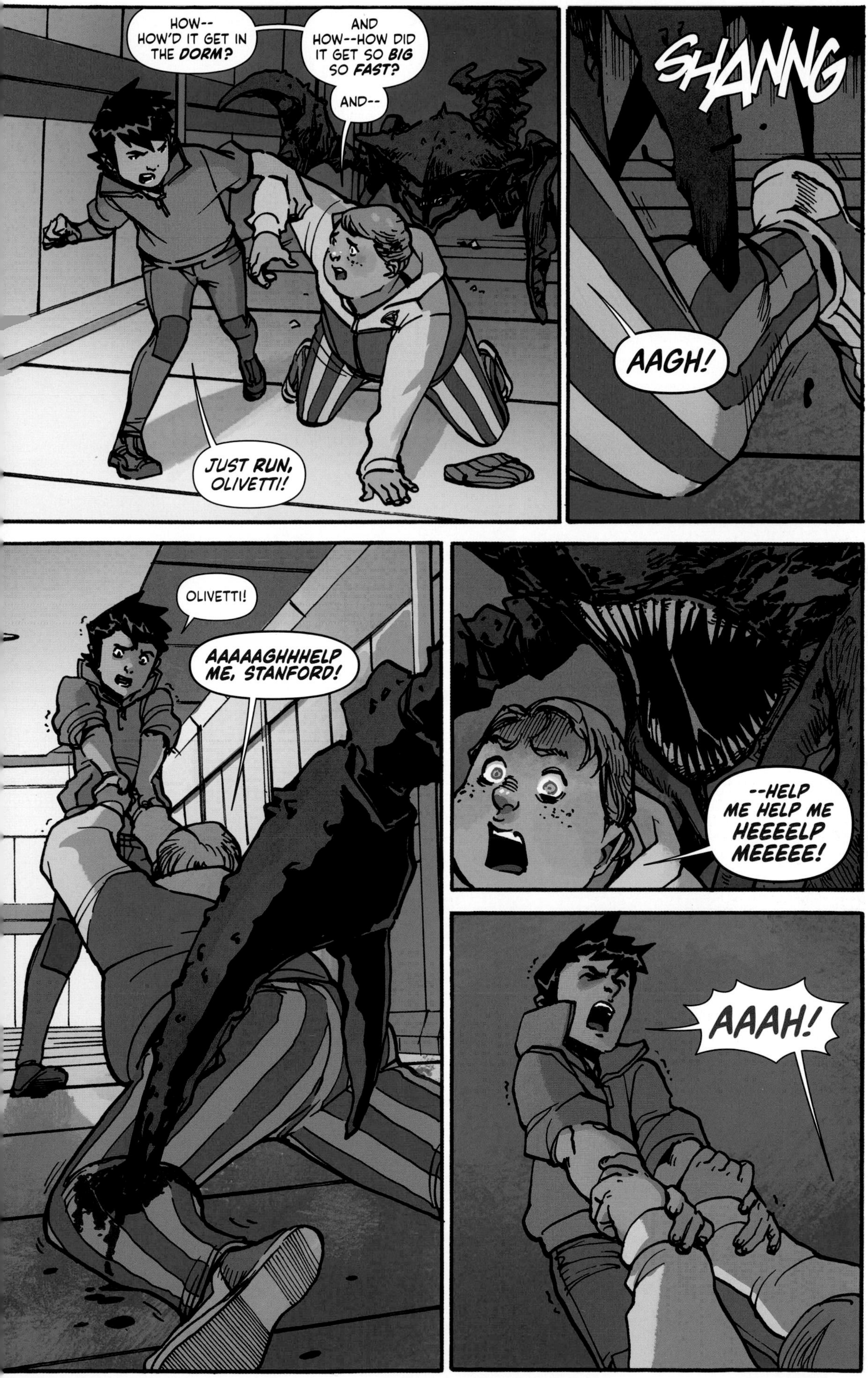
HOW--
HOW'D IT GET IN THE DORM?
AND HOW--HOW DID IT GET SO BIG SO FAST?
AND--
JUST RUN, OLIVETTI!
SHANNG
AAGH!
OLIVETTI!
AAAAAGHHHELP ME, STANFORD!
--HELP ME HELP ME HEEEELP MEEEEE!
AAAH!

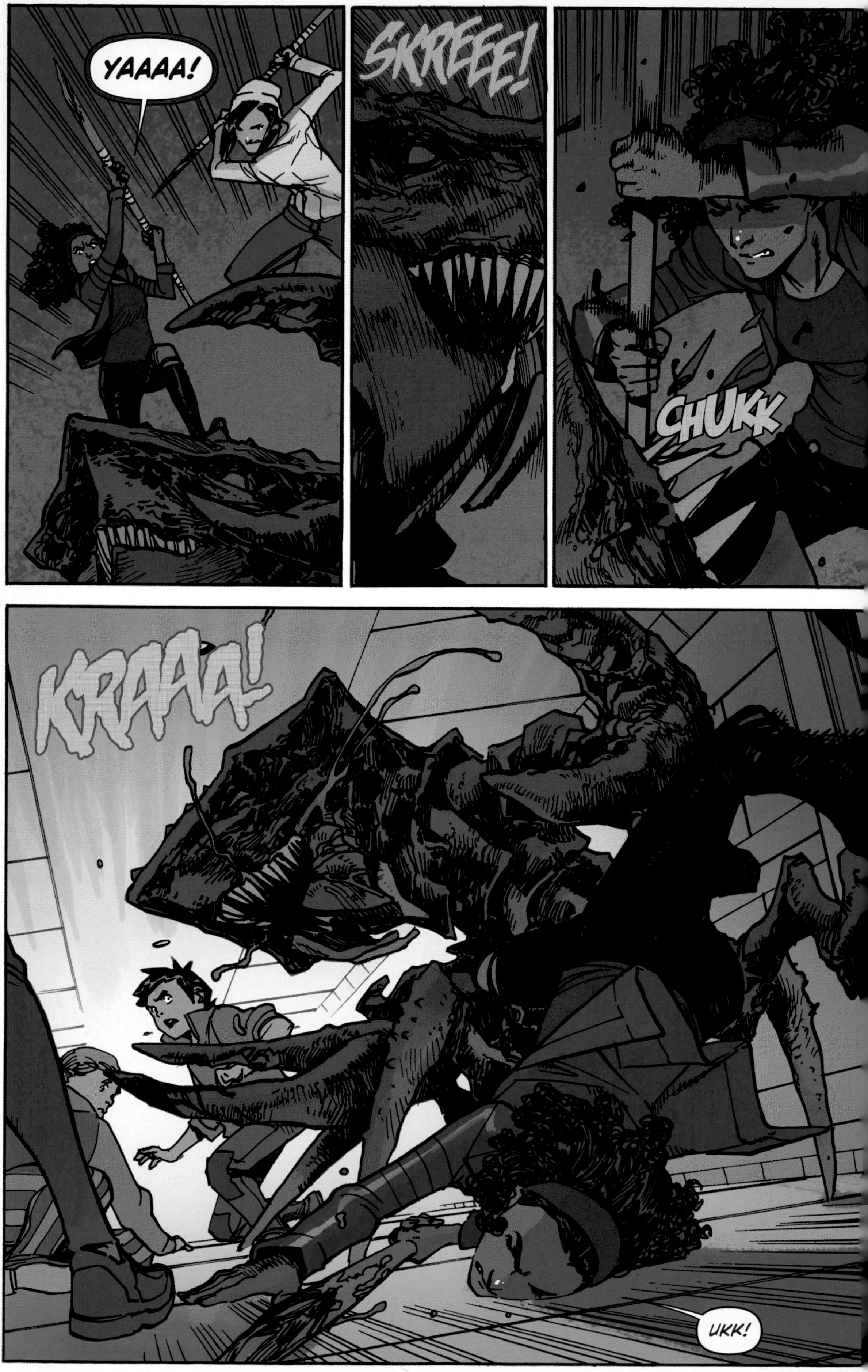
YAAAA!
SKREEE!
CHUKK
KRAAA!
UKK!

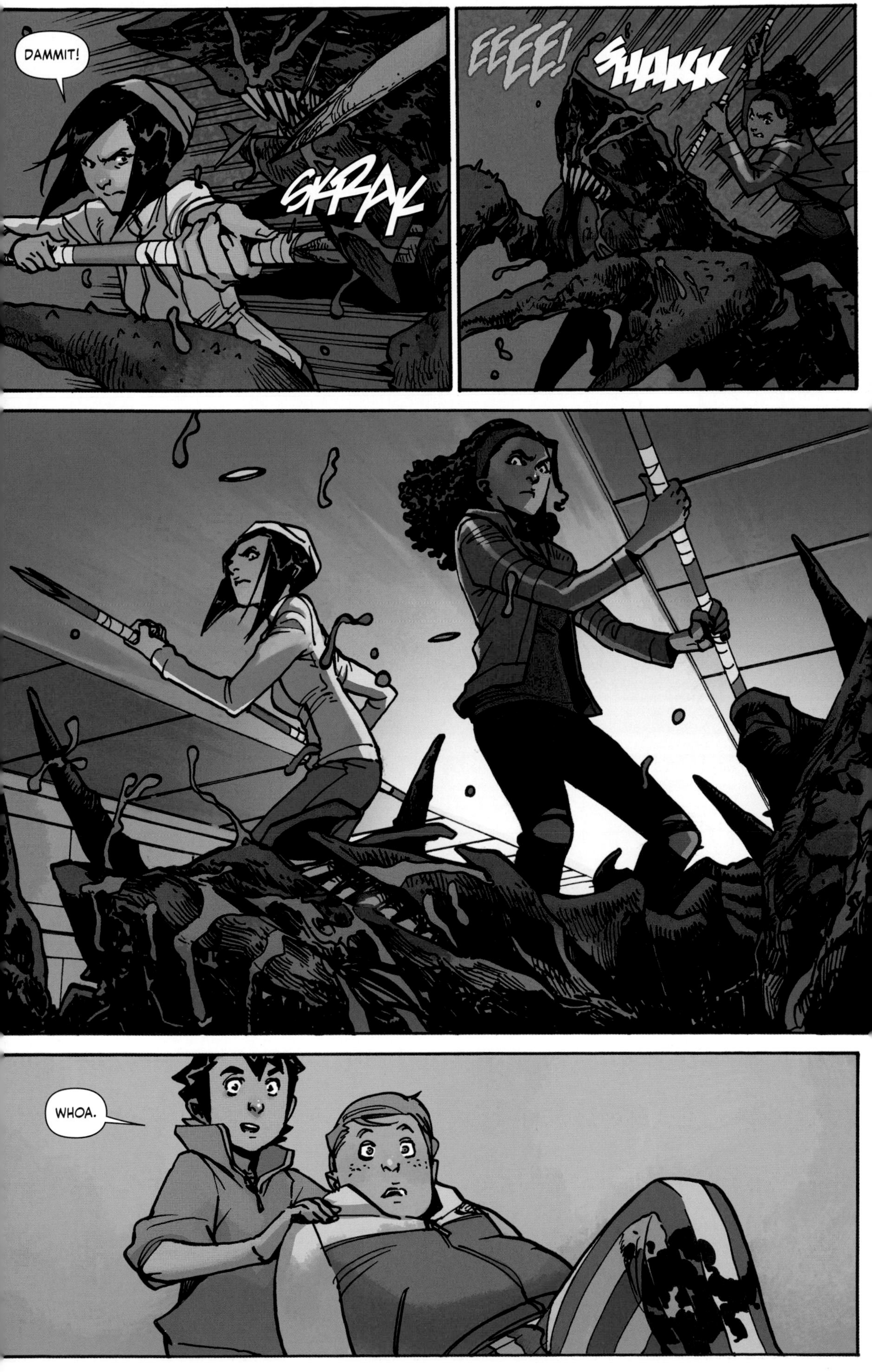
DAMMIT!
SKRAK
EEEE!
SHAKK
WHOA.

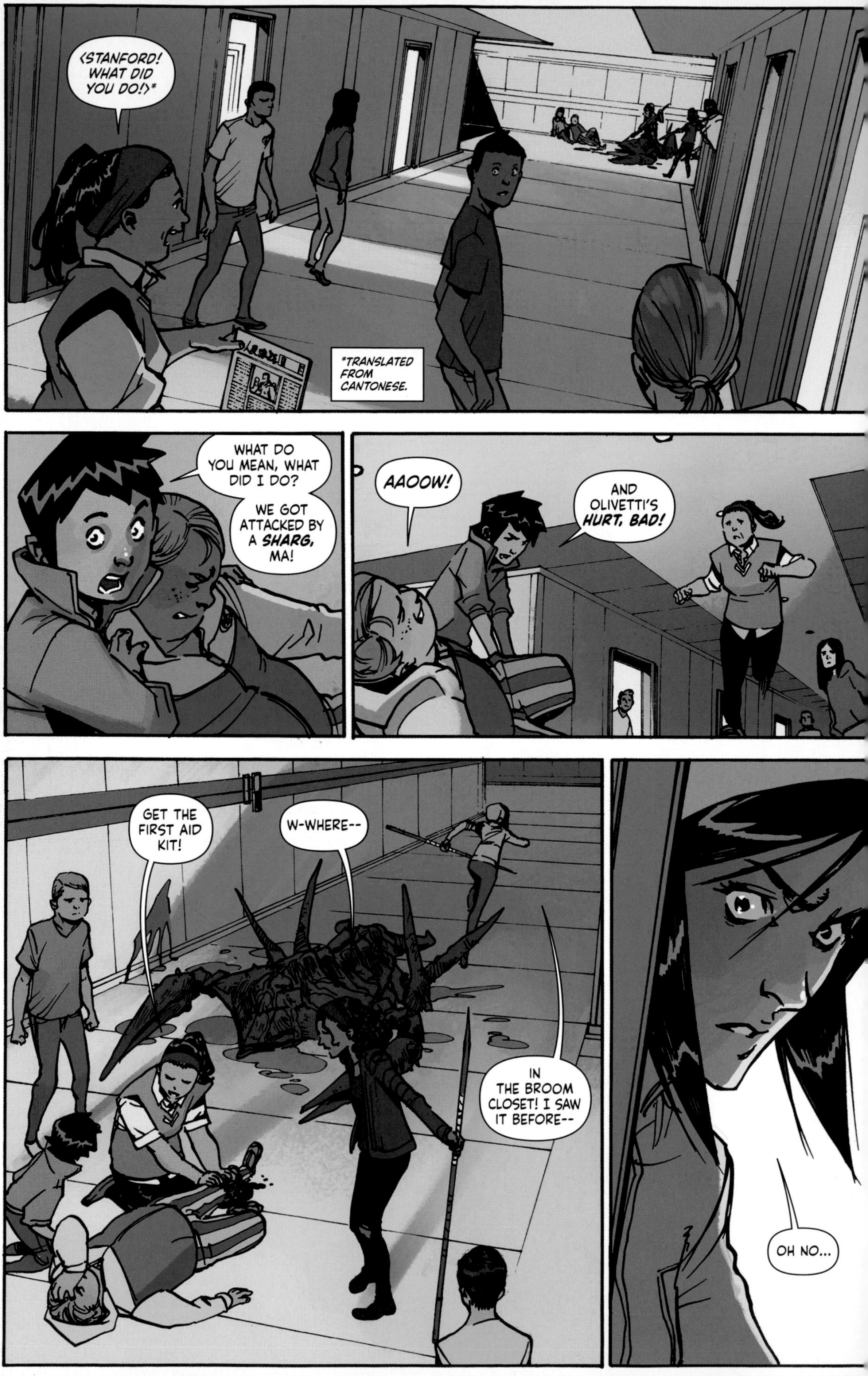

‹STANFORD! WHAT DID YOU DO!›*
*TRANSLATED FROM CANTONESE.
WHAT DO YOU MEAN, WHAT DID I DO?
WE GOT ATTACKED BY A SHARG, MA!
AAOOW!
AND OLIVETTI'S HURT, BAD!
GET THE FIRST AID KIT!
W-WHERE--
IN THE BROOM CLOSET! I SAW IT BEFORE--
OH NO...

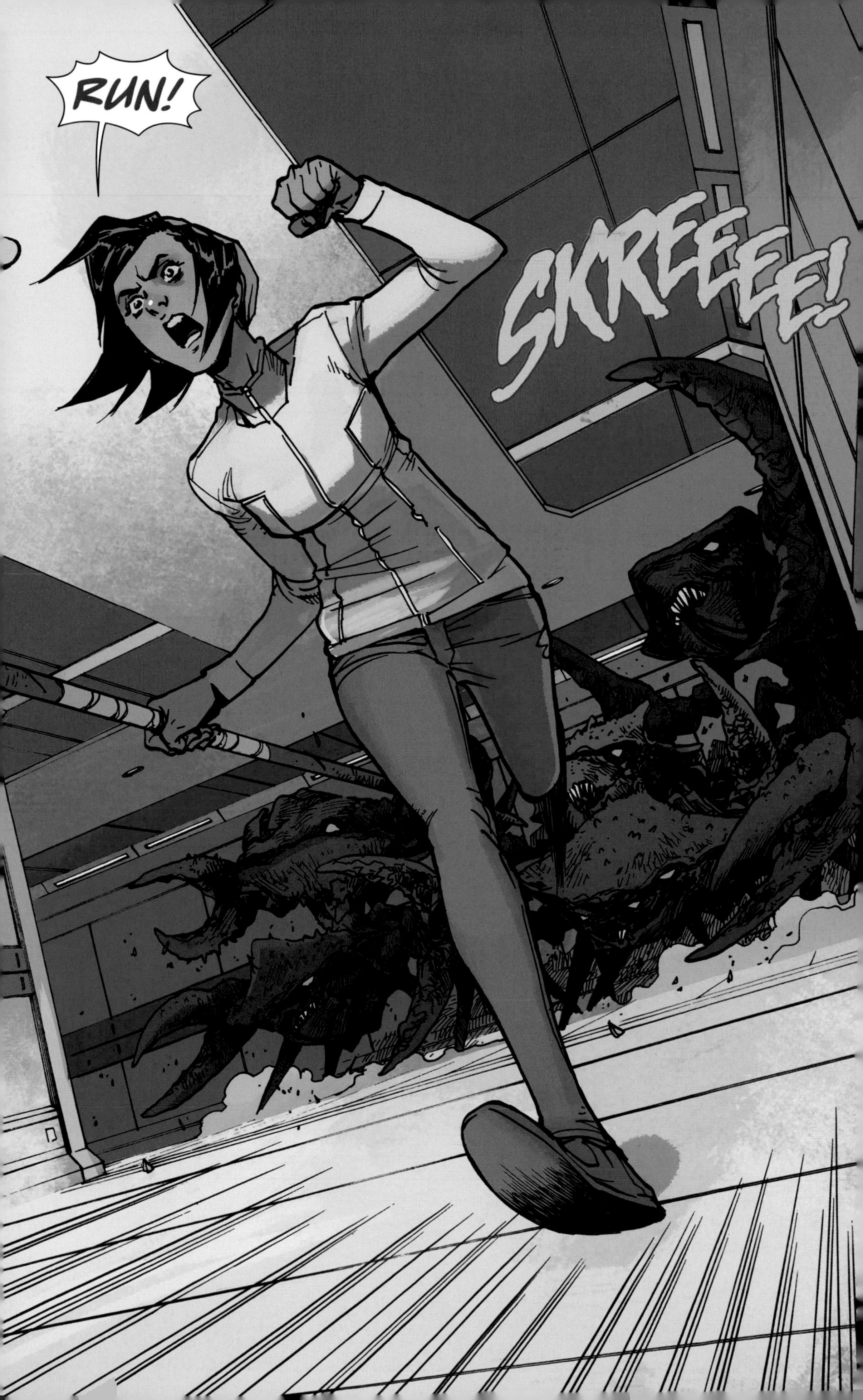
RUN!
SKREEEEE!

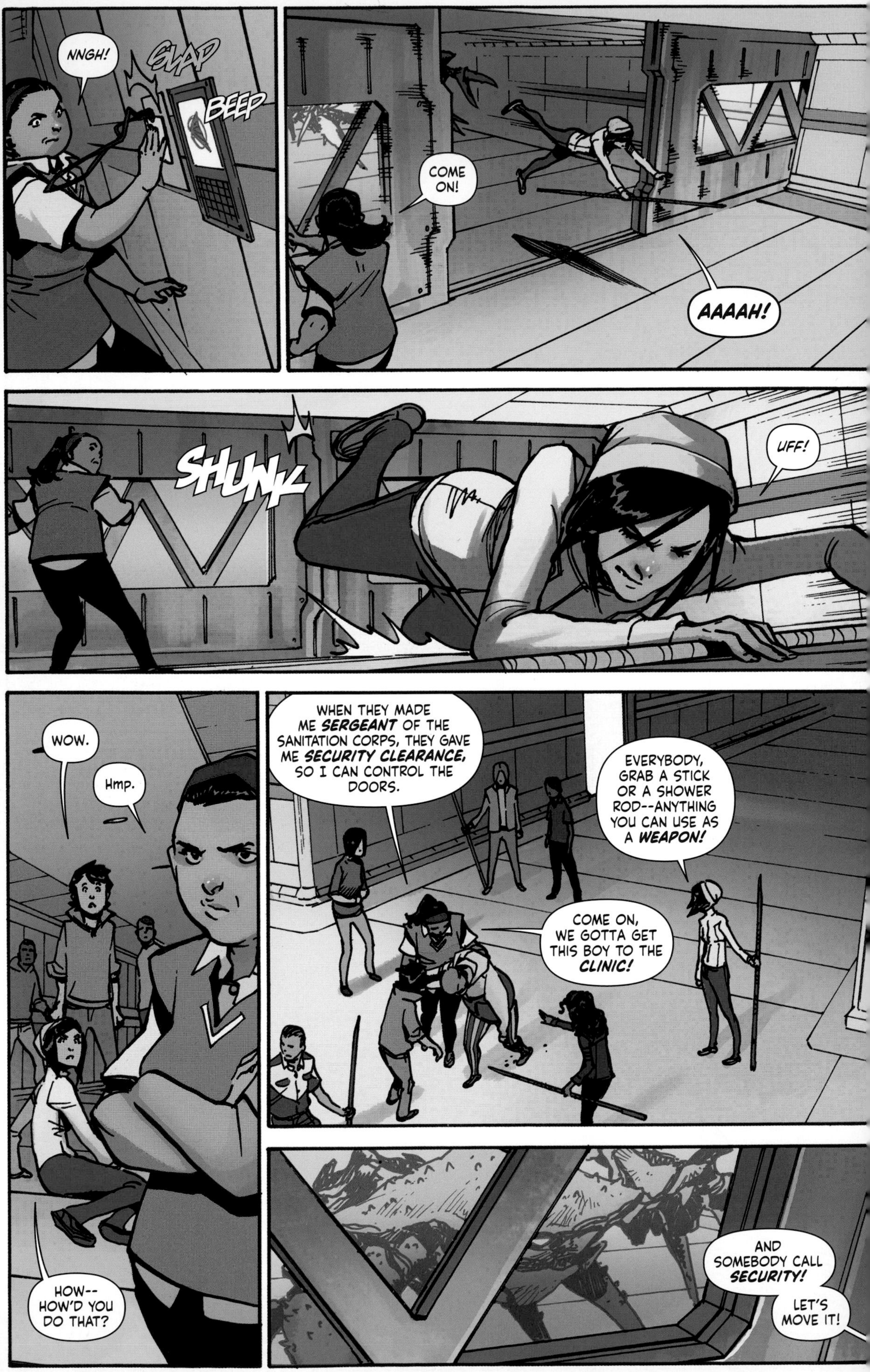
NNGH!
SLAP
BEEP
COME ON!
AAAAH!
SHUNK
UFF!
WOW.
Hmp.
HOW-- HOW'D YOU DO THAT?
WHEN THEY MADE ME SERGEANT OF THE SANITATION CORPS, THEY GAVE ME SECURITY CLEARANCE, SO I CAN CONTROL THE DOORS.
EVERYBODY, GRAB A STICK OR A SHOWER ROD--ANYTHING YOU CAN USE AS A WEAPON!
COME ON, WE GOTTA GET THIS BOY TO THE CLINIC!
AND SOMEBODY CALL SECURITY!
LET'S MOVE IT!

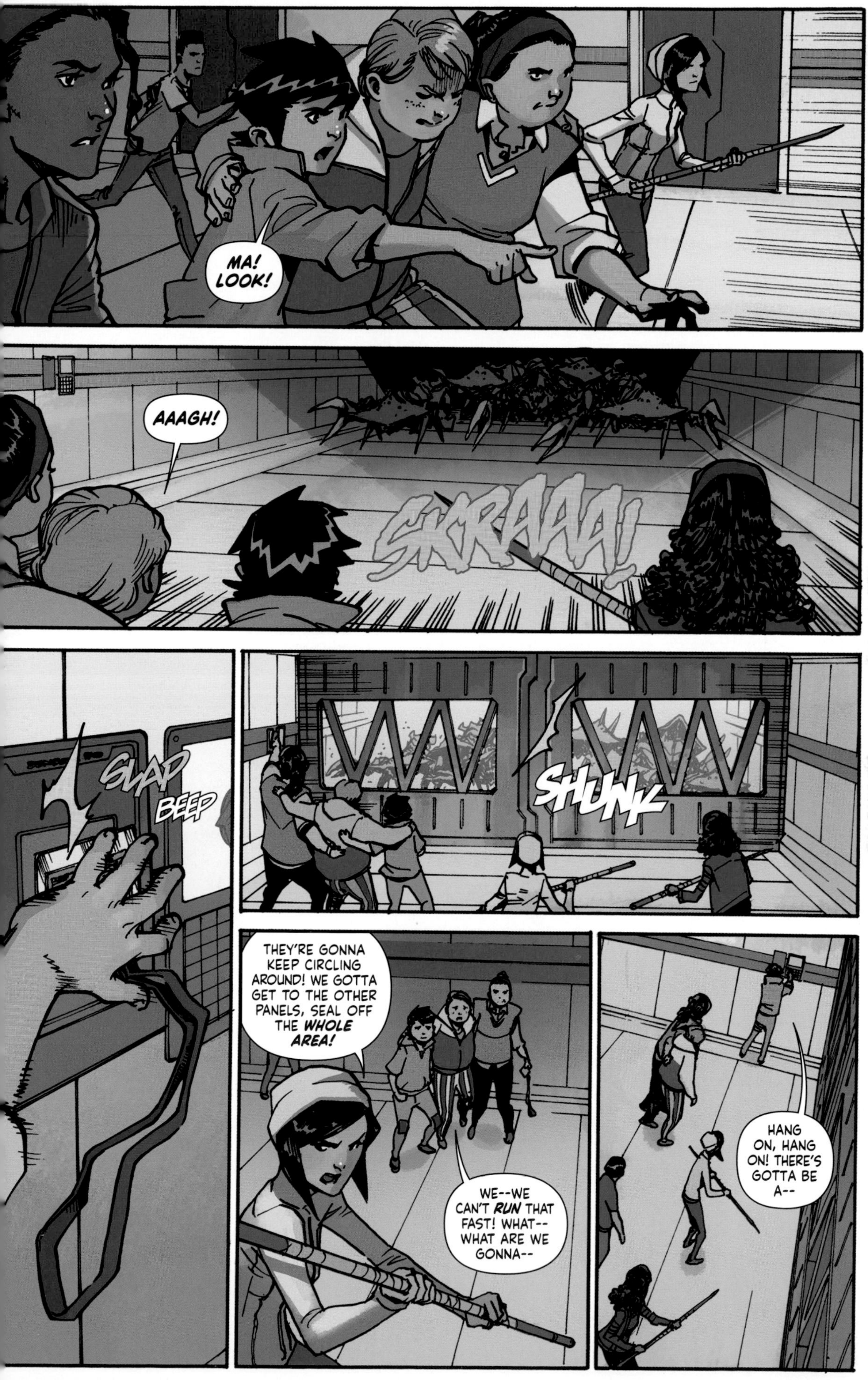
MA! LOOK!
AAAGH!
SKRAAAA!
SLAP
BEEP
SHUNK
THEY'RE GONNA KEEP CIRCLING AROUND! WE GOTTA GET TO THE OTHER PANELS, SEAL OFF THE *WHOLE AREA!*
WE--WE CAN'T *RUN* THAT FAST! WHAT--WHAT ARE WE GONNA--
HANG ON, HANG ON! THERE'S GOTTA BE A--

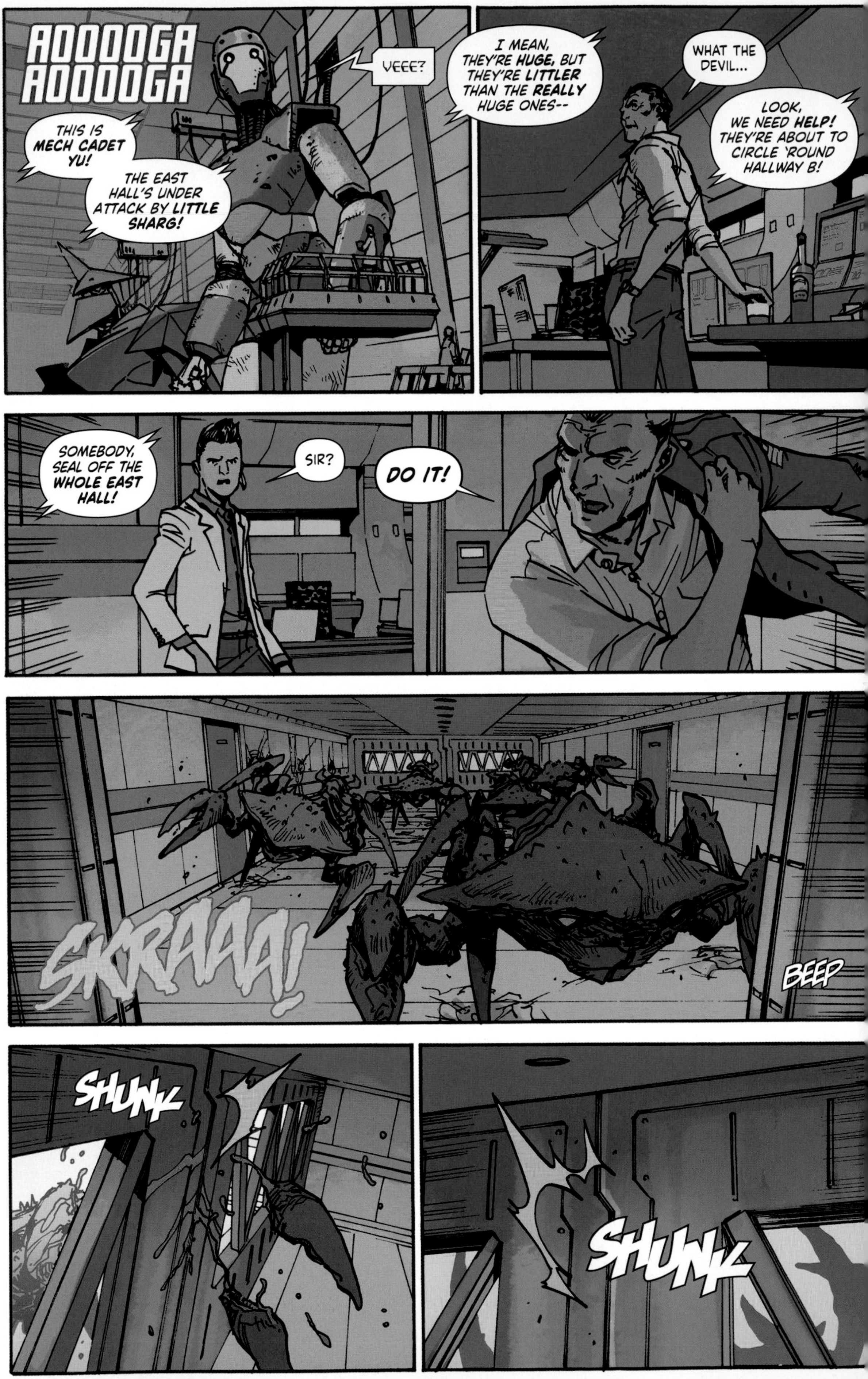
AOOOOGA AOOOOGA
THIS IS MECH CADET YU!
THE EAST HALL'S UNDER ATTACK BY LITTLE SHARG!
VEEE?
I MEAN, THEY'RE HUGE, BUT THEY'RE LITTLER THAN THE REALLY HUGE ONES--
WHAT THE DEVIL...
LOOK, WE NEED HELP! THEY'RE ABOUT TO CIRCLE 'ROUND HALLWAY B!
SOMEBODY, SEAL OFF THE WHOLE EAST HALL!
SIR?
DO IT!
SKRAAAA!
BEEP
SHUNK
SHUNK

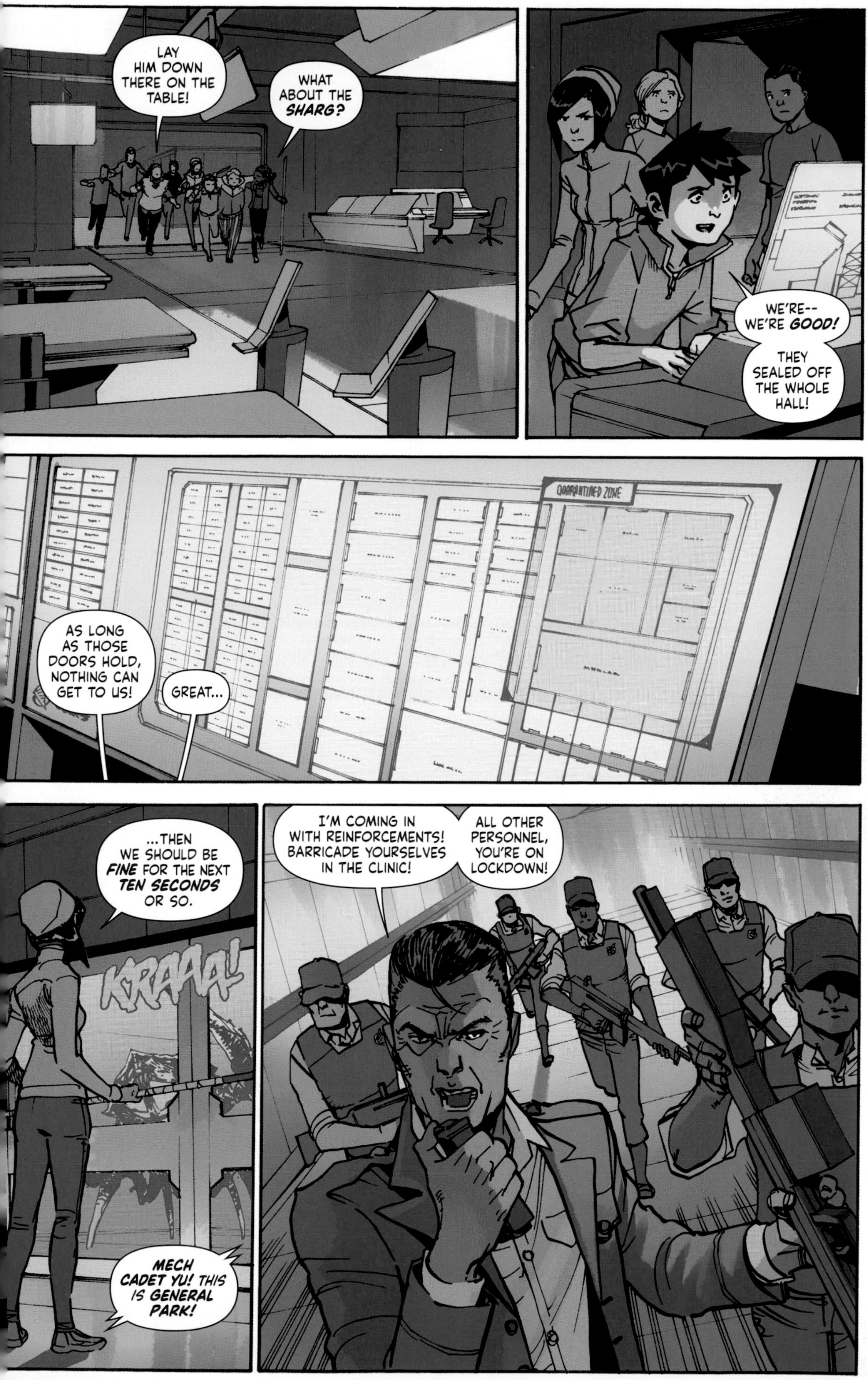
LAY HIM DOWN THERE ON THE TABLE!
WHAT ABOUT THE SHARG?
WE'RE-- WE'RE GOOD!
THEY SEALED OFF THE WHOLE HALL!
QUARANTINED ZONE
AS LONG AS THOSE DOORS HOLD, NOTHING CAN GET TO US!
GREAT...
...THEN WE SHOULD BE FINE FOR THE NEXT TEN SECONDS OR SO.
KRAAA!
MECH CADET YU! THIS IS GENERAL PARK!
I'M COMING IN WITH REINFORCEMENTS! BARRICADE YOURSELVES IN THE CLINIC!
ALL OTHER PERSONNEL, YOU'RE ON LOCKDOWN!

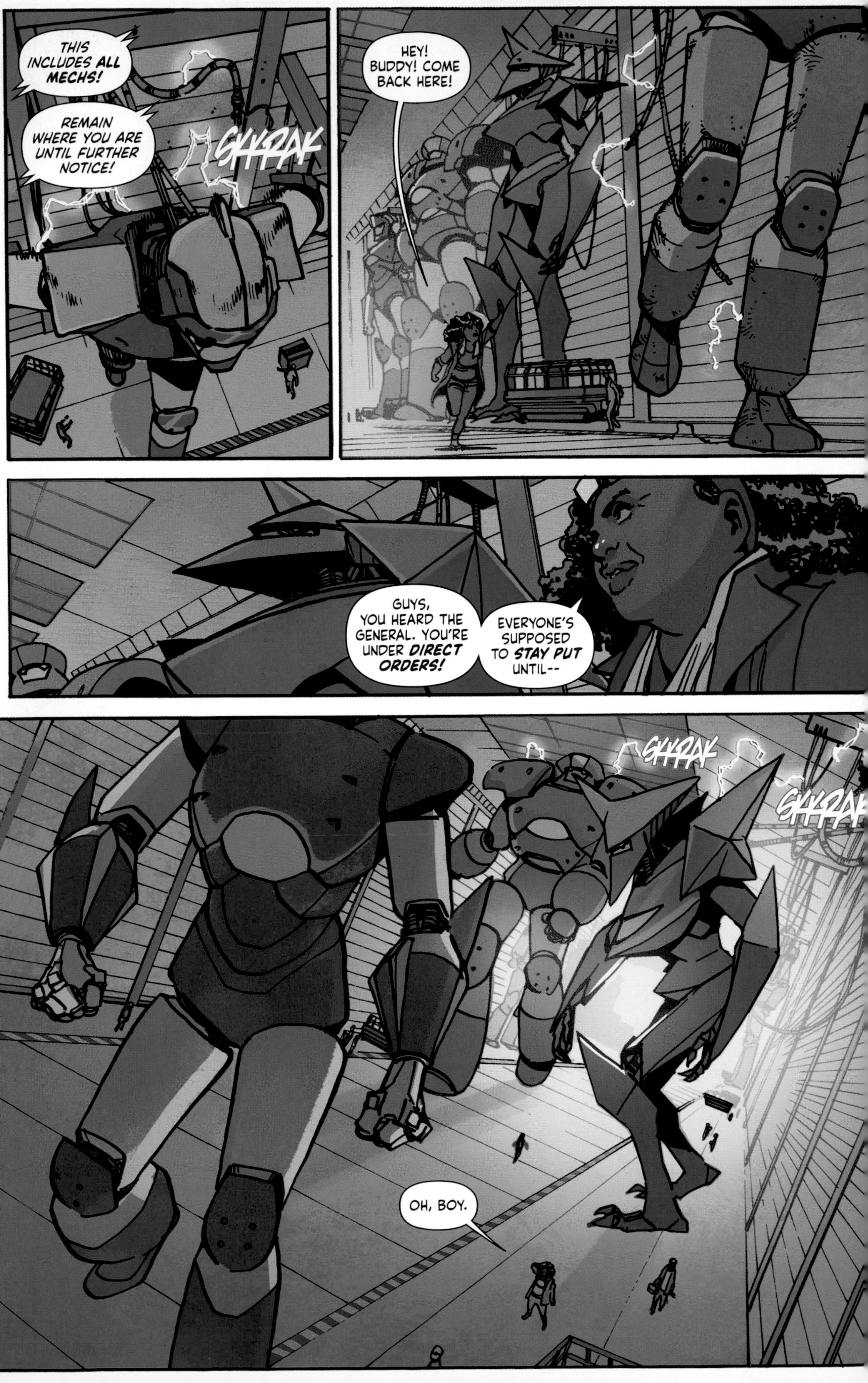
THIS INCLUDES ALL MECHS!
REMAIN WHERE YOU ARE UNTIL FURTHER NOTICE!
SKKRAK
HEY! BUDDY! COME BACK HERE!
GUYS, YOU HEARD THE GENERAL. YOU'RE UNDER DIRECT ORDERS!
EVERYONE'S SUPPOSED TO STAY PUT UNTIL--
SKKRAK
SKKRAK
OH, BOY.

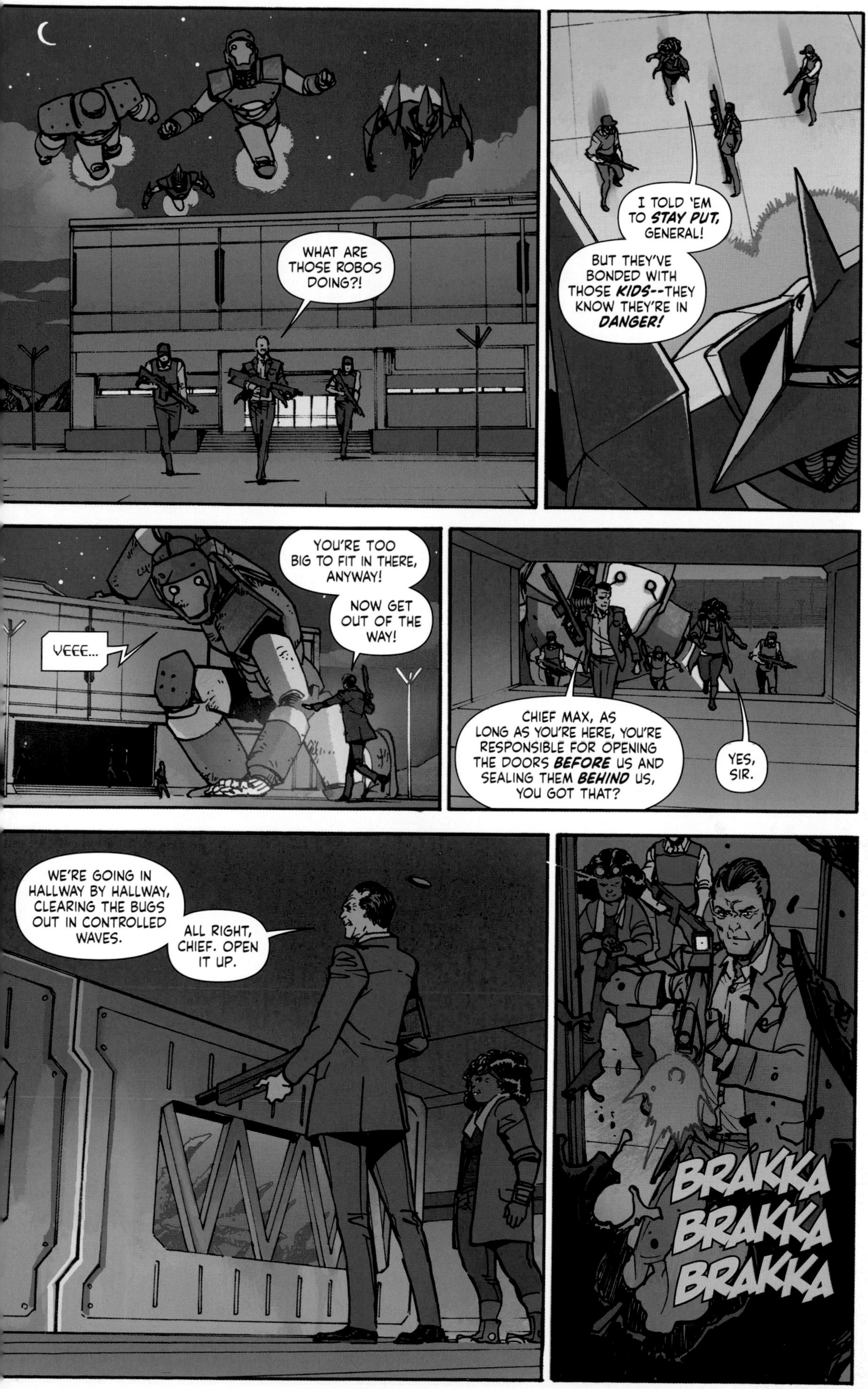
WHAT ARE THOSE ROBOS DOING?!
I TOLD 'EM TO STAY PUT, GENERAL!
BUT THEY'VE BONDED WITH THOSE KIDS--THEY KNOW THEY'RE IN DANGER!
YOU'RE TOO BIG TO FIT IN THERE, ANYWAY!
NOW GET OUT OF THE WAY!
VEEE...
CHIEF MAX, AS LONG AS YOU'RE HERE, YOU'RE RESPONSIBLE FOR OPENING THE DOORS BEFORE US AND SEALING THEM BEHIND US, YOU GOT THAT?
YES, SIR.
WE'RE GOING IN HALLWAY BY HALLWAY, CLEARING THE BUGS OUT IN CONTROLLED WAVES.
ALL RIGHT, CHIEF. OPEN IT UP.
BRAKKA
BRAKKA
BRAKKA

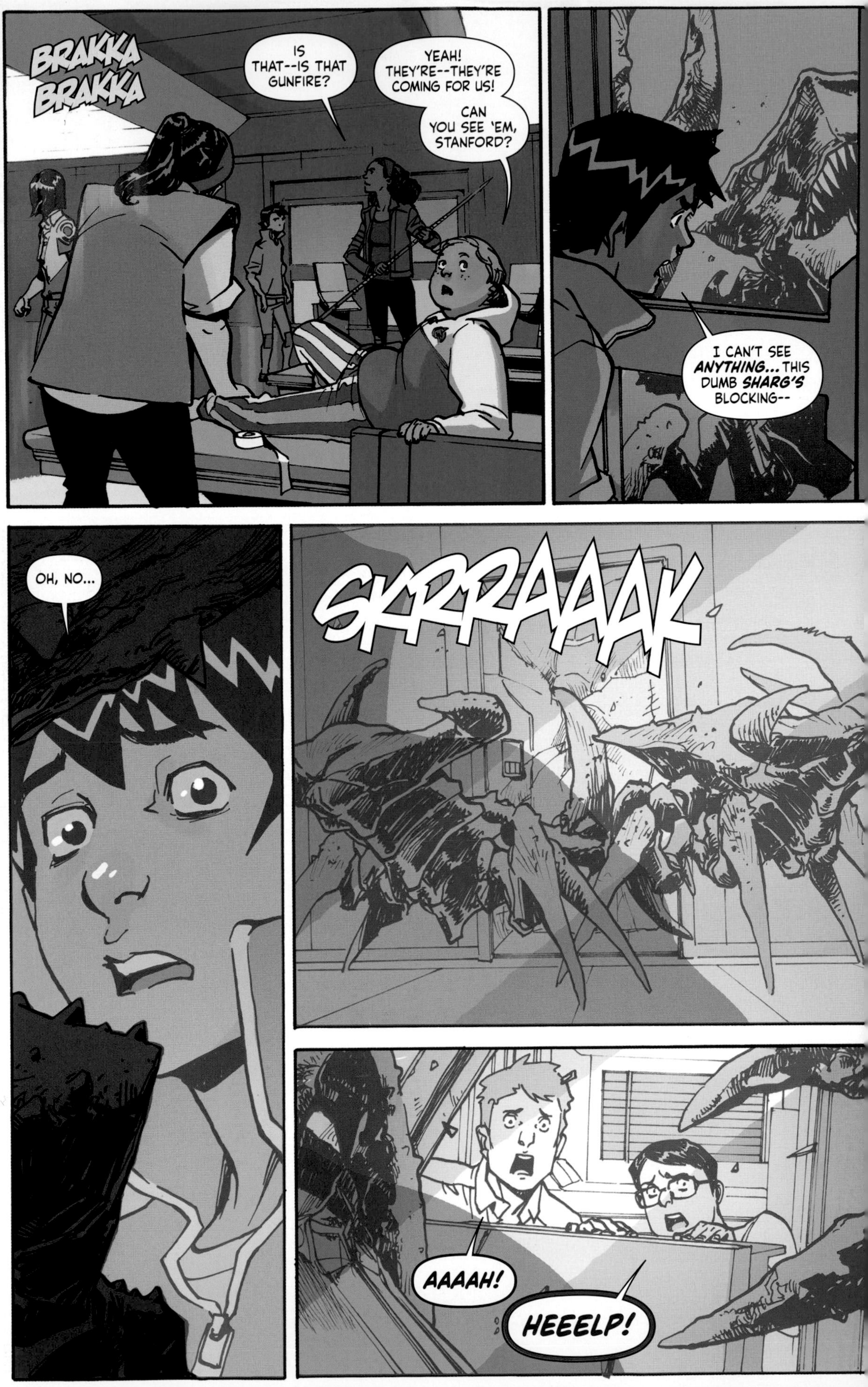
BRAKKA BRAKKA
IS THAT--IS THAT GUNFIRE?
YEAH! THEY'RE--THEY'RE COMING FOR US!
CAN YOU SEE 'EM, STANFORD?
I CAN'T SEE ANYTHING... THIS DUMB SHARG'S BLOCKING--
OH, NO...
SKRRAAAK
AAAAH!
HEEELP!

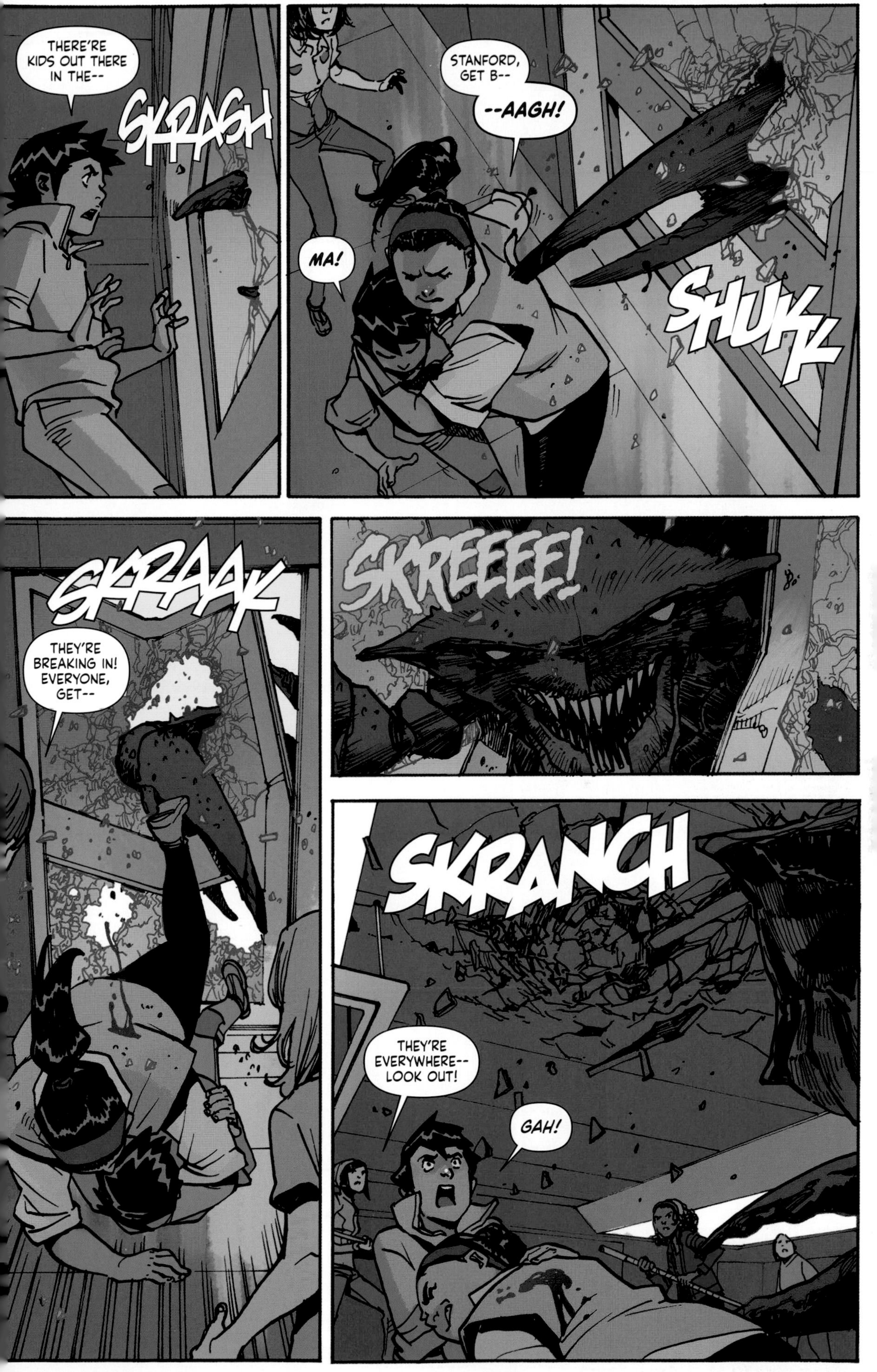

THERE'RE KIDS OUT THERE IN THE--
SKRASH
STANFORD, GET B--
--AAGH!
MA!
SHUKK
SKRAAK
THEY'RE BREAKING IN! EVERYONE, GET--
SKREEEE!
SKRANCH
THEY'RE EVERYWHERE-- LOOK OUT!
GAH!

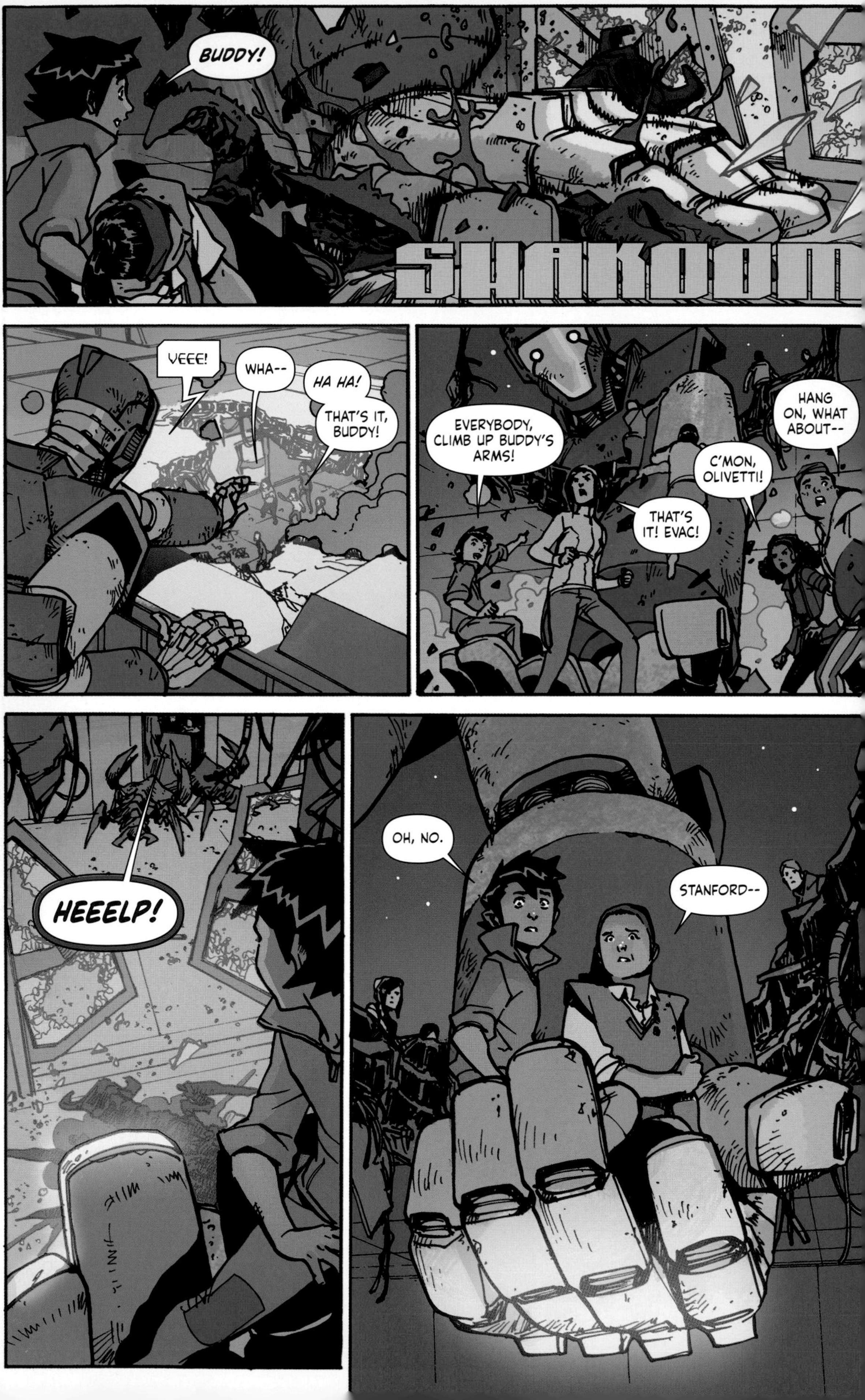
BUDDY!
SHAKOOM
VEEE!
WHA--
HA HA!
THAT'S IT, BUDDY!
EVERYBODY, CLIMB UP BUDDY'S ARMS!
THAT'S IT! EVAC!
C'MON, OLIVETTI!
HANG ON, WHAT ABOUT--
HEEELP!
OH, NO.
STANFORD--

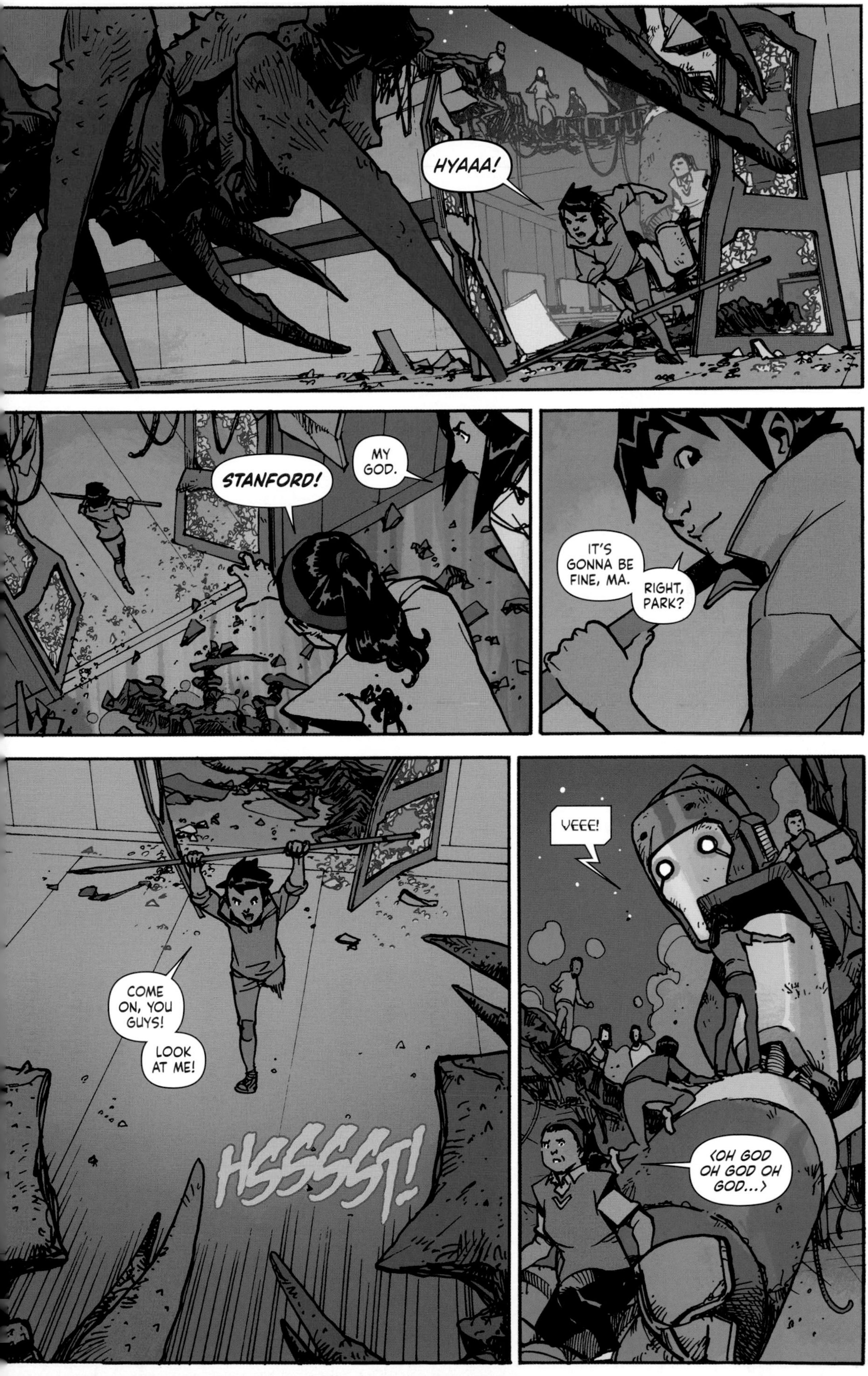
HYAAA!
STANFORD!
MY GOD.
IT'S GONNA BE FINE, MA.
RIGHT, PARK?
COME ON, YOU GUYS!
LOOK AT ME!
HSSSST!
VEEE!
<OH GOD OH GOD OH GOD...>

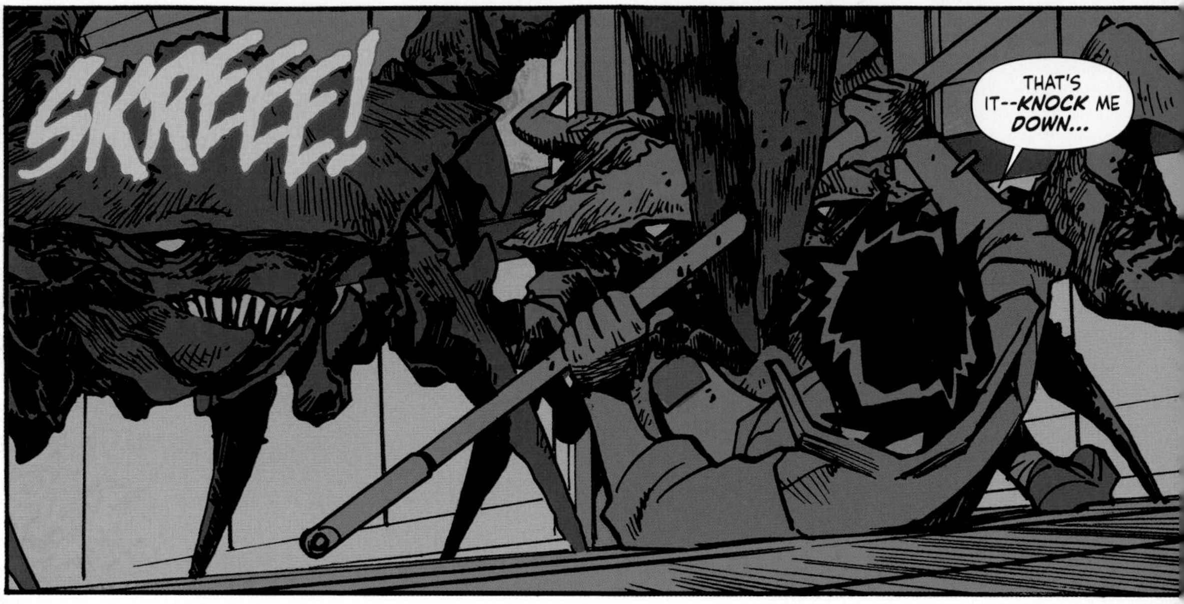
SKREEE!
THAT'S IT--KNOCK ME DOWN...

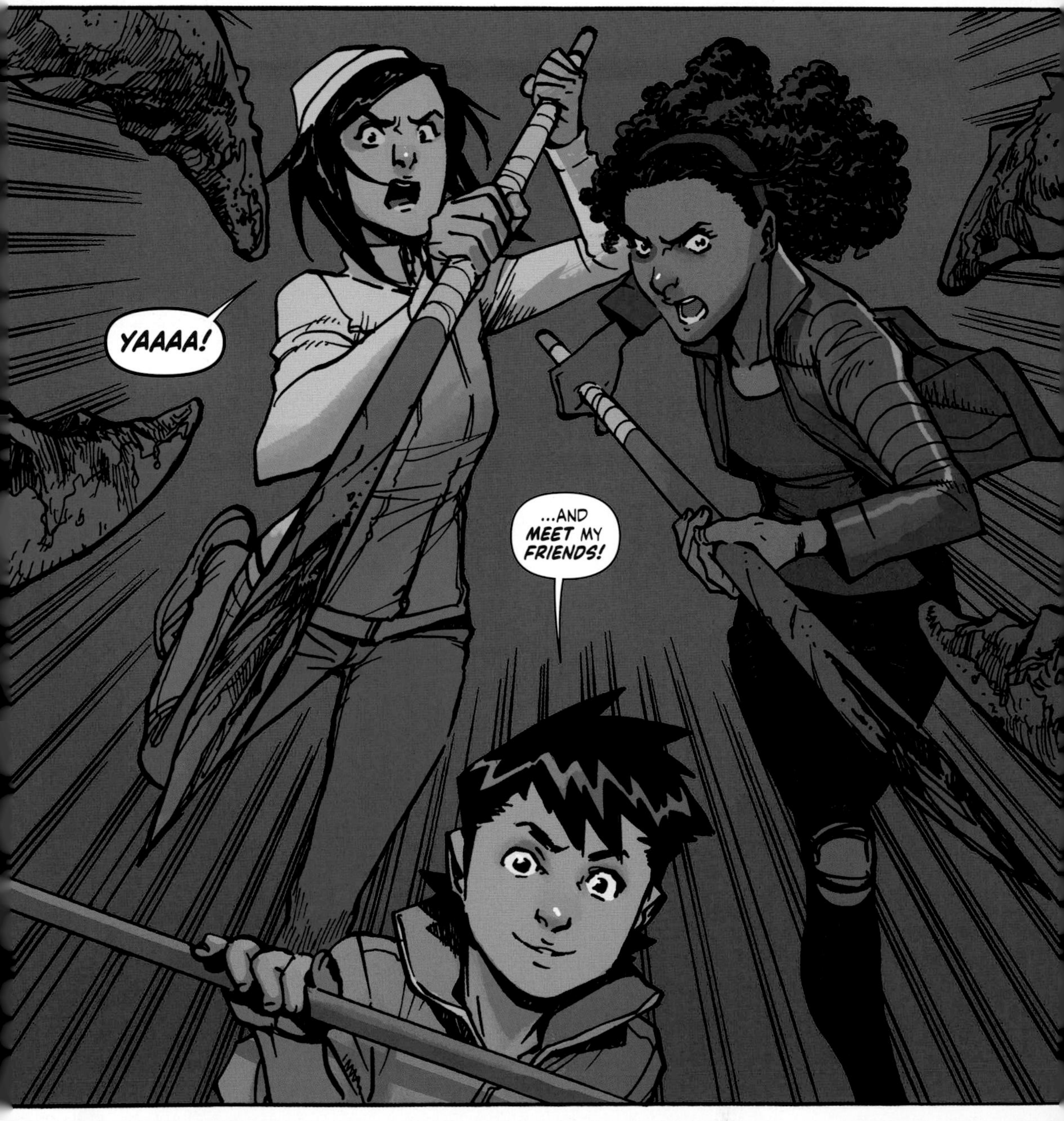
YAAAA!
...AND MEET MY FRIENDS!

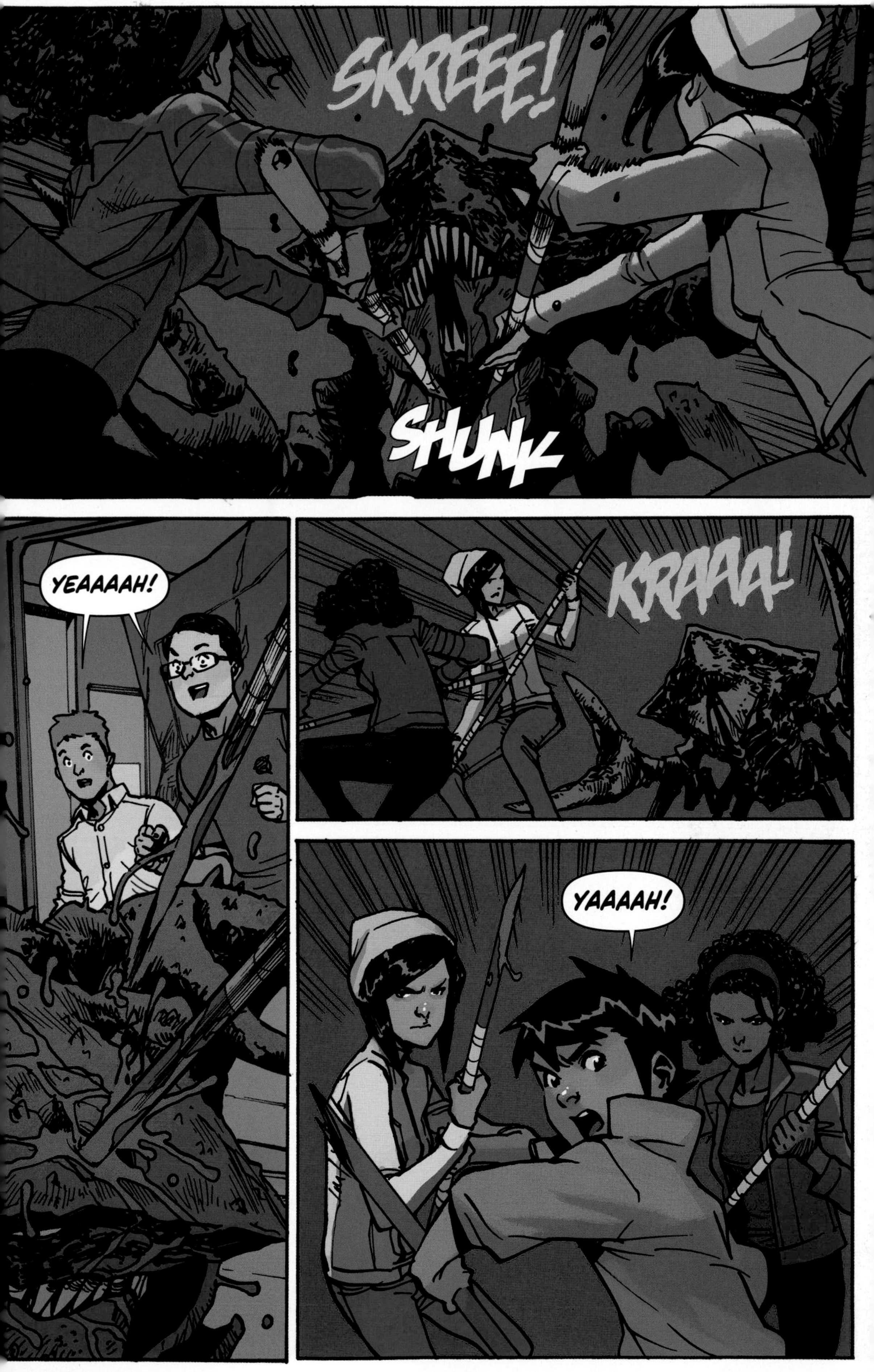
SKREEE!
SHUNK
YEAAAAH!
KRAAA!
YAAAAH!

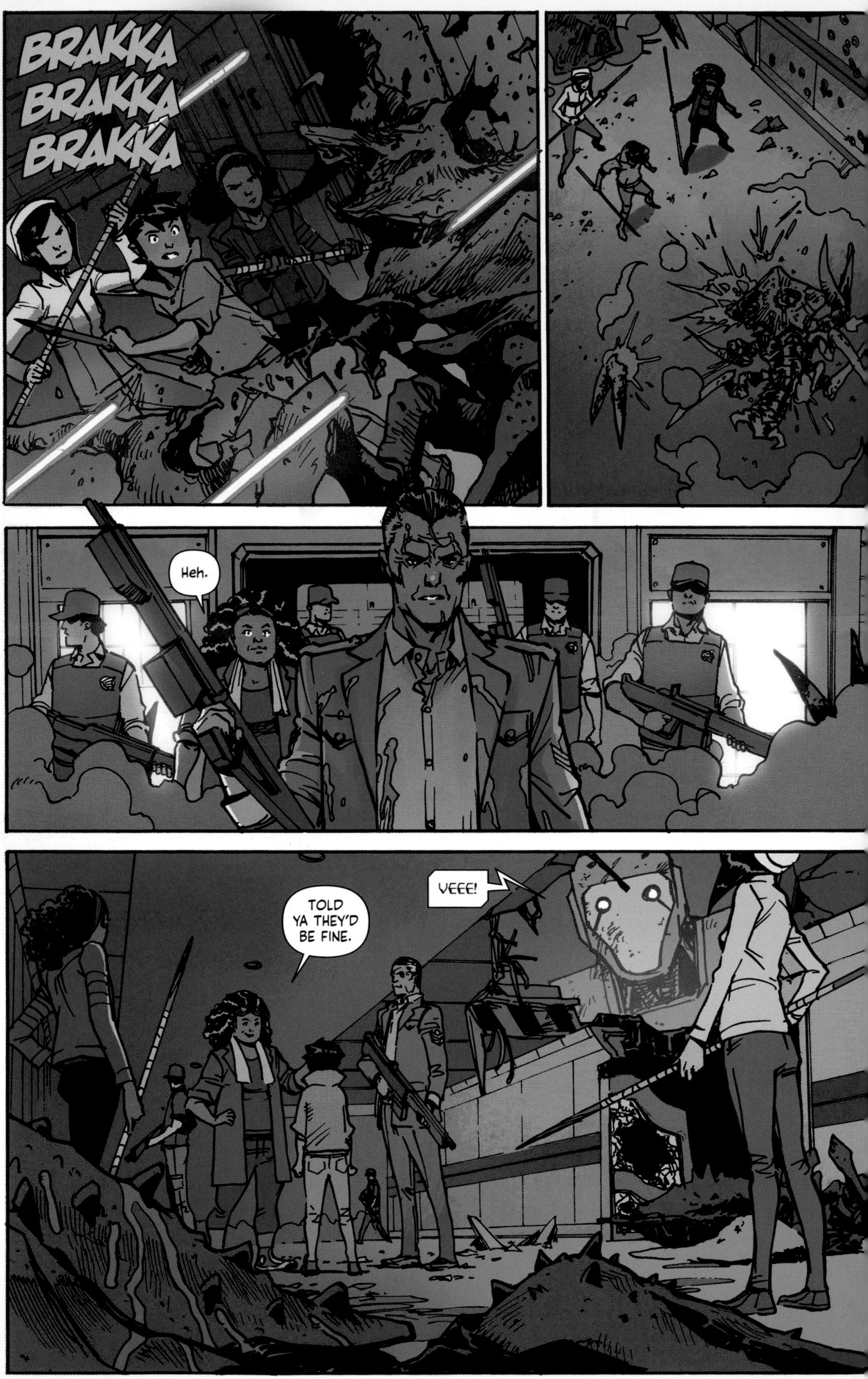
BRAKKA
BRAKKA
BRAKKA
Heh.
TOLD YA THEY'D BE FINE.
VEEE!

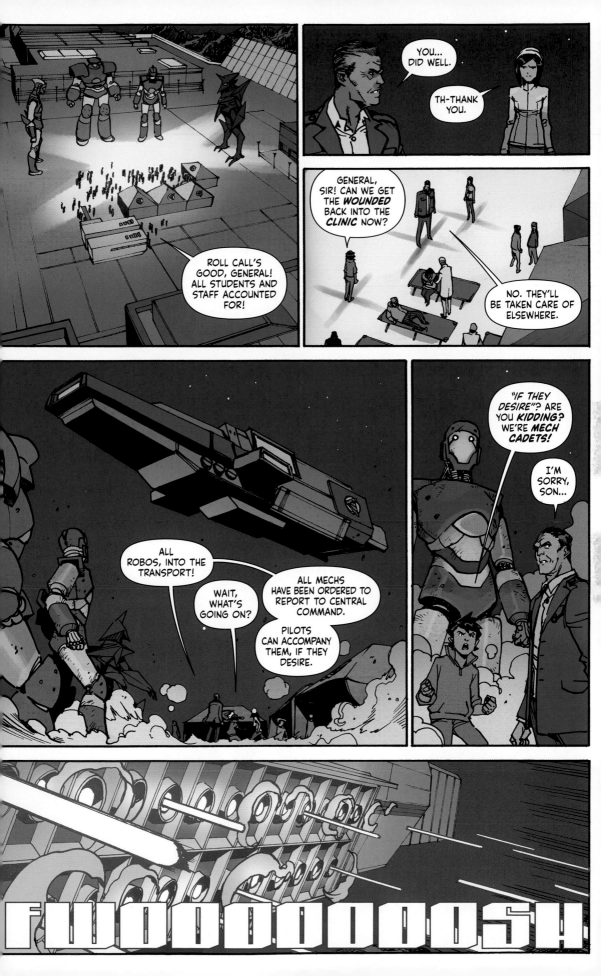

YOU... DID WELL.

TH-THANK YOU.

ROLL CALL'S GOOD, GENERAL! ALL STUDENTS AND STAFF ACCOUNTED FOR!

GENERAL, SIR! CAN WE GET THE *WOUNDED* BACK INTO THE *CLINIC* NOW?

NO. THEY'LL BE TAKEN CARE OF ELSEWHERE.

ALL ROBOS, INTO THE TRANSPORT!

WAIT, WHAT'S GOING ON?

ALL MECHS HAVE BEEN ORDERED TO REPORT TO CENTRAL COMMAND.

PILOTS CAN ACCOMPANY THEM, IF THEY DESIRE.

"IF THEY *DESIRE*"? ARE YOU *KIDDING*? WE'RE *MECH CADETS*!

I'M SORRY, SON...

FWOOOOOOOOSH!

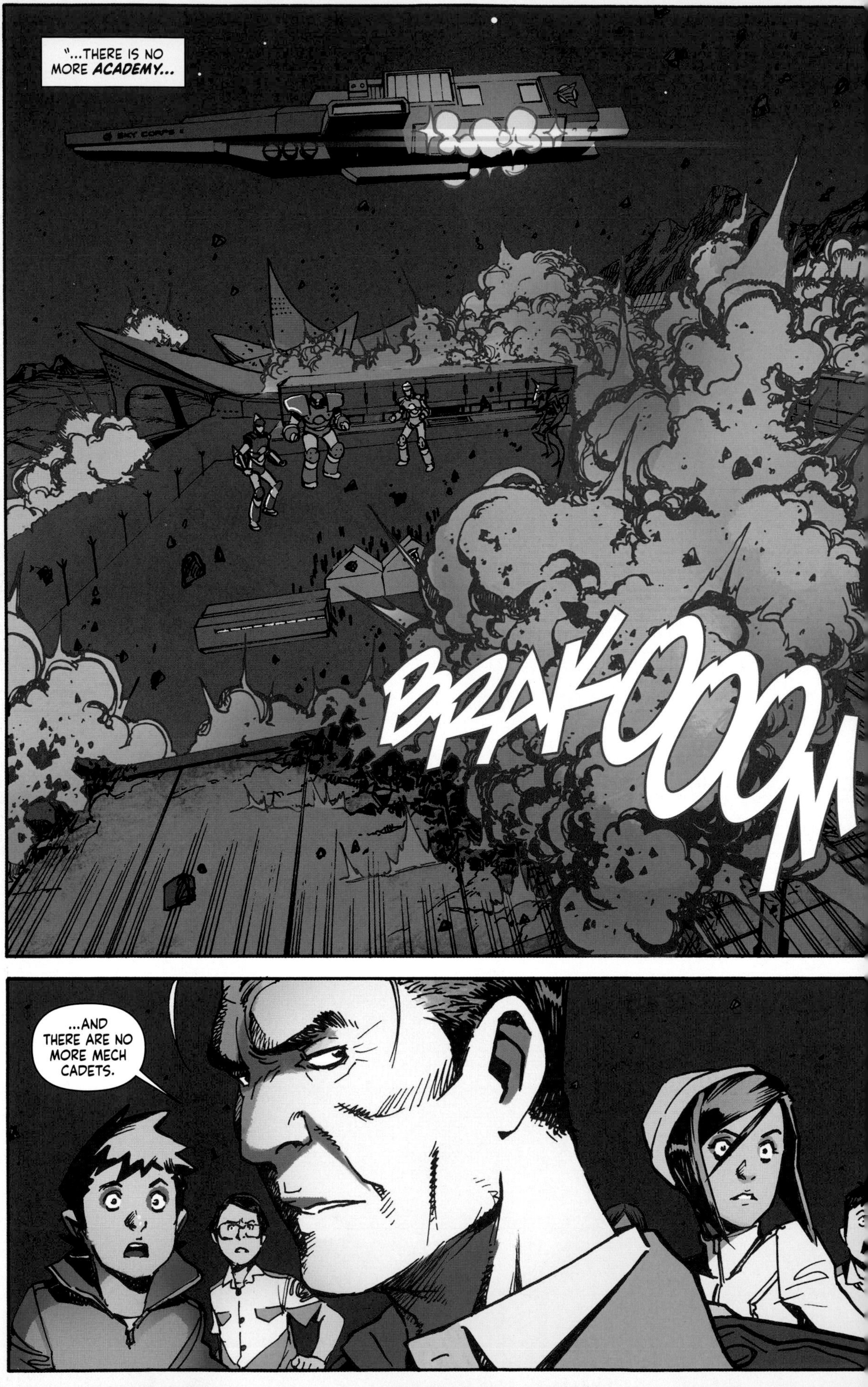
"...THERE IS NO MORE ***ACADEMY...***
BRAKOOOM
...AND THERE ARE NO MORE MECH CADETS.

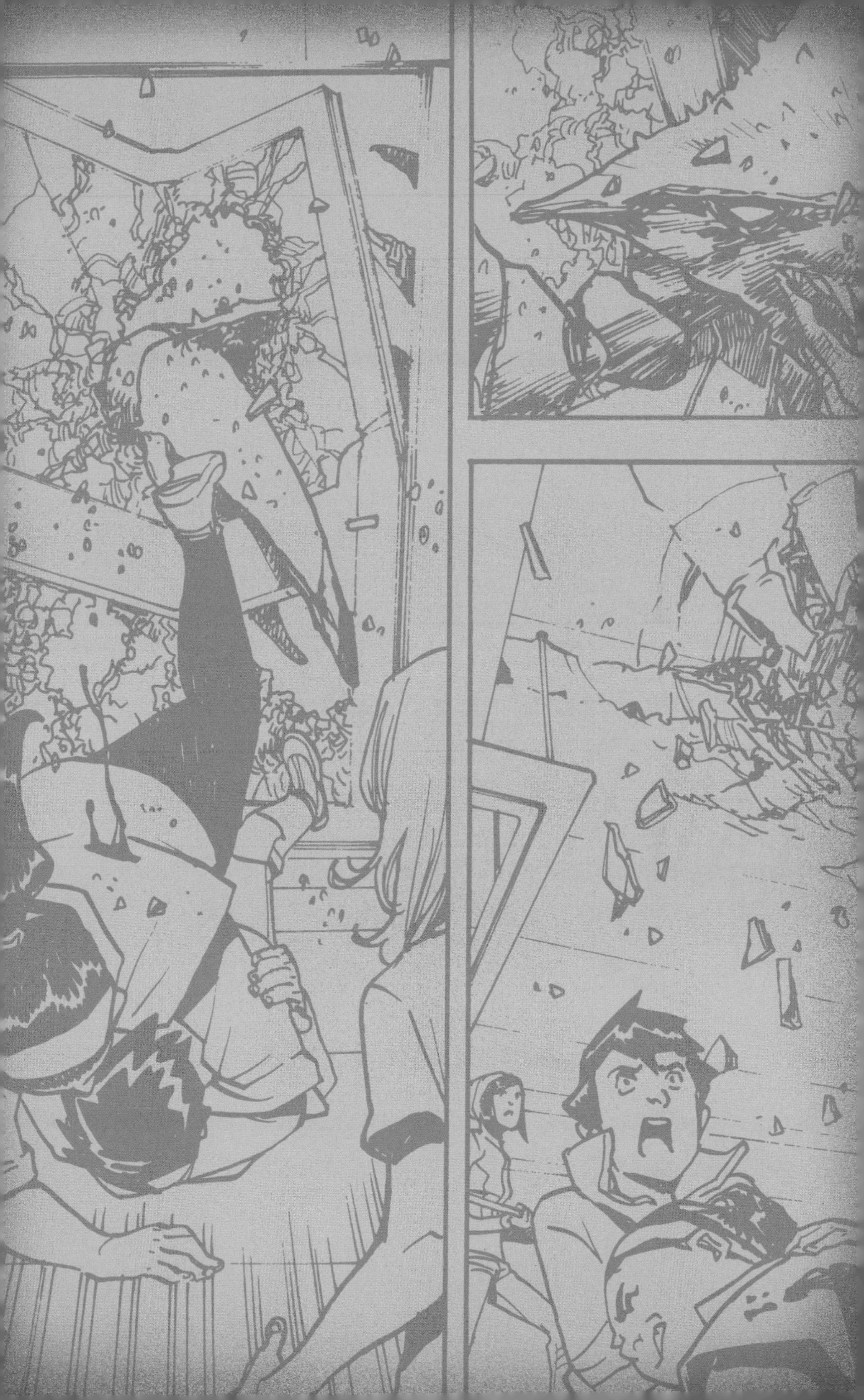

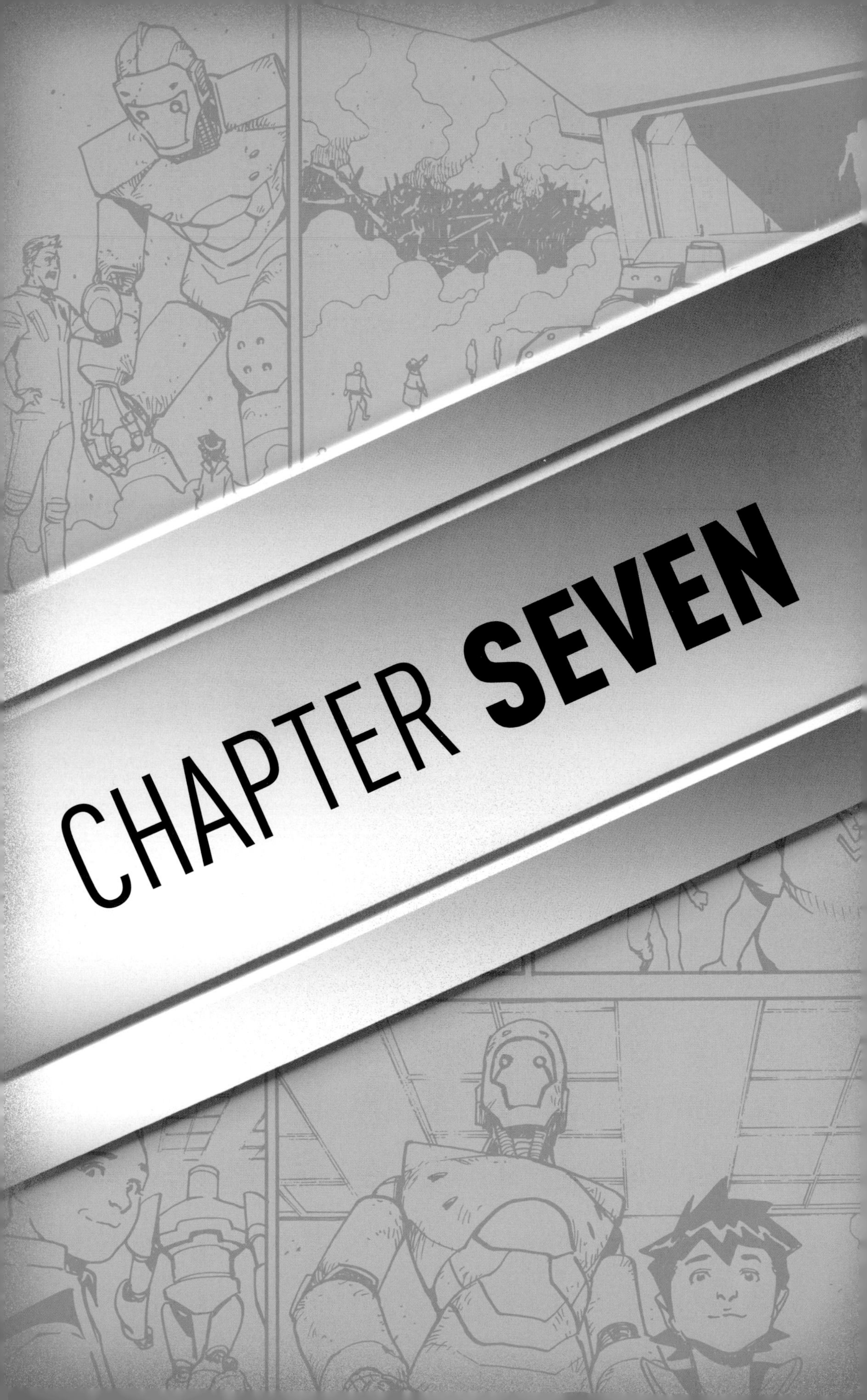

CHAPTER SEVEN

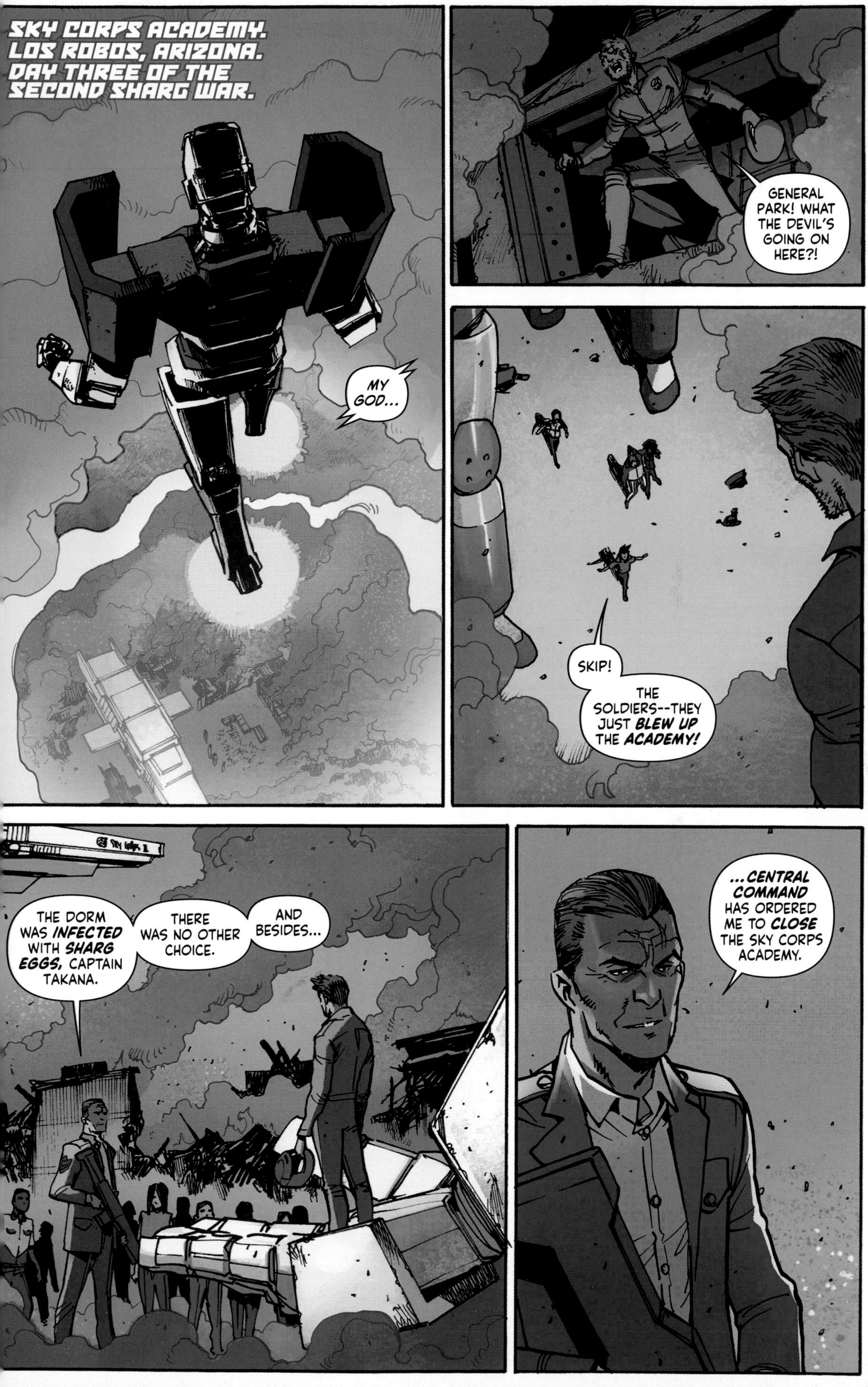
SKY CORPS ACADEMY.
LOS ROBOS, ARIZONA.
DAY THREE OF THE
SECOND SHARG WAR.
MY GOD...
GENERAL PARK! WHAT THE DEVIL'S GOING ON HERE?!
SKIP!
THE SOLDIERS--THEY JUST BLEW UP THE ACADEMY!
THE DORM WAS INFECTED WITH SHARG EGGS, CAPTAIN TAKANA.
THERE WAS NO OTHER CHOICE.
AND BESIDES...
...CENTRAL COMMAND HAS ORDERED ME TO CLOSE THE SKY CORPS ACADEMY.

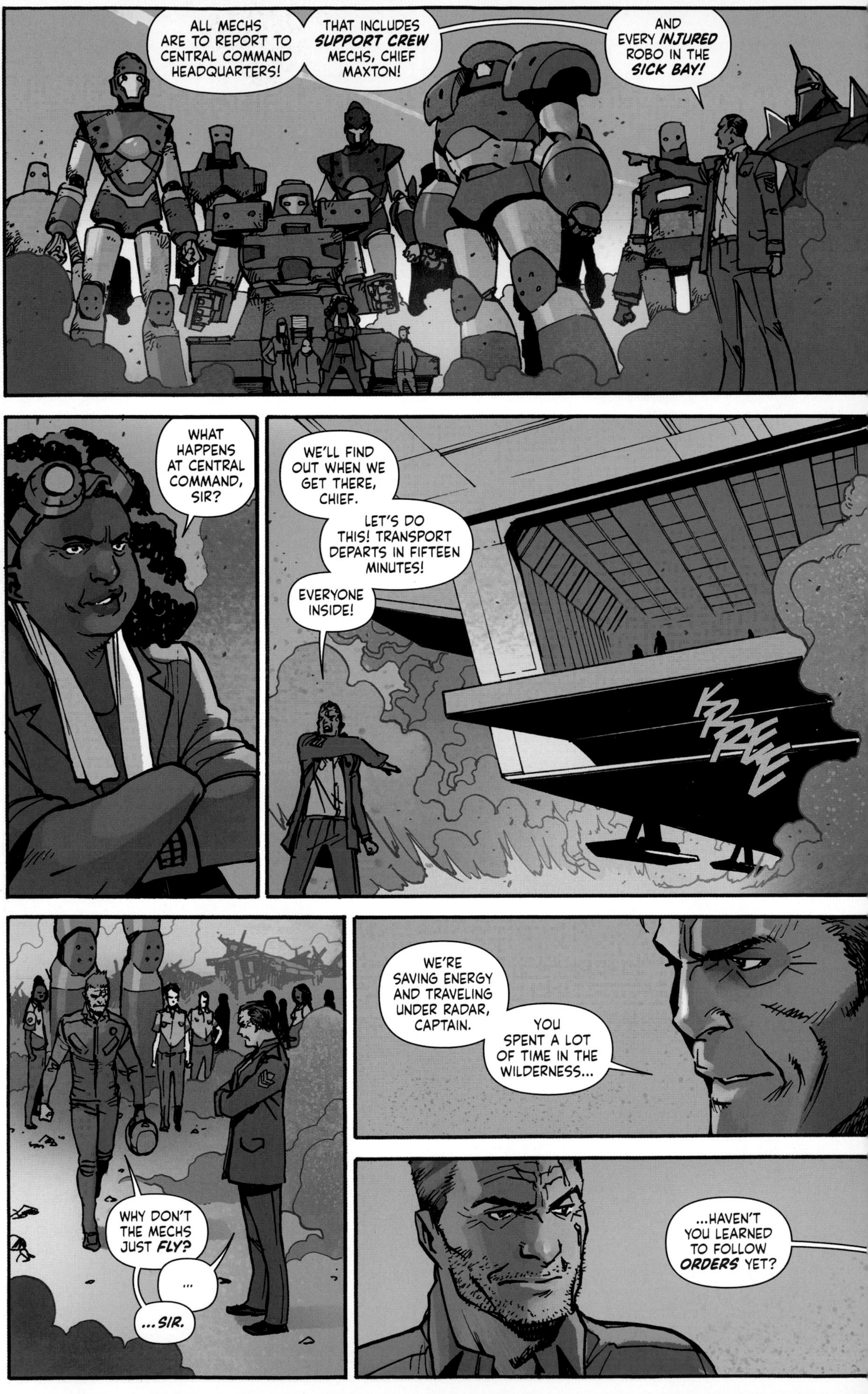
ALL MECHS ARE TO REPORT TO CENTRAL COMMAND HEADQUARTERS!
THAT INCLUDES SUPPORT CREW MECHS, CHIEF MAXTON!
AND EVERY INJURED ROBO IN THE SICK BAY!
WHAT HAPPENS AT CENTRAL COMMAND, SIR?
WE'LL FIND OUT WHEN WE GET THERE, CHIEF.
LET'S DO THIS! TRANSPORT DEPARTS IN FIFTEEN MINUTES!
EVERYONE INSIDE!
KRREEE
WHY DON'T THE MECHS JUST FLY?
...
...SIR.
WE'RE SAVING ENERGY AND TRAVELING UNDER RADAR, CAPTAIN.
YOU SPENT A LOT OF TIME IN THE WILDERNESS...
...HAVEN'T YOU LEARNED TO FOLLOW ORDERS YET?

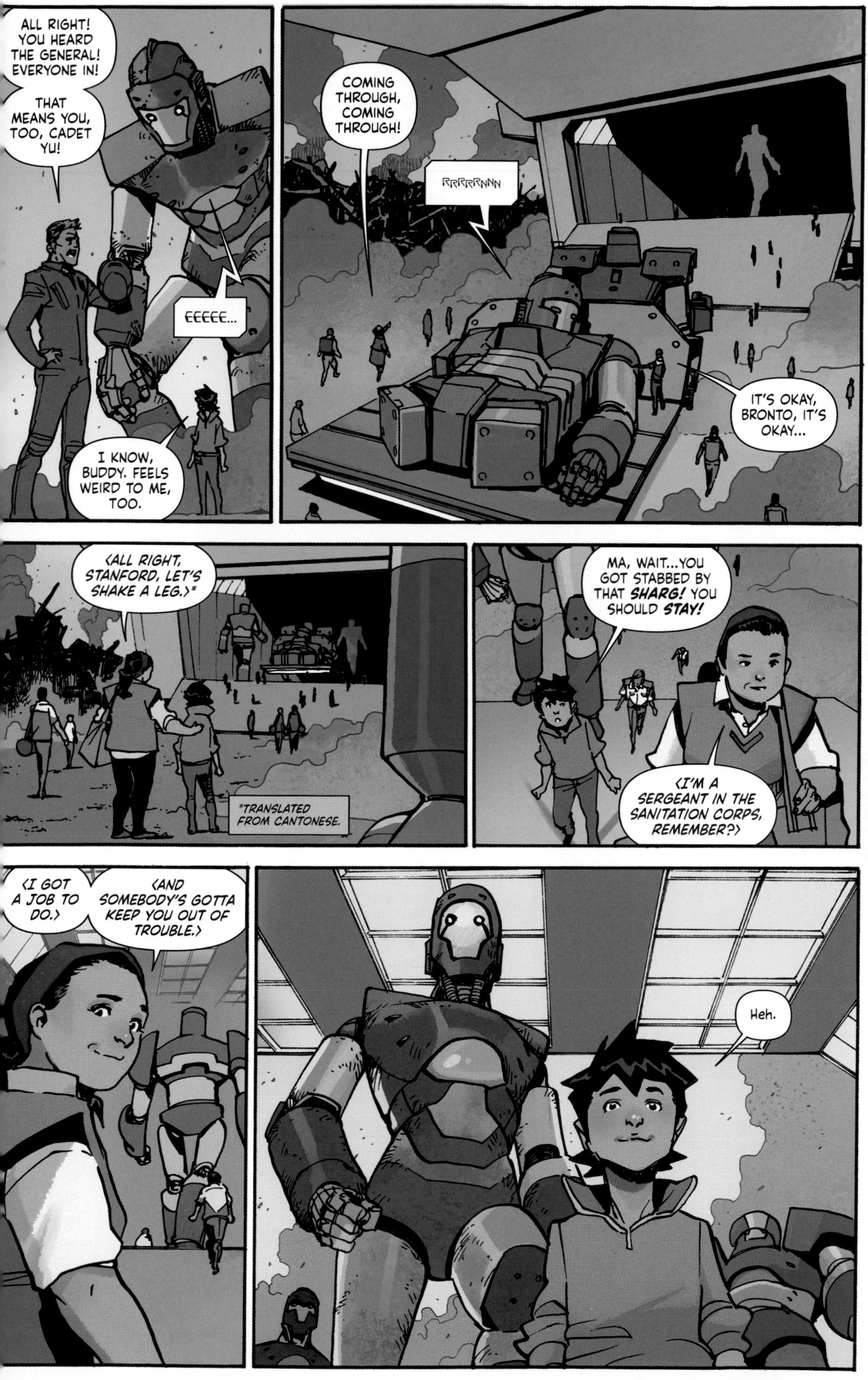
ALL RIGHT! YOU HEARD THE GENERAL! EVERYONE IN!
THAT MEANS YOU, TOO, CADET YU!
EEEEE...
I KNOW, BUDDY. FEELS WEIRD TO ME, TOO.
COMING THROUGH, COMING THROUGH!
RRRRRNNN
IT'S OKAY, BRONTO, IT'S OKAY...
<ALL RIGHT, STANFORD, LET'S SHAKE A LEG.>*
*TRANSLATED FROM CANTONESE.
MA, WAIT...YOU GOT STABBED BY THAT SHARG! YOU SHOULD STAY!
<I'M A SERGEANT IN THE SANITATION CORPS, REMEMBER?>
<I GOT A JOB TO DO.>
<AND SOMEBODY'S GOTTA KEEP YOU OUT OF TROUBLE.>
Heh.

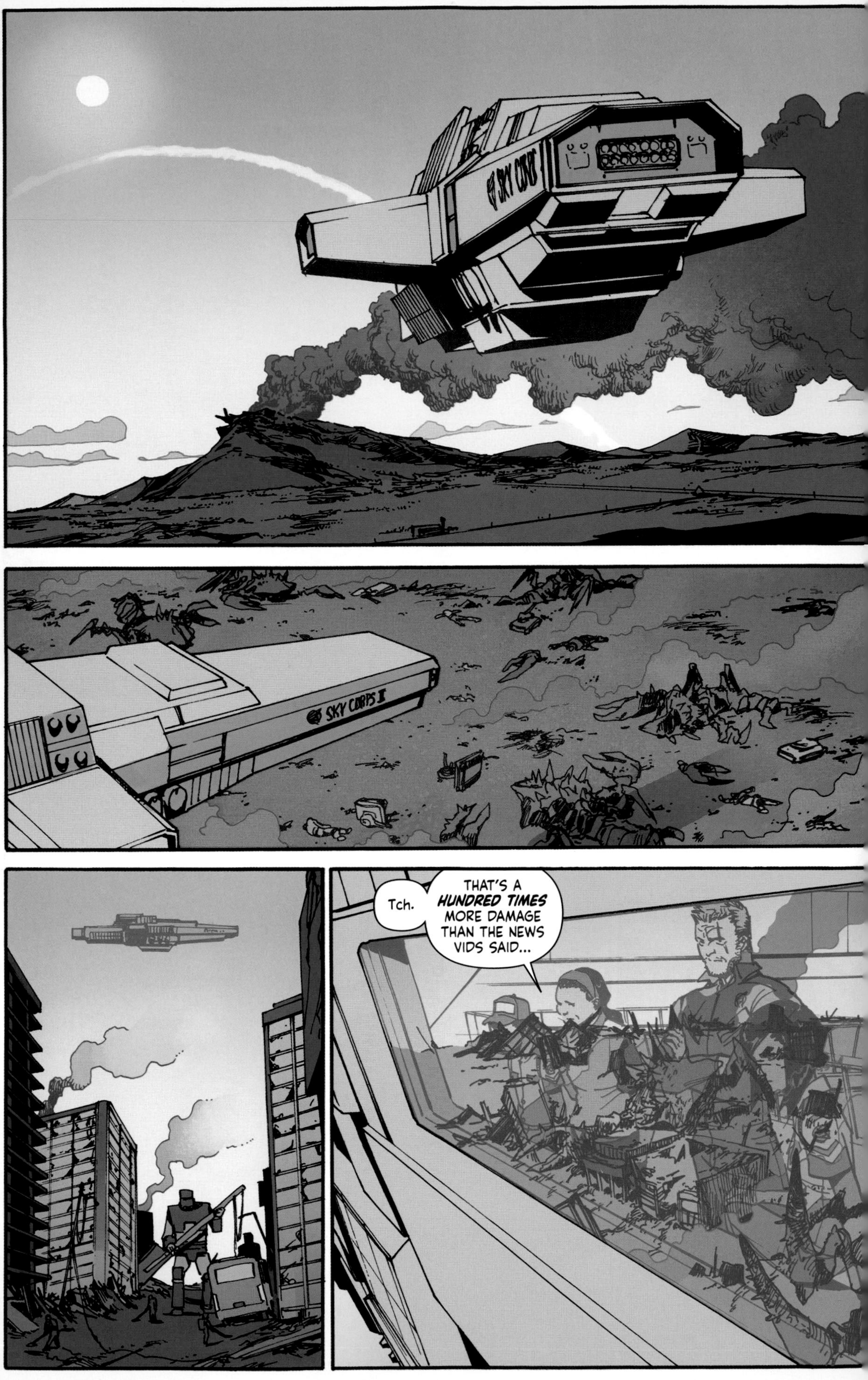
SKY CORPS
SKY CORPS II
Tch.
THAT'S A HUNDRED TIMES MORE DAMAGE THAN THE NEWS VIDS SAID...

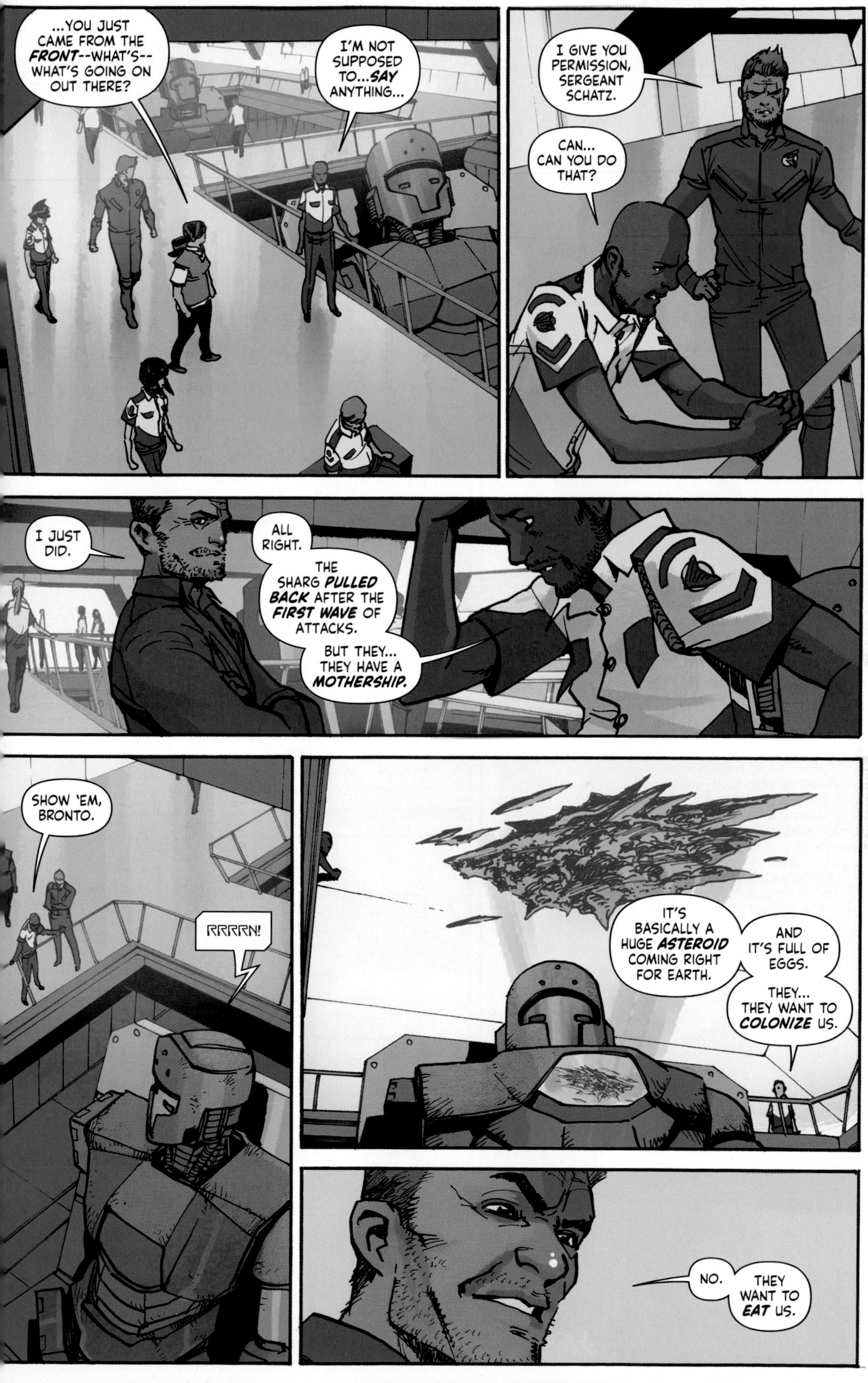
...YOU JUST CAME FROM THE FRONT--WHAT'S--WHAT'S GOING ON OUT THERE?
I'M NOT SUPPOSED TO...SAY ANYTHING...
I GIVE YOU PERMISSION, SERGEANT SCHATZ.
CAN... CAN YOU DO THAT?
I JUST DID.
ALL RIGHT.
THE SHARG PULLED BACK AFTER THE FIRST WAVE OF ATTACKS.
BUT THEY... THEY HAVE A MOTHERSHIP.
SHOW 'EM, BRONTO.
RRRRN!
IT'S BASICALLY A HUGE ASTEROID COMING RIGHT FOR EARTH.
AND IT'S FULL OF EGGS.
THEY... THEY WANT TO COLONIZE US.
NO.
THEY WANT TO EAT US.

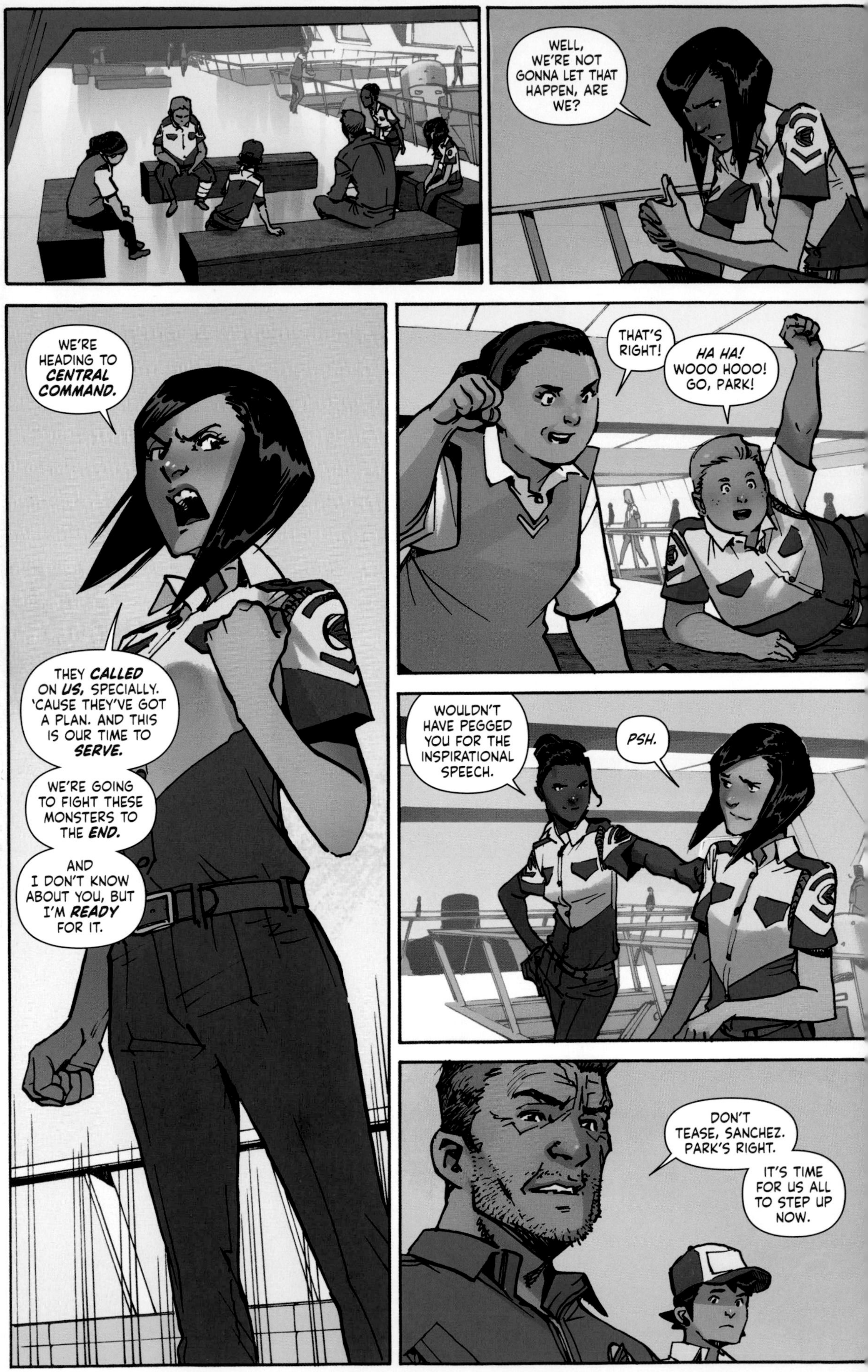
WELL, WE'RE NOT GONNA LET THAT HAPPEN, ARE WE?
WE'RE HEADING TO **CENTRAL COMMAND.**
THEY **CALLED** ON **US,** SPECIALLY. 'CAUSE THEY'VE GOT A PLAN. AND THIS IS OUR TIME TO **SERVE.**
WE'RE GOING TO FIGHT THESE MONSTERS TO THE **END.**
AND I DON'T KNOW ABOUT YOU, BUT I'M **READY** FOR IT.
THAT'S RIGHT!
HA HA! WOOO HOOO! GO, PARK!
WOULDN'T HAVE PEGGED YOU FOR THE INSPIRATIONAL SPEECH.
PSH.
DON'T TEASE, SANCHEZ. PARK'S RIGHT.
IT'S TIME FOR US ALL TO STEP UP NOW.

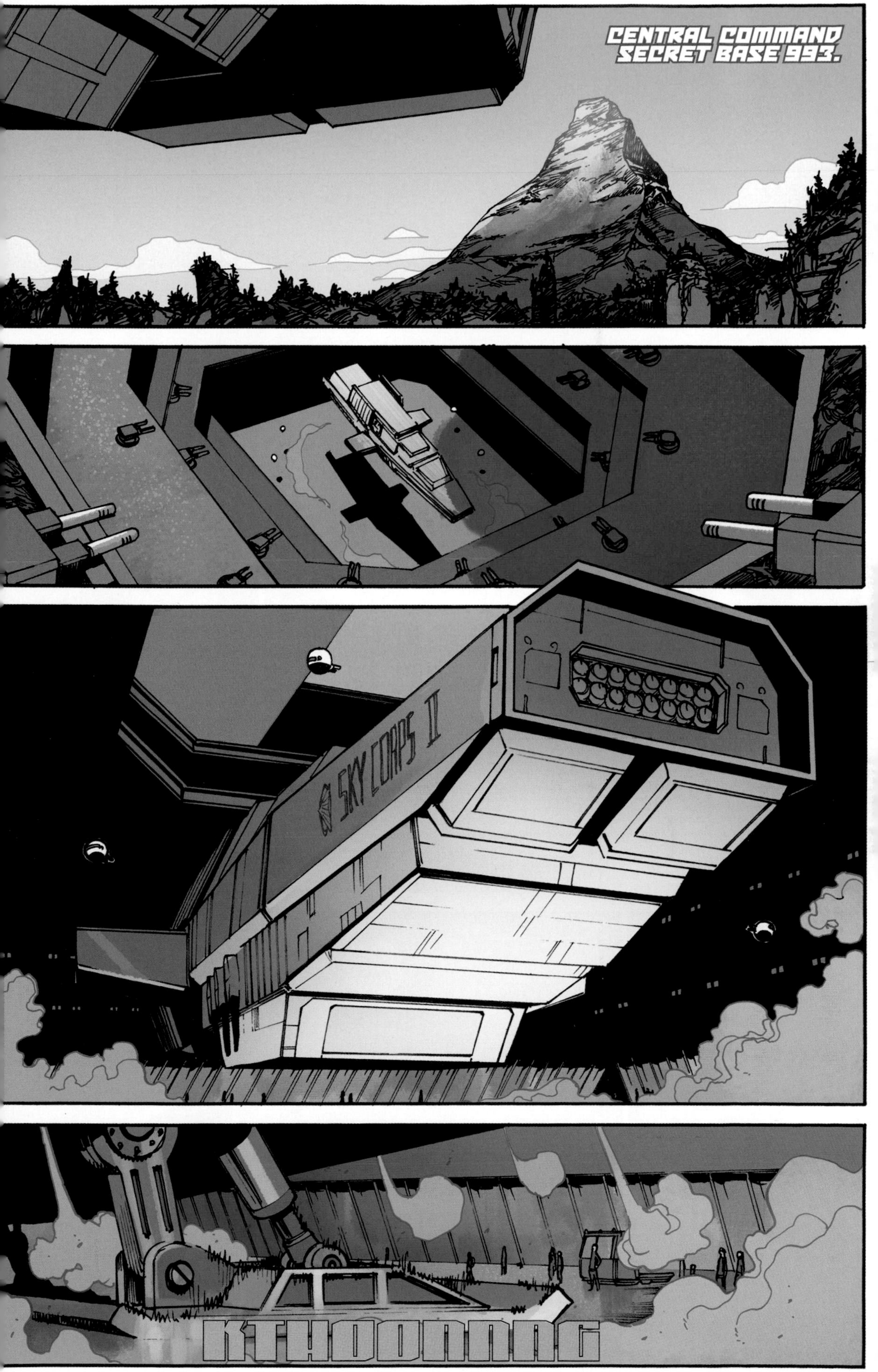
CENTRAL COMMAND
SECRET BASE 993.
SKY CORPS II
KTHOONNNG

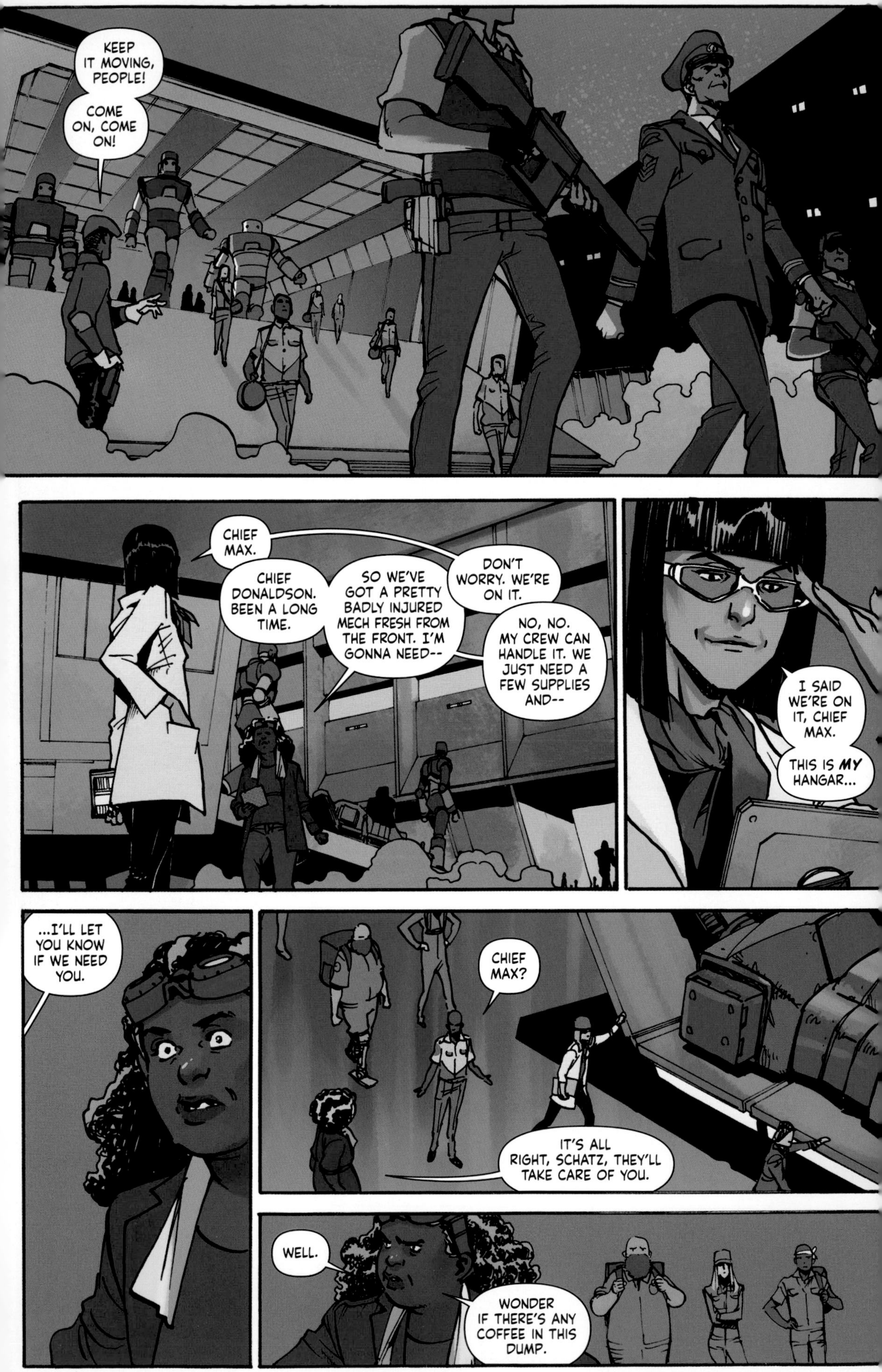
KEEP IT MOVING, PEOPLE!
COME ON, COME ON!
CHIEF MAX.
CHIEF DONALDSON. BEEN A LONG TIME.
SO WE'VE GOT A PRETTY BADLY INJURED MECH FRESH FROM THE FRONT. I'M GONNA NEED--
DON'T WORRY. WE'RE ON IT.
NO, NO. MY CREW CAN HANDLE IT. WE JUST NEED A FEW SUPPLIES AND--
I SAID WE'RE ON IT, CHIEF MAX.
THIS IS *MY* HANGAR...
...I'LL LET YOU KNOW IF WE NEED YOU.
CHIEF MAX?
IT'S ALL RIGHT, SCHATZ, THEY'LL TAKE CARE OF YOU.
WELL.
WONDER IF THERE'S ANY COFFEE IN THIS DUMP.

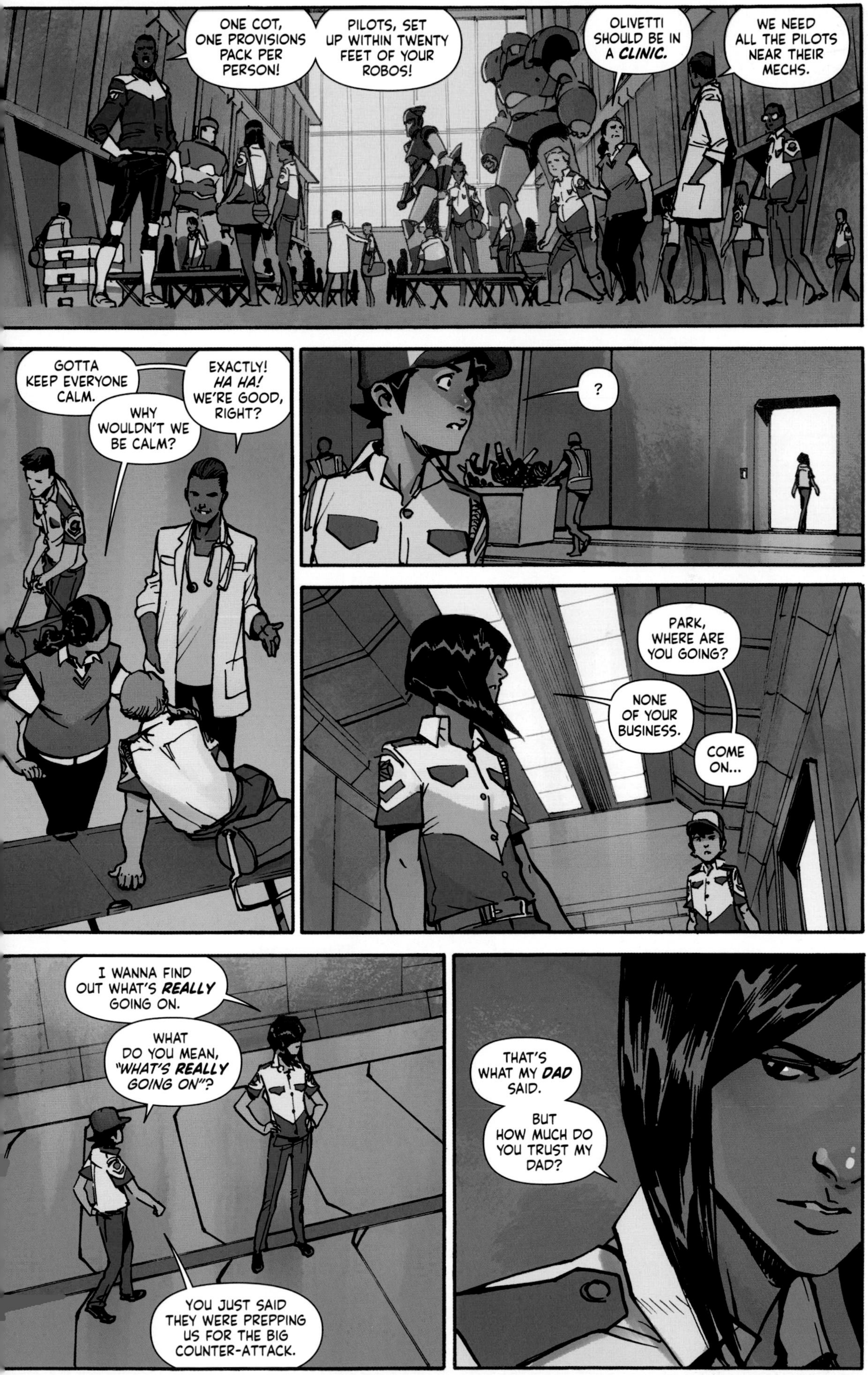

ONE COT, ONE PROVISIONS PACK PER PERSON!
PILOTS, SET UP WITHIN TWENTY FEET OF YOUR ROBOS!
OLIVETTI SHOULD BE IN A *CLINIC.*
WE NEED ALL THE PILOTS NEAR THEIR MECHS.
GOTTA KEEP EVERYONE CALM.
WHY WOULDN'T WE BE CALM?
EXACTLY! *HA HA!* WE'RE GOOD, RIGHT?
?
PARK, WHERE ARE YOU GOING?
NONE OF YOUR BUSINESS.
COME ON...
I WANNA FIND OUT WHAT'S ***REALLY*** GOING ON.
WHAT DO YOU MEAN, *"WHAT'S **REALLY** GOING ON"?*
YOU JUST SAID THEY WERE PREPPING US FOR THE BIG COUNTER-ATTACK.
THAT'S WHAT MY ***DAD*** SAID.
BUT HOW MUCH DO YOU TRUST MY DAD?

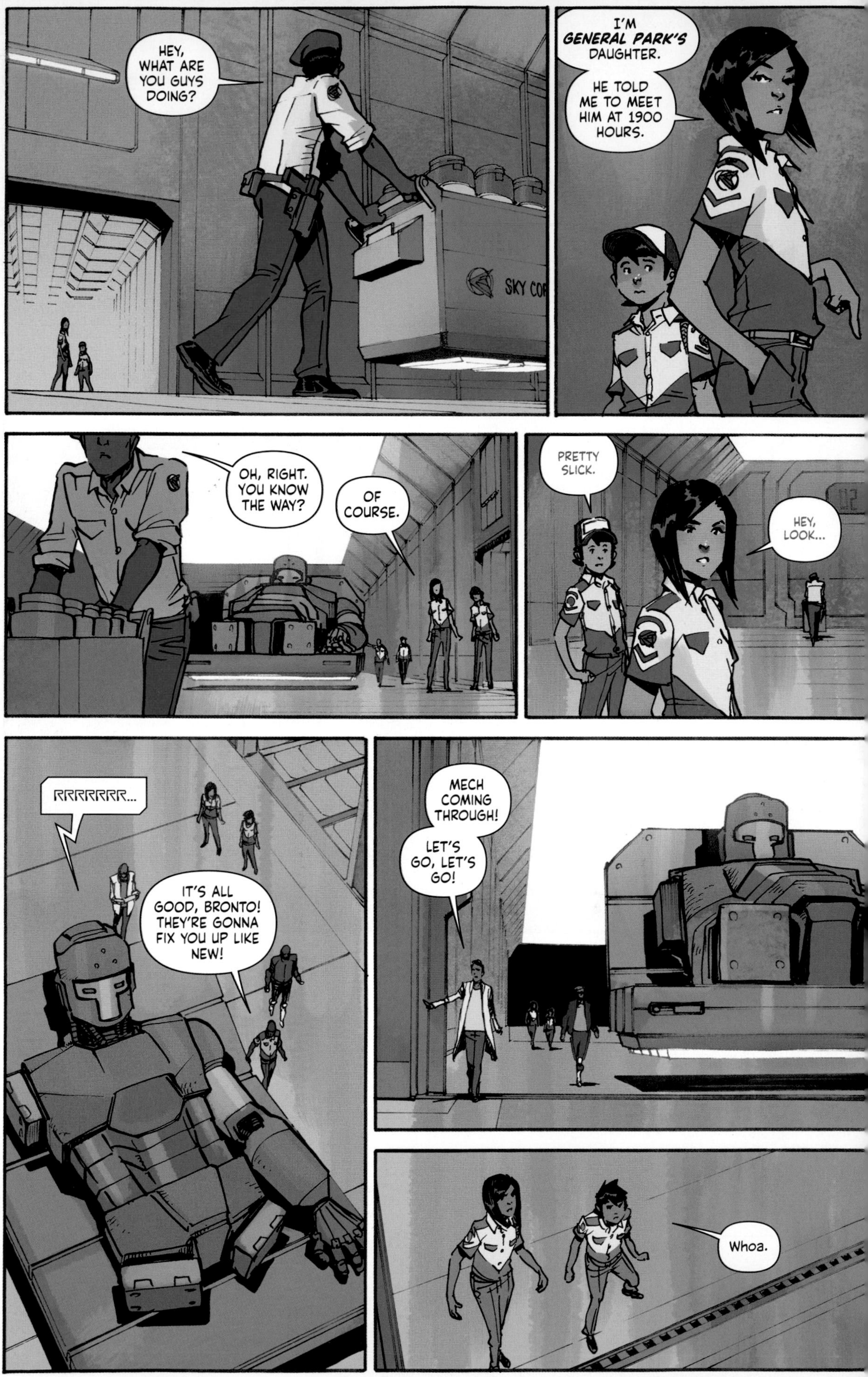
HEY, WHAT ARE YOU GUYS DOING?
SKY COR
I'M GENERAL PARK'S DAUGHTER.
HE TOLD ME TO MEET HIM AT 1900 HOURS.
OH, RIGHT. YOU KNOW THE WAY?
OF COURSE.
PRETTY SLICK.
HEY, LOOK...
RRRRRRRR...
IT'S ALL GOOD, BRONTO! THEY'RE GONNA FIX YOU UP LIKE NEW!
MECH COMING THROUGH!
LET'S GO, LET'S GO!
Whoa.

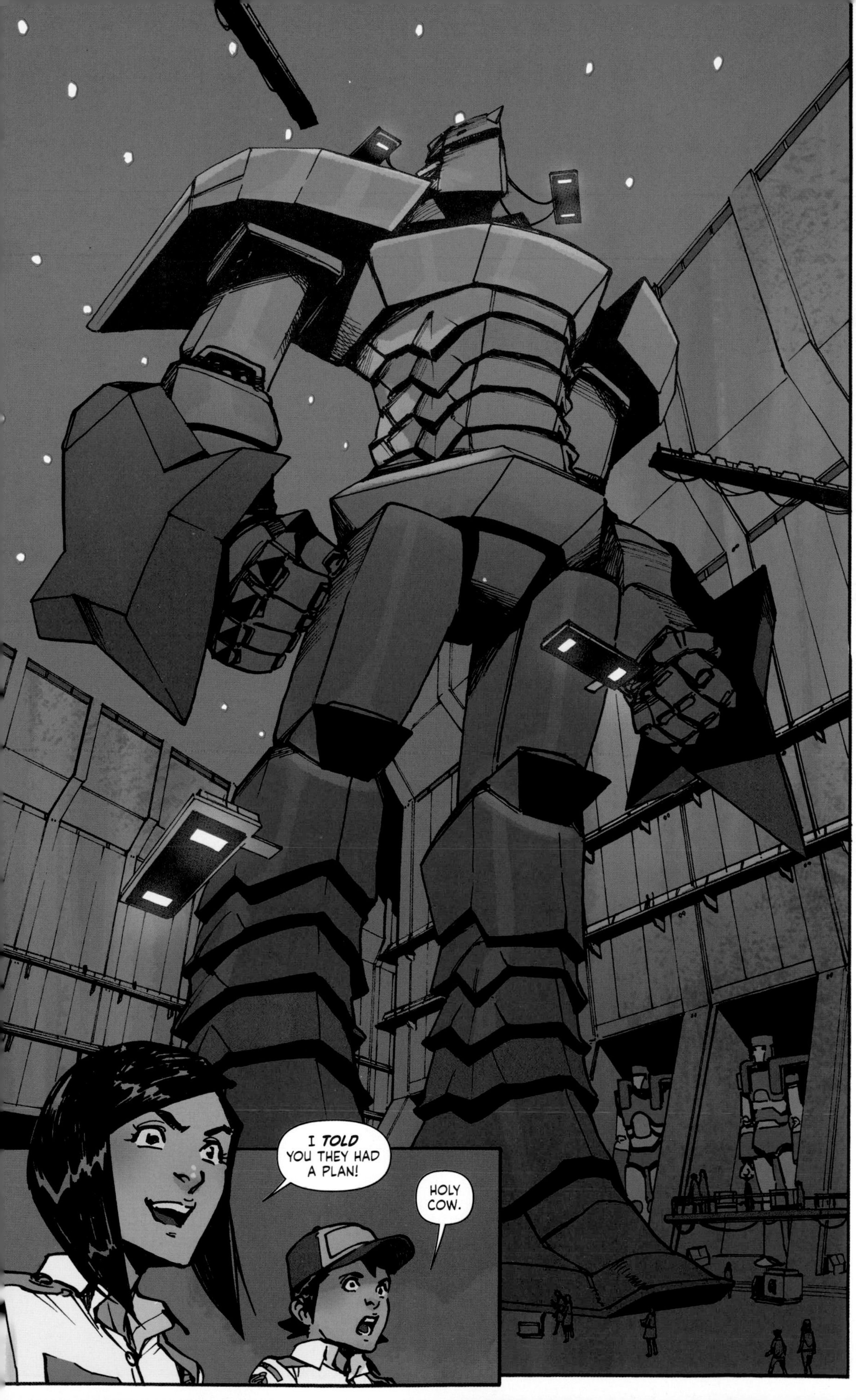
I TOLD YOU THEY HAD A PLAN!
HOLY COW.

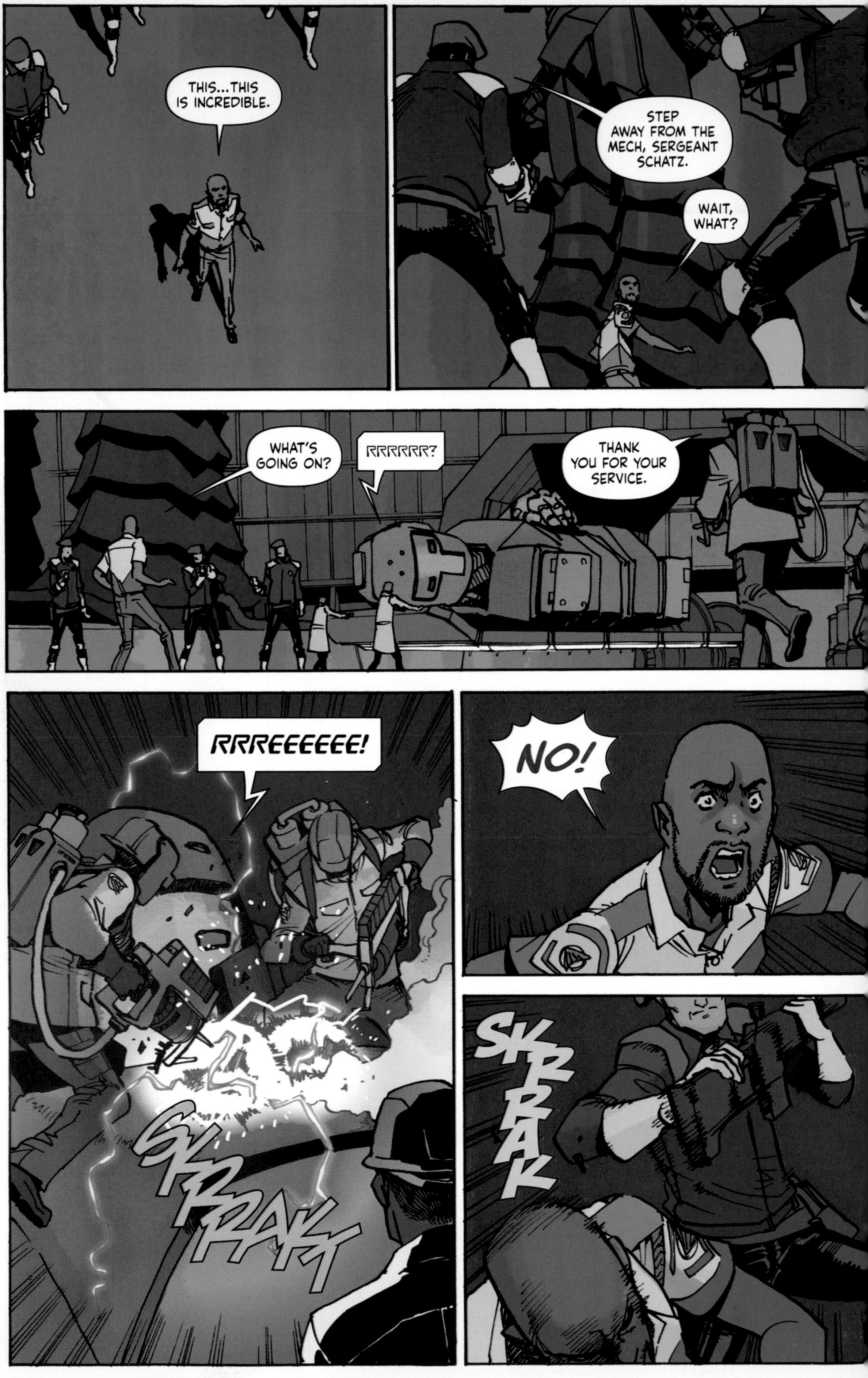
THIS...THIS IS INCREDIBLE.
STEP AWAY FROM THE MECH, SERGEANT SCHATZ.
WAIT, WHAT?
WHAT'S GOING ON?
RRRRRRR?
THANK YOU FOR YOUR SERVICE.
RRREEEEEEE!
SKRAKT
NO!
SKRAK

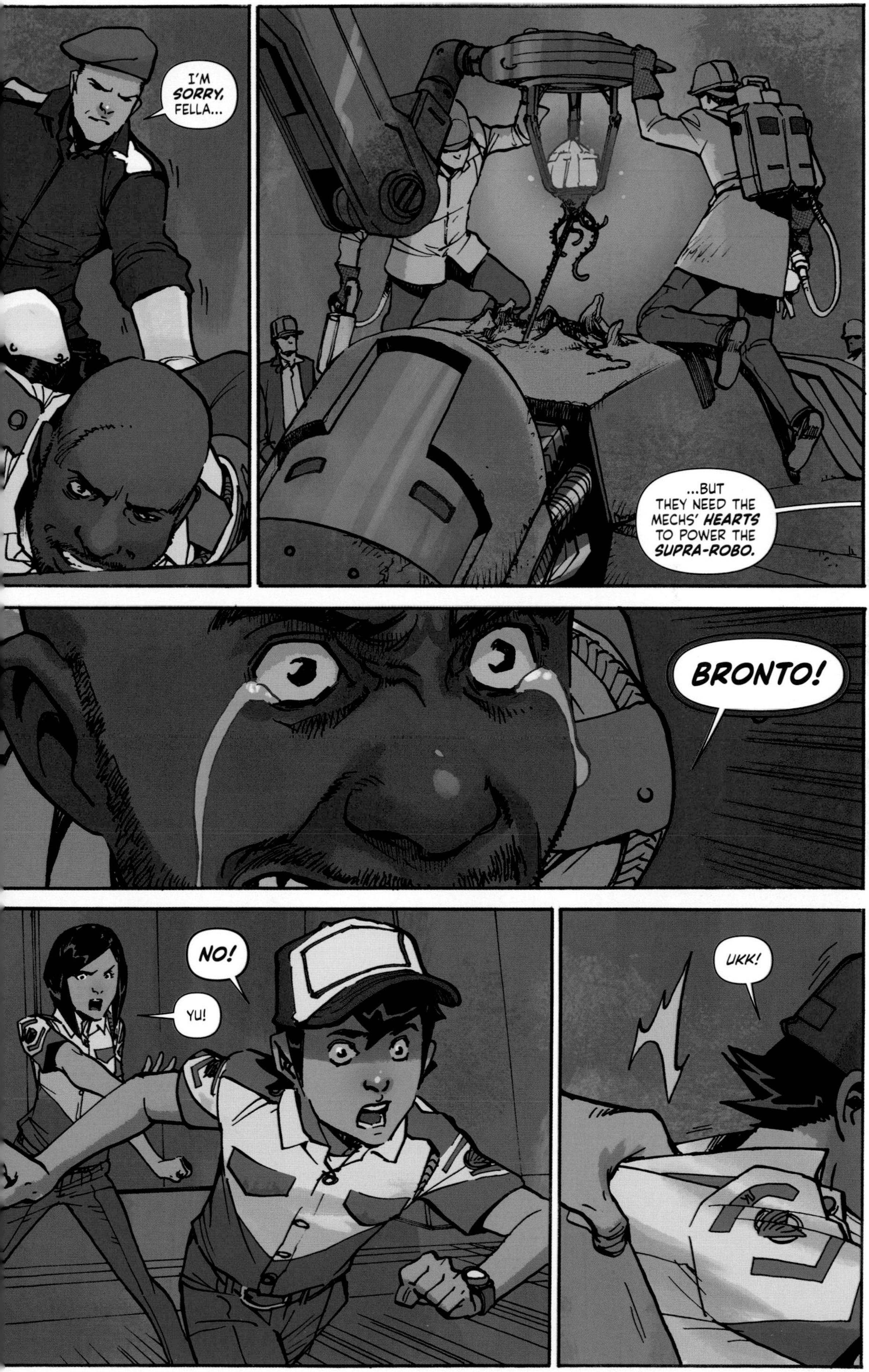
I'M SORRY, FELLA...
...BUT THEY NEED THE MECHS' HEARTS TO POWER THE SUPRA-ROBO.
BRONTO!
NO!
YU!
UKK!

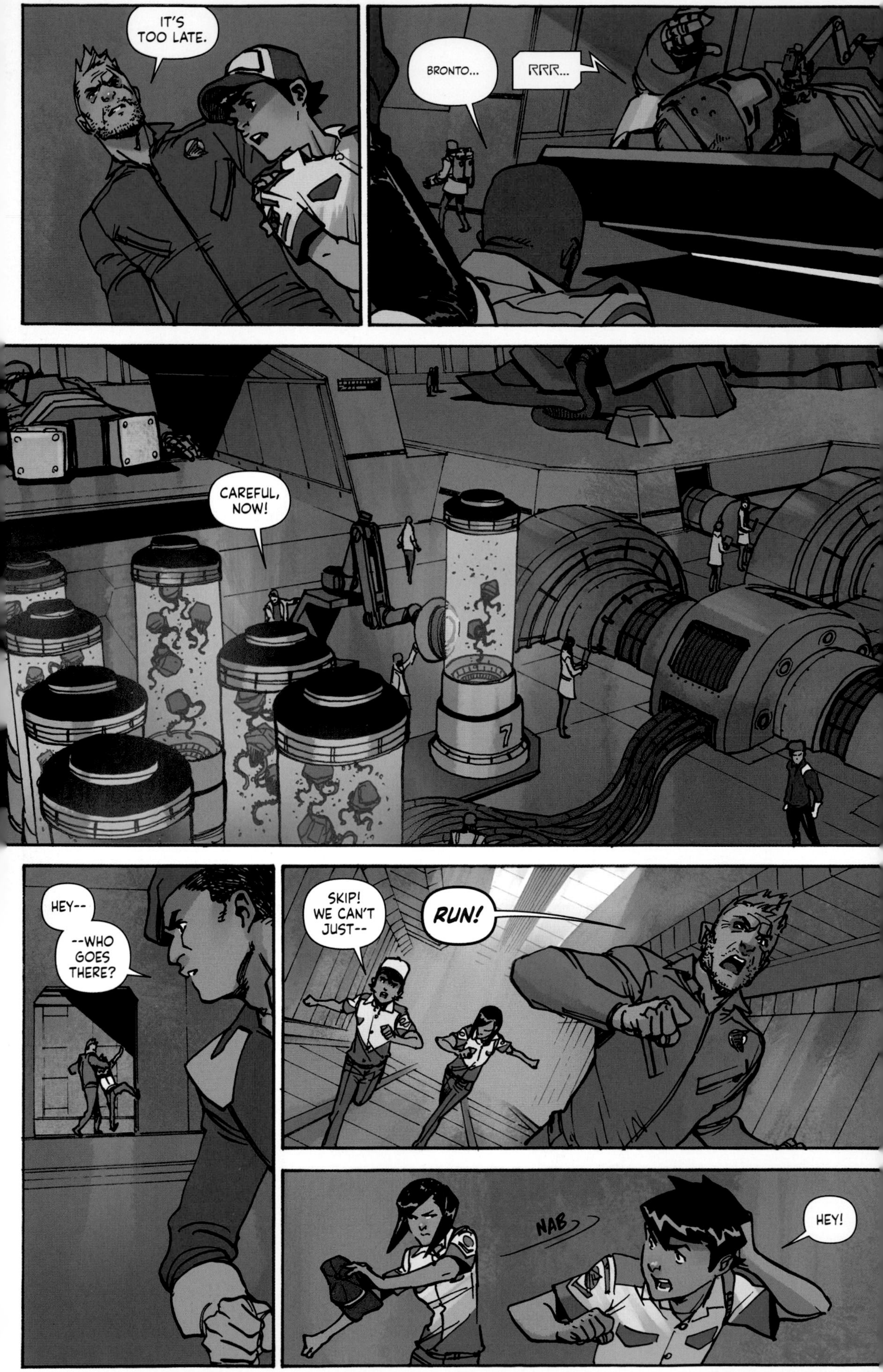
IT'S TOO LATE.
BRONTO...
RRR...
CAREFUL, NOW!
7
HEY--
--WHO GOES THERE?
SKIP! WE CAN'T JUST--
RUN!
NAB
HEY!

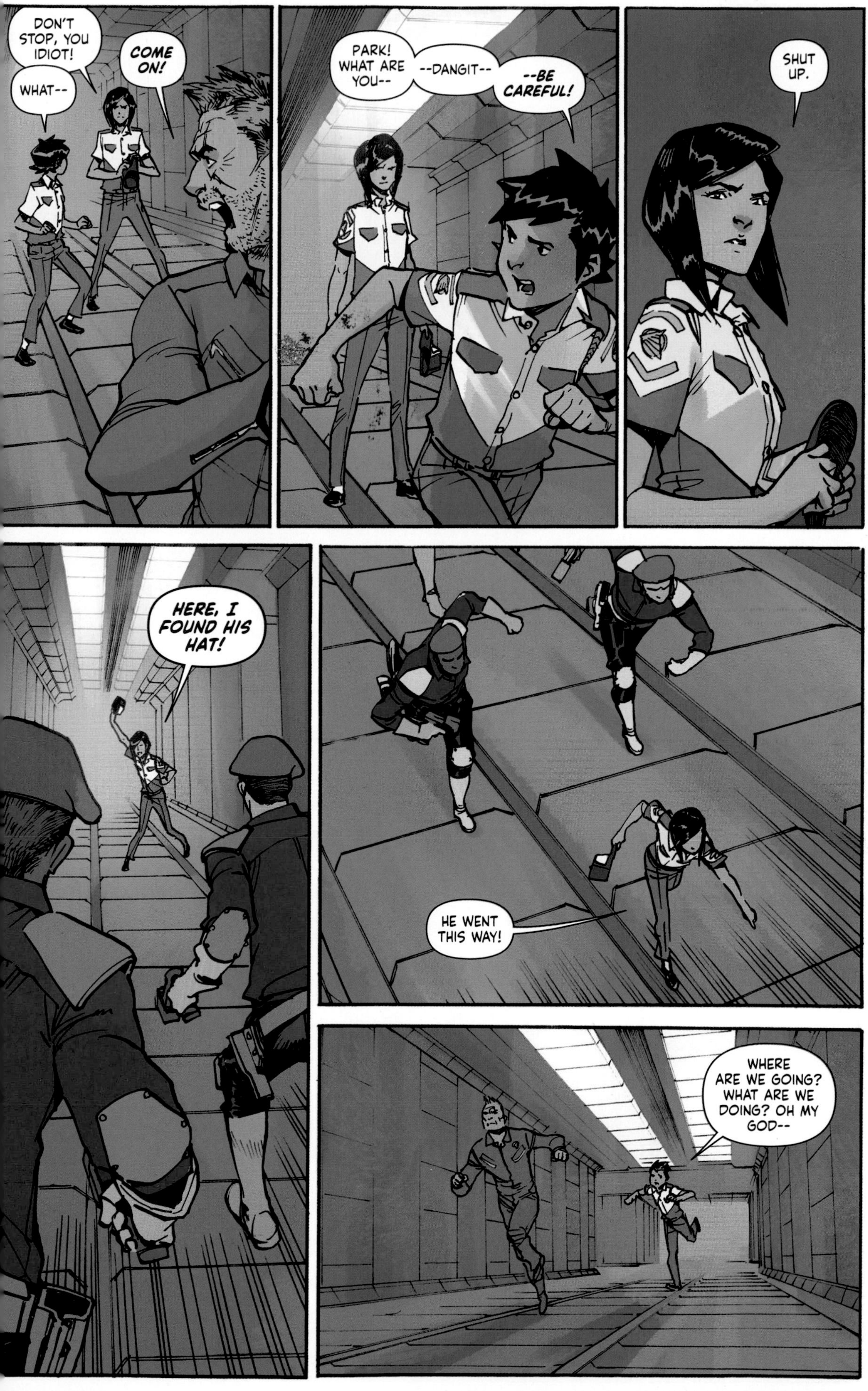
DON'T STOP, YOU IDIOT!
WHAT--
COME ON!
PARK! WHAT ARE YOU--
--DANGIT--
--BE CAREFUL!
SHUT UP.
HERE, I FOUND HIS HAT!
HE WENT THIS WAY!
WHERE ARE WE GOING? WHAT ARE WE DOING? OH MY GOD--

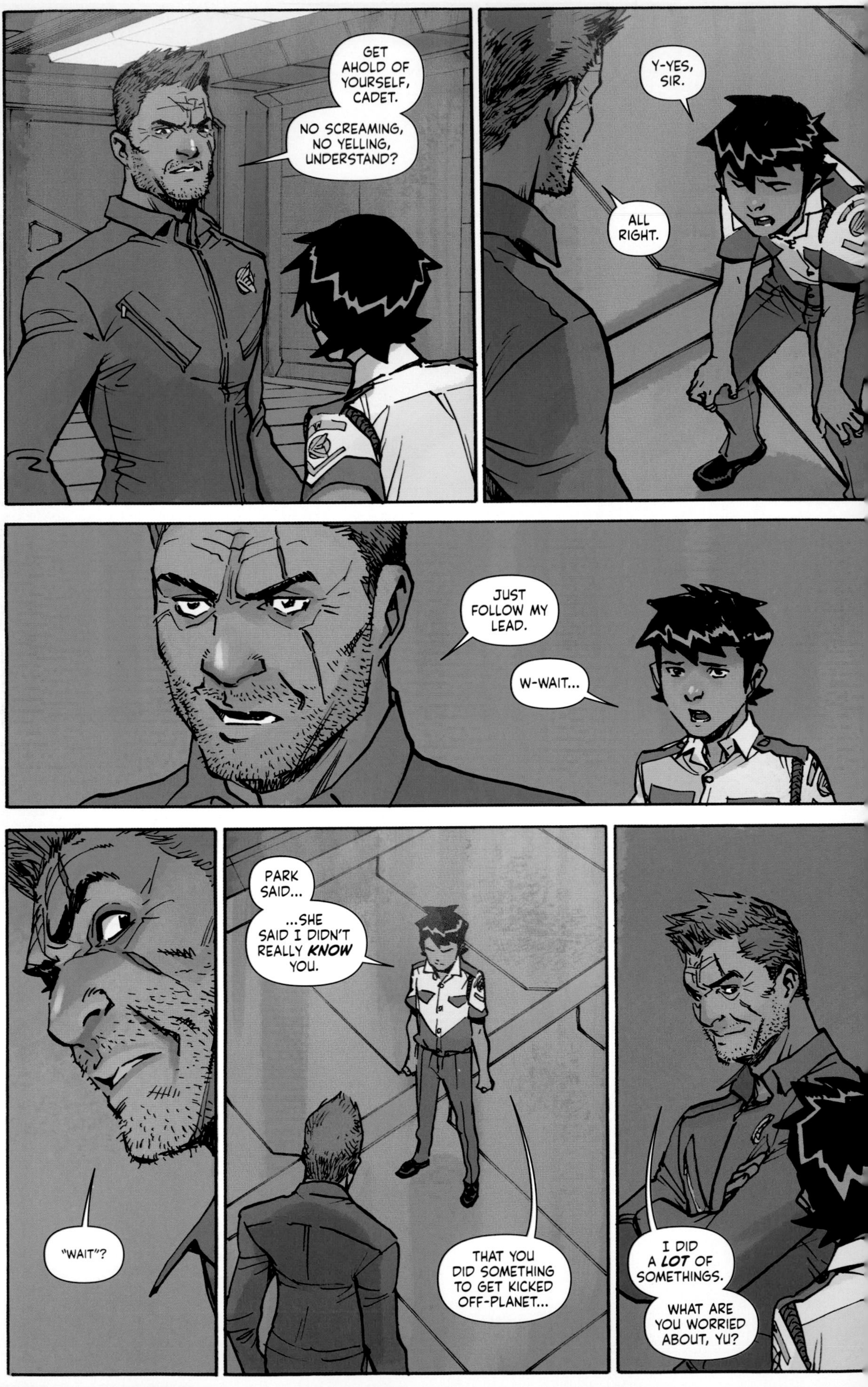
GET AHOLD OF YOURSELF, CADET.
NO SCREAMING, NO YELLING, UNDERSTAND?
Y-YES, SIR.
ALL RIGHT.
JUST FOLLOW MY LEAD.
W-WAIT...
"WAIT"?
PARK SAID...
...SHE SAID I DIDN'T REALLY *KNOW* YOU.
THAT YOU DID SOMETHING TO GET KICKED OFF-PLANET...
I DID A *LOT* OF SOMETHINGS.
WHAT ARE YOU WORRIED ABOUT, YU?

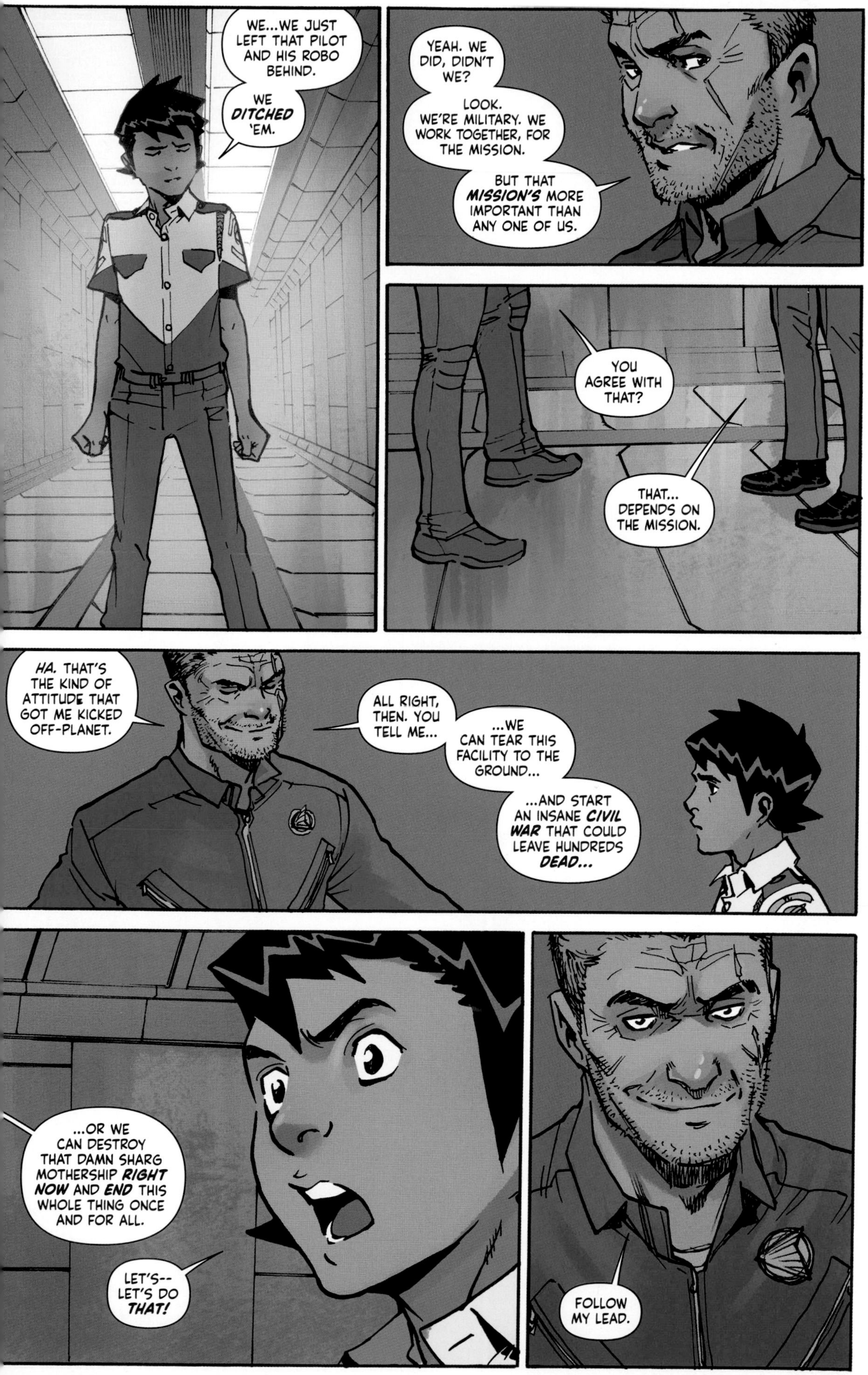
WE...WE JUST LEFT THAT PILOT AND HIS ROBO BEHIND.
WE DITCHED 'EM.
YEAH. WE DID, DIDN'T WE?
LOOK. WE'RE MILITARY. WE WORK TOGETHER, FOR THE MISSION.
BUT THAT MISSION'S MORE IMPORTANT THAN ANY ONE OF US.
YOU AGREE WITH THAT?
THAT... DEPENDS ON THE MISSION.
HA. THAT'S THE KIND OF ATTITUDE THAT GOT ME KICKED OFF-PLANET.
ALL RIGHT, THEN. YOU TELL ME...
...WE CAN TEAR THIS FACILITY TO THE GROUND...
...AND START AN INSANE CIVIL WAR THAT COULD LEAVE HUNDREDS DEAD...
...OR WE CAN DESTROY THAT DAMN SHARG MOTHERSHIP RIGHT NOW AND END THIS WHOLE THING ONCE AND FOR ALL.
LET'S-- LET'S DO THAT!
FOLLOW MY LEAD.

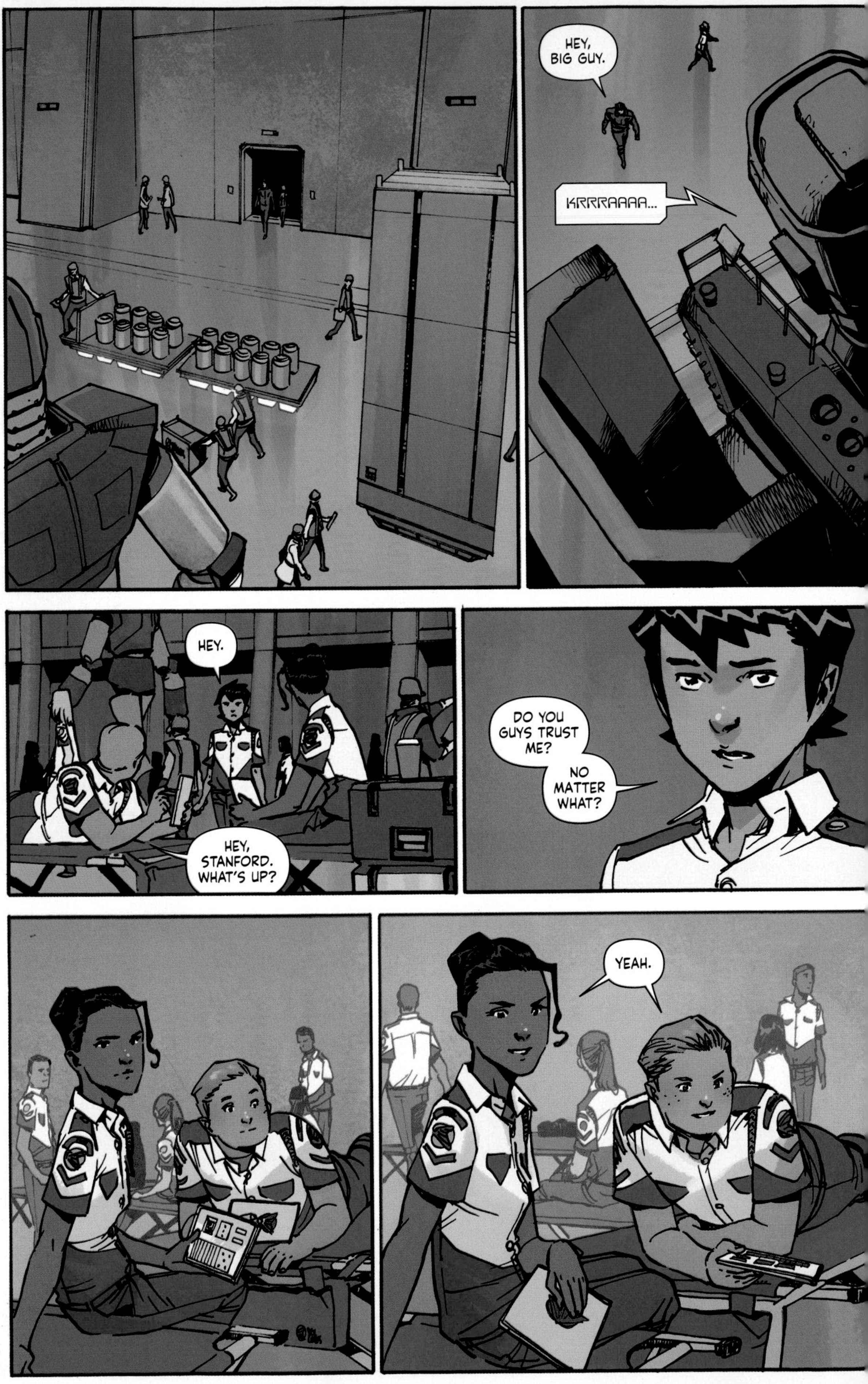
HEY, BIG GUY.
KRRRAAAA...
HEY.
HEY, STANFORD. WHAT'S UP?
DO YOU GUYS TRUST ME?
NO MATTER WHAT?
YEAH.

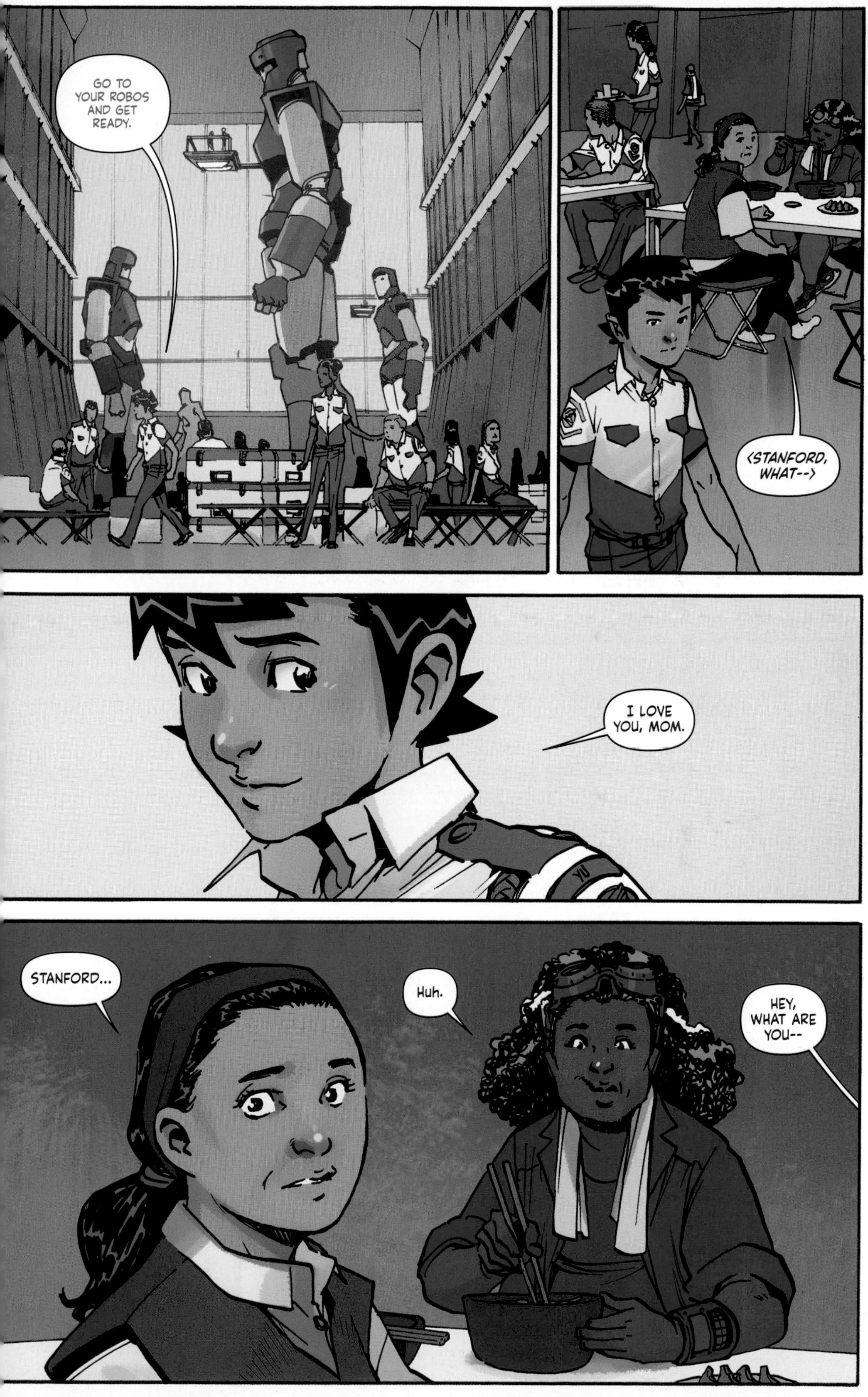

GO TO YOUR ROBOS AND GET READY.
<STANFORD, WHAT-->
I LOVE YOU, MOM.
STANFORD...
Huh.
HEY, WHAT ARE YOU--

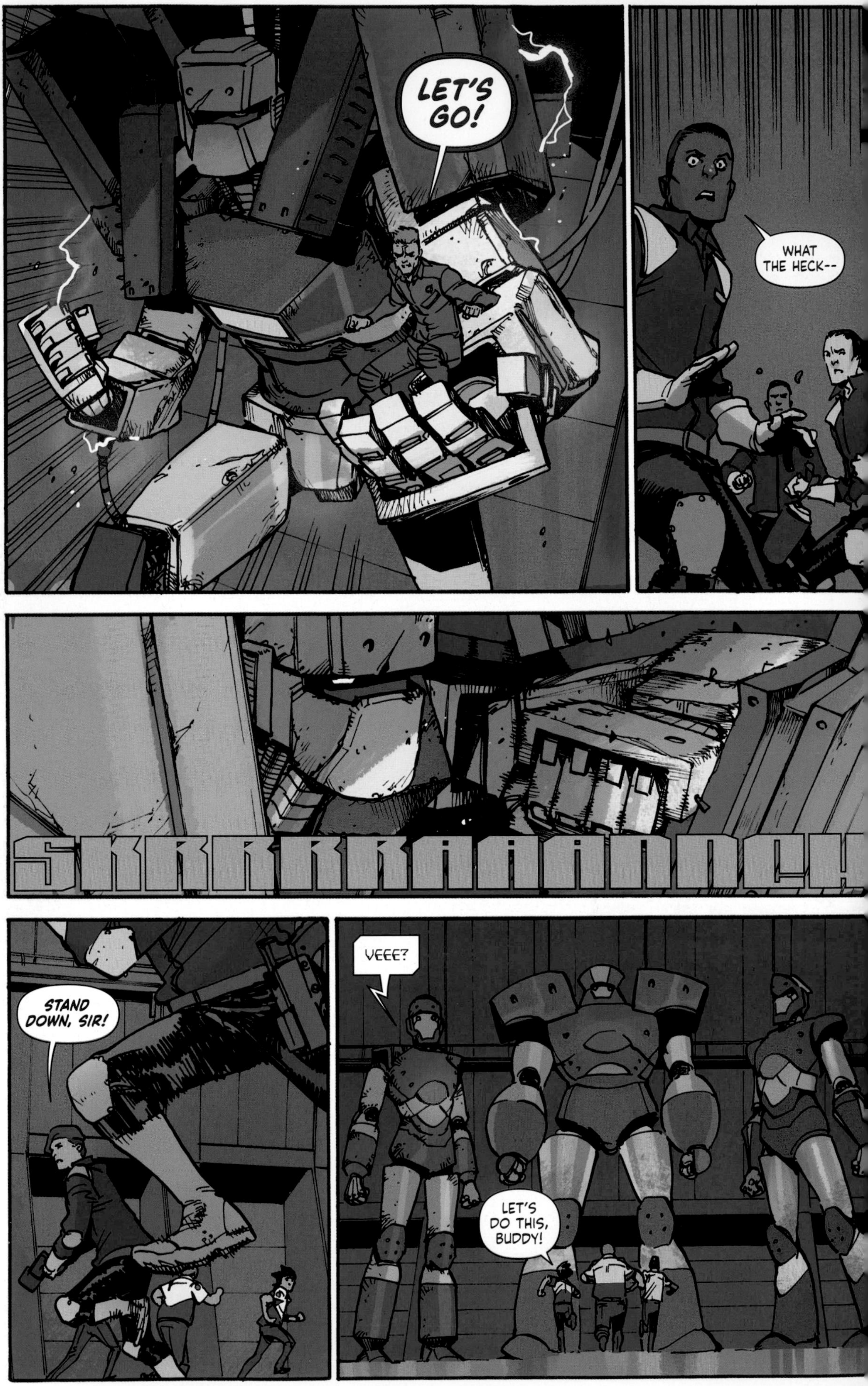
LET'S GO!
WHAT THE HECK--
SKRRRRAAAANNCH
STAND DOWN, SIR!
VEEE?
LET'S DO THIS, BUDDY!

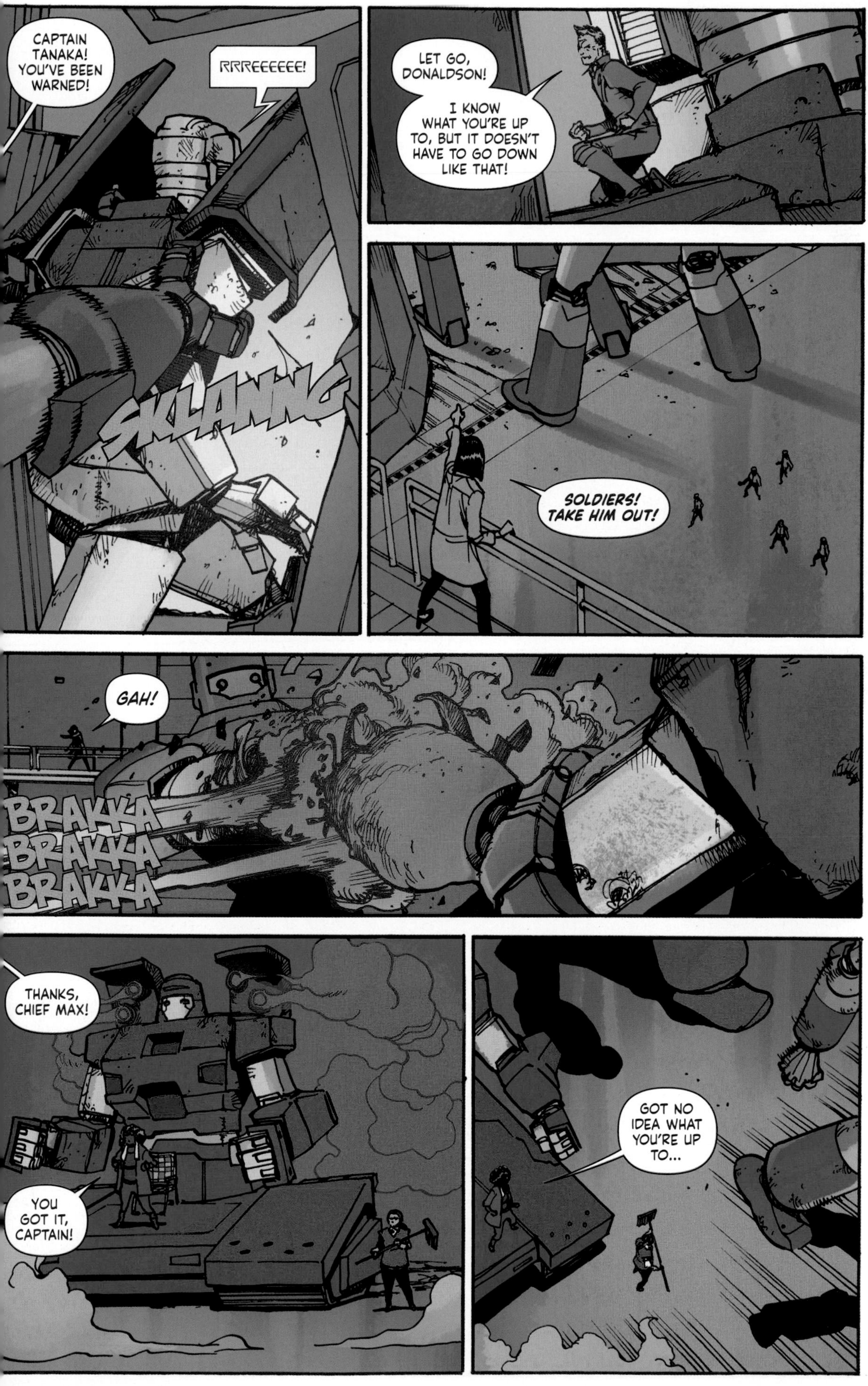
CAPTAIN TANAKA! YOU'VE BEEN WARNED!
RRRREEEEEEE!
SKLANNG
LET GO, DONALDSON!
I KNOW WHAT YOU'RE UP TO, BUT IT DOESN'T HAVE TO GO DOWN LIKE THAT!
SOLDIERS! TAKE HIM OUT!
GAH!
BRAKKA BRAKKA BRAKKA
THANKS, CHIEF MAX!
YOU GOT IT, CAPTAIN!
GOT NO IDEA WHAT YOU'RE UP TO...

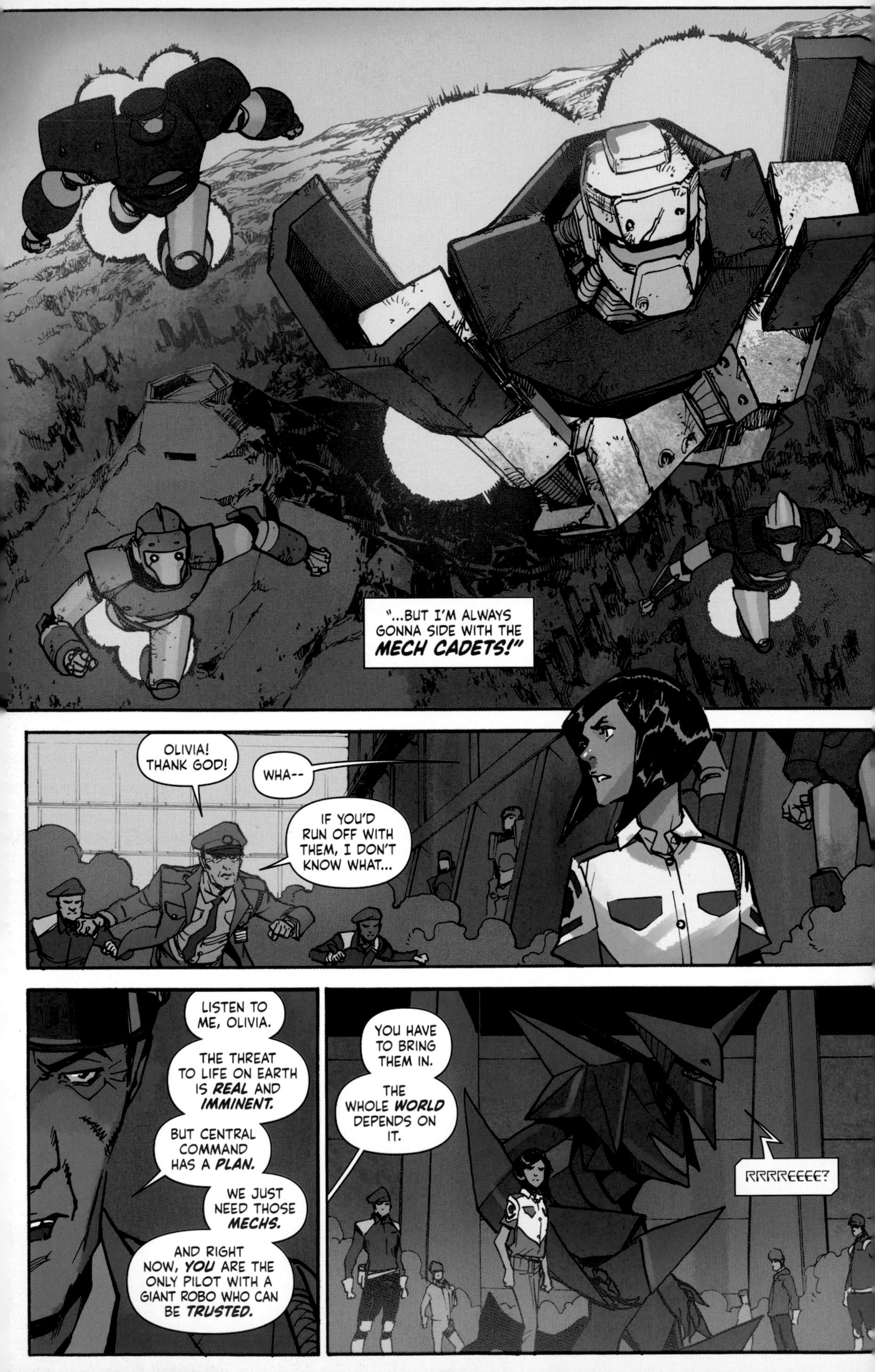
"...BUT I'M ALWAYS GONNA SIDE WITH THE MECH CADETS!"
OLIVIA! THANK GOD!
WHA--
IF YOU'D RUN OFF WITH THEM, I DON'T KNOW WHAT...
LISTEN TO ME, OLIVIA.
THE THREAT TO LIFE ON EARTH IS REAL AND IMMINENT.
BUT CENTRAL COMMAND HAS A PLAN.
WE JUST NEED THOSE MECHS.
AND RIGHT NOW, YOU ARE THE ONLY PILOT WITH A GIANT ROBO WHO CAN BE TRUSTED.
YOU HAVE TO BRING THEM IN.
THE WHOLE WORLD DEPENDS ON IT.
RRRREEEE?

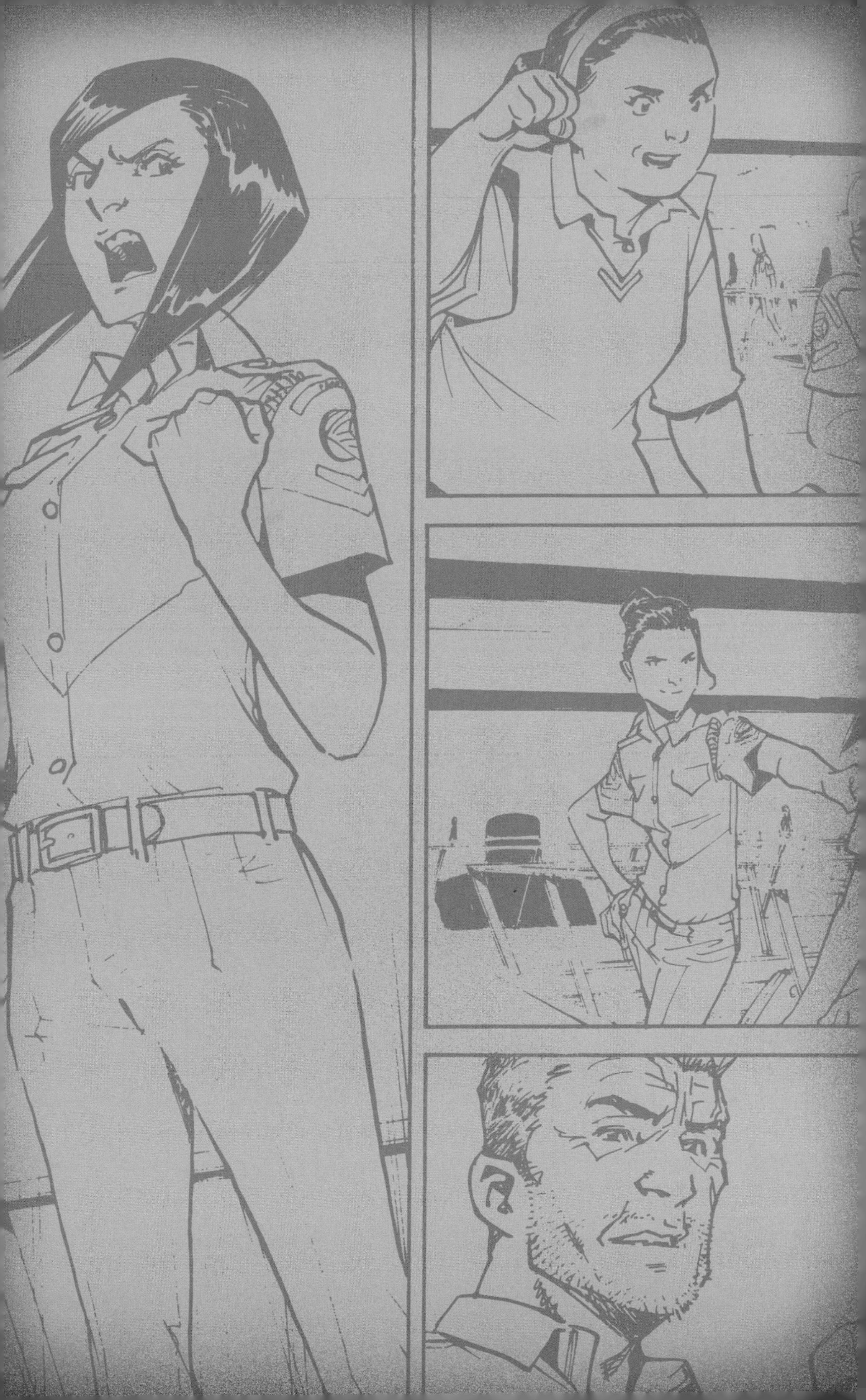

CHAPTER EIGHT

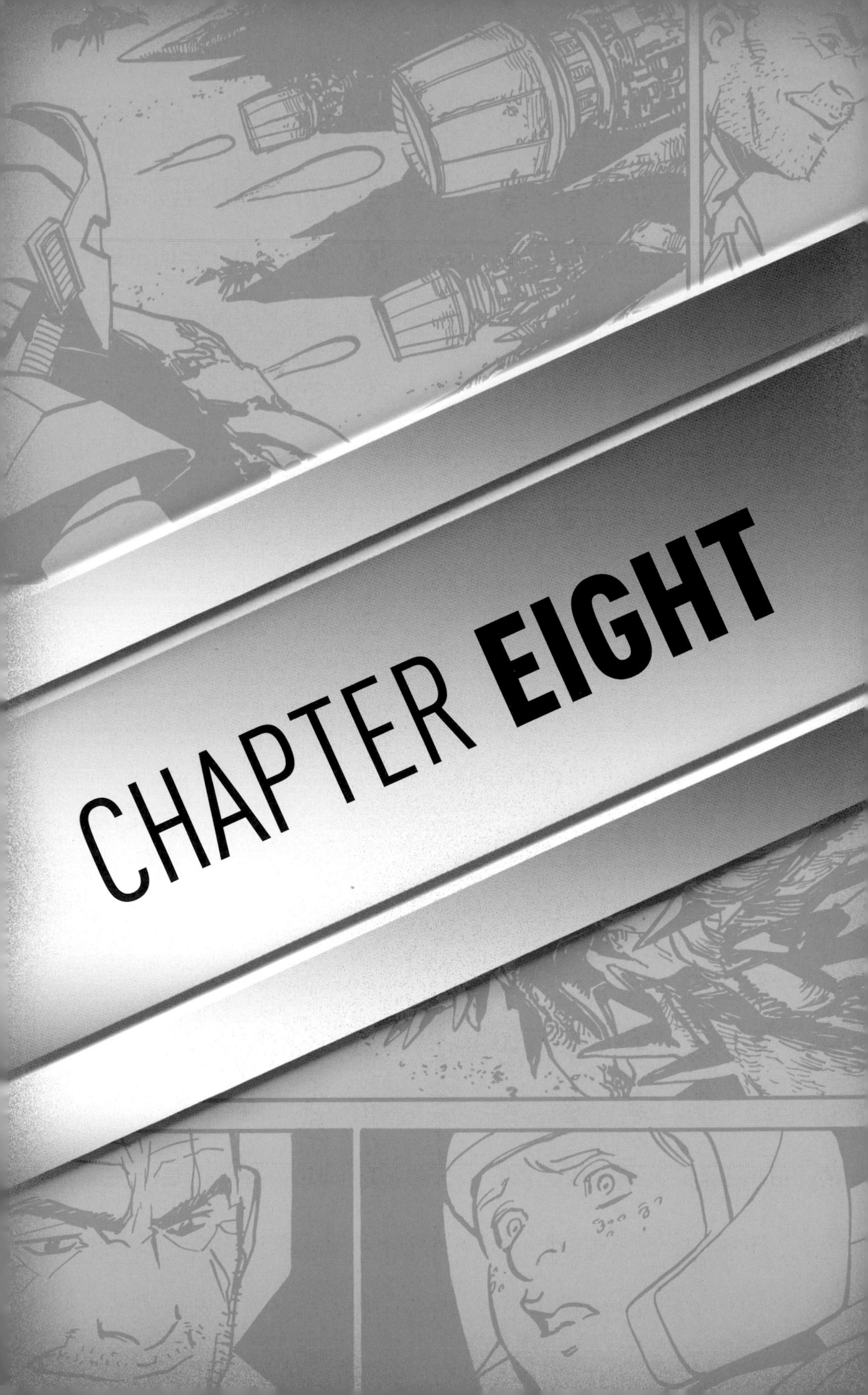

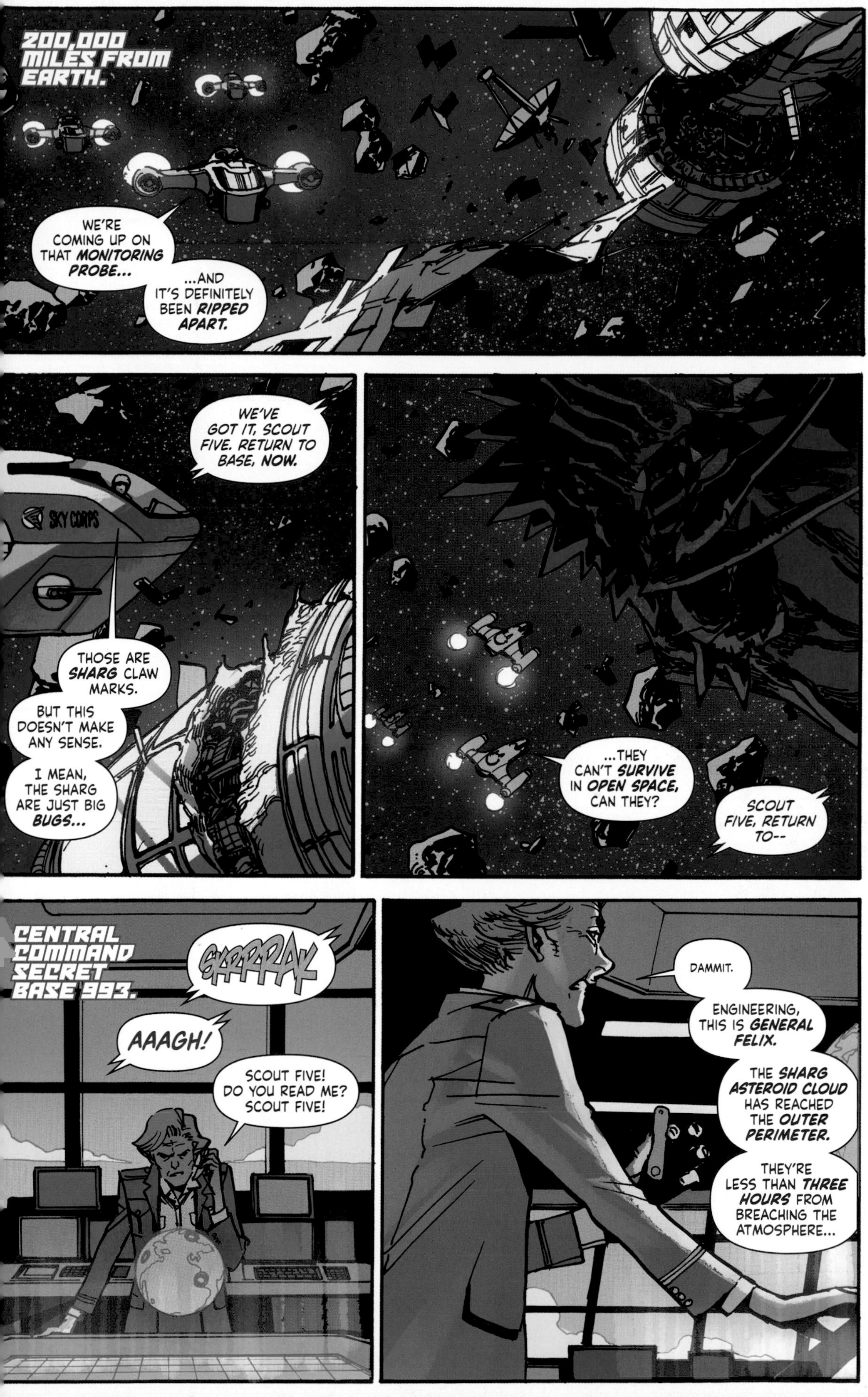
200,000 MILES FROM EARTH.
WE'RE COMING UP ON THAT MONITORING PROBE...
...AND IT'S DEFINITELY BEEN RIPPED APART.
WE'VE GOT IT, SCOUT FIVE. RETURN TO BASE, NOW.
SKY CORPS
THOSE ARE SHARG CLAW MARKS.
BUT THIS DOESN'T MAKE ANY SENSE.
I MEAN, THE SHARG ARE JUST BIG BUGS...
...THEY CAN'T SURVIVE IN OPEN SPACE, CAN THEY?
SCOUT FIVE, RETURN TO--
CENTRAL COMMAND SECRET BASE 993.
SKRRRRAK
AAAGH!
SCOUT FIVE! DO YOU READ ME? SCOUT FIVE!
DAMMIT.
ENGINEERING, THIS IS GENERAL FELIX.
THE SHARG ASTEROID CLOUD HAS REACHED THE OUTER PERIMETER.
THEY'RE LESS THAN THREE HOURS FROM BREACHING THE ATMOSPHERE...

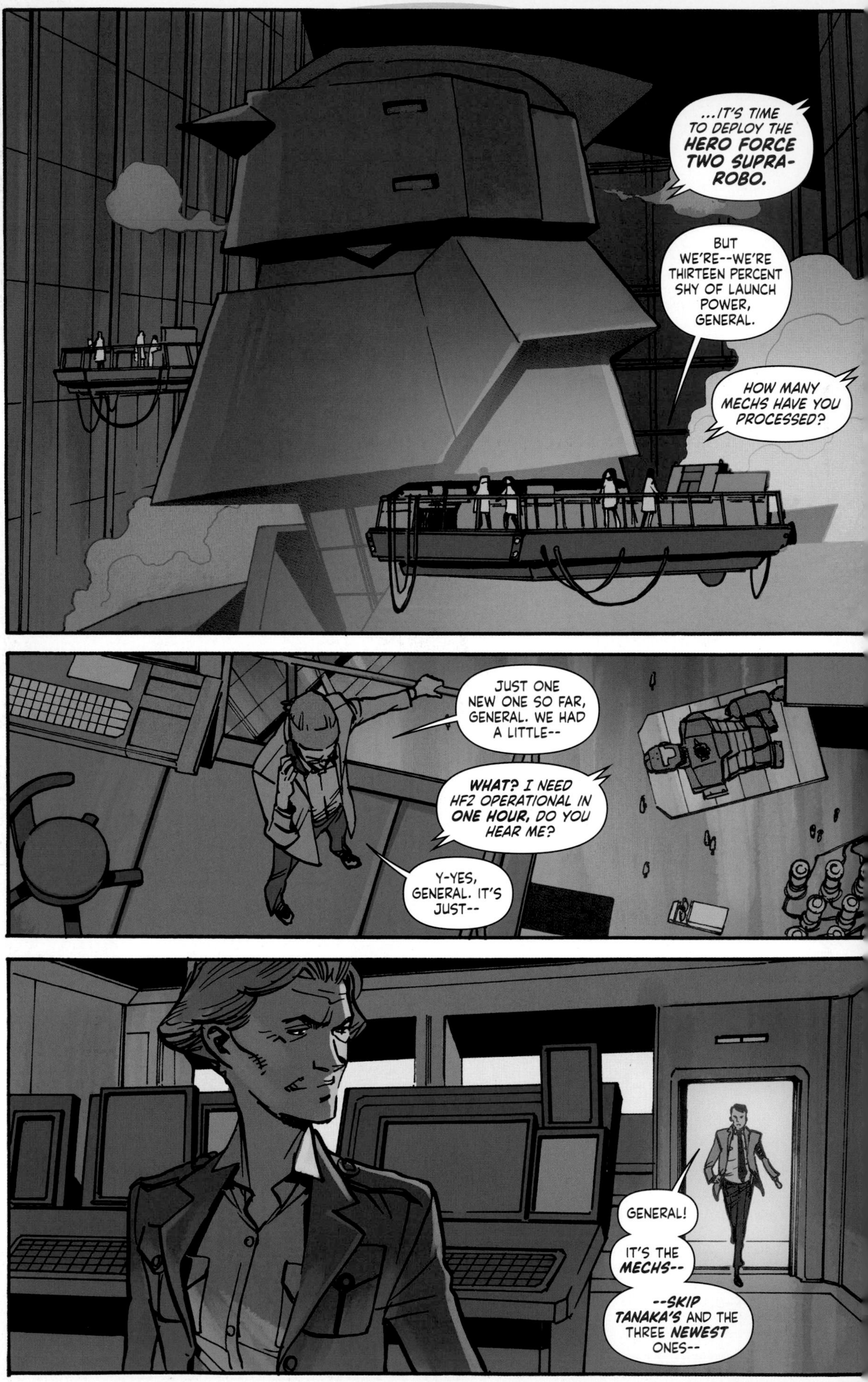
...IT'S TIME TO DEPLOY THE HERO FORCE TWO SUPRA-ROBO.
BUT WE'RE--WE'RE THIRTEEN PERCENT SHY OF LAUNCH POWER, GENERAL.
HOW MANY MECHS HAVE YOU PROCESSED?
JUST ONE NEW ONE SO FAR, GENERAL. WE HAD A LITTLE--
WHAT? I NEED HF2 OPERATIONAL IN ONE HOUR, DO YOU HEAR ME?
Y-YES, GENERAL. IT'S JUST--
GENERAL!
IT'S THE MECHS--
--SKIP TANAKA'S AND THE THREE NEWEST ONES--

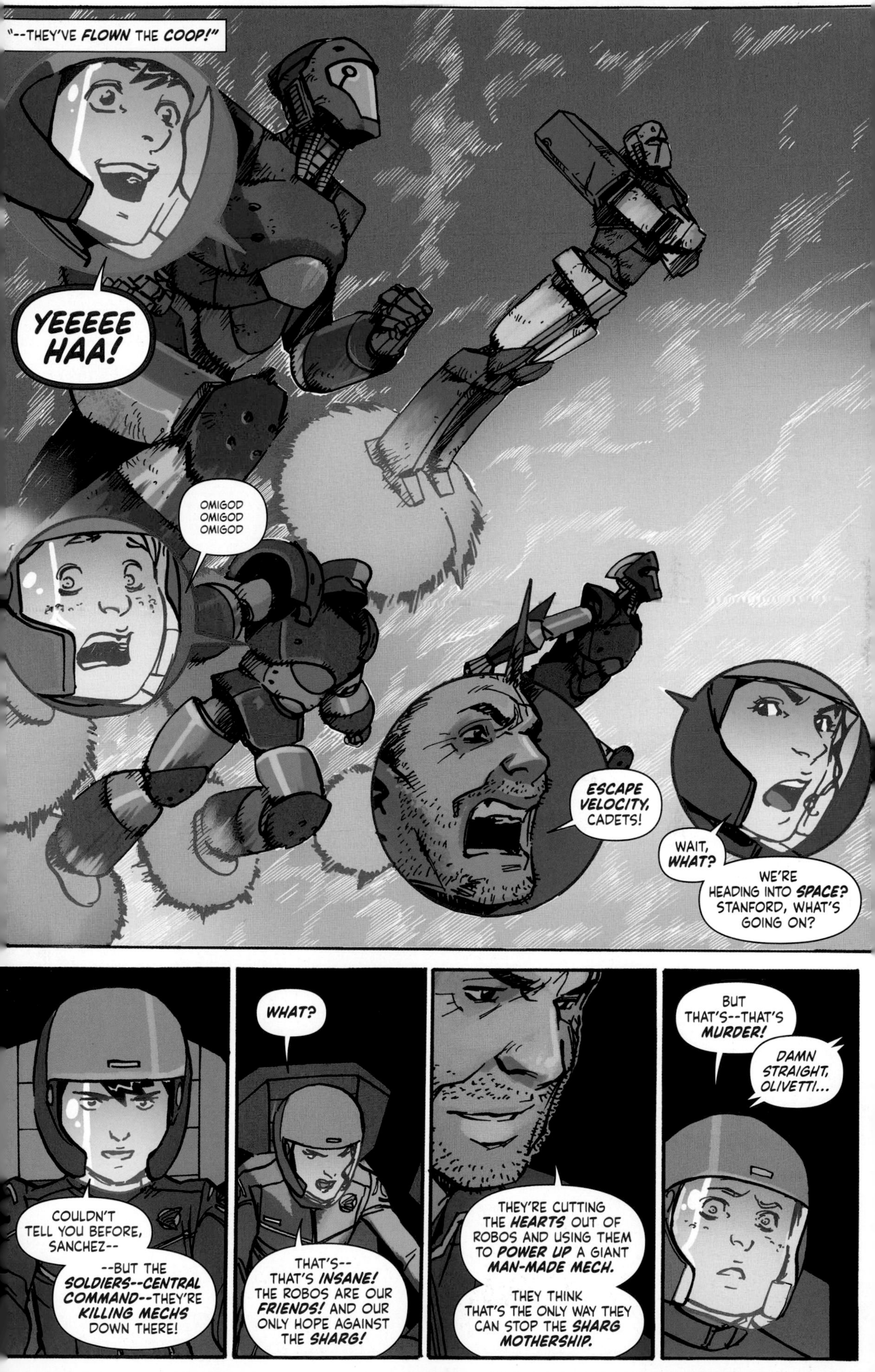
"--THEY'VE FLOWN THE COOP!"
YEEEEE HAA!
OMIGOD OMIGOD OMIGOD
ESCAPE VELOCITY, CADETS!
WAIT, WHAT?
WE'RE HEADING INTO SPACE? STANFORD, WHAT'S GOING ON?
COULDN'T TELL YOU BEFORE, SANCHEZ--
--BUT THE SOLDIERS--CENTRAL COMMAND--THEY'RE KILLING MECHS DOWN THERE!
WHAT?
THAT'S--THAT'S INSANE! THE ROBOS ARE OUR FRIENDS! AND OUR ONLY HOPE AGAINST THE SHARG!
THEY'RE CUTTING THE HEARTS OUT OF ROBOS AND USING THEM TO POWER UP A GIANT MAN-MADE MECH.
THEY THINK THAT'S THE ONLY WAY THEY CAN STOP THE SHARG MOTHERSHIP.
BUT THAT'S--THAT'S MURDER!
DAMN STRAIGHT, OLIVETTI...

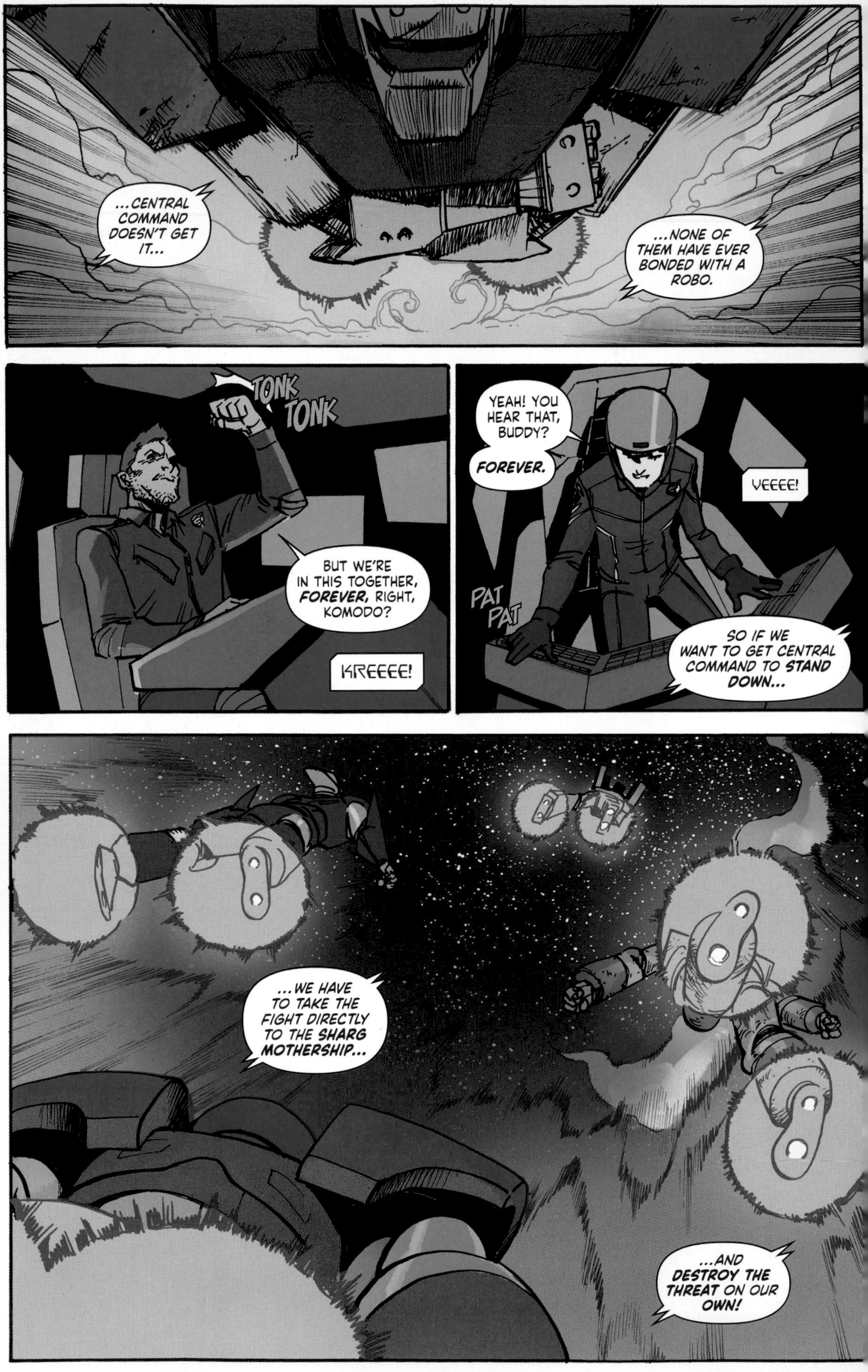
...CENTRAL COMMAND DOESN'T GET IT...
...NONE OF THEM HAVE EVER BONDED WITH A ROBO.
TONK TONK
BUT WE'RE IN THIS TOGETHER, FOREVER, RIGHT, KOMODO?
KREEEE!
YEAH! YOU HEAR THAT, BUDDY?
FOREVER.
VEEEE!
PAT PAT
SO IF WE WANT TO GET CENTRAL COMMAND TO STAND DOWN...
...WE HAVE TO TAKE THE FIGHT DIRECTLY TO THE SHARG MOTHERSHIP...
...AND DESTROY THE THREAT ON OUR OWN!

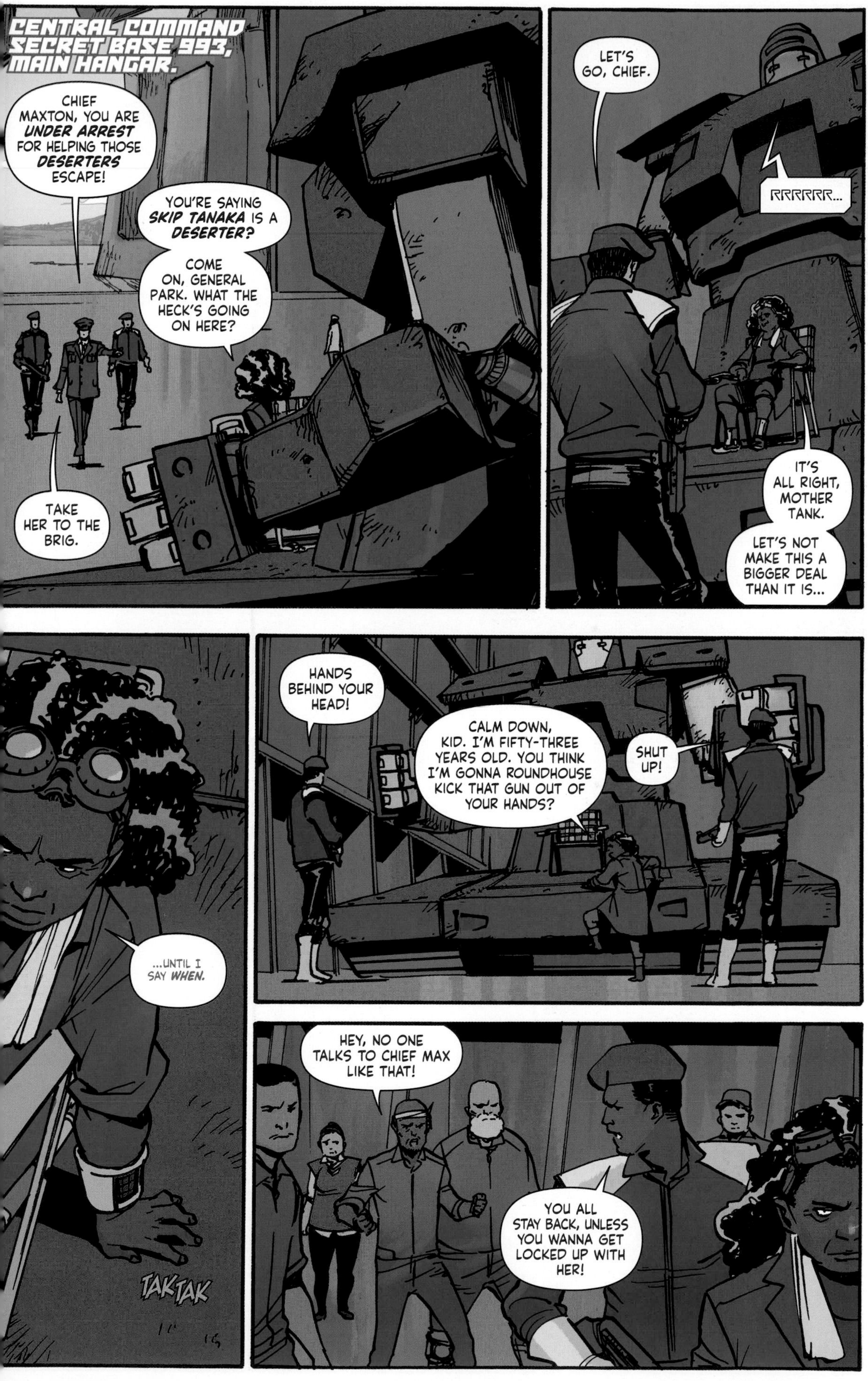
CENTRAL COMMAND SECRET BASE 993, MAIN HANGAR.
CHIEF MAXTON, YOU ARE *UNDER ARREST* FOR HELPING THOSE *DESERTERS* ESCAPE!
YOU'RE SAYING *SKIP TANAKA* IS A *DESERTER?*
COME ON, GENERAL PARK. WHAT THE HECK'S GOING ON HERE?
TAKE HER TO THE BRIG.
LET'S GO, CHIEF.
RRRRRR...
IT'S ALL RIGHT, MOTHER TANK.
LET'S NOT MAKE THIS A BIGGER DEAL THAN IT IS...
...UNTIL I SAY *WHEN.*
TAKTAK
HANDS BEHIND YOUR HEAD!
CALM DOWN, KID. I'M FIFTY-THREE YEARS OLD. YOU THINK I'M GONNA ROUNDHOUSE KICK THAT GUN OUT OF YOUR HANDS?
SHUT UP!
HEY, NO ONE TALKS TO CHIEF MAX LIKE THAT!
YOU ALL STAY BACK, UNLESS YOU WANNA GET LOCKED UP WITH HER!

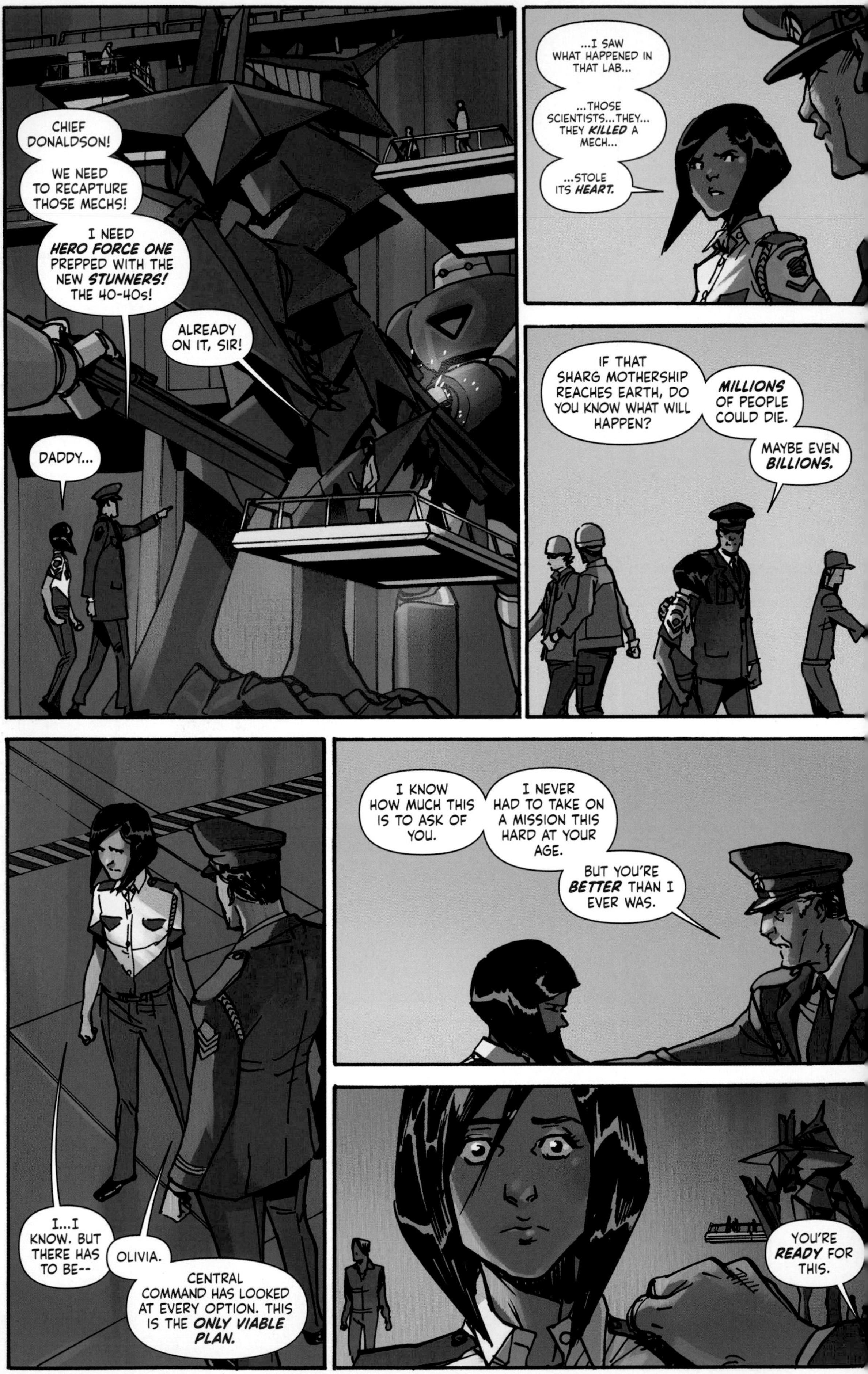
CHIEF DONALDSON!
WE NEED TO RECAPTURE THOSE MECHS!
I NEED HERO FORCE ONE PREPPED WITH THE NEW STUNNERS! THE 40-40s!
ALREADY ON IT, SIR!
DADDY...
...I SAW WHAT HAPPENED IN THAT LAB...
...THOSE SCIENTISTS...THEY... THEY KILLED A MECH...
...STOLE ITS HEART.
IF THAT SHARG MOTHERSHIP REACHES EARTH, DO YOU KNOW WHAT WILL HAPPEN?
MILLIONS OF PEOPLE COULD DIE.
MAYBE EVEN BILLIONS.
I...I KNOW. BUT THERE HAS TO BE--
OLIVIA.
CENTRAL COMMAND HAS LOOKED AT EVERY OPTION. THIS IS THE ONLY VIABLE PLAN.
I KNOW HOW MUCH THIS IS TO ASK OF YOU.
I NEVER HAD TO TAKE ON A MISSION THIS HARD AT YOUR AGE.
BUT YOU'RE BETTER THAN I EVER WAS.
YOU'RE READY FOR THIS.

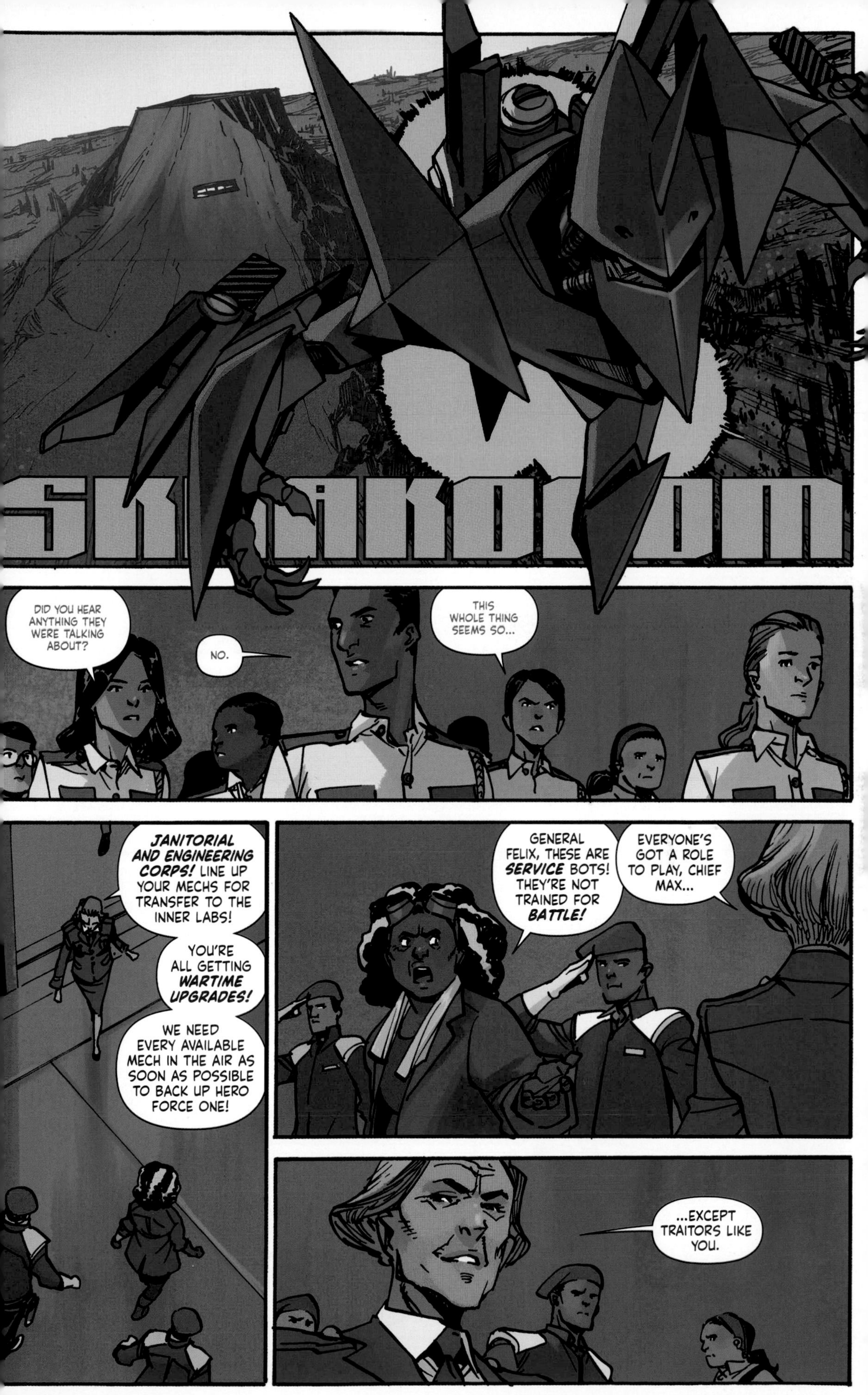
SKRAKOOOM
DID YOU HEAR ANYTHING THEY WERE TALKING ABOUT?
NO.
THIS WHOLE THING SEEMS SO...
JANITORIAL AND ENGINEERING CORPS! LINE UP YOUR MECHS FOR TRANSFER TO THE INNER LABS!
YOU'RE ALL GETTING WARTIME UPGRADES!
WE NEED EVERY AVAILABLE MECH IN THE AIR AS SOON AS POSSIBLE TO BACK UP HERO FORCE ONE!
GENERAL FELIX, THESE ARE SERVICE BOTS! THEY'RE NOT TRAINED FOR BATTLE!
EVERYONE'S GOT A ROLE TO PLAY, CHIEF MAX...
...EXCEPT TRAITORS LIKE YOU.

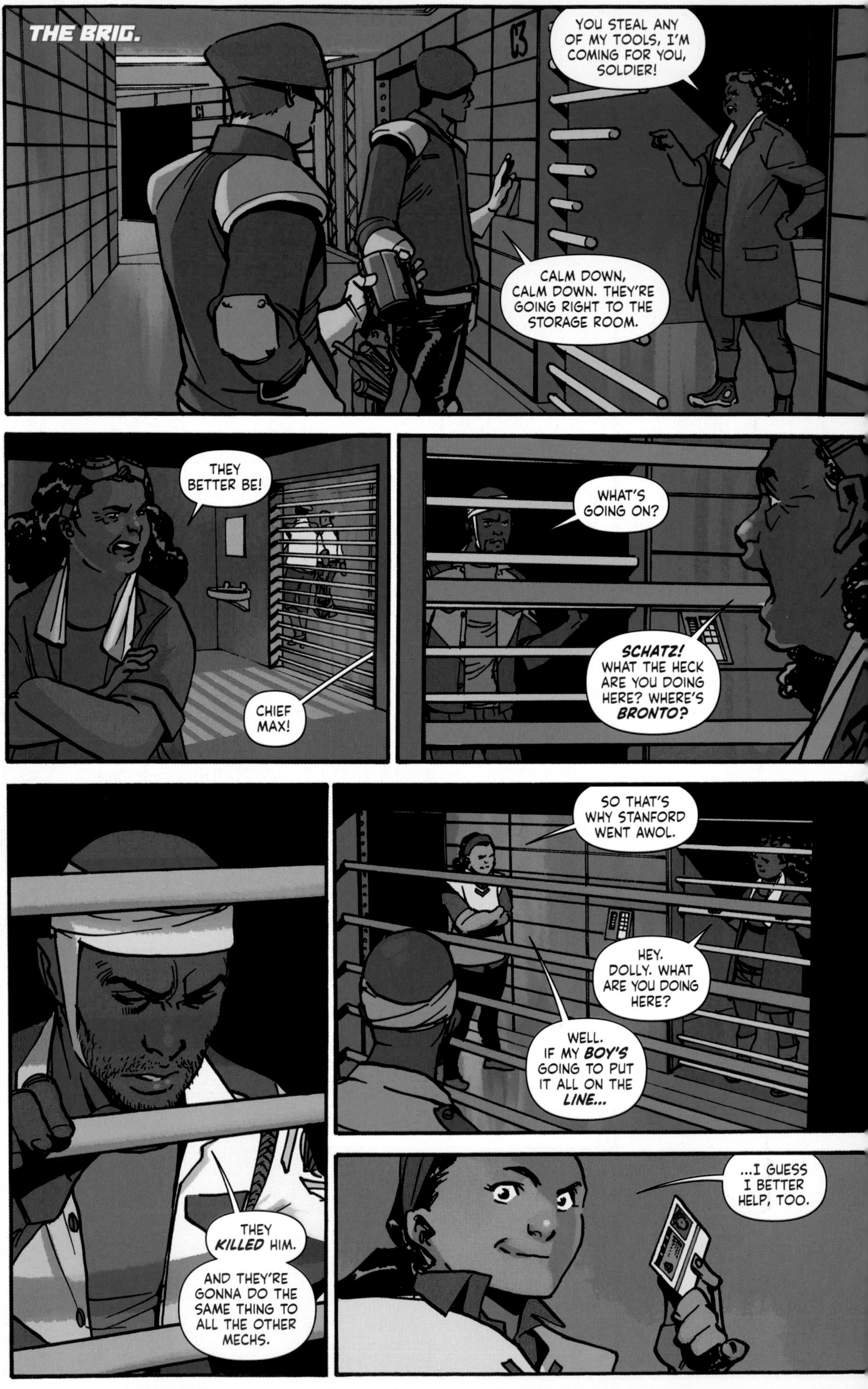
THE BRIG.
YOU STEAL ANY OF MY TOOLS, I'M COMING FOR YOU, SOLDIER!
CALM DOWN, CALM DOWN. THEY'RE GOING RIGHT TO THE STORAGE ROOM.
THEY BETTER BE!
CHIEF MAX!
WHAT'S GOING ON?
SCHATZ! WHAT THE HECK ARE YOU DOING HERE? WHERE'S BRONTO?
THEY KILLED HIM.
AND THEY'RE GONNA DO THE SAME THING TO ALL THE OTHER MECHS.
SO THAT'S WHY STANFORD WENT AWOL.
HEY. DOLLY. WHAT ARE YOU DOING HERE?
WELL. IF MY BOY'S GOING TO PUT IT ALL ON THE LINE...
...I GUESS I BETTER HELP, TOO.

OH, NO...

TRAINING'S OVER, CADETS...

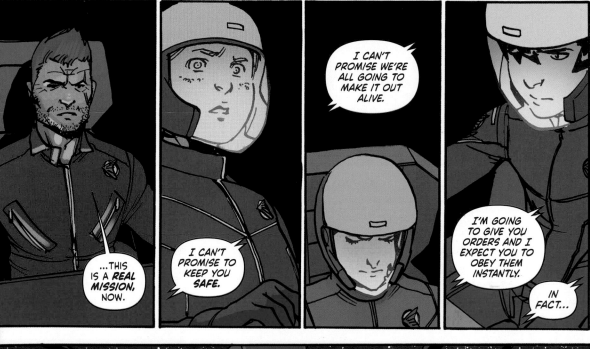

...THIS IS A *REAL MISSION*, NOW.

I CAN'T PROMISE TO KEEP YOU SAFE.

I CAN'T PROMISE WE'RE ALL GOING TO MAKE IT OUT ALIVE.

I'M GOING TO GIVE YOU ORDERS AND I EXPECT YOU TO OBEY THEM INSTANTLY.

IN FACT...

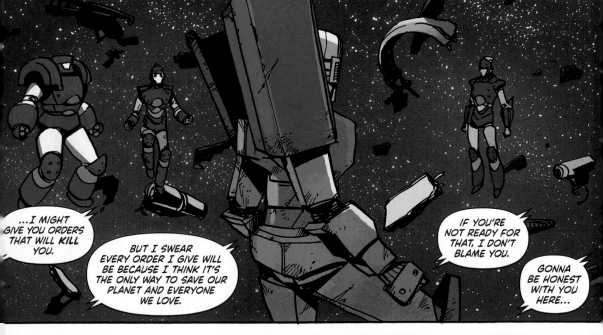

...I MIGHT GIVE YOU ORDERS THAT WILL *KILL* YOU.

BUT I SWEAR EVERY ORDER I GIVE WILL BE BECAUSE I THINK IT'S THE ONLY WAY TO SAVE OUR PLANET AND EVERYONE WE LOVE.

IF YOU'RE NOT READY FOR THAT, I DON'T BLAME YOU.

GONNA BE HONEST WITH YOU HERE...

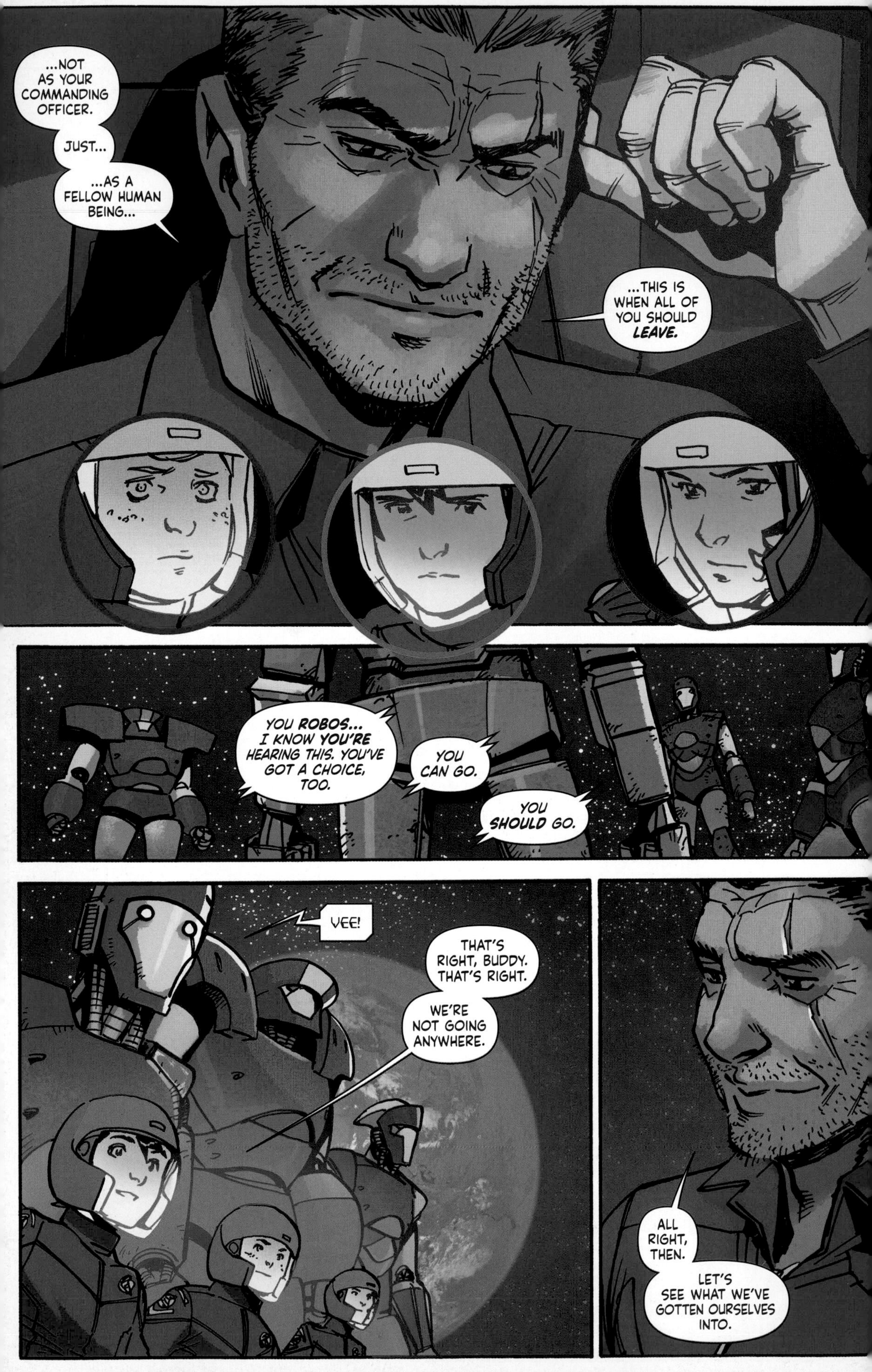
...NOT AS YOUR COMMANDING OFFICER.
JUST...
...AS A FELLOW HUMAN BEING...
...THIS IS WHEN ALL OF YOU SHOULD LEAVE.
YOU ROBOS... I KNOW YOU'RE HEARING THIS. YOU'VE GOT A CHOICE, TOO.
YOU CAN GO.
YOU SHOULD GO.
VEE!
THAT'S RIGHT, BUDDY. THAT'S RIGHT.
WE'RE NOT GOING ANYWHERE.
ALL RIGHT, THEN.
LET'S SEE WHAT WE'VE GOTTEN OURSELVES INTO.

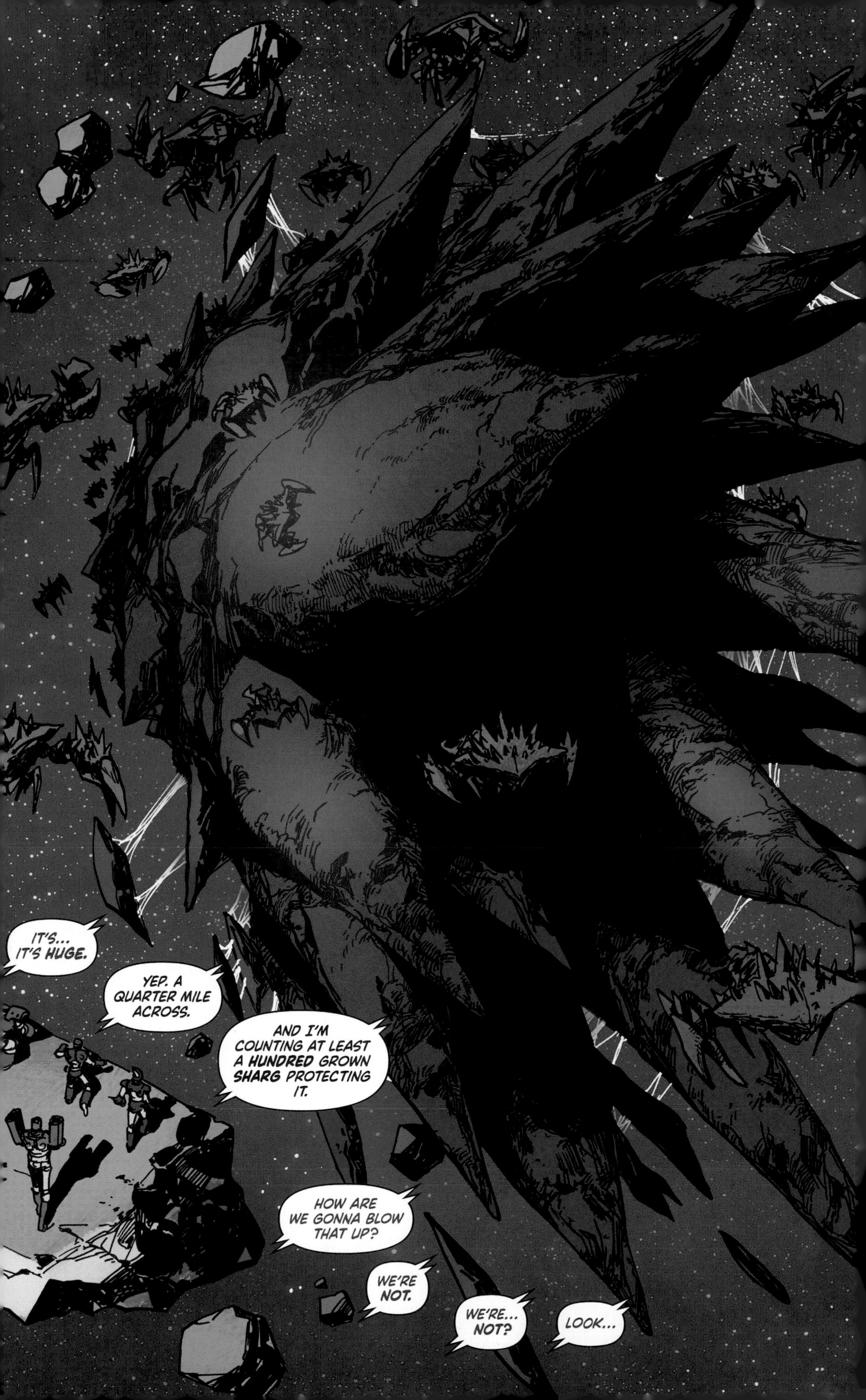
IT'S... IT'S **HUGE.**
YEP. A QUARTER MILE ACROSS.
AND I'M COUNTING AT LEAST A **HUNDRED** GROWN **SHARG** PROTECTING IT.
HOW ARE WE GONNA BLOW THAT UP?
WE'RE **NOT.**
WE'RE... **NOT?**
LOOK...

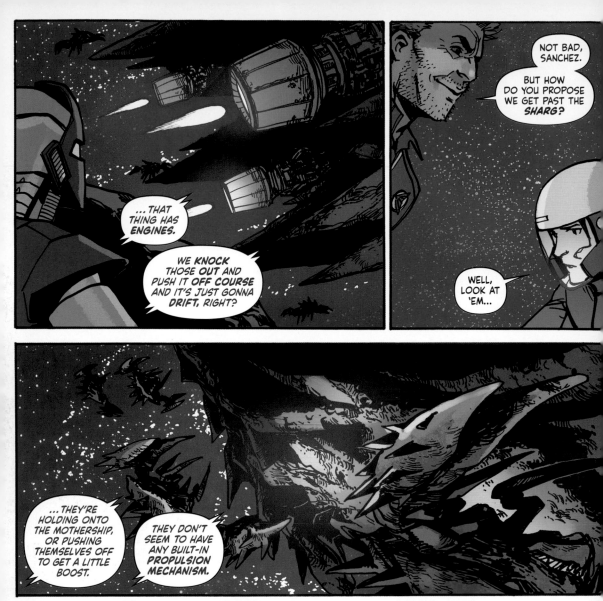

...THAT THING HAS ENGINES.

WE KNOCK THOSE OUT AND PUSH IT OFF COURSE AND IT'S JUST GONNA DRIFT, RIGHT?

NOT BAD, SANCHEZ.

BUT HOW DO YOU PROPOSE WE GET PAST THE SHARG?

WELL, LOOK AT 'EM...

...THEY'RE HOLDING ONTO THE MOTHERSHIP, OR PUSHING THEMSELVES OFF TO GET A LITTLE BOOST.

THEY DON'T SEEM TO HAVE ANY BUILT-IN PROPULSION MECHANISM.

I'M PLOTTING SOME TRAJECTORIES FOR US...ANY CONCERNS IN THE MEANTIME?

JUST ONE...

...I THOUGHT THEY WERE JUST BIG BUGS, RIGHT?

EXACTLY. WE'RE FASTER AND MORE MANEUVERABLE.

BUT THEY OUTNUMBER US A HUNDRED TO THREE.

IF YOU GET CAUGHT, IT'S OVER.

SO WHO THE HECK BUILT THOSE ENGINES?

GREAT QUESTION.

HOW 'BOUT WE ALL DO OUR BEST TO LIVE LONG ENOUGH TO FIND OUT SOME DAY?

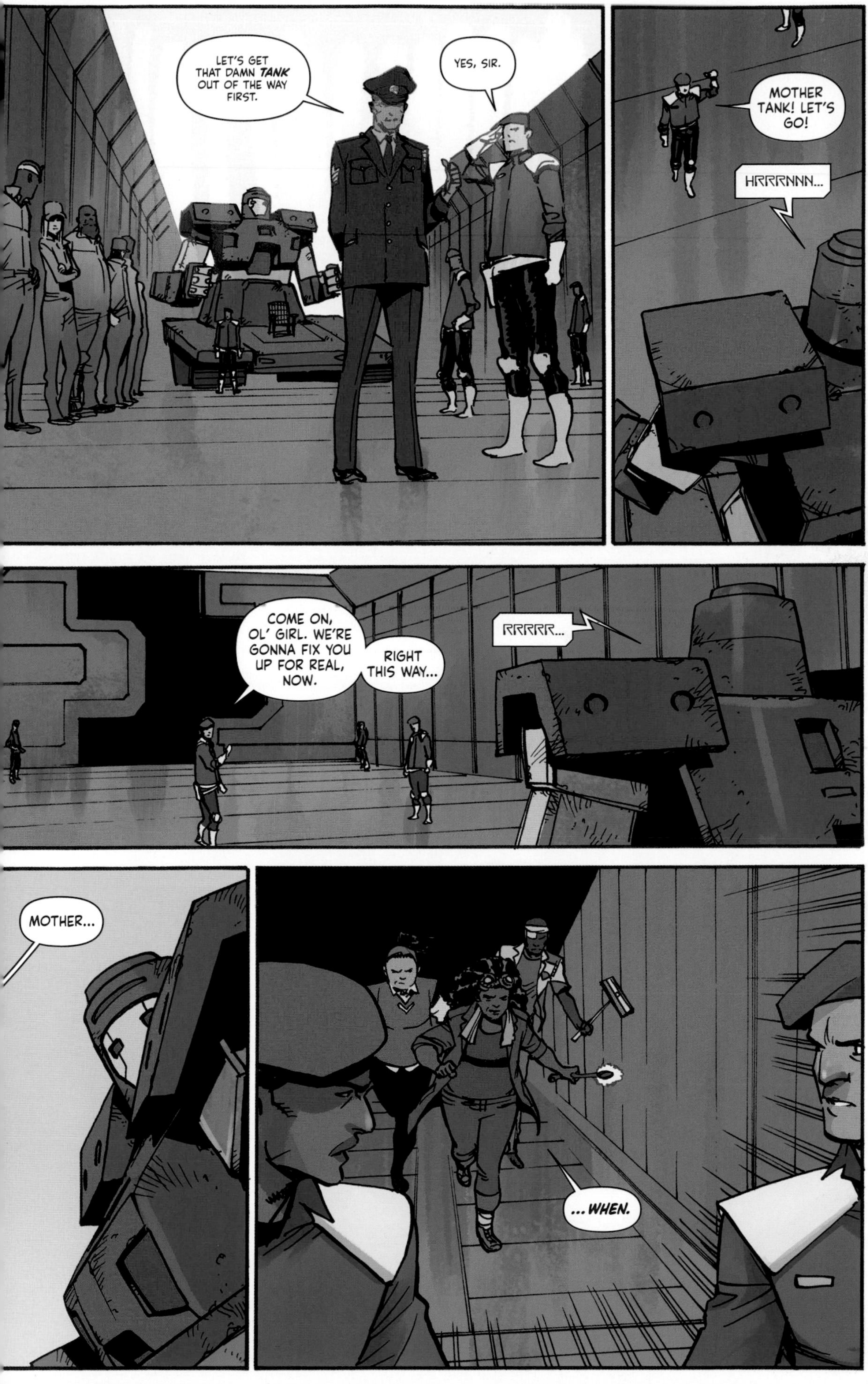
LET'S GET THAT DAMN TANK OUT OF THE WAY FIRST.
YES, SIR.
MOTHER TANK! LET'S GO!
HRRRNNN...
COME ON, OL' GIRL. WE'RE GONNA FIX YOU UP FOR REAL, NOW.
RIGHT THIS WAY...
RRRRR...
MOTHER...
...WHEN.

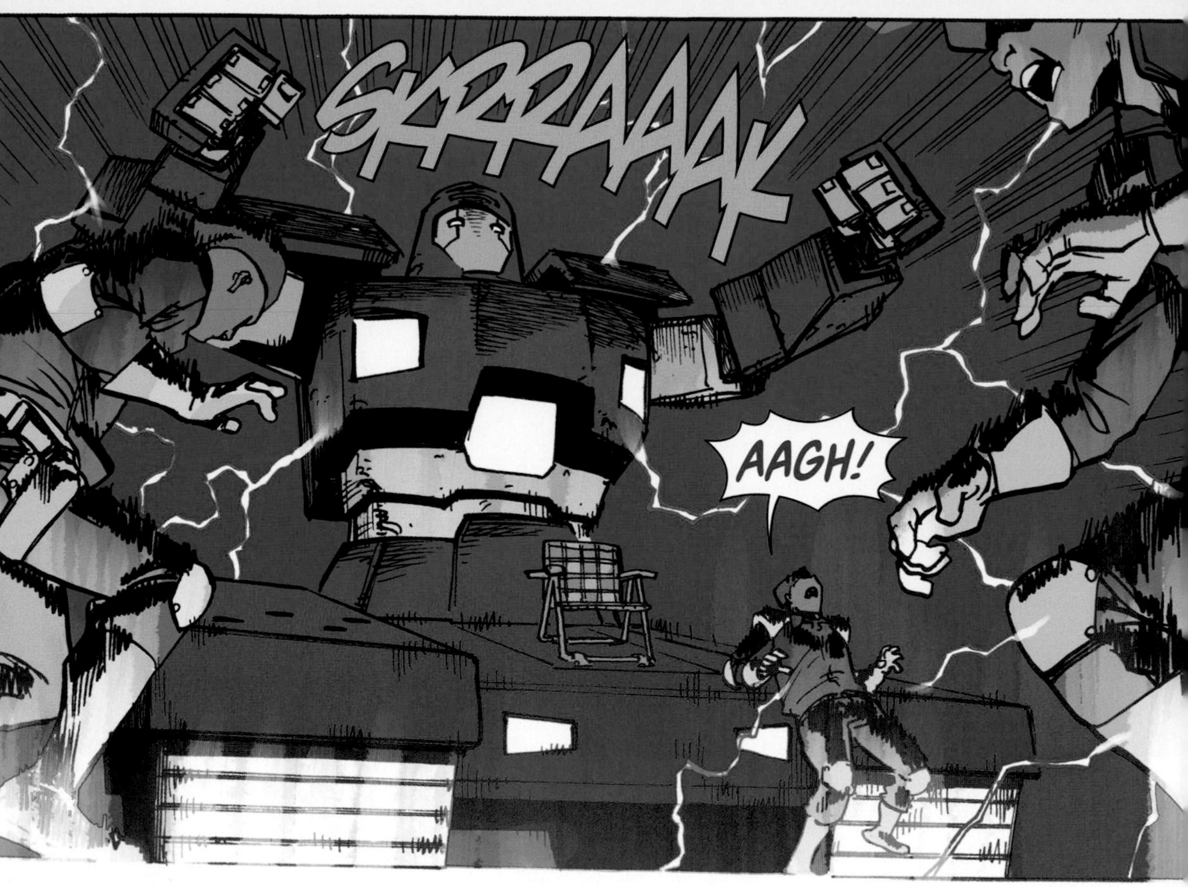
SKRRAAAK
AAGH!

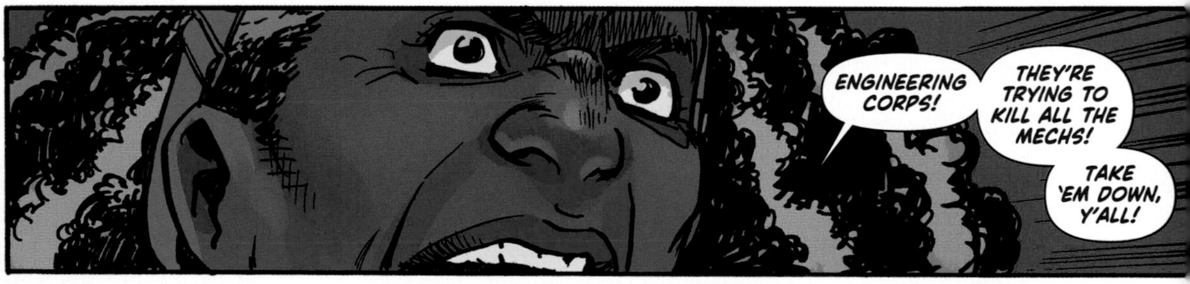
ENGINEERING CORPS!
THEY'RE TRYING TO KILL ALL THE MECHS!
TAKE 'EM DOWN, Y'ALL!

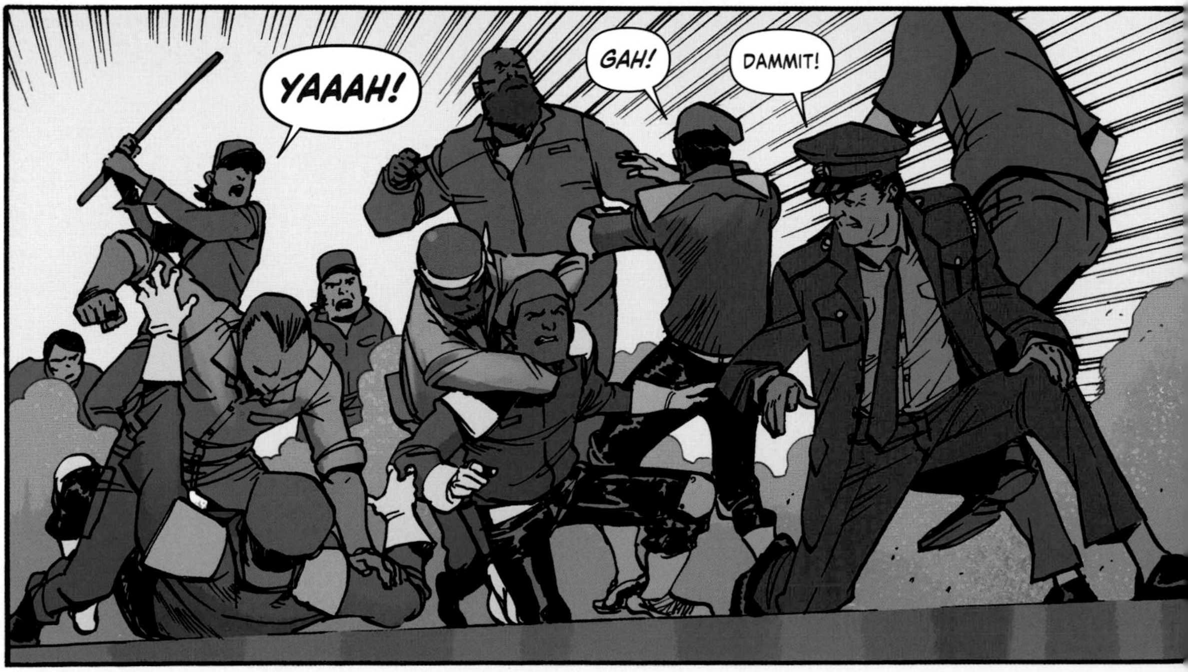
YAAAH!
GAH!
DAMMIT!

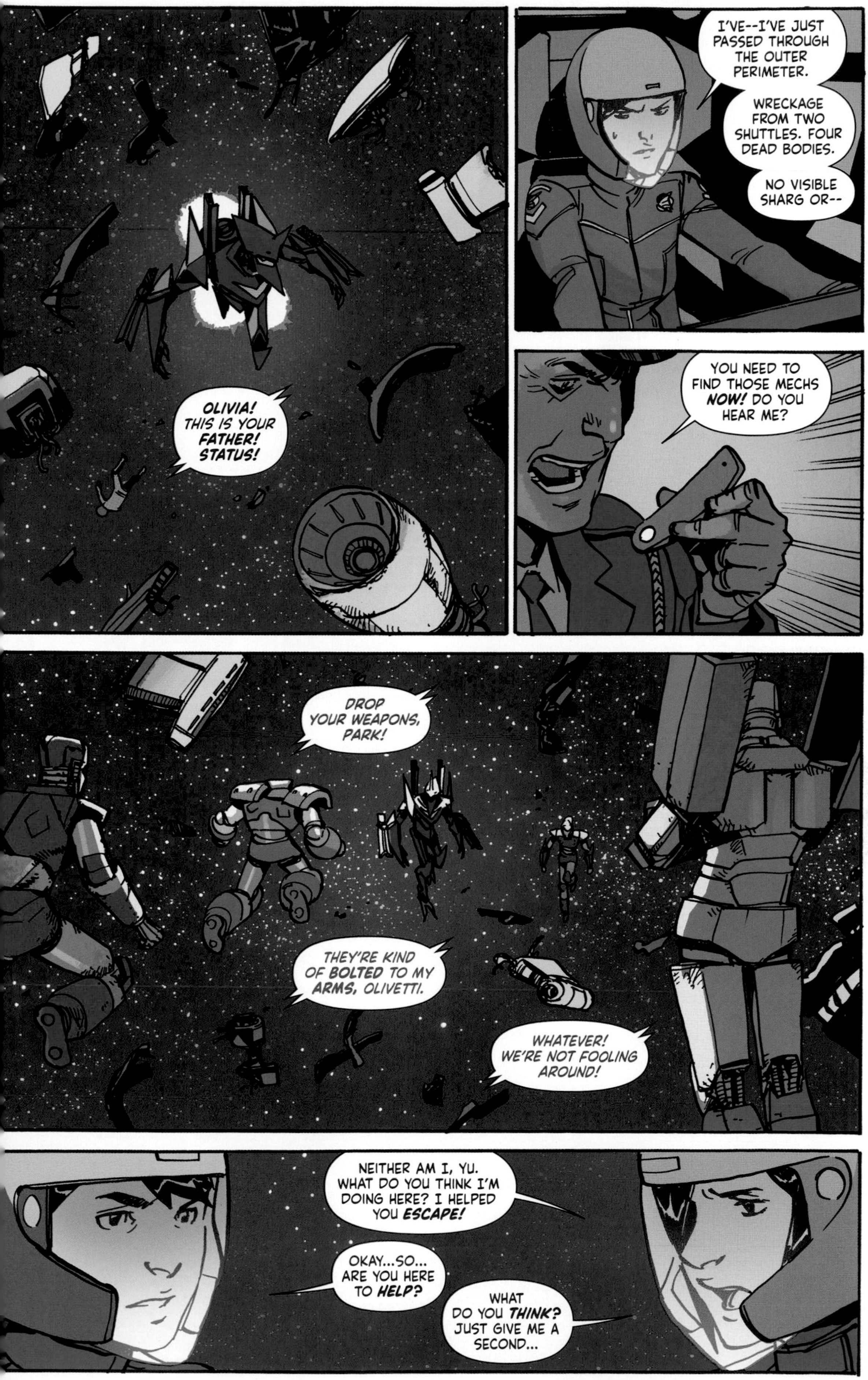
I'VE--I'VE JUST PASSED THROUGH THE OUTER PERIMETER.
WRECKAGE FROM TWO SHUTTLES. FOUR DEAD BODIES.
NO VISIBLE SHARG OR--
OLIVIA! THIS IS YOUR FATHER! STATUS!
YOU NEED TO FIND THOSE MECHS NOW! DO YOU HEAR ME?
DROP YOUR WEAPONS, PARK!
THEY'RE KIND OF BOLTED TO MY ARMS, OLIVETTI.
WHATEVER! WE'RE NOT FOOLING AROUND!
NEITHER AM I, YU. WHAT DO YOU THINK I'M DOING HERE? I HELPED YOU ESCAPE!
OKAY...SO... ARE YOU HERE TO HELP?
WHAT DO YOU THINK? JUST GIVE ME A SECOND...

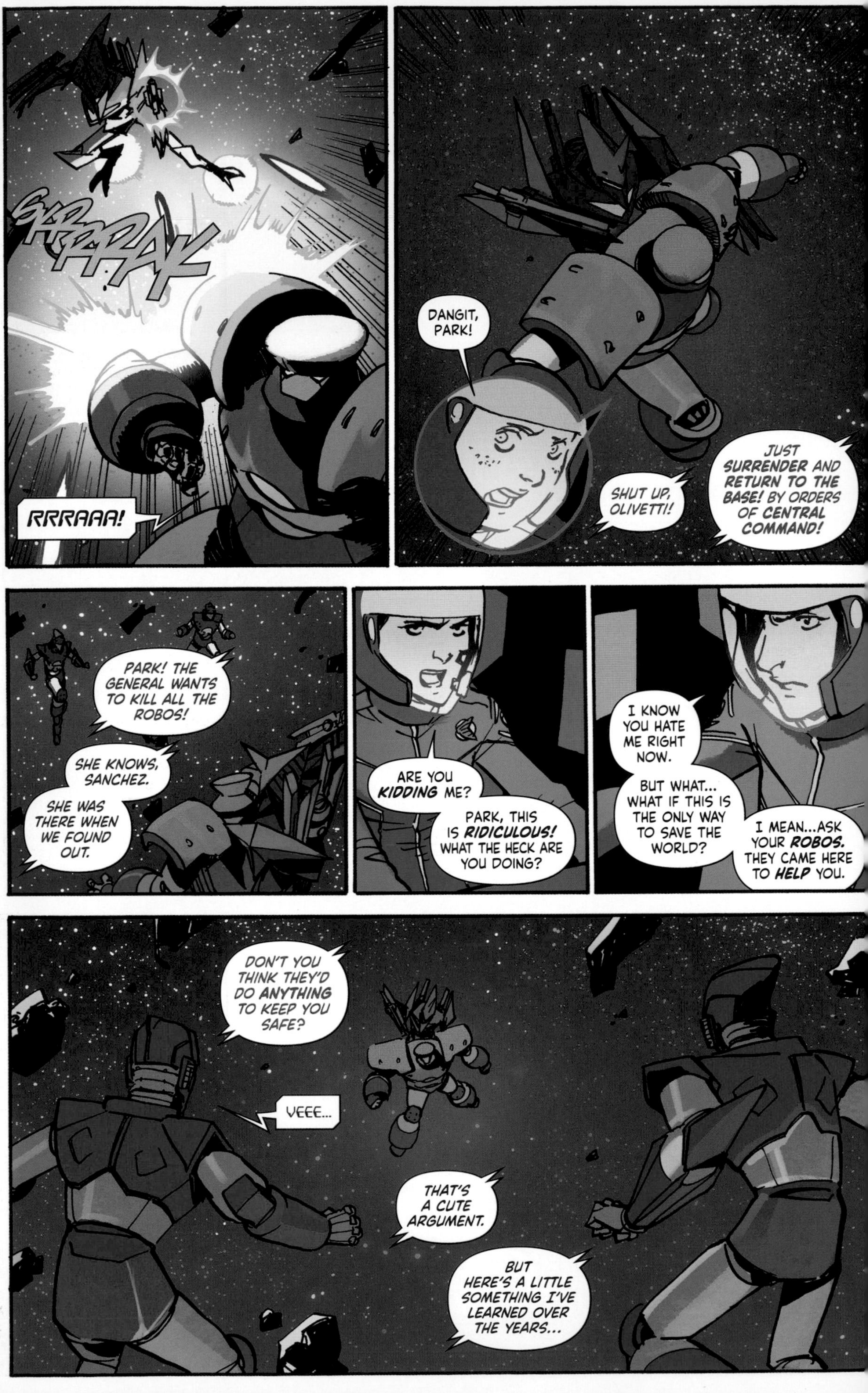
SKRRRAK
RRRAAA!
DANGIT, PARK!
SHUT UP, OLIVETTI!
JUST SURRENDER AND RETURN TO THE BASE! BY ORDERS OF CENTRAL COMMAND!
PARK! THE GENERAL WANTS TO KILL ALL THE ROBOS!
SHE KNOWS, SANCHEZ.
SHE WAS THERE WHEN WE FOUND OUT.
ARE YOU KIDDING ME?
PARK, THIS IS RIDICULOUS! WHAT THE HECK ARE YOU DOING?
I KNOW YOU HATE ME RIGHT NOW.
BUT WHAT... WHAT IF THIS IS THE ONLY WAY TO SAVE THE WORLD?
I MEAN...ASK YOUR ROBOS. THEY CAME HERE TO HELP YOU.
DON'T YOU THINK THEY'D DO ANYTHING TO KEEP YOU SAFE?
VEEE...
THAT'S A CUTE ARGUMENT.
BUT HERE'S A LITTLE SOMETHING I'VE LEARNED OVER THE YEARS...

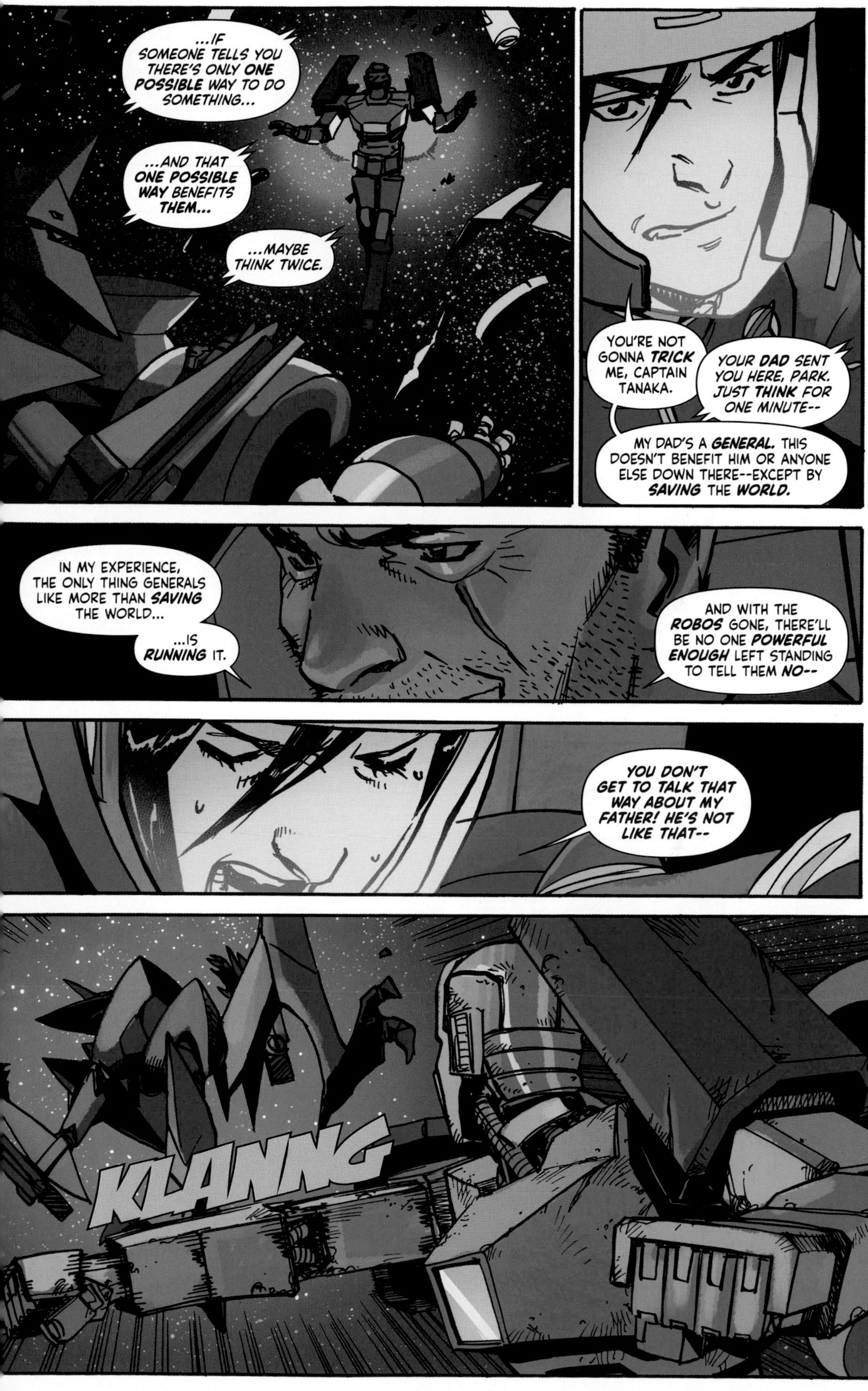

...IF SOMEONE TELLS YOU THERE'S ONLY ONE POSSIBLE WAY TO DO SOMETHING...
...AND THAT ONE POSSIBLE WAY BENEFITS THEM...
...MAYBE THINK TWICE.
YOU'RE NOT GONNA TRICK ME, CAPTAIN TANAKA.
YOUR DAD SENT YOU HERE, PARK. JUST THINK FOR ONE MINUTE--
MY DAD'S A GENERAL. THIS DOESN'T BENEFIT HIM OR ANYONE ELSE DOWN THERE--EXCEPT BY SAVING THE WORLD.
IN MY EXPERIENCE, THE ONLY THING GENERALS LIKE MORE THAN SAVING THE WORLD...
...IS RUNNING IT.
AND WITH THE ROBOS GONE, THERE'LL BE NO ONE POWERFUL ENOUGH LEFT STANDING TO TELL THEM NO--
YOU DON'T GET TO TALK THAT WAY ABOUT MY FATHER! HE'S NOT LIKE THAT--
KLANNG

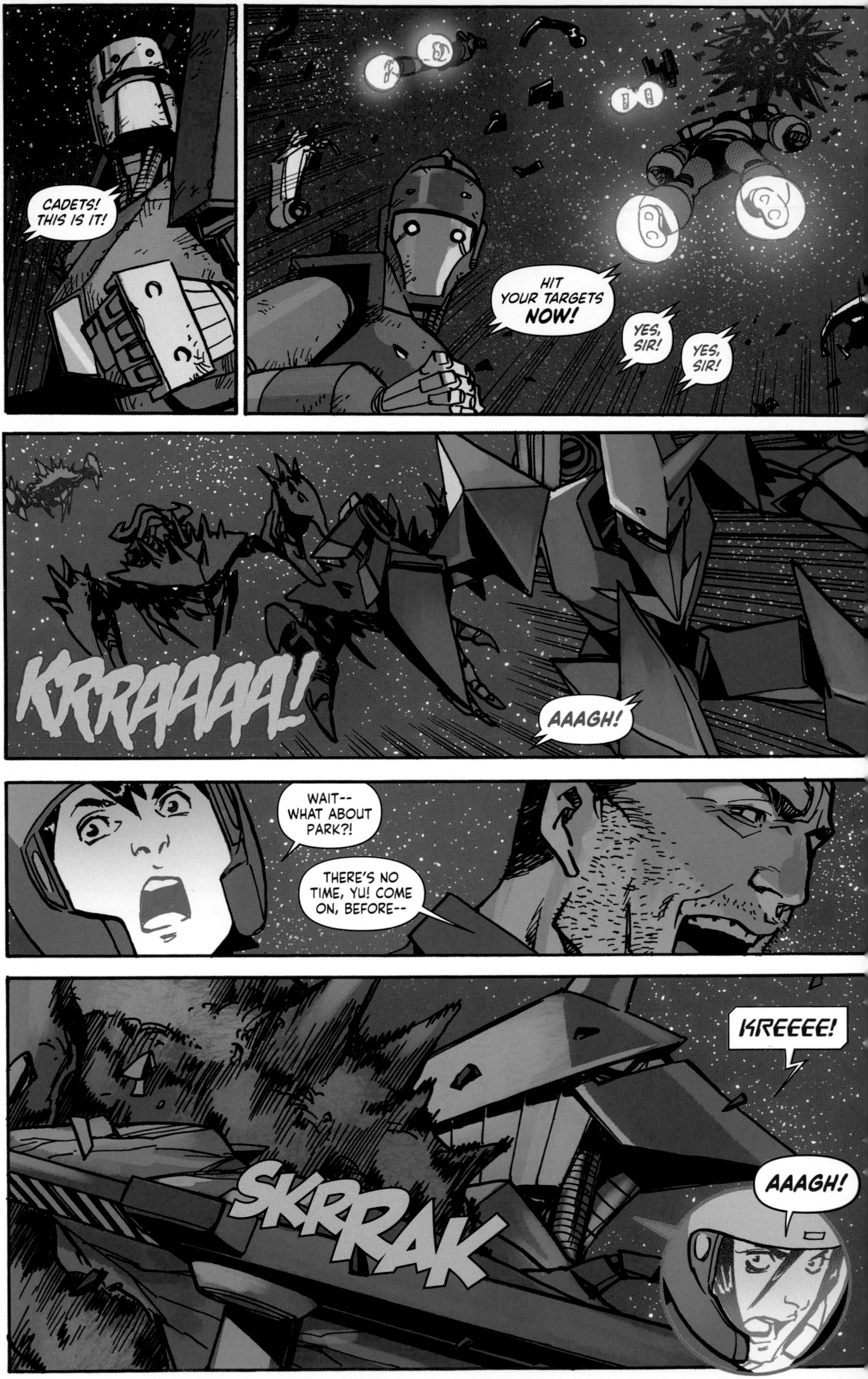
CADETS! THIS IS IT!
HIT YOUR TARGETS NOW!
YES, SIR!
YES, SIR!
KRRAAAAA!
AAAGH!
WAIT-- WHAT ABOUT PARK?!
THERE'S NO TIME, YU! COME ON, BEFORE--
KREEEE!
SKRRAK
AAAGH!

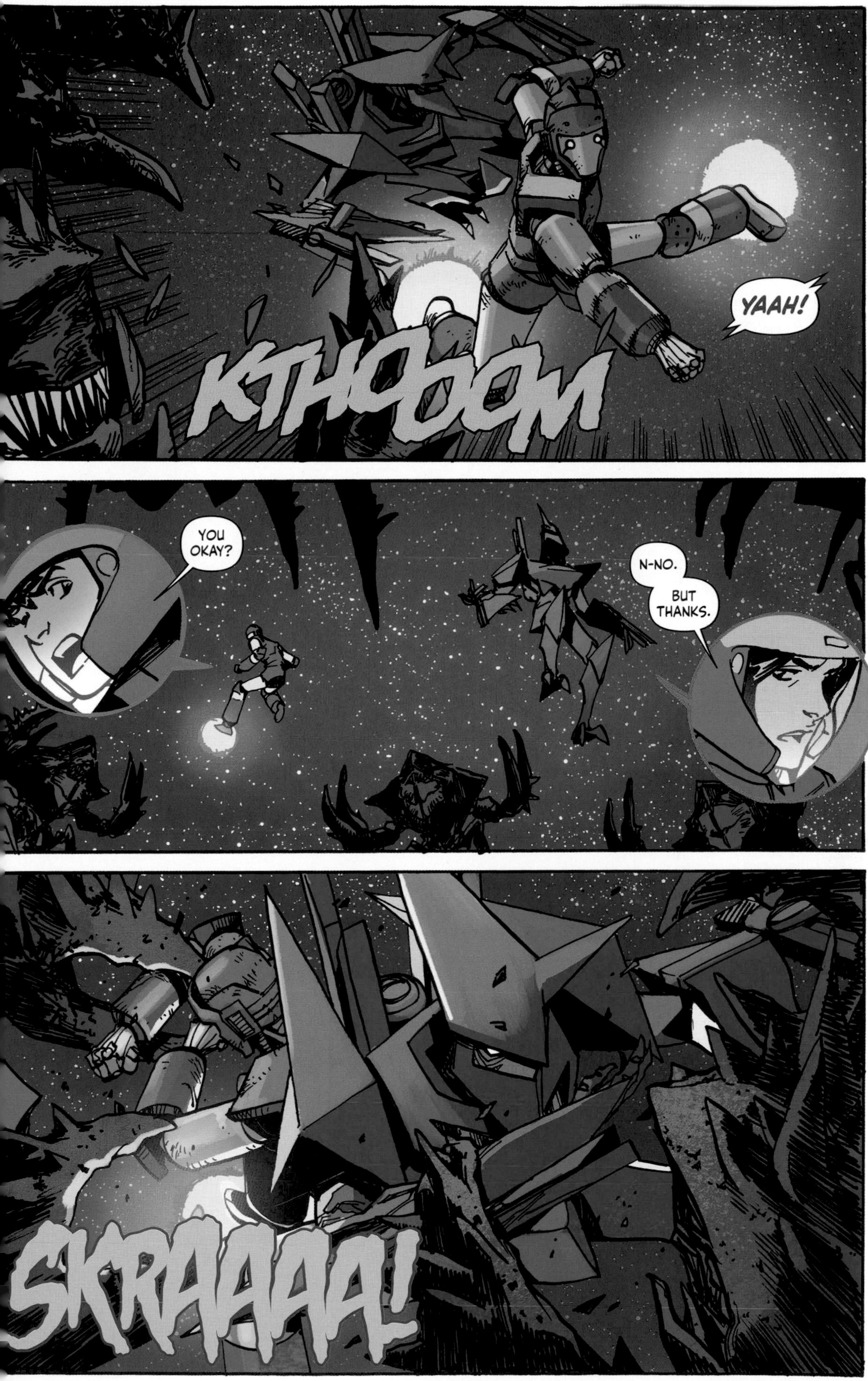
YAAH!
KTHOOOM
YOU OKAY?
N-NO.
BUT THANKS.
SKRAAAA!

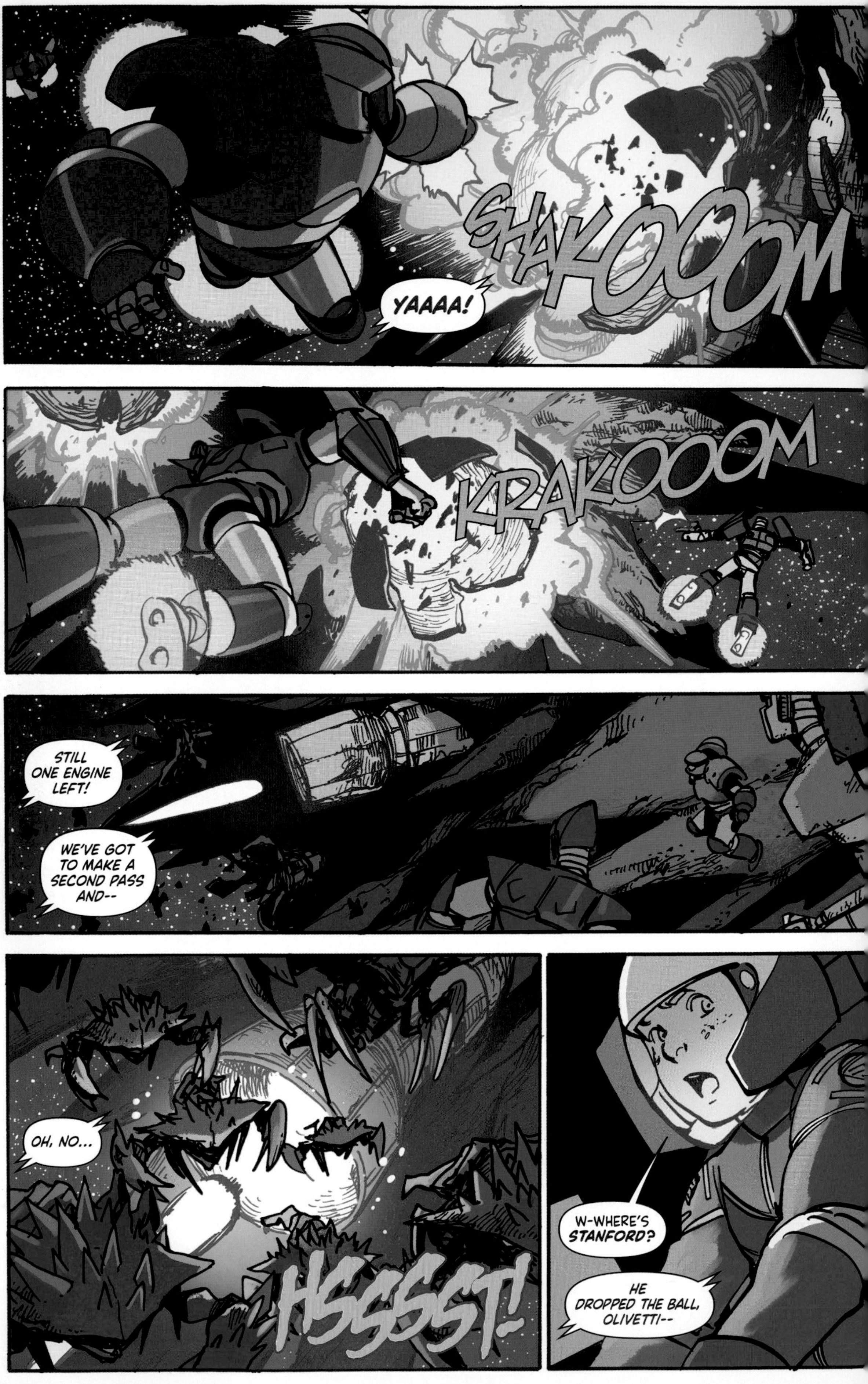
SHAKOOOOM
YAAAA!
KRAKOOOOM
STILL ONE ENGINE LEFT!
WE'VE GOT TO MAKE A SECOND PASS AND--
OH, NO...
HSSSST!
W-WHERE'S STANFORD?
HE DROPPED THE BALL, OLIVETTI--

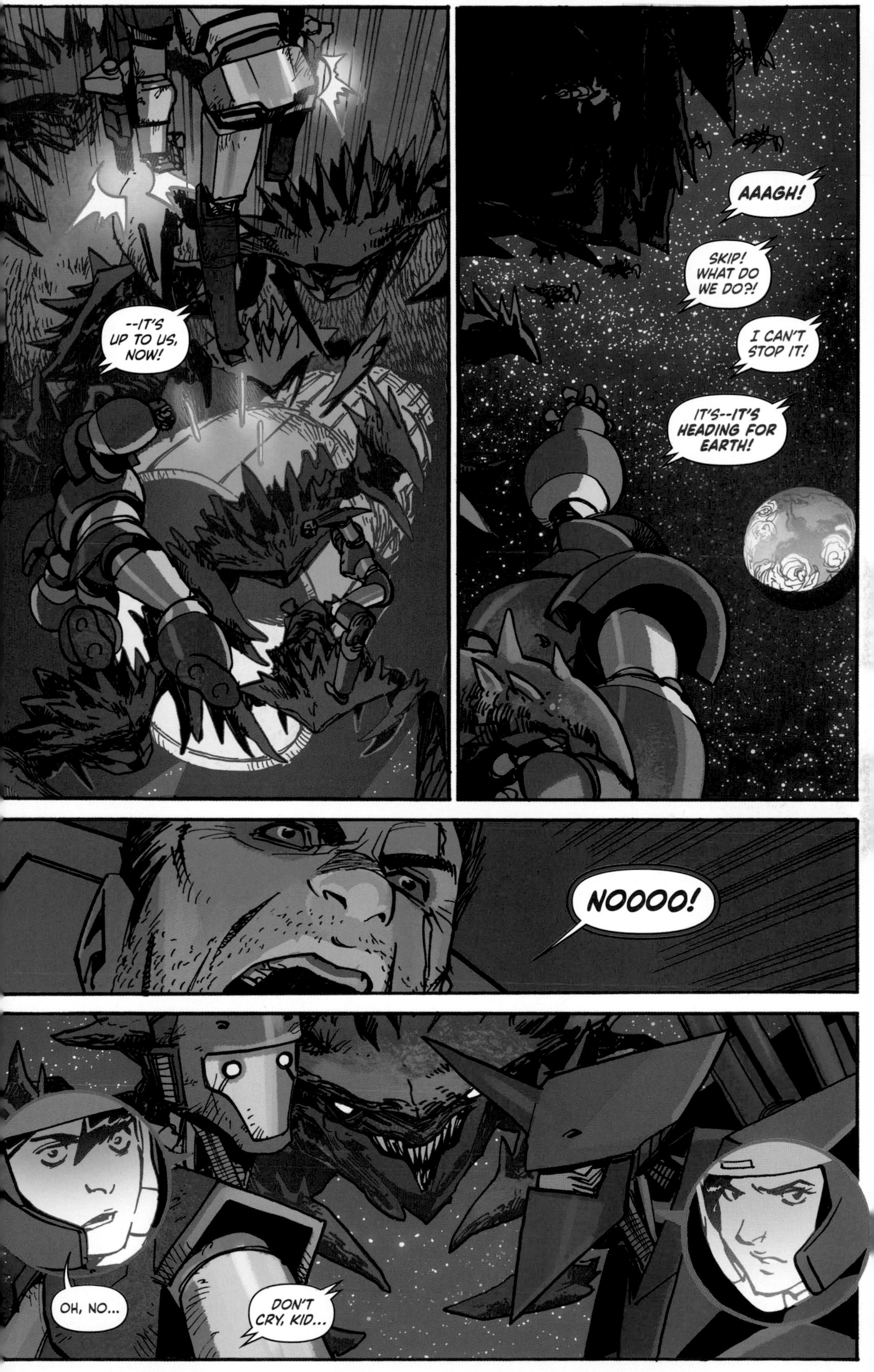
--IT'S UP TO US, NOW!
AAAGH!
SKIP! WHAT DO WE DO?!
I CAN'T STOP IT!
IT'S--IT'S HEADING FOR EARTH!
NOOOO!
OH, NO...
DON'T CRY, KID...

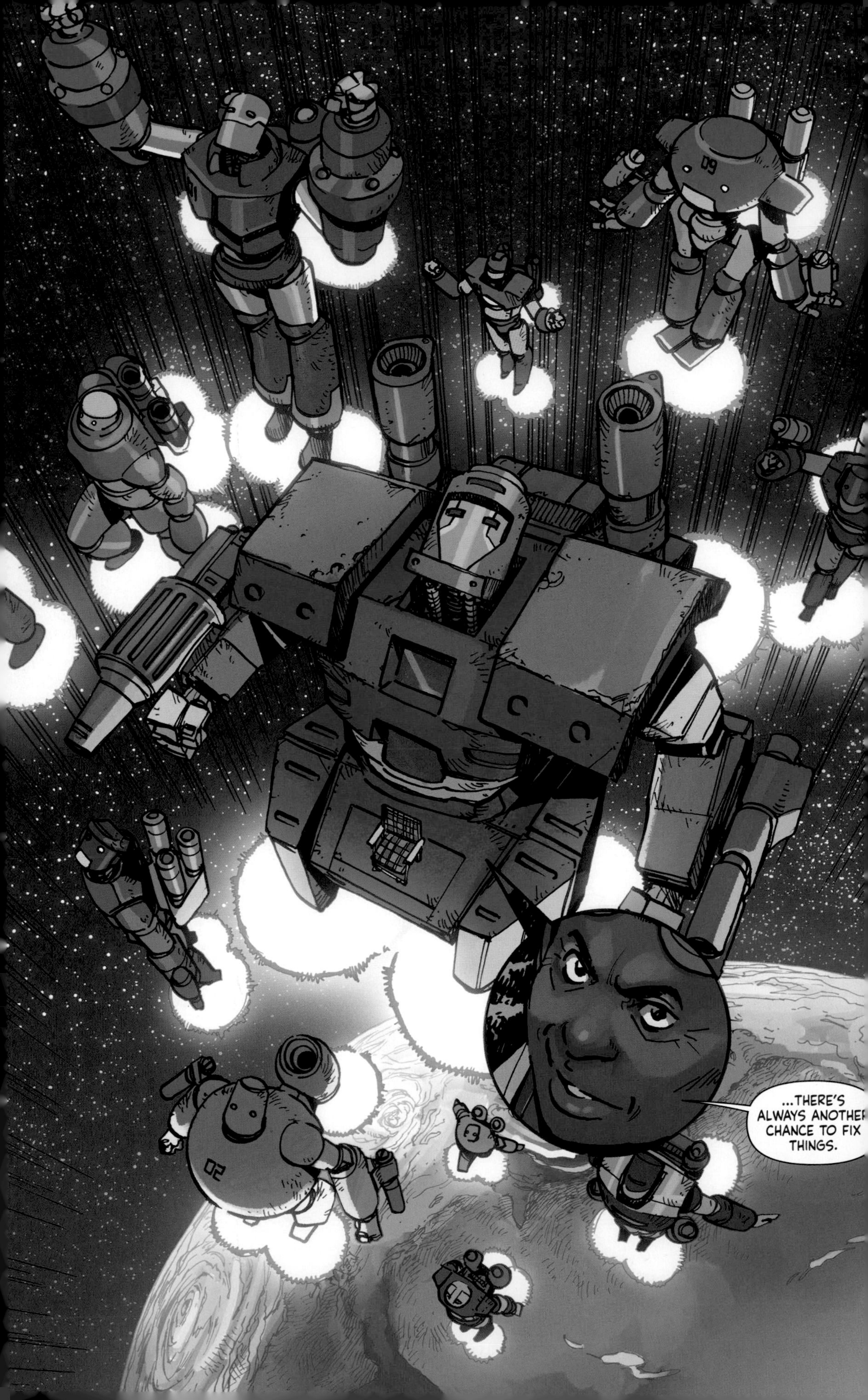
...THERE'S ALWAYS ANOTHER CHANCE TO FIX THINGS.

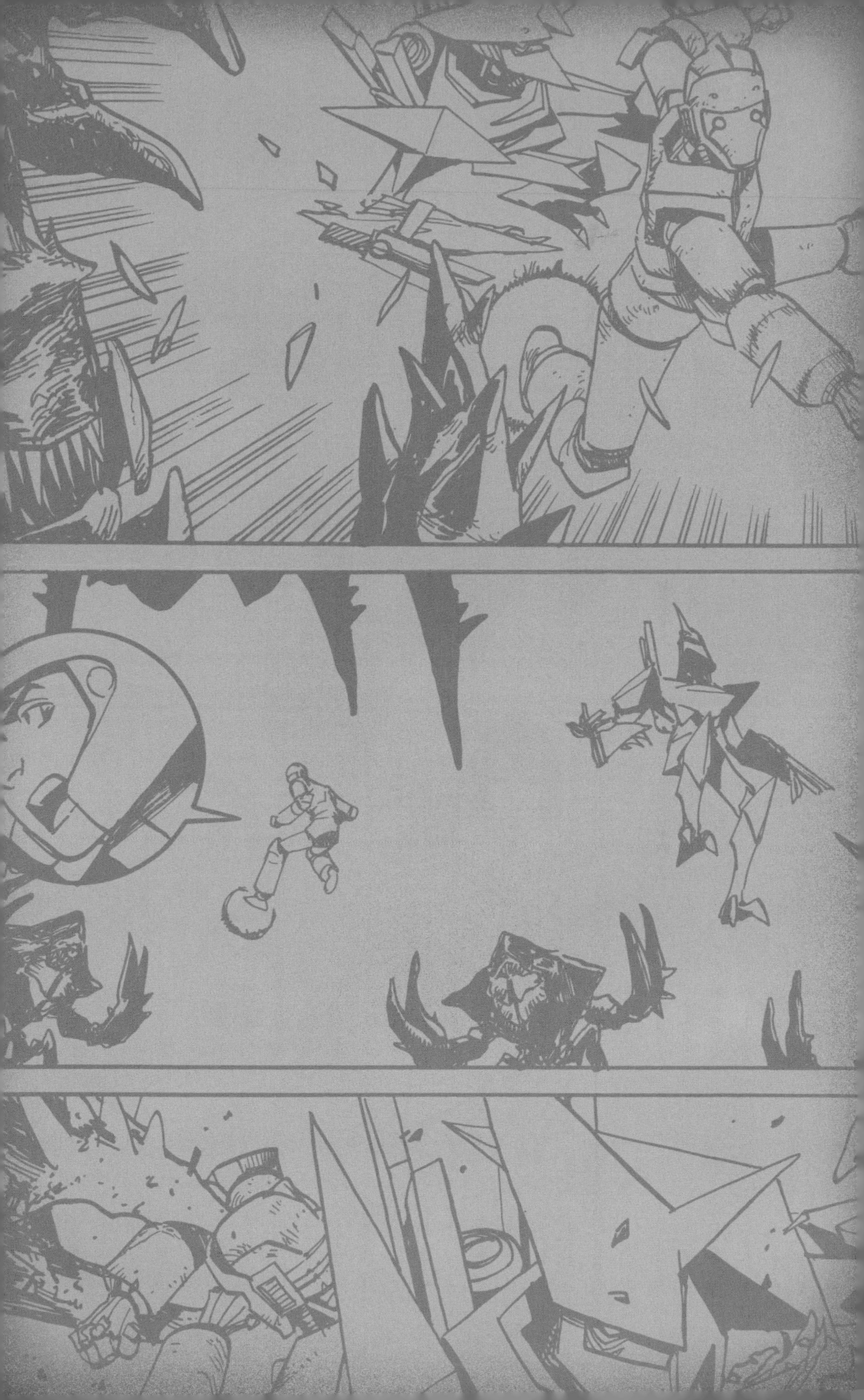

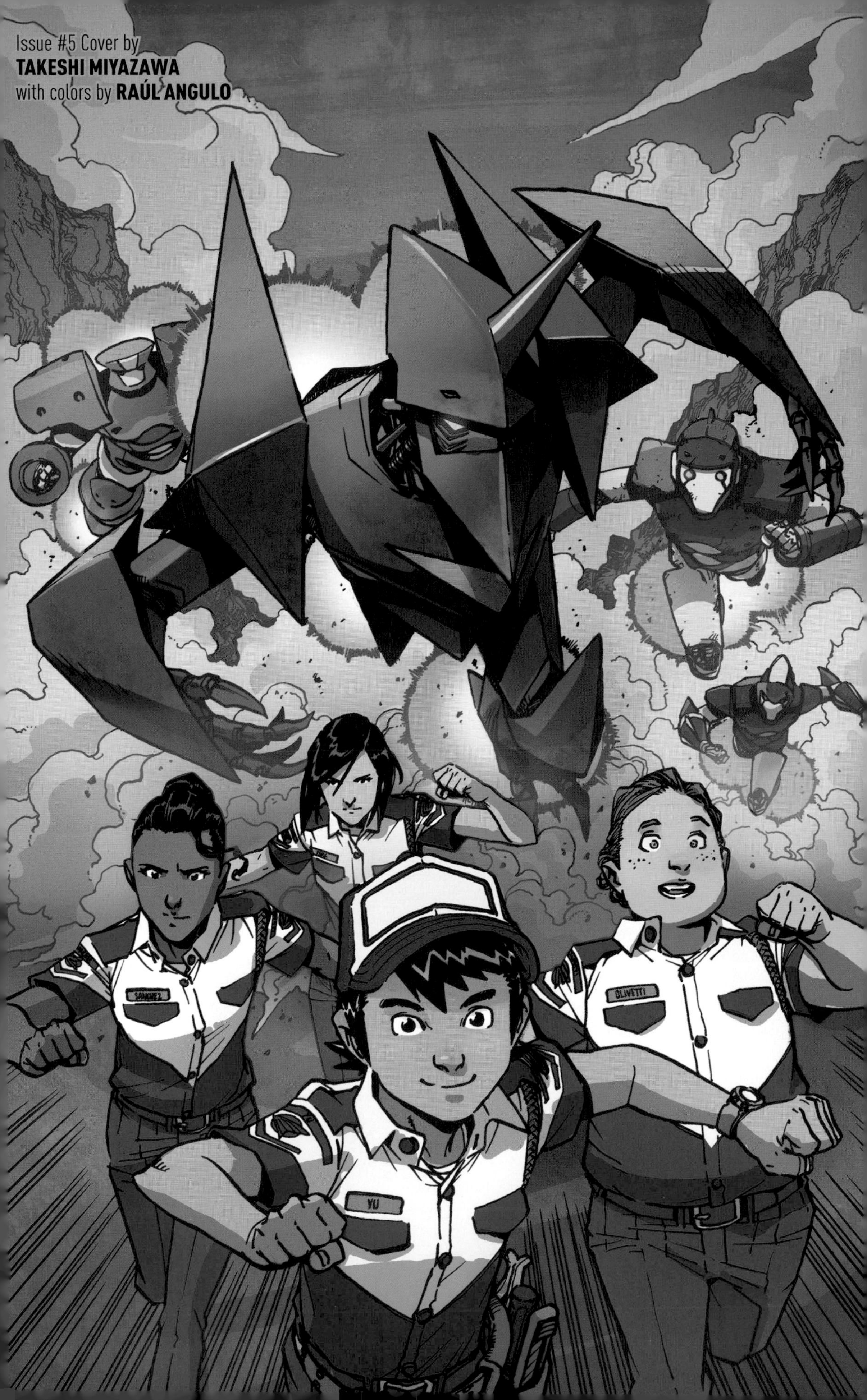
SANCHEZ
OLIVETTI
YU
Issue #5 Cover by
TAKESHI MIYAZAWA
with colors by **RAÚL ANGULO**

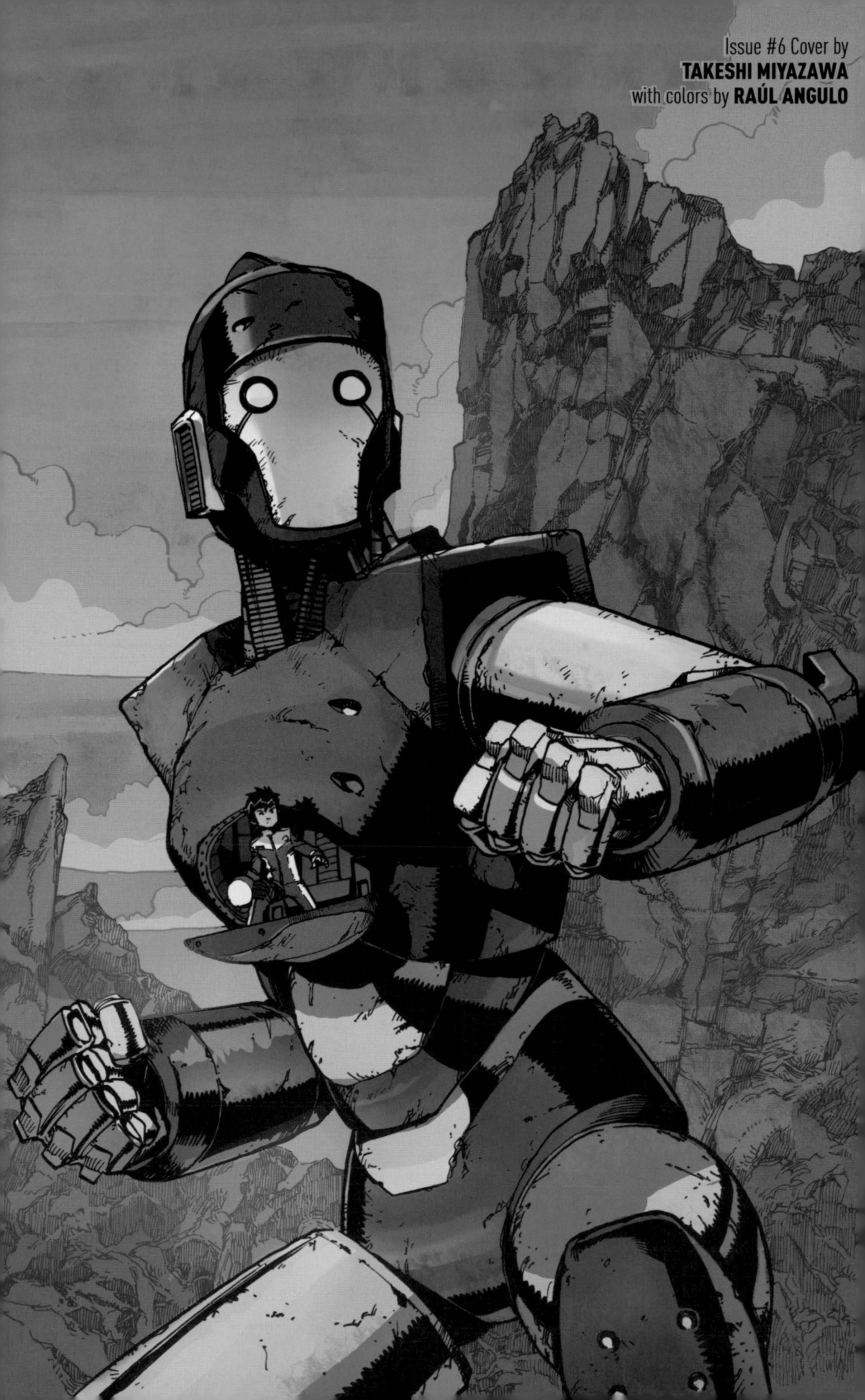

Issue #6 Cover by
TAKESHI MIYAZAWA
with colors by **RAÚL ANGULO**

Issue #7 Cover by
TAKESHI MIYAZAWA
with colors by **RAÚL ANGULO**

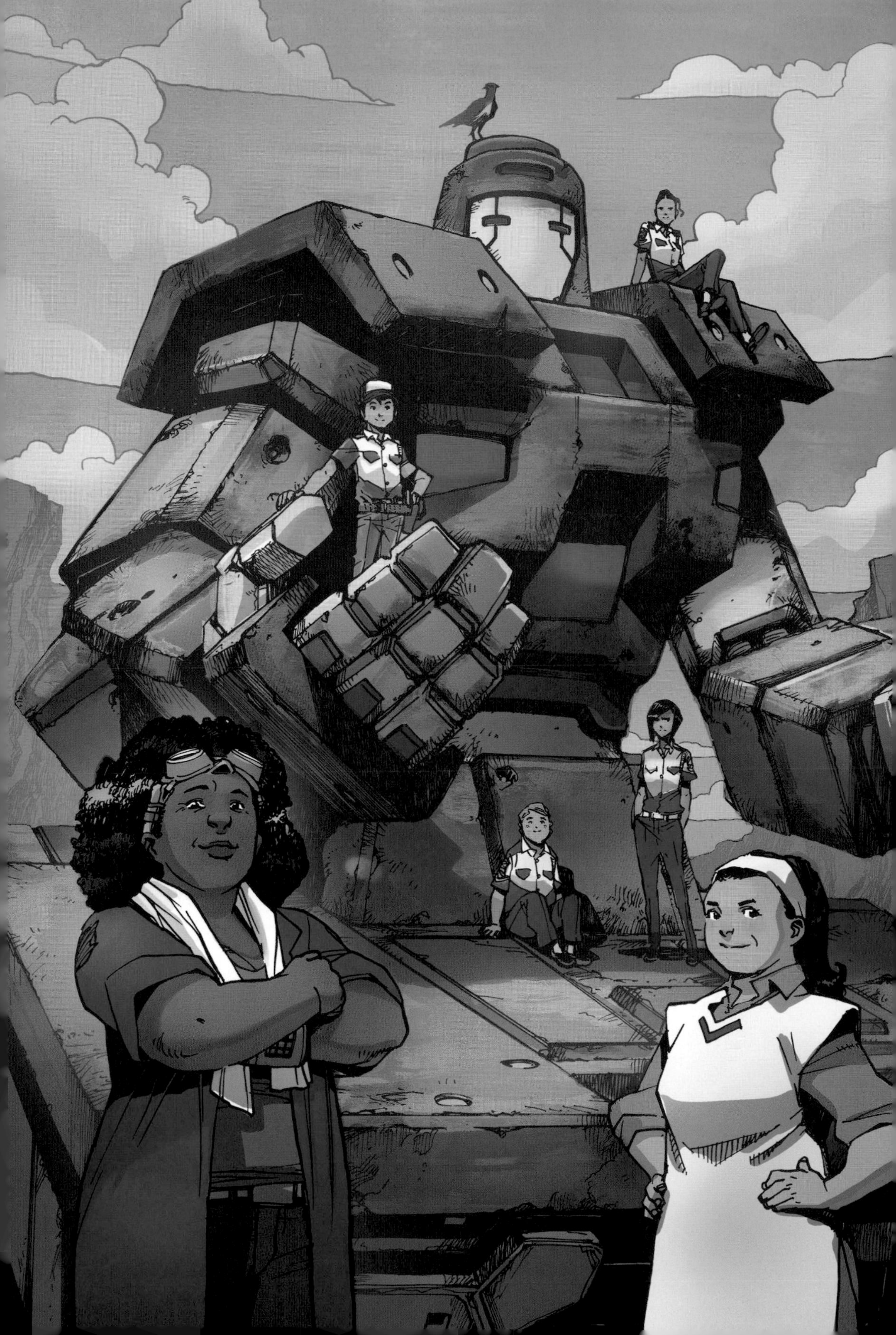

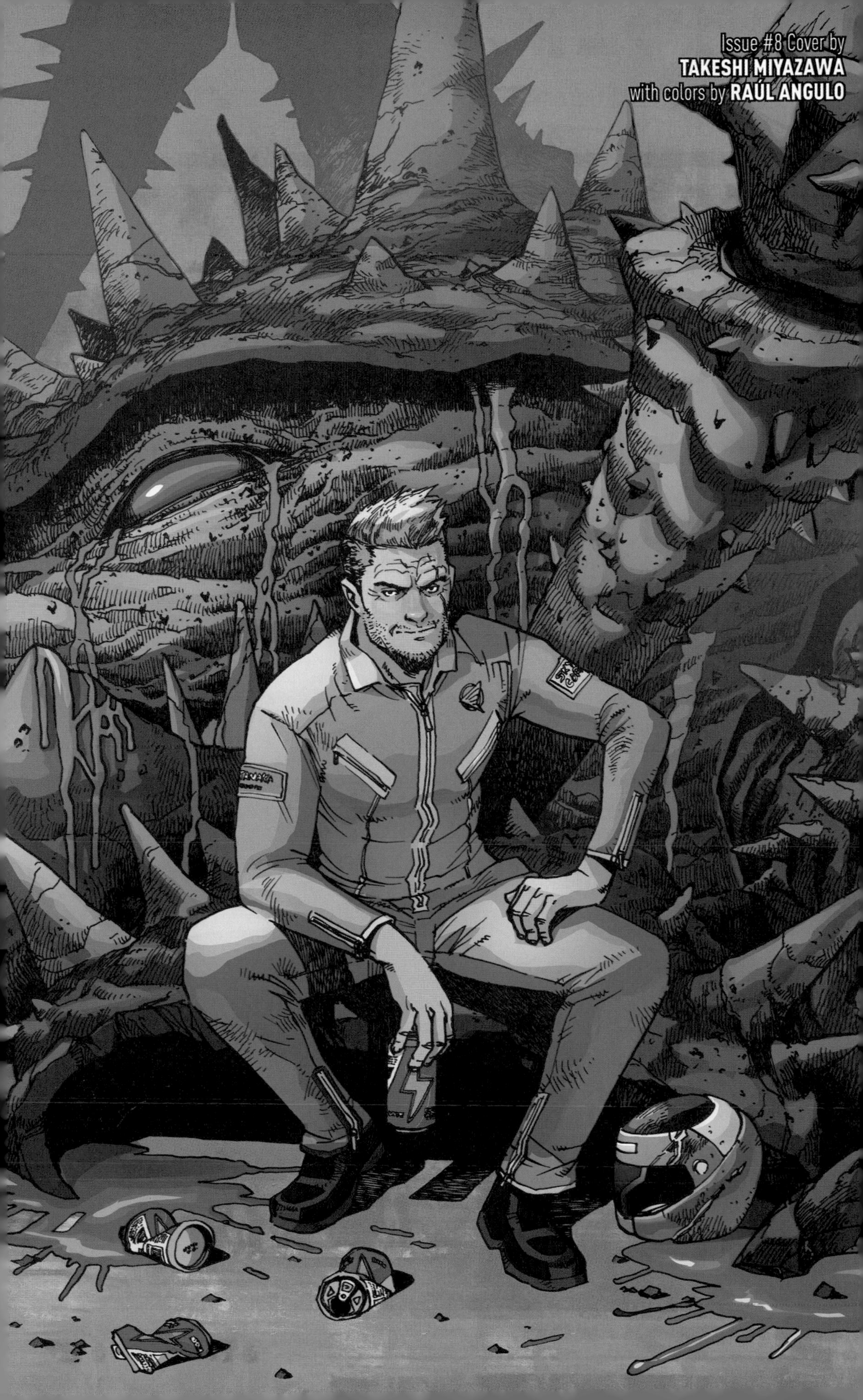
TANAKA

Issue #8 Cover by
TAKESHI MIYAZAWA
with colors by **RAÚL ANGULO**

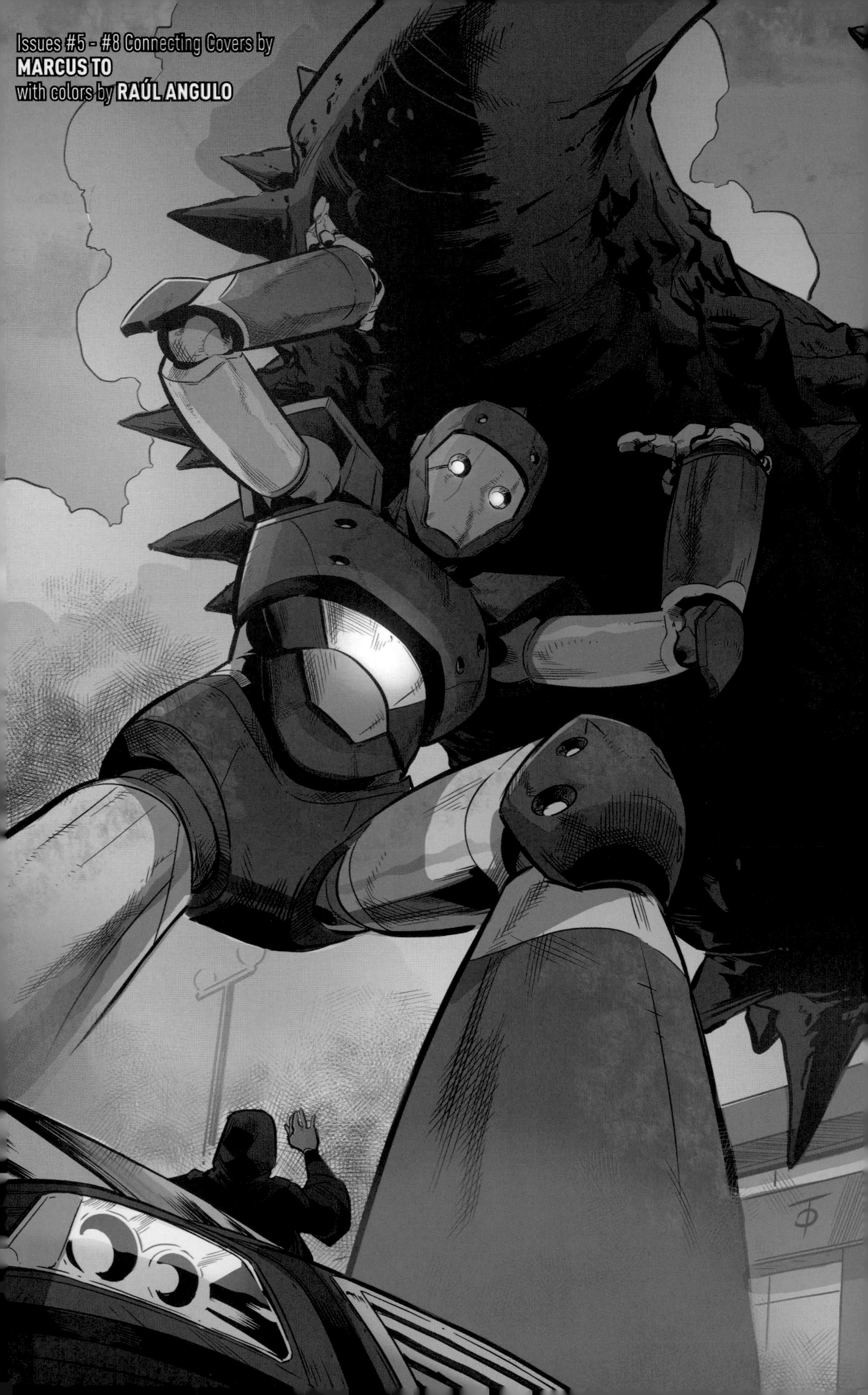

Issues #5 - #8 Connecting Covers by
MARCUS TO
with colors by **RAÚL ANGULO**

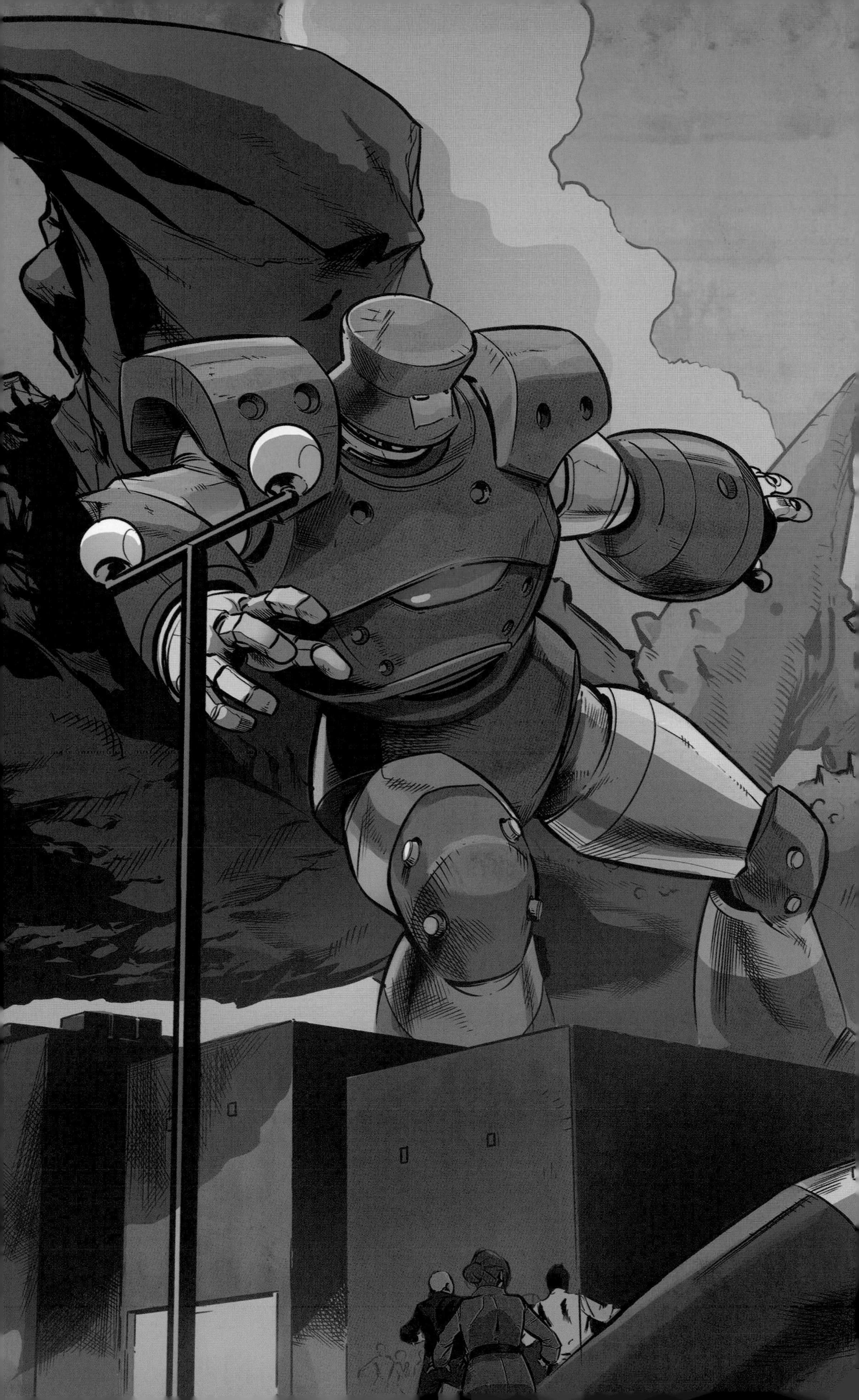

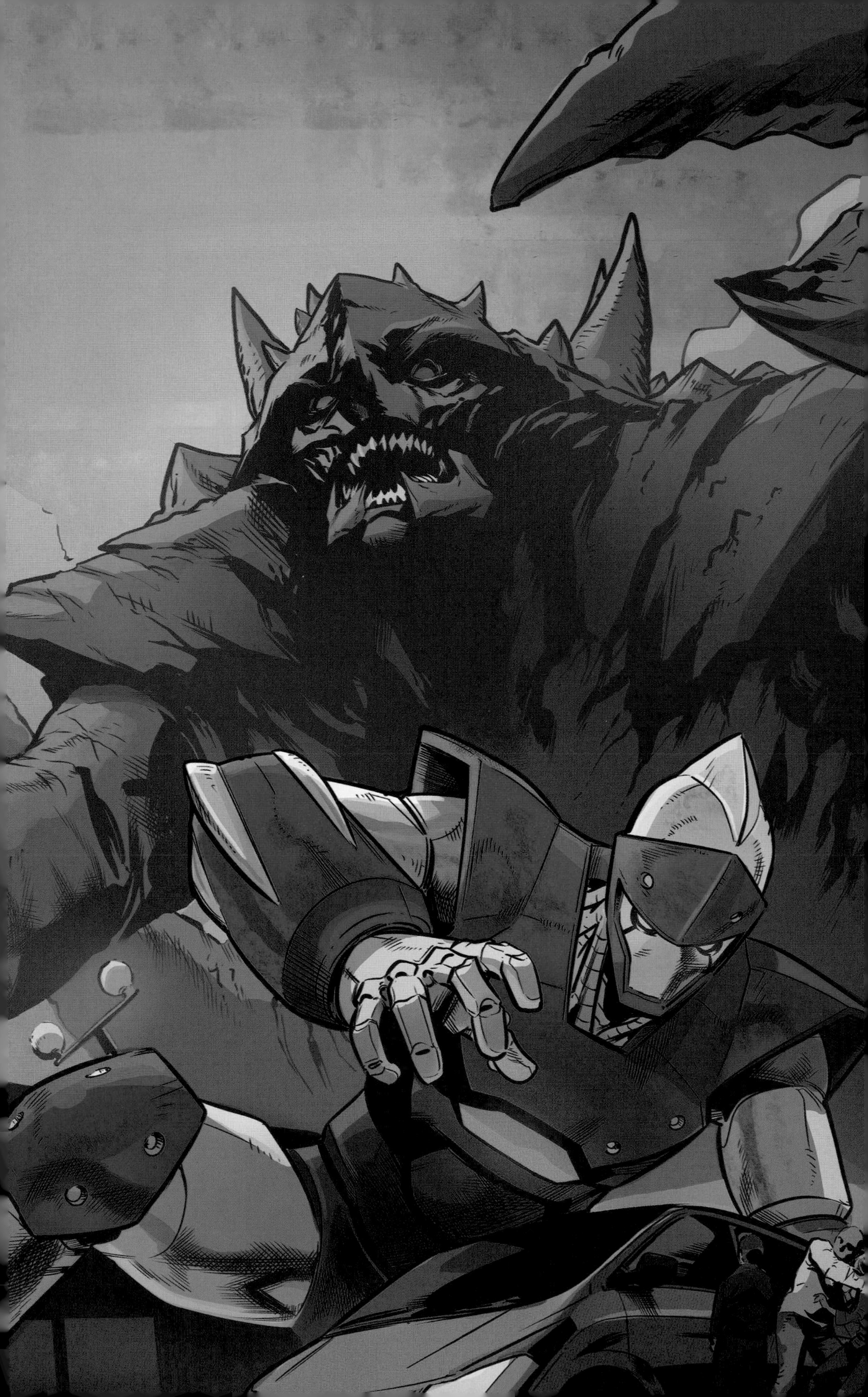

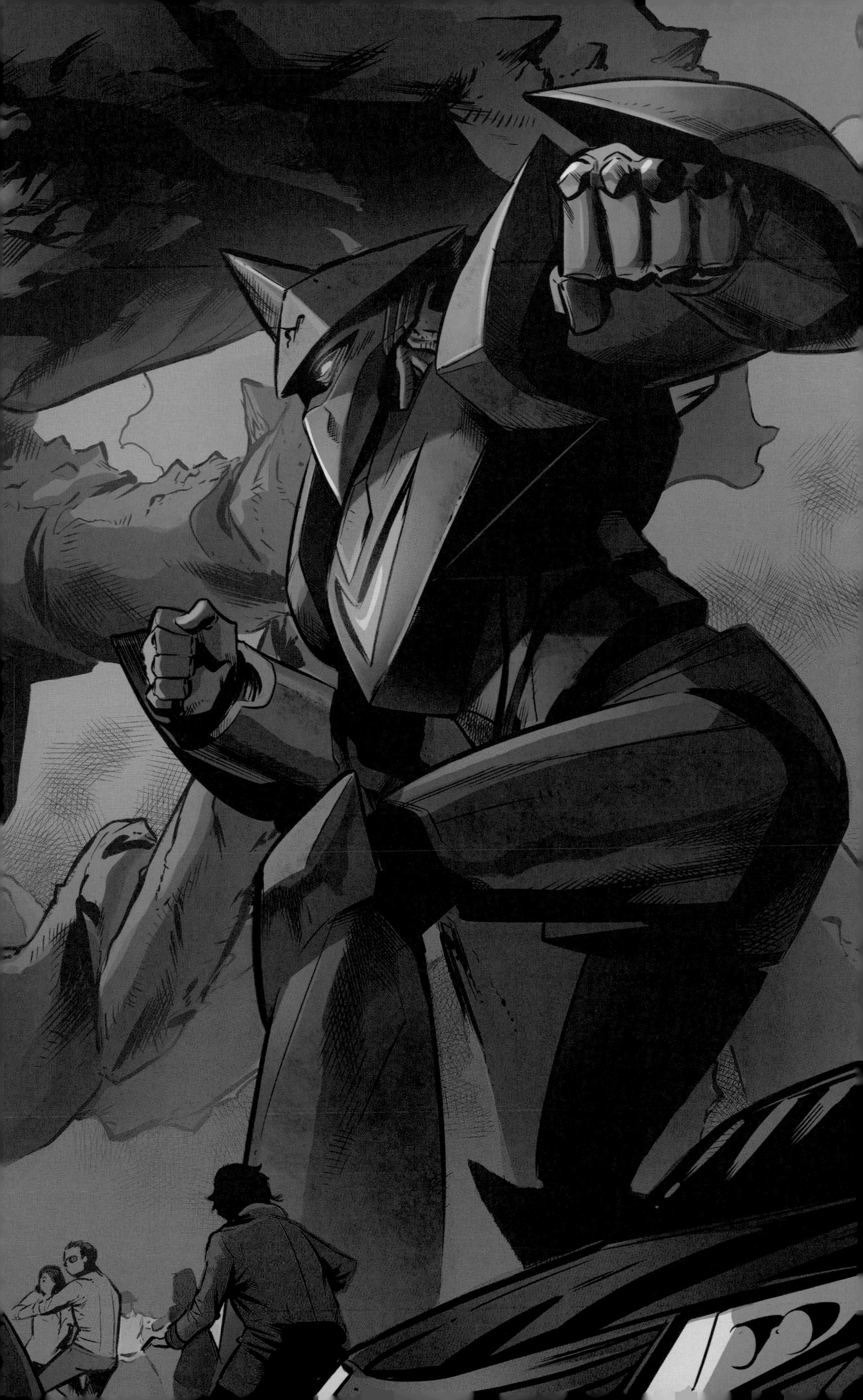

Issue #5 Unlocked Retailer Variant Cover by
DAN MORA
with colors by **RAÚL ANGULO**

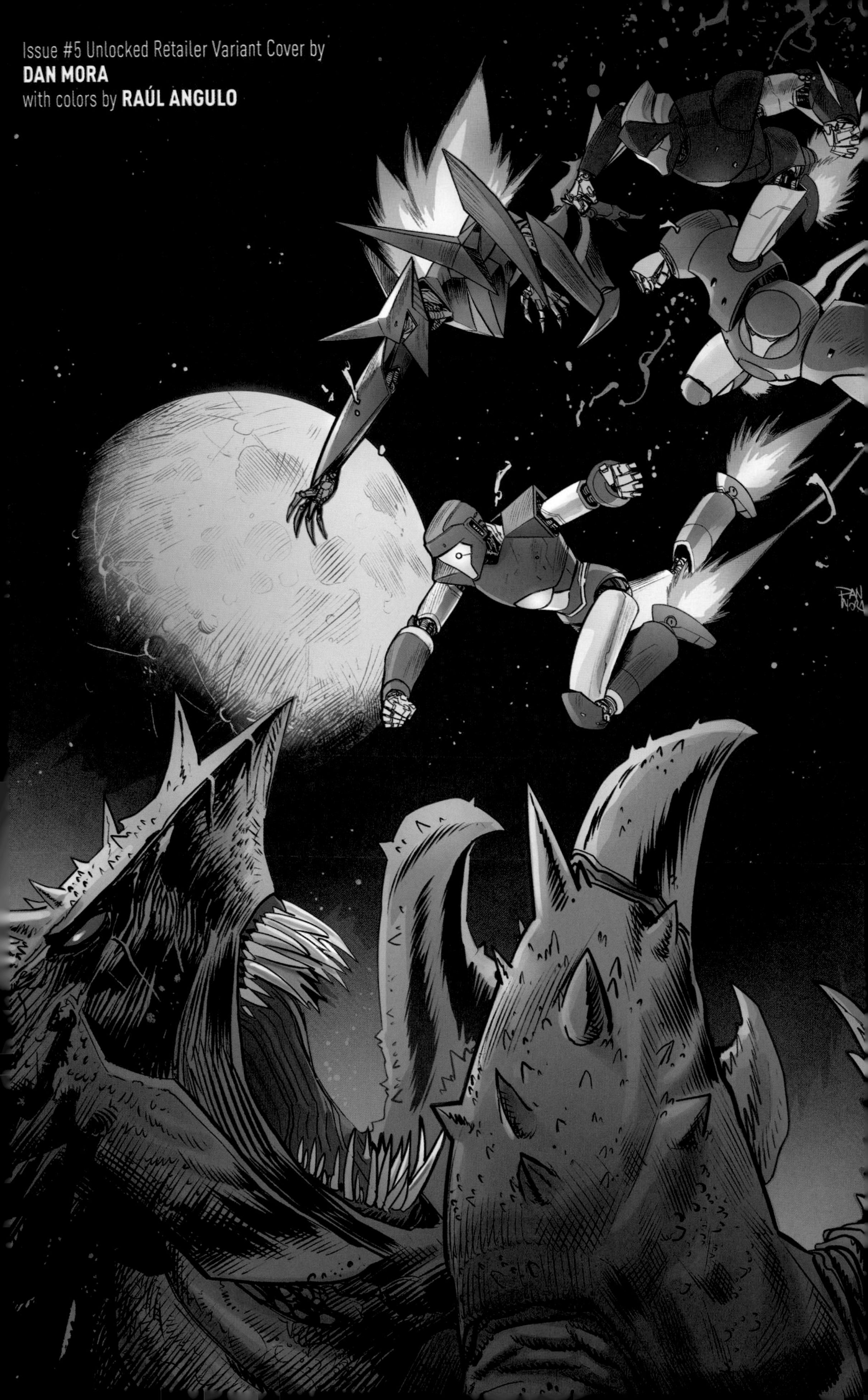
DAN MORA

Mech Cadet Yu
SKETCHBOOK
HERO FORCE MARK II CONCEPT ART BY
TAKESHI MIYAZAWA

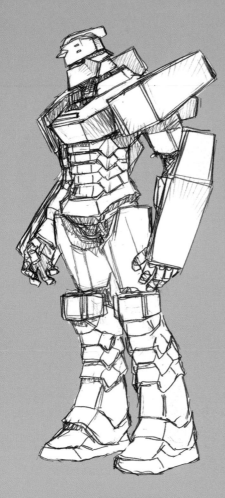

VERSION 1.0

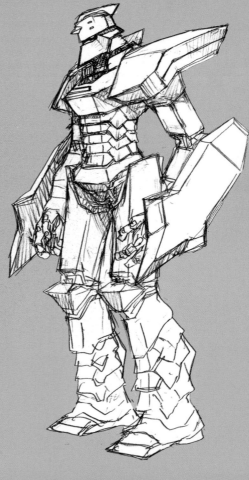

VERSION 2.0

DISCOVER
VISIONARY CREATORS

THE
WOODS
JAMES TYNION IV • MICHAEL DIALYNAS
VOL. 1
THE ARROW

"The Spire is fantastic! My kind of genre free-for-all."
—BRIAN K. VAUGHAN
(Saga)
THE
SPIRE
SIMON SPURRIER
JEFF STOKELY
ANDRÉ MAY

MARK WAID • PETER KRAUSE
IRREDEEMABLE
AFTERWORD BY
GRANT MORRISON

J.G.
JONES
MARK
WAID
STRANGE
FRUIT
Foreword by
ELVIS MITCHELL

MICHAEL ALAN NELSON
DAN MORA
GABRIEL CASSATA
HEXED
THE HARLOT & THE THIEF VOLUME ONE

ABNETT & CULBARD
WILD'S
END
FIRST LIGHT
"IT'S REALLY GREAT!"
JEFF LEMIRE

AVAILABLE AT YOUR LOCAL COMICS SHOP AND BOOKSTORE
WWW.**BOOM-STUDIOS**.COM

James Tynion IV

The Woods
Volume 1
ISBN: 978-1-60886-454-6 | $9.99 US
Volume 2
ISBN: 978-1-60886-495-9 | $14.99 US
Volume 3
ISBN: 978-1-60886-773-8 | $14.99 US

The Backstagers
Volume 1
ISBN: 978-1-60886-993-0 | $14.99 US

Simon Spurrier

Six-Gun Gorilla
ISBN: 978-1-60886-390-7 | $19.99 US

The Spire
ISBN: 978-1-60886-913-8 | $29.99 US

Weavers
ISBN: 978-1-60886-963-3 | $19.99 US

Mark Waid

Irredeemable
Volume 1
ISBN: 978-1-93450-690-5 | $16.99 US
Volume 2
ISBN: 978-1-60886-000-5 | $16.99 US

Incorruptible
Volume 1
ISBN: 978-1-60886-015-9 | $16.99 US
Volume 2
ISBN: 978-1-60886-028-9 | $16.99 US

Strange Fruit
ISBN: 978-1-60886-872-8 | $24.99 US

Michael Alan Nelson

Hexed The Harlot & The Thief
Volume 1
ISBN: 978-1-60886-718-9 | $14.99 US
Volume 2
ISBN: 978-1-60886-816-2 | $14.99 US

Day Men
Volume 1
ISBN: 978-1-60886-393-8 | $9.99 US
Volume 2
ISBN: 978-1-60886-852-0 | $9.99 US

Dan Abnett

Wild's End
Volume 1: First Light
ISBN: 978-1-60886-735-6 | $19.99 US
Volume 2: The Enemy Within
ISBN: 978-1-60886-877-3 | $19.99 US

Hypernaturals
Volume 1
ISBN: 978-1-60886-298-6 | $16.99 US
Volume 2
ISBN: 978-1-60886-319-8 | $19.99 US

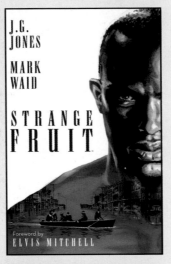

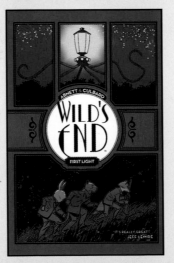